PRAISE FOR PARIS IN RUINS

Meticulously rese... ...omen whose families were caugh... ...eply moving and suspenseful ~~ ... ...plendor Before the Dark: A Novel of t... ...Nero

M.K. Tod's elegant style and uncanny eye for time and place again shine through in her riveting new tale, *Paris in Ruins* ~~ Jeffrey K. Walker author of *No Hero's Welcome*

Tod is not only a good historian, but also an accomplished writer ... a gripping, well-limned picture of a time and a place that provide universal lessons ~~ *Kirkus Reviews.*

A riveting story of patriotism, treachery and bravery set against the Siege of Paris when the courage of gently raised women like Camille and Mariele knows no bounds ~~ Patricia O'Reilly, author of *The First Rose of Tralee*

A wonderful, compelling novel of the literal horrors of conflict arising from both war and revolution, seamlessly joined by the loyalty and friendship of Camille and Mariele that never wavers but grows despite the destruction of their comfortable and safe world. ~~ Margaret Scott Chrisawn, Ph.D., author of *The Emperor's Friend*

An exquisitely crafted story combining poignancy and passion that follows the lives of two strong women and their families during the horrendous 1870 siege of Paris. ~~ Patricia Sands, bestselling author of *Drawing Lessons*

M.K. Tod's Paris in Ruins conjures a compelling story from the historical catastrophes that befell Paris in 1870 and 1871, when a German Army conquered the city, then Frenchmen turned on each other in a revolution that devolved into a bloody civil war. A triumph of historical fiction! ~~ David O. Stewart, bestselling author of *The Paris Deception*.

PARIS IN RUINS

M.K. TOD

HEATH STREET PUBLISHING

The author M.K. Tod may be contacted at mktod@bell.net. For more
information visit www.mktod.com.

Author's Note: This is a work of fiction. Names, characters, places and incidents
are a product of the author's imagination. Locales and public names are
sometimes used for atmospheric purposes. Any resemblance to actual people,
living or dead, or to businesses, companies, events, institutions or locales is
completely coincidental.

Cover design by Jenny Toney Quinlan, Historical Editorial

Paris In Ruins / M.K. Tod — 1st ed.

ISBN: Book 978-0-9919670-4-9;
Electronic Book 978-0-9919670-5-6

À vaillant cœur rien d'impossible. ~~ Jacques Cœur
For a valiant heart nothing is impossible.

PREFACE

Paris In Ruins is set during the Franco-Prussian War, the Siege of Paris, and the Paris Commune. What were these momentous events that played a part in shaping French history? Before embarking on writing the novel, I needed to answer this question.

By the summer of 1870, Napoleon III, nephew of Napoleon I, had presided over France for twenty-two years, first as president and then as emperor. During that time, he expanded the French empire, modernized the economy, expanded the railways and the merchant marine, and negotiated significant trade agreements with Britain and other European countries. He also dismantled and rebuilt large parts of Paris to create the boulevards and buildings that remain to this day and give the city its distinctive style.

For some—the aristocrats, the Catholic Church, military and political leaders, the influential artists and writers of the day, and the upper middle class—life was good. However, the gap between rich and poor had widened. Over half the population lived with poverty and destitution. Even for the working class, life was increasingly difficult. The people were restless. Protests bubbled beneath the surface, occasionally spilling over onto the streets in riots and demonstrations. According to one account, people assembled every night on the Boulevards, singing the Marseillaise, destroying property, their leaders inflaming the crowds with sedition.

On the military front, Napoleon III allied with Britain in the Crimean War, defeated the Austrian empire in the Franco-Austrian war, and defended the Papal States against annexation by Italy. But the increasing militarism of Prussia and its desire to unite all German states into one country threatened Napoleon III's regime. Otto von Bismarck, Chancellor of Prussia, reportedly said: "I knew that a Franco-Prussian war must take place before a united Germany was formed."

Prussia engineered a crisis that threatened France and by the middle of July 1870, the two countries were at war. Prussian forces were superior in numbers, leadership, and technology. On September 2nd, Napoleon III surrendered after huge losses at the Battle of Sedan. By September 15th, the Prussian army reached the outskirts of Paris. By the 19th, Paris was totally surrounded. The siege lasted until the end of January 1871.

Two months later, radical republicans overthrew the government and established the Paris Commune. For ten weeks, the Commune carried out acts of murder, assassination, pillage, robbery, blasphemy, and terror, until finally expiring in blood and flames.

EARLY SEPTEMBER 1870 – CAMILLE

CAMILLE NOISETTE PULLED a drab cape around her shoulders and stared at her image in the gilt-edged mirror. For the evening's outing she had borrowed a simple, loose-fitting skirt from Monique, her maid, as well as a homespun linen blouse that fastened at the neck with a ragged piece of ribbon. To complete the outfit, she had braided her hair loosely and covered it with a kerchief.

Satisfied that she now looked like someone from the working class, Camille opened her bedroom door a few inches. The corridor was empty. She slipped out, tiptoed toward a narrow archway, and hurried down the backstairs.

As promised, André Laborde was waiting in the shadows on the south side of the house. Instead of the elegant, well-fitting clothes he wore to Madame Lambert's weekly salon, he was dressed like a shopkeeper in a plain woolen jacket, baggy pants, and a cloth cap that might have been run over by a carriage. His normally close-shaven face was rough with stubble.

"You're ready," he said. "And you certainly look the part."

"I had to leave by the servants' entrance to avoid my father and brothers," Camille replied. "If asked, my maid will tell them

I've gone to bed with a headache. Let's walk this way." She pointed at a wooden gate. "There's an alleyway leading to the street. Now tell me, where exactly are we going?"

André shoved his hands into his pockets. "I listened to Auguste Blanqui two days ago at a radical club called *La Patrie en Danger*," he replied. "Blanqui believes our country is in danger and was urging his followers to overthrow the new government. From what I understand, he thinks that such a revolution should be carried out by a small group of collaborators." André frowned. "Men like him must be watched carefully. Their actions could escalate into another uprising. With Prussia intent on conquering Paris, France needs stability not further unrest." His voice had grown agitated. "I apologize, Mademoiselle Noisette. You can tell that I'm passionate about our country. But I don't wish to alarm you. Tonight, I plan to attend a different republican club. Having you along will allow me to mingle more easily."

"Really?"

At Madame Lambert's most recent salon, André had mentioned visiting one of the republican clubs known for stirring unrest among the working class. Camille had been intrigued at the thought that a successful man like him, who was relatively new to Parisian society, would risk his reputation in that way. On impulse, she had asked to attend the next meeting with him. She had been surprised when he had agreed.

"Yes," he nodded. "You can charm just about anyone. However, given the way we're dressed, we'll have to speak like working-class people. Do you think you can do that?"

Working class clothing and speech—clearly the evening had a purpose. "I believe I can," she replied. "But tell me why you're so interested in what's going on at these clubs."

André let out a long slow breath. "I'm seeking information to pass along to others, but I'm not at liberty to tell you who they are. If tonight goes well, that may change."

How unusual, she thought. *Are we to be spies among our fellow citizens?* The serious tone of André's voice along with the implication of future involvement made her respond with gravity. "I'll follow your lead then, shall I?"

"That would be best. And you should call me André. I'll introduce you as Henriette . . . Henriette Giraud. Will that suit you?"

Camille nodded. "Are we to be married or merely sweethearts?"

"Sweethearts. Otherwise people will expect me to know much more about you." André linked his arm with hers. "And now we need to walk quickly. The club meets near the Palais Royal at eight, and the best time to mingle is before the proceedings begin."

HALF AN HOUR LATER, Camille followed André as he negotiated a path through the small circular tables lining the sidewalk on rue Molière. Despite news that Paris would soon be surrounded by the Prussian army, passionate conversation and great bursts of laughter filled the air as customers consumed beer, wine, or cognac and ate with gusto. A ragged child lingered near the tables, holding out a hand for a coin or a crust of bread.

André led her through the front door of Restaurant Polignac into an oak-paneled room where candles flickered, and the scent of roasting meat filled the air. When he asked where the meeting was taking place, the waiter jerked his head toward the back of the room and a winding staircase that led to the second floor. As they neared the top of the stairs, Camille heard angry voices.

"Are you sure this is the right place?" she whispered.

"Definitely. I wonder what the debate is about?"

"It sounds to me like a fight is brewing, not a debate."

Immediately inside the door was a man wearing a red

kerchief around his neck. He held out his cap. "Haven't seen you before, Monsieur. Are you new to the cause?"

André dropped a few coins into the cap. "Been at Club La Lanterne, but it's too radical for me."

His gruff voice surprised Camille. It sounded like he had suddenly sickened with a cold.

The man nodded. "You and Madame will find many here who feel as you do. Pay no attention to the clamoring going on. Some people just want to hear themselves talk."

Although the room was large, it felt confined by the sloping roof. Rough wooden tables of various sizes filled the space, some set with chairs, others with long wooden benches. Through the haze of bitter cigarette smoke, Camille could see bottles of wine and cups of coffee on some of the tables and stacks of dirty plates on the floor in one corner. An odor of sweat and grease permeated the air.

Except for a few wealthy-looking Parisians, the crowd was a mix of bourgeoisie and working class. These different groups mingled together in conversation, the noise level rising as points were made and fists thumped in agreement. Here and there, men and women called out greetings to one another, and a dog yelped as a man kicked the scrawny animal away from the fireplace. In the far corner, a loose-limbed man danced a lively jig to the sound of a mouth organ.

André guided her toward a group of men clustered around a woman with an angular face and thin lips. "*Bonsoir, messieurs et mesdames*," he said, offering his hand in greeting. "My name is André Bourdin, and this is my fiancée, Henriette Giraud."

The men shook André's hand, and the woman nodded. "Louise Michel," she said.

Camille observed the woman's fitted black jacket and the wide red ribbon that was knotted just beneath the collar and pinned with a silver brooch. Louise Michel had the look of a schoolteacher—authoritative and severe.

"I am delighted to meet you, Madame," André offered a stilted greeting in the same rough voice. "I've heard much about you, but I thought you were with the Vigilance Committee of Montmartre."

"Madame Michel is here as a guest this evening, Monsieur Bourdin," said a man with graying hair and plump cheeks.

"What do you know of our Vigilance Committee, Monsieur?" Louise Michel asked.

André clasped his hands behind his back. "I've heard that it's one of the leading republican groups, Madame. And that you are an important part of its success."

Louise Michel tilted her head. "And you, Monsieur? Do you share our desire to strengthen the role of working men and women in our great republic?"

"Certainly, Madame," André replied. "Working people are not getting a fair share of our government's money and effort."

Louise turned toward Camille. "Mademoiselle Giraud, are you sympathetic to our concerns?"

"I am, Madame." Camille spoke in a soft voice and avoided looking directly into the woman's eyes. She hoped this more subservient manner would be convincing. "André has explained many things to me. Yours is a good cause."

"It could be your cause too, Mademoiselle. You should come to our meetings. We need women like you."

Camille pursed her lips. "My mistress might disapprove, Madame, and I can't afford to lose my job. I work very long hours." She slipped her arm around André's and pulled him close. "André and I barely have time to see one another. But when we marry, things will be different, won't they, sweetheart?"

The man with plump cheeks cleared his throat. "If you will excuse us, Monsieur, Mademoiselle, the meeting must now begin."

While the proceedings got underway, André led Camille to

the back of the room. Administrative matters were followed by a series of brief speeches criticizing the new government and lamenting the state of Paris. It seemed to Camille that there was no agenda to guide the discussion, nor anyone in charge until the man with gray hair and plump cheeks climbed onto the raised platform and called for order.

"Ladies and gentlemen! Quiet, please!" He tapped his glass with a pocketknife and waited for the crowd to quiet. "Tonight, we have Madame Louise Michel as our guest. Many of you will know of her struggle for the rights of women. She is also head of the Montmartre Women's Committee, and there is a rumor going around that she will soon join the National Guard. Please welcome her."

A roar of applause filled the room. "Is this who you came to see?" Camille whispered to André.

"Yes," he said. "I will tell you more later."

Louise Michel's speech was full of inflammatory language and exhortations for Parisians to rise up and establish a commune, a people's government. Camille listened intently as the woman declared that the time for parliamentary devices had passed, enemies of the republic should be punished, banks should be for ordinary citizens, not merely for business and the wealthy, and the army should be commanded by the people. She was astonished to see most in attendance hanging on every word.

Michel's eyes blazed. She raised a clutched fist in the air with defiance. "Do we trust our politicians?"

"No!" came the audience's reply.

"Will the government look after the people?"

"No!" came a second roar from many in the room.

"Does an emperor surrender like Napoleon did?" Louise Michel's eyes flashed.

"Never!"

"Do we have the right to determine our destiny?"

"Yes!"

Louise Michel pulled a red scarf from her pocket and waved it high above her head. "Who will save France? Who will save Paris?"

"*Vive la Commune!*" the crowd roared. "*Vive la France!*"

"I'VE NEVER SEEN anything like that before," Camille said not long after leaving the restaurant.

The evening was unseasonably warm, and it seemed that all of Paris had left their homes to walk the streets or meet with friends at one of the many outdoor cafés. As they turned onto the rue de Rivoli, she heard a violin playing "Oh, Quand Je Dors," the music both poignant and romantic.

"Neither have I," André replied. "A passionate woman can be a dangerous woman." He chuckled. "Please don't mistake my meaning. I am in favor of passionate women. However, Louise Michel is destined to be an influential woman." His voice turned serious once more. "The force of her words and her conviction will inflame the people. And hence, she may become dangerous to the future security of Paris."

"Is this merely your opinion?"

"No." André linked his arm with hers. "It's the opinion of a number of worried citizens in government, industry, and the military who are fearful of the radicals. The coming siege will present ideal conditions for unrest to boil over. Louise Michel and others like her must be carefully watched. No sane Parisian wishes to experience another revolution."

"So, you intend to watch her, do you?"

"Actually, I hope you will watch her and report your findings to me."

"Me?" Camille was so astonished, she almost stumbled.

"Yes, you. I think you're perfect for the role."

At this point, they were halfway across the Pont Royal. On

the other side of the Seine, Haussmann-style buildings with their distinctive mansard roofs and rows of equally spaced windows graced Quai Voltaire. Camille stopped and turned to face André. "Don't be ridiculous, Monsieur Laborde. I would be revealed as a society woman in an instant."

"I preferred it when you called me André."

Camille disengaged her arm from his. "Be serious, André. If you and your friends, whoever they are, want to watch this woman, you need to find someone of her kind."

He removed his cap and leaned against the railing. "What we need is someone we trust who is clever enough to take on this responsibility. Your role would be to watch Madame Michel at the Montmartre Vigilance Committee meetings and report to me what you've heard and seen. No one doubted your disguise tonight, did they? If she recognizes you, you can say you were inspired by her speech. This is important, Camille. Tell me that you will at least consider it."

Although he looked like a man out for a stroll with little on his mind except pleasure, Camille had never heard him speak so passionately. Radicals, unrest, revolution—the possibilities were frightening. Her father had been a young man during the uprising of 1848. He told stories of the barricades throughout the city, the fires and destruction that followed, and the angry mobs that converged on the palace to overthrow King Louis-Philippe. After the king's abdication, dissent between the bourgeoisie and the working class led to a second uprising where the army forcefully quashed the workers. Over three thousand lives had been lost. Would this be the fate of Paris once more?

"All right," she said quietly. "Let me think about your request. I will send a note tomorrow. I assume you don't want me to disclose this evening's events to anyone."

"Thank you, Camille. And yes, I need . . . we need your discretion."

2

SEPTEMBER 15, 1870 – CAMILLE

CAMILLE WAS SITTING in the library at a narrow writing desk, planning the week's menu, when her father returned from the train station.

"They're off?" she asked her father.

"Yes. A few last-minute crises, however, I got everyone on the train with the promise of sending along your mother's Indian shawl and the foot powder she uses to keep her feet from itching. Can you organize that?"

She nodded. In addition to her mother, Camille's two sisters and her youngest brother were leaving Paris for the safety of Lyon.

"Your mother is wise to leave the city," her father said. He picked a piece of lint off his jacket. "I could force you to go, you know."

"I know, Papa. But you agreed I could be useful here. I promise I won't cause any problems."

Charles Noisette grunted. "Make sure you don't. While your bold approach to life amuses me, there are limits, and I won't put up with you exceeding them." He crossed the room and looked out the window.

The family often gathered in the library after dinner. According to custom, her father and brothers—Bertrand, Victor, and Paul—sat in a grouping of settee and chairs next to a curved section of floor-to-ceiling bookcases. The women took places elsewhere: Camille at her needlework in a plumply cushioned chair next to the fireplace; her mother, Laure, and Louise at the card table for a game of piquet. Although she disliked needlework, the task left her free to listen to the men's conversation.

"Where are your brothers?" her father asked.

"Bertrand has gone to the bank, and Victor said something about a sick parishioner."

Her father sat on the settee and sighed. "I'm glad to have that turmoil over and done with," he said. "I have a few meetings arranged and need to visit the ammunition works. Bertrand promised to join me there. Will you be fine on your own?"

"Of course, Father. There's no need to worry about me. I have much to organize now that Maman and the others have left. I want to simplify things. I hope you're agreeable to that decision."

Her father waved his hand, as if dismissing one of the servants. "Of course. Do what you think best. You're the sensible one of my daughters. Buy from our regular providers. I have funds set aside for the time when they will no longer offer goods on account. Let me know when you need them."

Her father was planning ahead, as usual. "I will. Bertrand and I are going to Madame Lambert's this evening. Would you like to come with us? I believe Mariele de Crécy will be there." Camille placed the cap on her pen. "You know, in school she was rather timid and bland, but I'm beginning to like her. Bertrand has made an excellent choice."

"Yes, yes. The de Crécys are a fine family. But I won't attend tonight. Bertrand is unhappy with me, and I don't wish to spoil his evening." Her father pulled on his lower lip. "He wants to join the National Guard, but I've said no because I need his help."

Camille set down her pen. "Bertrand told me. But don't you think he will feel less of a man if he's unable to do his duty? You don't want him accused of cowardice, do you?" For a man who was so clever in business, her father's treatment of his favorite son often lacked understanding.

Charles Noisette rubbed his chin. "Hmm. I hadn't considered that."

Camille picked up her pen, removed its cap, and dipped it in the inkwell. She did not reply.

LATER THAT AFTERNOON, Camille went to her father's small study, seeking his stamp for a letter she'd written on his behalf. The sun streamed through a south-facing window, catching dust motes in its path. A globe sat on a table next to a heavy leather chair. Camille remembered her father spinning the globe when she was little and telling stories of whatever country her finger landed upon—tales of the Sahara Desert, the lost temples of Cambodia, America's Wild West, the vast lands of Siberia. Her favorite had been the story of the Taj Mahal in India built to honor Shah Jahan's never-ending love for his wife Mumtaz. Camille spun the globe and let one finger rest gently against it until it stopped. Prussia.

That's not a very good omen.

Papers covered her father's desk. Camille was about to investigate them when footsteps sounded from beyond the doorway. She turned, ready to greet her father or possibly Bertrand, but the footsteps continued along the corridor and down the stairs.

She exhaled slowly, then picked up a piece of paper stamped with a government seal and glanced at the contents. As she scanned the next page and then a third, she raised her eyebrows. *What on earth is Father up to now?*

She didn't linger, reading only enough to know her father was in possession of confidential papers concerning military plans for war with Prussia. Another set of papers, containing mostly figures, was more difficult to understand; a few columns seemed to show projected monthly volumes while another column had been labeled INCOME. Scrawled on the margins in a hand she didn't recognize were the words *munitions, supplies,* and *uniforms* along with a series of initials. Beside each set of initials was the symbol for francs followed by an amount.

Was he paying people for something? Did the initials connote investments? He was always talking about contacts he had in both business and government. Those contacts had been instrumental in securing large development projects during Baron Haussmann's renovation of Paris—lucrative projects that had secured a fortune for the Noisette family.

Camille looked more closely. One set of initials was PDC. Philippe de Crécy? Was the father of Bertrand's fiancée involved? She knew they'd worked together three years earlier on preparations for the Universal Exposition. Perhaps new opportunities had arisen, and her father wanted to solidify his connection with an influential man like Philippe de Crécy through marriage.

She shook her head. Her father was always scheming.

IN THE DAYS THAT FOLLOWED, Camille went out with purpose, shopping for food, visiting the small group of friends who had remained in the city, stopping at Red Cross headquarters, where wounded soldiers welcomed anyone who would chat with them. With no one to guide or admonish her, she chose her own activities, feeling an increasing sense of commitment to the security of Paris. Accustomed to frivolity, to spending without concern, to gossip and idle conversation, such feelings surprised her. She confided these newfound emotions of duty, responsibility, and resolve to no one except her sister Juliette.

Less than a year apart in age, Camille and her younger sister were inseparable. At sixteen, Juliette's sparkling eyes, rosy cheeks, and red lips had been considered signs of emerging beauty, and their mother had proclaimed that her third daughter would have many suitors. Marie Louise Noisette had even boasted of securing a marriage to a member of the aristocracy. That prediction had shattered when the doctor advised that Juliette's lack of appetite, increasing thinness, and delicate, almost transparent skin were signs of consumption. There was no hope for a cure, only the gradual wasting away of her life. A few weeks after her nineteenth birthday, Juliette had died.

Camille had been devastated. Following the funeral, she had remained in her bedroom for days staring out the window. No one could penetrate her grief. Victor had offered to pray with her. Her mother had counseled fortitude. Her father had told her that Juliette would want her to get back to the business of living. But it wasn't until her brother Bertrand had forced her to go riding with him, that she'd found a way forward.

They had ridden along the bridle paths of the Bois de Boulogne where sunlight filtered through the trees and squirrels darted left or right to avoid the horses' hooves. Feeling the wind on her face, Camille had gradually increased the pace to a full trot. Her horse readily lengthened his stride and she urged him to go faster.

"Slow down," Bertrand shouted. "If you fall, you could break your neck."

Ignoring her brother, Camille swerved to avoid a puddle. Hooves thundered against the beaten path. A slender branch slashed her face. Her eyes watered with the pain and a trickle of blood ran down one cheek. Camille leaned forward. She thought of nothing except staying in the saddle.

For some reason, that ride had been a turning point. From that day, Camille had vowed to live life for two. She often spoke to her sister, not aloud but in her thoughts. Such conversations gave her comfort.

The transformation of Paris is alarming, Juliette. In the Bois, hundreds of enormous trees have been cut down to provide barricades and fuel. The park itself is now home to thousands of sheep, so the government can feed the people of Paris. And you would be amazed at how quickly the military has acted. Thousands of soldiers have dug temporary fortifications around the city walls. Semaphore stations are in place atop the Arc de Triomphe, the Panthéon, and Montmartre so we can communicate with the forts surrounding the city. Now that the Louvre is empty of its treasures, the galleries house arms and ammunition. Papa and Bertrand have converted one of our factories to make cartridges needed by our troops. The two of them are busy day and night.

Surprisingly, life goes on—people continue to promenade, dine out, shop, gossip. In the evenings, we attend the theater and soirees and salons. No one knows how long it will be before the Prussians attack. I feel a new sense of purpose, Juliette. I hope to do whatever I can to help our city survive.

THE FOLLOWING THURSDAY, Camille went to Madame Lambert's salon. In keeping with her mood, she wore a plain taupe dress that revealed a white underskirt edged with ruffles. After greeting their hostess, she watched Bertrand hurry off toward a small group of people that included his fiancée. Camille remained at the entrance, surveying the assembled crowd and listening to the rise and fall of conversation.

The most striking aspect of the salon was its color: rich red silk covered the walls; red drapes hung at the windows and interior doorways; Persian carpets with red accents covered the wooden floors. With creamy white doors and ceilings, and accent pieces—consoles, side tables, pedestals—in polished mahogany, the effect was one of luxury and plush, soothing comfort.

While the room was arranged with clusters of seating to foster different conversations, it was customary for guests to move from one place to another as the evening progressed. In the middle of the room, Gustave Moreau and Edouard Manet were seated with a few other painters, including Berthe Morisot and her sister. A group of men, whose grim faces suggested a serious topic, sat near the fireplace. Next to a window over-looking the courtyard, Camille noticed her father whispering to his mistress. For a moment, she thought it might be amusing to join them and ask a few awkward questions.

Camille caught a glimpse of André Laborde and thought of their recent outing. He was clearly a man of a more serious nature than she'd imagined. When they'd been introduced, she had admired his confident bearing and lively eyes. Although he had flirted with her that evening, he hadn't pursued her in any way. She drifted in André's direction, stopping to greet a few guests before settling on a tufted chair a few feet away from him. While the men espoused their views on the military situa-tion, she thought about André's request.

"My opinion of General Trochu," one man said, "is that he's better at theory than action, so our military forces are like a flock of sheep without shepherds. Trochu has close to three hundred thousand men under his command and little to show for it."

Others chimed in with their opinions. Eventually, a man with bushy eyebrows asked, "Will the National Guard fight? Monsieur Laborde, you've joined the Guard, what do you think?"

The question startled Camille. She had no idea that André had joined the National Guard. Not that he needed her permission, of course. If he hadn't been engaged in responding, she would have demanded to know the details. Any day now, she expected Bertrand to announce the same news. The thought of her favorite brother taking up arms sent a shiver down her spine.

"Well," André said, "I'm certainly prepared to fight as soon as I'm trained. For the moment, however, our duties are unclear, and since we are organized by arrondissement, much effort goes into coordination. But there are many brave men among us who are ready to take up arms."

"And what's the word on supplies?" the same man continued, the curled ends of his mustache twitching. "With more than a million people in the city, we will need enormous food supplies, to say nothing of weapons, ammunition and fuel. The trains coming into Paris won't run much longer."

"As far as I'm concerned, we have too many useless mouths to feed," grumbled an older man with rheumy eyes. "The government should have organized an exodus; instead, we permitted thousands of people to enter the city."

Madame Lambert joined the group. "You men only think of war. A most serious matter for those of the fairer sex is the suspension of *La Gazette Rose*," she said. "The Vicomtesse de Renneville has stated most emphatically that the security of Paris is more important than her fashion magazine, and I am certain other publications will soon follow suit. What are we women to do?"

Although laughter followed, the conversation soon returned to the perilous state of Paris.

"Our leaders have been too busy organizing a new republic and ensuring positions of power for themselves," said Ernest Garnier, whose bald head and white beard conferred an air of authority.

Camille knew Garnier and his son Jules, who was developing a reputation as a portrait artist. She leaned forward. "And what do you think of our new government, Monsieur Garnier?" she asked. "Will these men be able to lead us through such difficult times?"

"Our government has too many republicans with radical views for my liking," Ernest Garnier replied. "And too many neophytes. This is a time for men of experience, not men who merely know how to appeal to the masses."

Garnier's reply reminded her of the speeches she'd heard at the republican club. "And the women, Monsieur? How do you feel the women can best be of service?"

"Well, the actresses of the Comédie-Française have turned the theater into a convalescent hospital, and there's a rumor that Sarah Bernhardt will do the same with the Odéon. Perhaps they will need volunteers. No doubt Bernhardt's relationship with Kératry will enable her to get all the necessary supplies." Garnier's eyes twinkled.

Camille had no idea why the men laughed in response. She made a mental note to ask Bertrand on the way home.

"But to answer your question, Mademoiselle, I don't believe actresses are suitable companions for a young lady like you," Garnier continued, bringing the lighthearted moment to an end. "Women like you should stay at home and leave the worrying to us."

Despite the man's condescending attitude, Camille smiled to acknowledge his opinion. A few seconds later, she felt a tap on her shoulder. When she turned to look, André tilted his head and gestured at a window next to a potted palm. She waited until the next round of conversation got underway before joining him.

"That conversation was becoming tedious," André said. "Too many men who think they could do a better job. I doubt any of them have military experience. I need a breath of air. Will you join me on the balcony?"

"When did you join the Guard?" Camille asked after they moved onto the balcony. "I didn't realize you planned to do so."

André stared at the street below, where a dog sniffed the ground beneath a lamppost. "I feel it's my duty. I'm not a man who desires combat, but the times call for extraordinary measures. If men like me refuse to enlist, the National Guard will be dominated by extreme factions who believe in over-throwing the government."

Camille pressed her lips together. "How will Paris withstand the kind of siege those men are expecting? There won't be enough food for everyone. The shops and trades won't have enough business. The poor . . . I can't imagine what the poor will do. Life is difficult enough for them now. And the Prussians . . ." Suddenly, she felt as if she couldn't breathe.

"Do you wish me to be frank?" André's tone remained neutral.

"Of course."

"Paris can withstand a siege until the level of suffering demands surrender. It's September. The weather is warm, and for the moment, we have an abundance of food. Come November or December, the poor will be dying in the streets from cold and starvation. People like us will find ways to manage, but others will soon run out of money. Think of the little children who'll be affected and the women whose husbands will lose their livelihood, or even their lives. Those people won't be able to keep a roof over their heads. And to make matters worse, the radicals might seize the opportunity to create further turmoil. We could even face another revolution."

"You make it sound dire, Monsieur and I applaud your deci-sion to enlist. As for me, I hope to volunteer at one of the hospitals."

"You don't plan to heed Monsieur Garnier's words, then."

"No, Monsieur. His opinions are firmly entrenched in the past. Fortunately, my father permits me a little more liberty. I chose to remain in Paris in order to be useful."

"I'm certain you will be more than useful." He turned to face her. "Will you go to the meetings in Montmartre?"

After attending the club at Restaurant Polignac, she'd spent hours considering André's request, weighing the dangers against her desire to contribute to the country's future and the bolder approach to living she'd adopted since Juliette's death. Ultimately, she had sent him a letter confirming her participation.

"Yes. I gave you my word, Monsieur. I'll attend the next meeting and let you know what happens."

He did not smile. "Don't write anything down. Tell me in person."

3

SEPTEMBER 23, 1870 – MARIELE

"I KNOW you don't want to leave Paris, Evangeline. We've had this discussion several times already. However, I insist. Everything is arranged."

Mariele de Crécy paused at the top of the stairs, where her parents' suites were located across the hall from each other. Based on his tone, her father's frustration was about to boil over —an infrequent occurrence. He was usually courteous and composed when speaking with his wife.

"And I've told you many times that I don't want to leave. I want to be here for when Robert comes home," her mother replied.

Mariele imagined the stubborn look that would be on her mother's face: lips pulled tight; eye flashing; chin set. Her parents were increasingly at odds. She wondered whether that was the fate of most marriages and how she and Bertrand could avoid such an outcome.

"Has it not occurred to you that I have serious reasons for this decision?" her father continued. "You and Mariele will be in danger if you remain. Danger, Evangeline. In my mind, it's not merely a possibility, but a certainty. I am privy to information that others are not, and while I cannot disclose this knowledge, I can take actions to protect my family. You *must* leave Paris tonight. I've made special arrangements. Do not fight me any further."

Mariele waited for her mother's reply, but the words were indistinct, followed by the sound of crying and her father's murmured words of comfort. With her hand on the carved newel post, she turned and tiptoed along the wide corridor toward her bedroom.

"Mariele!" her father called a few seconds later.

She stopped and turned back to face him. "Yes, Papa?"

The hallway wasn't well lit, nonetheless she could see that he looked rumpled, as though he'd slept in his clothes, an astonishing state for a man who was always so impeccably dressed. Indeed, he looked like a man who hadn't slept at all. Philippe de Crécy narrowed his eyes and glared at her. She knew that look, a look that used to make her cower.

"Were you listening to us?"

"Yes, Papa. I'm sorry. I know that was rude. I came upstairs to finish my packing and—"

"Well, then," her father interrupted, "you know how important it is to leave Paris tonight. I expect you to cooperate and to help your mother."

"Yes, Papa." She paused. Confronting her father when he was in this sort of mood was risky. Nevertheless, the desire for an answer outweighed her normal caution. "How is it that you know such things and can arrange for special papers?"

His scowl deepened. "That's none of your business."

"Forgive me, Papa, but you are sending Maman and me away. You expect us to cross the Prussian lines. If anything goes wrong, we could be in serious danger." She squared her shoulders. "I'm not a child. I believe I have a right to know that your information is reliable."

Her father tugged at his chin. "I know you're not a child,

Mariele," he said, his tone a fraction softer. "However, in this instance, you'll just have to trust me."

Trust. She'd always trusted her father. He was wise and for the most part kind to his children. She'd grown up in wealthy circumstances, never lacking for anything material. With her father's guidance and influence, Mariele and her brothers, Robert and Theo, could anticipate a similar future.

"Can you tell Bertrand what you know?"

"No, not Bertrand. Not anyone." He took a step closer. "I shared confidential information with your mother. Information you were not intended to hear."

"I promise I won't disclose anything." She hated being the object of her father's displeasure, but the circumstances surrounding their departure from Paris were so unusual, she hadn't hesitated to eavesdrop. "And you're not coming with Maman and me?"

"No, but I will take you to the rendezvous point. You must be ready no later than ten p.m."

WITH THE PROMISE of acquiring new clothes once they reached Rouen, Mariele packed only one suitcase and concentrated her efforts on essentials and small items like earrings and ribbons and toiletries. Bertrand had given her a photo, and she tucked that in along with one of Theo and Robert and another of the whole family taken when they were on holiday at the seaside.

Mariele paused her packing and crossed to the window. With a west-facing view, the bedroom had become warm. She unlatched the fastener, opened both sides of the window, and leaned out for a breath of air, admiring the pebbled pathways and neatly clipped sections of the garden and courtyard, which were surrounded by trees and thick bushes bearing tinges of autumn colors. *When will our lives return to normal?* she wondered.

A few minutes later, Mariele returned to her packing, adding two more books, a fan, and one of the shawls she'd received from Bertrand at their engagement party. She looked around. On a table beside the chaise was a letter which had arrived just that morning. She picked it up and read it once more.

MY DEAR MARIELE,

I do hope it's acceptable to use your given name. Writing to my future sister-in-law as Mademoiselle de Crécy seems far too formal, and I already feel that we will become dear friends.

Bertrand told me last night that you and your mother are leaving this evening. Such a bold step, although I'm sure your father has thought the matter through carefully. Rouen is certain to be safer than Paris. You and your maman will be comfortable there and will have no need to be concerned with these awful Prussians. And do not worry about Bertrand. I will remind him of his duty to take care of himself for his bride-to-be.

While you are away, think of me helping at one of the hospitals that are springing up around the city. I plan to visit the Odéon Theatre where Sarah Bernhardt is creating a new site to treat wounded soldiers. I believe I have sufficient talent to be of some use.

When this dreadful siege is over, we will further our friendship. I do so long for someone to be as true a friend as my dear sister Juliette.

I hope your travels are swift and free from danger.

Written in haste,

Camille Noisette

ON IMPULSE, Mariele tucked the letter into her suitcase and fastened the straps.

∾

AT TEN P.M., Mariele and her mother donned heavy cloaks and descended the stairs to the ground floor foyer, where their bags were waiting. Her father led them outside, closing the door with a soft thud. Thick clouds obscured the light of the moon, and, with streetlamps no longer lit, the night was dark and close. *Perfect for leaving Paris*, Mariele thought. *If I actually wanted to leave.*

She glanced back over her shoulder at the house she had lived in since the age of three—a four-storied house of grand proportions situated near the entrance to Parc Monceau. Light glowed softly at the salon windows on the main floor and from the window of her mother's dressing room. Soon, Suzette would light a candle to make her way upstairs to the fourth floor, and Theo might be enjoying a final glass of wine in the library before bed. Mariele would miss him. She tried not to think about whether he would enlist in the National Guard and put himself in danger like so many other young Parisian men.

"Quickly now," her father urged. "We can't be late."

Using connections with senior officials at the Ministry of War and the British Embassy, her father had secured a *laissez-passer* signed by General Trochu permitting two women to exit Paris. They would travel as Yvonne and Patricia Williams, the wife and adopted daughter of one of four Englishmen leaving Paris to return to the safety of London. Heading west out of the city, they would have to cross both French and Prussian lines.

With a valise in each hand, her father escorted them along a series of side streets and dusty alleys toward the Grand Hôtel on the Place du Palais-Royal, where they would meet the others. Only the pitter of rats broke the ominous quiet.

Mariele's eyes darted left and right. She had heard stories of other attempts to leave, few of which had been successful. There was a rumor of a couple who had been caught near Neuilly and accused of spying. They were now incarcerated in one of the country's most notorious prisons, and many Parisians were clamoring for their execution. Would that be her fate? A rush of bile stung her throat.

At the Grand Hôtel, a carriage flying the Union Jack and large white flags on either side of the driver's box seat was waiting in the courtyard. Four whiskered gentlemen were gathered around a pile of luggage and wicker hampers. As her father shook hands with each man, Mariele noted their serious faces and somber voices.

"Thank you, gentlemen," he said. "I'm grateful for your help."

"Think nothing of it, de Crécy. You've been good to us and to Britain. It's the least we can do," said a man wearing a top hat and red woolen scarf.

"Monsieur Williams, my wife, Evangeline, and our daughter, Mariele," Papa said.

"*Enchantée,*" Monsieur Williams replied. "You will be Yvonne and Patricia from now on."

"Yes, Monsieur," her mother said. "And thank you for your kindness."

"Does your daughter speak English?"

"Only a little, Monsieur."

"Best leave the talking to me, then. If we are questioned, I will say that I married a French woman and adopted her daughter. All right, gentlemen. Is everyone ready?"

Mariele watched her parents' stiff embrace and then, after a brisk hug from her father, climbed into the landau and settled onto a wooden bench covered in worn leather. With six occupants squeezed into a space meant for four, she was uncomfortably pressed against the metal sides, her knees almost touching the man sitting opposite. Wishing she were as slender as Camille, Mariele straightened her posture and pulled her lips into a smile.

"*Tout prêt?*" Monsieur Williams asked. Without waiting for a response, he banged on the door with his silver-tipped cane and shouted at the driver.

A whip cracked. Wheels creaked. The landau lurched, throwing Mariele against the corpulent man on her left, whom her father had addressed as Monsieur Danbury.

"Pardon, Monsieur," she said, noting a rather odious aroma of boiled onions and garlic emanating from the man.

"De rien, Mademoiselle."

And they were off.

TO MARIELE'S SURPRISE, no one stopped them as they traveled along rue de Rivoli and the Champs Élysées. She glimpsed a few people on the streets and a group of soldiers guarding the entrance to the Arc de Triomphe, but otherwise the cafés were closed, and only dim lights shone in the windows of nearby apartments. Beyond the Porte Maillot, the road narrowed, and the trees lining either side made the night seem even blacker. The carriage rumbled on. Each minute seemed to last an hour. As Mariele thought of all that could go wrong, her heart thumped so hard she thought it might burst.

A sudden shout pierced the night air.

"Stop!"

The horses neighed. The carriage slowed. When a shot rang out, Mariele jumped. She could barely make out the faces of her traveling companions but heard a swift intake of breath from Monsieur Danbury.

"Stay inside," Monsieur Williams whispered. "I have our papers. Madame, you and your daughter are to say nothing."

The coach door swung open, revealing two soldiers, one holding a lantern, the other a menacing rifle. They looked rough and disheveled, their uniforms anything but clean. Monsieur Williams climbed down from the coach.

"Who are you?" barked the soldier with the lantern.

"Englishmen and women," Williams said. "We have permission to leave France. I have our *laissez-passer* papers." He thrust them at the soldier. "My wife and daughter accompany me. We are returning to England."

"Permission to leave?" the soldier said. "Don't you know we're surrounded? No one can leave Paris." He laughed, a mirthless sound that was more like a dog's growl. "Keep your rifle on them," he said to his companion. "They might be spies. I'll take these papers to the captain."

Mariele held her hands tightly together in an effort to remain calm. Although every nerve in her body wanted to leap from the carriage and run, she knew they must act as though they had every right to leave the city. Maman's eyes were shut, and her hat, a stylish concoction of blue and tan, was askew. Mariele reached across the carriage to squeeze her mother's hand and, when Maman's eyes flew open, gave what she hoped was a reassuring smile.

The Seine slapped against the riverbanks. Minutes ticked by. No one spoke. With the coach door open, Mariele could see rough scrub at the roadside and an overturned wooden box in the dim glow of a lantern hanging from a nearby tree. An owl hooted. Farther away, the embers of a cooking fire glimmered.

The distant sound of cannon reminded Mariele of the dangers they would face beyond this French outpost. The audacity of their plans suddenly struck her as ridiculous. How could they hope to escape not one, but two checkpoints? Even if the French military allowed them passage, the Prussians were unlikely to be amenable. And what would happen to them should the Prussians discover their real identities?

Scrunch, scrunch, scrunch. Footsteps approached. Mariele held her breath.

"My captain says you are free to pass through, Monsieur," the soldier said. "But he cautions that the Prussians may send you and your friends back. And they won't treat you with any

courtesy. Be alert and vigilant. You are about to cross into a war
zone."

FROM THE FRENCH OUTPOST, their progress was slower, the
horses balking when shells exploded and the driver swerving
the carriage left or right to avoid potholes along the roadway.
The moon had broken free of the night's heavy clouds, and in its
spectral glow, Mariele noted the grim-faced tension of her
companions and was surprised to see her mother holding a
rosary, her lips moving rapidly but without sound.

"Not long now," Monsieur Williams said. "I'm told there's a
Prussian checkpoint at Rueil. And if it's inaccessible for any
reason, we can travel on to Saint-Germain-en-Laye. Let's follow
the same procedure. I'll do the talking."

Mariele wondered who had told Monsieur Williams the
locations of these checkpoints. Surely the disposition of
Prussian troops was not common knowledge. Would someone
at the French or British Embassy be privy to such crucial information? If so, why would they share it with Monsieur Williams?
Who exactly were these men Papa had chosen to be their traveling companions?

For the first time, she wondered about the exact nature of
her father's business dealings. As a child, she'd thought of him as
someone well known and important. Even as a young adult, she
had never associated specifics to his role other than a vague
notion that lawyers drew up contractual terms to protect their
clients. Were his relationships with men such as Monsieur
Williams of this nature, or were they more significant? She
would ask Papa this very question when they were together
again—if God and fortune permitted such an eventuality. A cold
wind assaulted the carriage. Mariele shivered.

"*Halten Sie sich!*" a harsh, grating voice called out.

The driver struggled to control the horses that reared and

whinnied and jostled the carriage to and fro. Once again
Monsieur Williams descended from the carriage. This time
moonlight permitted a glimpse of two stone cottages at the
road's edge, their windows glowing in the dark, smoke drifting
from each chimney. A wagon loaded with barrels was parked
alongside one of the cottages, and in a lean-to built of straw and
thick twigs, several Prussian soldiers lounged on the ground,
their weapons stacked against a wooden railing. A short
distance away was a line of canvas tents and more soldiers
grouped around a blazing fire. Flags flapped in the wind.
Mariele's heart shuddered.

She heard a mix of French, German, and English as
Monsieur Williams spoke with a steel-helmeted officer who
seemed to be in charge. Once again, the *laissez-passer* documents
were handed over. Once again, they waited.

By the time the officer returned, the horses had begun to
shuffle restlessly despite the driver's efforts to soothe them, and
Mariele worried that the two gray Percherons might decide to
bolt and cause the Prussian soldiers to open fire. She gripped
her hands tight and muttered a prayer for their safety.

At first, Monsieur Williams spoke calmly with the officer,
but gradually his voice grew louder, and his agitation—as
evidenced by the vigorous movement of the Englishman's arms
and head—increased. Mariele had no idea what was being said.
The Prussian's tone shifted to belligerence, and he clasped the
hilt of his sword. Williams made a calming motion with his
hands and backed away.

"They're taking us to Versailles for questioning," Monsieur
Williams whispered in French, looking meaningfully at Mariele
and her mother. "I will do my best to protect you. We will all be
blindfolded so that we gain no information on the strength or
disposition of the Prussian army."

One by one, each member of the party stepped out of the
carriage to be blindfolded. Mariele's mother moaned softly as

she looked at her daughter just before leaving the carriage, and then it was Mariele's turn. Black, tight, and reeking of sweat and dirt, her blindfold made the darkness complete. A rough hand pushed her back inside the carriage.

As each passenger returned to their seats, the carriage rocked back and forth until finally, the door slammed shut. Soldiers shouted in a guttural language Mariele didn't understand. A whip cracked. The carriage jerked forward. *Papa was wrong*, she thought. *If we'd stayed in Paris, we wouldn't be in the hands of the enemy.*

Instead, they were on their way to Versailles, which was now headquarters for the Prussian army. Monsieur Williams said he would do the talking, but what if they were separated? Under those circumstances, the likelihood of maintaining false identities as the wife and adopted daughter of an English gentleman was very slim.

The carriage gained speed, bouncing along the rough roadway, careening around corners. Maman gripped Mariele's hand. Someone coughed. No one spoke. How long would it take to reach their destination? An hour, perhaps; perhaps more. What if the Prussians had no respect for English citizens who were neutrals in a war between France and its Germanic neighbor? What if they were accused of being spies? Mariele felt caught in a vice that was tightening bit by bit.

The driver snapped the whip once more, urging the horses to greater speed on a straight stretch of road. Wind whistled through the cracks. Canvas flapped. A dog barked. A sudden rattle of planks beneath the wheels suggested they had just crossed a river. She tried to recall the terrain west of Paris and the way the Seine twisted back and forth, heading to the ocean. They had already crossed the river twice, but perhaps there was a third bridge on the way to Versailles. Her mind clogged like a thick soup.

Finally, the pace slowed. The driver called out. The carriage stopped, and Mariele heard the horses snorting, panting, hooves pawing the ground.

"Courage," Monsieur Williams whispered.

Yes, she thought. *Maman and I will definitely need courage.*

Mariele was roughly handled as the blindfold was removed, and she was forced to stand by a wrought-iron fence that was tipped in gold and at least twenty feet tall. When her mother joined her, Mariele held her hand.

"What will happen, Maman?" she whispered.

"Shh! Say nothing. Not a single word," her mother whispered in return.

With a hint of dawn piercing the sky, soldiers were visible everywhere—drilling, marching, cleaning rifles, polishing boots, shouting orders; many hundreds, if not thousands, gathered across the wide expanse of Versailles' grounds.

Mon Dieu, Mariele thought. *What will they do to us?*

4

SEPTEMBER 23, 1870 – MARIELE

"WHAT IS YOUR NAME?" the officer demanded.

"Yvonne Williams," her mother replied. "And this is my daughter, Patricia."

They were in a small room next to what might once have been a library, although Mariele had had only the briefest glimpse of that gold-studded space lined with shelves as they were marched along. Despite Monsieur Williams's protests, he had not been allowed to remain with them for questioning, and instead the men had been led away down a separate corridor. Not much larger than the laundry closet of their Paris home, the room where Mariele and her mother stood housed only a rough table and a few chairs. A single window faced a dark inner courtyard. On the wall were two sconces, each designed to hold three candles. Tonight, one candle illuminated the space with a feeble, flickering light. A drip of candlewax fell to the floor.

The man questioning them had a bulbous nose marked with spidery veins and hair so coarse it reminded her of straw. Mottled gray eyes regarded them with fierce determination. Mariele had no idea of his military rank, although the soldier who had escorted them had saluted with vigor before leaving.

"Fräulein, please tell me why you are leaving France." The officer spoke in English.

Her mother answered, "We go to England with my husband."

"I do not ask you, Madame. I ask your daughter."

"Sir, she is young and frightened. I am her mother."

"But she knows her age, yes?" He glared at Mariele. "Your age, Fräulein?"

Mariele, frantically trying to remember how to count in English, took several seconds to answer. "Nineteen, *mein Herr*. I be nineteen."

"I be nineteen, you say."

Mariele nodded. She was pleased with herself for remembering a little more English than the number nineteen. The soldier's eyes glittered as he rose from his chair, and he said nothing as he walked around the desk.

"Well, if you truly are the adopted daughter of an Englishman, you would know to say, 'I *am* nineteen,' so what is your real name, Fräulein?"

"Patricia . . . Patricia Williams," she said.

Smack. The soldier hit Mariele's mother across the face with the back of his hand. She stumbled, then steadied herself, a red welt rising quickly on her cheek. Her lips drained of color. *Smack.* The soldier hit the other cheek. Maman raised her hands to touch her face, then lifted her chin defiantly.

"We are Yvonne and Patricia Williams," she said.

Mariele held her mother's hand and repeated the statement. The soldier moved to stand directly in front of Mariele and raised his hand once again. Instinctively, she drew back to avoid his blow.

"No," her mother shouted. Her eyes darted here and there like a scared rabbit.

"No, Madame?" he said.

"We are not English," she said. "We are French. From Paris."

"Ah," he said. "I thought so," he continued in French. "And perhaps you are spies."

"No, Monsieur. We wish to escape the siege. My husband . . ."

"What about your husband?"

"He thought we would be safer outside Paris."

"Did he now?" The soldier placed one finger beneath her mother's chin and tilted her head up. "Did he now?" he repeated.

The man whirled away, strode toward the door, and bellowed down the hall. Within moments, boots thudded along the marble corridor and the soldier who had removed their blindfolds appeared. He snapped a salute.

"Herr Kapitän," he said.

In rapid German, the captain issued instructions, emphasizing his wishes with a jerk of his head.

"Jawohl, Herr Kapitän."

"Good luck," the captain said mockingly as the soldier led Mariele and her mother out the door.

THE SOLDIER SET a brisk pace along one corridor and then another and another before exiting through an arched doorway into a courtyard filled with troops on horseback. The air was thick with clouds of dirt kicked up as horses nickered and shuffled and flicked their tales with restless energy.

"Come!" the soldier said, his voice gruff and menacing.

They crossed the courtyard and approached another entrance to the palace. Beyond the massive doors, he motioned for them to proceed ahead of him and prodded each of them with his rifle as they hurried along the length of a wide interior gallery to a set of stairs that descended into a maze of passageways. Within minutes, Mariele was completely disoriented.

Flickering candles lit the way through narrow corridors with rough walls built of jagged stones placed haphazardly, as if this part of the palace was of no consequence. Most of the rooms they passed were dark and there was little sound except the clump of the soldiers boots and the occasional harsh cough.

Where is he taking us? Mariele wondered. She clutched her mother's hand and felt a slight answering squeeze.

"Halt!" The soldier thumped the butt of his rifle on the floor.

When Mariele turned, she noticed a doorway into a large, dimly lit room. The soldier motioned them inside. Still holding her mother's hand, Mariele took a few steps forward. Two lanterns hanging from wrought-iron hooks illuminated what was once a kitchen with two deep fireplaces, wooden shelves built into the walls, and a long trestle table running down the center of the room. A single pot hung from a chain beside the fire and a small stack of wood lay in a wicker basket.

At one end of the room was a wooden door fastened with a thick bolt. The soldier led them toward it, pulled back the bolt, and motioned them inside.

"You aren't going to leave us here, are you?" Mariele said.

No answer.

"Please, monsieur. When will we be allowed to leave?"

"There's no point in asking questions," her mother said. "He doesn't understand us."

The soldier backed away, closed the door, and slammed the bolt shut.

5

SEPTEMBER 24, 1870 – CAMILLE

"HOW COULD there be so many spies?" Camille asked after reading the latest news that morning. "Let me read to you what the *Gaulois* is saying: 'Spies are being arrested every half hour. Many mistakes have been made by overzealous citizens and police, but there is no doubt that a good many Germans are in Paris disguised in French uniforms. While some suggest they should be publicly shot, this newspaper proposes to have them imprisoned for the duration of the siege.'"

"Paris is home to many Germans," Bertrand replied after setting down his own newspaper. "Perhaps some harbor ill will for France, but I certainly don't believe they should be shot."

"Surely there aren't as many spies as the papers imply," Victor said, as he entered the room. He held a rosary in one hand but was otherwise dressed in regular clothes.

"Good morning, Victor," Camille responded. "Aren't you going to the church today?"

Victor shook his head. "I have a rare day off. What does my brother know about spies?"

"You might be right about the numbers, Victor. But I'd

rather have a few falsely imprisoned than many undermining the safety of our city." Bertrand drained the last of his coffee and stood up. "Father and I should be home this evening, but I'll send word if we're detained."

"Before you go, tell us how far you think Mariele and her mother have traveled," Victor asked. "I've been praying for them."

Bertrand slid his jacket on and began fastening the buttons. "It's hard to say. Conditions on the road may be difficult, and I have no idea how many checkpoints they will have encountered." He sighed. "I wish they'd left the city when Maman and the others did."

"I'm sure you're worried about them," Camille said.

"I didn't sleep last night. I kept imagining the dangers they might have encountered." Bertrand drew a silver watch from his pocket, flipped the catch, and checked the time. "I have to go. Camille, if you need any provisions, send me a note."

AFTER SHE FINISHED BREAKFAST, Camille retreated to her room, where cream-colored curtains and bedding created an oasis of calm. It was the seventh day of the siege, and the government had already issued many proclamations headlined with the rallying cry of *"Liberté, égalité, fraternité."* These included rules regarding the consumption of milk, bread, and meat as well as exhortations to Parisians to report soldiers who were drunk and citizens who propagated false news, exhortations to prevent the sale of liquor to soldiers on duty, and exhortations to defend the city at all costs.

Two days earlier, Camille had heard the first sounds of cannon firing from Prussian outposts, and now, as she dipped a brush into a small pot and leaned close to the mirror to spread the color evenly across her lips, she heard another deep rumble and lifted her head. A shiver ran along her shoulders, and she paused for a moment to consider the likelihood of danger.

According to the papers, the Prussians were within a few miles of Paris and had made their headquarters at Versailles. Much of the regular French army remained locked in prisoner-of-war camps close to the border with Prussia. Pockets of fighting had been reported at various forts guarding the city, but to date there had been no news of French successes. Bridges at Saint-Cloud, Sèvres, and Billancourt had been blown up, and there were rumors that Prussian artillery would soon be able to reach the Arc de Triomphe. Could Paris really be defended against so many bent upon its destruction? If not, how long would it be before the city was forced to surrender?

The house had fallen quiet. Camille glanced at the painting of her sister which hung next to her bed.

"What would you do, Juliette? Would you have gone to Lyon with Maman? Or would you be here with me? Here with me, I think. No doubt telling me not to be so foolish as to think I can help at a hospital."

She often spoke to her sister as if she were in the room. In the beginning her words were harsh. *Why did you die? Why did you leave me? How do you expect me to carry on without you?* But now, this one-way dialogue dealt with the plans she was considering or the consequences of choices she'd made. Camille didn't mind that there were no real answers. In her heart she knew what Juliette would have said.

She touched a felt cloth to one corner of her mouth to remove a smudge of color. Satisfied, she turned left and right to ensure her outfit was in order, then found her gloves and a parasol—a birthday gift from her father —to complement the dove gray of the dress she'd chosen for today's outing. *Purposeful, not frivolous*, she thought.

With her mother and older sister away and Bertrand and her

father preoccupied with business problems resulting from the siege, there was no one except Victor to consult about her plans, and since Camille knew he would disapprove, she hadn't bothered to mention them.

The gates of Paris had closed. No one was allowed in or out without permission and the proper documents. Fortified by a wall thirty feet high, a moat ten feet wide, and an outer ring of forts comprising a forty-mile circumference around the city, most Parisians were convinced of their impregnability. The Prussian army, however, had gradually surrounded Paris with a fifty-mile ring of troops and was now digging in, building their own fortifications while assembling the necessary tools of siege warfare: cannon, provisions, bridges, access to water, living quarters, fuel, medical facilities, and equipment. If André was right, the siege would be long and difficult. Some would not survive.

And yet the sense of noble fortitude required to withstand the wrong being perpetrated against her beloved Paris was almost exciting. She would do more than endure. She would excel at the demands of a siege, knowing that France was right to defend itself against Prussia the tyrant, and that Paris would prevail. Life would certainly change, and she would change with it. No inkling of doubt entered her mind.

Today her plan was to visit the Odéon Theatre and speak with Sarah Bernhardt. Approaching someone of such renown made her feel audacious. What if the great actress scoffed at her interest in volunteering? What if Bernhardt's plans were more gossip than substance? What if . . . Well, she had worried over these questions for two days already and had finally made up her mind. If Sarah Bernhardt had no interest, Camille would approach one of the other new hospitals springing up all over Paris in converted houses, apartments, hotels, and theaters, or the one recently opened at the Palais de l'Industrie.

~

"Do you know where I might find Madame Bernhardt?" Camille asked an old woman sweeping the black-and-white tiled floor of the theater's vestibule.

A puzzled look caused her to repeat the question, this time a little louder, and the woman waved at a narrow door tucked behind the grand staircase. *"Là-bas,"* she said. "Down there."

"Monique, why don't you wait for me here?" Camille said, pointing to a low bench. "I'm sure I won't be very long."

Following a dimly lit corridor that slanted downward, Camille reached the back of the theater and discovered a series of small rooms and a jumble of props and costumes as well as ladders, lamps, chairs, and a panel where tools of all sizes and shapes hung in an orderly fashion. A light glowed softly in the distance.

She took a few more steps. *"Bonjour,"* she called. "Is anyone here?"

"Oui, un instant," came the reply.

A minute later, a dark-haired beauty dressed in black emerged from a doorway, and although Camille could not see her face clearly, she knew from the mass of curls and statuesque posture that she was about to meet Sarah Bernhardt.

"Yes?" Bernhardt said. "If you are an actress, the theater is closed because of the war. I cannot help you. Life is difficult for anyone in the theater. You will have to make do, just as I am, as there are more important matters at hand." She arched her dark eyebrows and tilted her head as if expecting Camille to leave.

"My name is Camille Noisette, Madame, and I'm not an actress. However, I've heard you may soon open the Odéon as a hospital for our wounded, and I would like to help."

Bernhardt frowned and moved closer to Camille. "Where did you hear such a rumor?" The tone was dismissive, but the voice was pure as crystal.

"It's not true?" Camille asked.

"I didn't say that. I merely asked where you heard the rumor."

"I . . ." Was truth the right strategy? Would Sarah Bernhardt be offended if told of the gossip at Madame Lambert's salon? The actress's reputation held her to be impetuous and demanding, a woman of powerful connections and great willpower who was capable of daring risks to have her way. There was no point in lying. "I heard it at an evening salon. One of the gentlemen in attendance speculated that the Comte de Kératry would willingly help you."

Bernhardt laughed—a deep, throaty sound accompanied by a toss of her head. "Yes. That's exactly what people would say about me. And they're right. I am planning to open a hospital here, and I saw the comte yesterday. He is being most generous." The last sentence was accompanied by a sultry look.

"Well, I would like to help," Camille said. "I believe you will need volunteers, and although I'm not trained to nurse, I'm sure I can be useful."

Sarah Bernhardt tapped an index finger against her lips while surveying Camille from head to toe. "You don't look useful. You look like a young society woman accustomed to having others wait on her. Why would I need someone like that? You'd only get in the way. And I'm having enough difficulty as it is. Both the French Society for Aid to Wounded Soldiers and the French Army medical corps are in hopeless disarray."

It hadn't occurred to Camille that her station in life would be a reason for refusal, and for a moment she searched for an adequate reply. "I can . . . I can read to wounded soldiers," she said. "Or write letters. I can fetch supplies, fold linens, and spoon soup into the mouth of someone too weak to feed himself. I'm not afraid of hard work."

"Hmm. You're right. Those tasks might be useful. Do you know anyone who could provide supplies?"

"Such as?"

"Food, medicines, fuel, coffee, clothing, blankets. The hospital will need all sorts of things if we are to treat the wounded and help them heal. The Comte de Kératry told me definitively that they are expecting thousands of casualties, possibly tens of thousands. Many will die before they can be treated, but others we will save. They will all need to eat and drink and be kept warm."

"Tens of thousands, Madame? But how can that be? Paris is completely fortified."

Sarah crossed her arms. "Yes, but we can't defeat our enemy by hiding within the city walls. Our military will have to act. Casualties are inevitable. Even if we have some successes, the Prussian army has artillery that can reach greater distances than ours. Once they are ready, they will bombard our forts and, unless we surrender, the walls of the city will also be attacked."

"Surely, our army will retaliate."

"The comte says that General Trochu is a strategist, not a man of action. So, you see, Mademoiselle, we will need many supplies."

Camille thought of her father. He seemed to have connections in almost every line of business. "I might be able to secure some supplies."

"Excellent. I have meetings planned with several of my friends who have remained in Paris, but I could see you again on Wednesday, late afternoon—perhaps five o'clock—and if everything is satisfactory, we can make an agreement."

"Thank you, Madame. Five o'clock on Wednesday."

"*Au revoir*, Mademoiselle Noisette. Your visit has been most interesting."

～

CAMILLE FOUND her father in the library reading *La Presse* while drifts of cigar smoke circled above his head. A few other newspapers lay scattered at his feet. Although a fire had been laid, the room was cold and damp because the family had agreed to conserve supplies of wood and coal for as long as possible.

"Father?"

"Yes?" he muttered without looking up.

"I've volunteered to help at the new hospital being set up by Sarah Bernhardt."

He lowered the newspaper and peered at her. "Volunteered? At a hospital run by Sarah Bernhardt? What do you know about hospitals? Or about Madame Bernhardt, for that matter? And why would I allow my daughter to do such a thing?"

Camille bristled at his words but knew not to spark a quarrel. Her mother often cautioned with an old proverb: *le miel est doux, mais l'abeille pique.* Honey is sweet, but the bee stings.

"Father, you know I'm strong and capable. Several of my friends have volunteered, and I wish to do my part. How would you feel if Bertrand or Victor were wounded and had no one to help them? There have already been skirmishes beyond the city gates, and Madame Bernhardt said more than three hundred wounded soldiers have been brought into Paris for treatment."

"That's what doctors are for."

"But you know there aren't enough to go around. And even when the doctors do come, they can only spare a few moments for each soldier. Men will soon be dying of neglect." Camille had no idea whether her last statement was true but felt it enhanced the argument.

"Well, *ma chérie*, I admire your sentiments. As long as you're cautious and the work doesn't interfere with your duties here, you have my blessing."

"Thank you, Papa." She rarely called him Papa anymore. Instead, she had followed the custom established by Victor and Bertrand, who used the more formal term Father.

Her father picked up the newspaper once more, and Camille took a few steps toward the door before turning back. She had told Sarah Bernhardt that she could be useful. Securing supplies would prove it.

"Is there something else?" he asked.

"The hospital will need supplies." A neutral statement. Perhaps her father would offer without her asking.

"I'm sure it will."

"You and Bertrand are collecting various supplies. I believe I heard you mention that this would enable future profits if the siege lasts a long time. And so . . ."

"And so?"

Blunt and bold. That was the way to deal with her father. "I thought you would want to make a contribution."

"Why would I do that?"

"Well, it seems that the press is only too eager to vilify anyone who collects large supplies of food and essentials while others in the city suffer, especially our soldiers. Such a contribution would enhance your reputation." And now the statement that would signal her position. Not exactly a threat. More of a moral imperative. "You wouldn't want that damaged in any way, would you?"

"You're not suggesting I'm acting this way, are you?"

She did think he might be acting this way. Her father always had an eye to his own advantage. But there was no point in being confrontational. If she pushed too hard, he would balk at any contribution, and the wounded would be deprived of necessary help. Time to soften the approach.

"Of course not, Father. But a generous donation would certainly be noticed and positively described in the press. Your colleagues in government would be grateful, don't you think?"

"Hmm. You may have a point. I'll meet with Bertrand and determine what we can spare."

"Apparently the Meniers are supplying chocolate, and the Rothschilds have offered wine and brandy." Camille deliberately named two of the wealthiest families in all of France.

"I see," her father said. He tugged on a corner of his mustache. "Leave it with me."

6

SEPTEMBER 28, 1870 – CAMILLE

A LITTLE AFTER five on Wednesday afternoon, Camille reached the Odéon and walked into chaos. Boxes were stacked four or five in height. A pile of lumber leaned against one wall. She noted sacks of lentils and rice and rich-smelling coffee, bolts of cloth, and small piles of sawdust. Two pigeons had found their way in from the street and were pecking at some rice that had spilled onto the floor. She heard shouting and a hammer banging and the faint sound of a piano playing "La Marseillaise."

Expecting to find Madame Bernhardt in the same room backstage, she had to search for more than fifteen minutes before finding the actress directing a carpenter who was installing shelves at one end of the auditorium.

"Make them deep, Monsieur," Bernhardt said. "They are to hold linens and blankets. Ah, you've returned, Mademoiselle Noisette. Clearly you are persistent, a trait I admire."

"Thank you, Madame." Camille waved her hand at the work underway in the auditorium. "You've been busy."

Bernhardt pushed back a lock of curly hair and secured it with a pin. "Yes. Now that the war office has accepted my request to establish a military ambulance, I wish to be ready as quickly as possible. The comte is sending supplies in a few days' time. He told me they will come from the palace, where the empress had stored enough for months and months of siege. As you might imagine, news of her actions would inflame our fellow Parisians. I've also secured sources for raisins, sardines, lentils, butter, and eggs. The ambassador for the Netherlands will be sending three hundred nightshirts and a hundred sets of sheets."

"I'm astonished, Madame. You have worked miracles." As she looked around at the transformation that had taken place, Camille wondered if Sarah Bernhardt had other benefactors like Kératry.

Bernhardt laughed. "Tomorrow I plan to visit the Palais de l'Industrie to secure lint and linen for binding wounds. Now, you must meet my dear friend Madame Guerard. She keeps the keys to the theater, the medicine stores, food stores, linen supplies, and the small room containing casks of wine and brandy. I've known her since I was fifteen, and she has agreed to help with our little venture. Madame Guerard!" Sarah called to a tall, slender woman wearing a madras gown embellished with red leaves. "Madame, please come and meet our first volunteer."

If Madame Guerard was in possession of the keys, it was clear Sarah Bernhardt had great confidence in this particular friend. An aura of calm seemed to emanate from the woman, and Camille suspected that her keen gray eyes missed very little.

After introductions, Bernhardt said, "Do you have any news for me, Mademoiselle Noisette?" Her words were accompanied by a playful smile.

"I do. I've found a source for flour and sugar. One hundred pounds of flour and twenty pounds of sugar. This same source will also provide coffee." Camille had been astonished when her father explained the offer, which was far more generous than she had anticipated.

"Are you able to give me a name so I can thank the individual in person?"

"I . . . well, yes, I think I can tell you. It's my father who has offered these goods. I'm sure he would be delighted to hear from you."

"*Bon.* Very good. If you give me the address, I will write to him later today. Can you begin tomorrow? We're transforming the dressing rooms into storerooms. Madame Guerard is in charge. She will take you there and explain what's required. We have a lot to do, and the wounded will soon arrive."

ANDRÉ WAS WAITING with a horse and carriage when Camille appeared a little after six p.m. When he had learned that she planned to take a fiacre home, he had offered to drive her himself. Although they were unchaperoned, the carriage top was down to add a modicum of propriety.

"Your horse hasn't been confiscated." Camille said as she accepted André's hand.

"Not yet. The bank managed to secure a special permit for me. I don't know how long it will last."

"My father has done the same, although he was forced to give up his best ones."

André nodded. "What was the hospital like?"

"Bustling with activity. There will be beds everywhere: in the auditorium, the lounge, the bar, and even the foyer."

"Who will nurse the wounded?" he asked.

"Madame Bernhardt and her friend Madame Guerard will do that. And I believe the actress Marie Colombier also plans to nurse. Madame Bernhardt will oversee everything. She has an astonishing amount of energy. Once we have our first wounded to look after, I will help by reading to those who are conscious and giving comfort to those who are suffering."

"Your father permits this?"

"Not only does he approve, but he has also donated some supplies."

André steered the small carriage around a mound of discarded vegetables. "Well, make sure you're careful. The Prussians have begun mounting armaments south of the city, and our streets may soon be vulnerable to attack. Unless armies from the provinces arrive in the next few weeks, traipsing back and forth to the Odéon will be dangerous."

His words made her realize how precarious the situation had become. She stopped smiling. "I'll be careful."

They rode in silence for a while, a silence broken by the sounds of cannon from beyond the city's walls and street vendors hawking their wares. Normalcy vied with conflict in a world turned upside down.

"You're very quiet tonight," she said.

"I have three full weeks of training starting Monday."

She frowned. "And that's all you're going to tell me? I'm your confidant, in case you've forgotten."

He smiled a little, then shook the reins to encourage his horse to move past a barricade. "I don't know how I feel about it, really. Once we're trained, I'm committed to being on duty three times each week. Whether or not I see action will depend on Prussia and on our politicians."

"Our politicians?"

"Yes. If they negotiate peace before the Prussian army gets close enough to bombard Paris, it's unlikely I'll ever get beyond manning the ramparts. But if not . . ."

Camille didn't press him any further. "Well, don't do anything foolish."

André pulled to a stop in front of the Noisette home. "I'll meet you here tomorrow evening and take you to the foot of Montmartre. It's too far for you to walk the whole way at night. You can tell me what happened as I drive you home." He held her gloved hand in his and looked into her eyes. "This is serious work," he said. "And you will need your wits about you. You can still say no, if you'd prefer."

Serious work. Wits about you. His words rattled her. She gathered a cloak of bravado around her. "I said I would do it. Do you doubt me now?"

"Tomorrow night, then." He released her hand.

"Tomorrow at seven."

7

SEPTEMBER 1870 – MARIELE

HER MOTHER HAD WEPT when they were first enclosed in the small, dirty room that might once have been a scullery. Since the room was primarily below ground, only the barest hint of sunlight shone through the grimy window Mariele could reach only by standing on her tiptoes. After spreading her cloak on the stone floor, she and her mother had sat down to wait.

Other than a whiskered man who delivered food twice a day and removed the chamber pot once a day, they had seen no one since the officer had accused them of spying. Yet every hour they heard the sounds of war: the boom of cannon, the high-pitched whine of flares, the shouts of officers drilling their men, and late at night the raucous singing of drunken soldiers. And every morning, before the sun was up, a rooster crowed.

The stench and damp of their room had seeped into Mariele's very being. She took her mother's clammy hand in hers and rubbed it briskly. "You're cold, Maman. Perhaps we should walk about for a bit and try to warm ourselves."

Her mother continued to stare blankly and said nothing. By now, her hair and clothes were bedraggled, and smudges of dirt marked her face and hands. She looked much older than her age.

The bolt slid back, and the door opened. As was his custom, the whiskered man did not speak. He merely laid two metal bowls on the floor and closed the door with a loud clang. Mariele listened as the man's footsteps faded away and an eerie silence descended once more. She picked up one of the bowls and stirred the broth with her finger, noting a small piece of meat and a few wrinkled peas. She was famished.

"It looks more edible than yesterday's," she said. "And the smell isn't too unpleasant." She sipped the broth, trying not to gag on the greasy scum floating on the surface. "It might be beef soup. Try it, Maman. You need to eat something."

"I don't think I can eat," her mother said.

"You must eat something, Maman. It will be a long time before anyone comes again."

"We'll never get out of here," she said with a moan.

Mariele had expected her normally decisive and authoritative mother to be more resilient. This lethargic, defeated woman was so out of character. "Don't say that. The captain might be a brute, but I'm sure he won't just abandon us here." She said this with as much conviction as she could muster and surprised herself with her own sense of fortitude. Perhaps she had some of her father in her after all.

"I hope you're right," her mother said, clutching Mariele's hand. "I should be the strong one, not you. I'm sure someone will come."

THAT EVENING MARIELE and her mother were taken to a large office overlooking the gardens of Versailles, where a man who introduced himself as Major Werner offered them a seat and poured three cups of coffee. The major had dark brown eyes and a thin mustache that mimicked the line of his eyebrows, as though an artist had drawn all of them with the slash of black paint.

"You are suspected of spying," he said in French, his voice cool and detached. "A most serious charge. I could have you shot just like that." The snap of the major's fingers produced a sharp, explosive sound.

After waiting a few moments for her mother to speak, Mariele said, "We are not spies, Monsieur."

"No? And tell me, Mademoiselle, why should I believe you? You and your mother, if indeed she is your mother, were traveling with forged documents under false identities. You are French. Prussia is at war with France."

What story should she tell? Could she arouse the major's sympathy yet remain close to the truth? Major Werner's face had settled into a frown, and she wondered what sort of man he was. Kind? Harsh? Cruel? There was no way to tell. Whatever the case, in order for him to believe her, she needed to project confidence. Mariele braced her shoulders.

"We merely wanted to leave Paris for safety in Rouen," she said. "My grandfather lives there. We planned to stay with him. My mother and I are ordinary people, Monsieur. You must believe me."

Mariele jumped when Major Werner smacked his fist on the table. "Ordinary people do not have access to forged documents. But government spies do. You talk with too much confidence, Mademoiselle. Most young women in your circumstances would be cowering with fear."

To Mariele's surprise, her mother lifted her head and began to speak.

"My daughter speaks the truth." She reached for Mariele's hand. "My father is dying. I haven't been to Rouen for almost a year, and his last wish is to see his only daughter one more time. Can you not have some pity for us, Major?"

Her mother continued to embellish. Forcing herself to nod

sympathetically while keeping her face devoid of emotion, Mariele admired the way her mother lied, speaking to the major through tears and fluttering her eyelashes as though on the verge of fainting. When she was finished, the major drummed his fingers on the table and examined the papers before him, one of which bore an official-looking stamp of a winged creature with a scepter and crown. He gave a thin smile.

"You will stay with me, Mademoiselle, so I can question you further. Your mother will return to your room." He gave an order in German, and the soldier waiting next to the door jerked Mariele's mother by the arm.

"Please, Major Werner," her mother placed her hands together as if she were praying. "Don't separate us. My daughter is young. She needs her mother."

These pleas had no effect, and she was dragged from the room shouting, "Let me go! Please, Major. Don't hurt my daughter."

As her mother's screams slowly faded away, Mariele's mouth felt dry. Her heart tumbled uncontrollably. In an attempt to curb her trembling, she clasped her hands together tightly. What would he do? Why separate them? Did he plan to compare their answers? Would her responses satisfy him? If not, what would be the consequences? Panic was a hair's breadth away.

Major Werner smiled. A few moments later, he spoke as if nothing had happened. "Now, Mademoiselle. Tell me your name."

Major Werner's questions were at times simple, at other times complicated. *Where do you live? What school did you attend? How old are you? What is your father's name? Your grandfather's address in Rouen? Why did you leave Paris? How many siblings do you have?* He often asked the same question again and again, thumping his fist whenever she hesitated. Soon Mariele was exhausted.

"Your brother Robert. How old is he?"

"Twenty-four."

"What does he do?"

"He's a soldier," she whispered. It was the first time the major had asked this question, and Mariele feared the answer would inflame the man further. And yet she dared not lie, for if her mother was also being questioned and answered differently, they might never be released.

"A soldier! *Verdammt noch mal!* A fucking soldier. How many Prussians did he kill?"

Mariele took a deep breath. "I don't know, Monsieur. I haven't..."

"You haven't what?" The major leaned across the desk, his face so close she could see the pores on his long, narrow nose.

"I haven't seen him since July."

The major drummed his fingers on the desk. The sound of his nails striking the wooden surface felt ominous.

"Johann!" he shouted.

When the young soldier appeared, the major waved his hand dismissively. "She's yours. Take her away. And bring the mother back with you."

Why had the major spoken French to a soldier who was obviously German? Did he mean to frighten her more than he already had?

"Please, Major Werner. My mother is distraught. If you need answers to any more questions, you can ask me."

The major waved his hand once more but said nothing.

Johann hauled her out of the room. In the corridor, he tied her hands behind her back and shoved her forward. Mariele stumbled but did not fall. Another shove. Another stumble. Although he'd looked innocent enough when she'd first laid eyes on him, the young soldier's behavior frightened her. Did he mean to harm her? Would anyone hear her if she screamed? And if they did, would they come to her aid?

8

SEPTEMBER 1870 – MARIELE

BY THE TIME they reached the room where Mariele and her mother were being held, she had fallen several times, her nose and face bloodied in the process. While Johann had not molested her, he had smacked her face and thrust her against the door so hard her head was spinning.

"Mariele? Are you all right, *ma chérie?*" her mother cried out as soon as Mariele stumbled into the room.

Johann muttered something in German before throwing Mariele to the floor. Her mother scuttled over and wiped her face gently with her petticoat.

"*Kommen Sie!*" Johann shouted, gesturing to make himself understood.

"Go, Maman. I'm all right. Just tell the truth. That's what I did. Just tell the truth."

Johann pulled her mother into a standing position, slapped her face, and pushed her out the door.

Alone in the dark room, Mariele sobbed. Their situation was hopeless. The major had no compassion for their plight and had given the impression that he wouldn't stop until he had the information he wanted. But what was that information? She had told him the truth. What more could she do?

With her hands still tied, she struggled to reach a sitting position, then using a combination of pushing and wiggling, she shifted her body so she could lean against the wall. Why had her father urged them to leave Paris? They were in more danger now than they might ever have been had they stayed in the city. Could Maman withstand Major Werner's questioning? Would she make a mistake and bring more suspicion their way?

Sick with worry, she tried to think of something positive, imagining Theo and her father asleep in their beds, the clock ticking softly while embers flickered in the fire. Bertrand would also be asleep. She knew he had been concerned about the journey, but with very little mail getting through, he wouldn't expect to hear from her for quite some time. And never could he have imagined their current circumstances. She brought his face to mind, the feel of his steady arm, the few kisses they had shared.

It seemed like hours before Maman returned, and when she did, she was weeping uncontrollably. After the door closed, Mariele shuffled close enough to lie against her and whisper soothing words.

"Hush, Maman. We'll be all right. I'm sure the major is just trying to frighten us. Papa would not have let us leave Paris if he thought we would be in danger. Shh. Shh."

A long time passed before the weeping stopped.

WERNER INTERVIEWED Mariele and her mother separately on three more occasions, and although he varied the questions, his approach remained menacing and relentless. Each time, on the way back to their place of confinement, Johann threatened

Mariele, taking pleasure from her fear, hitting her if she stumbled, striking her face, and twisting her arm until she thought it might break. Every day her mother appeared more listless, alternating between weeping and sitting in silence, slumped against the wall. Despite Mariele's questions concerning her treatment and her efforts to cheer her, her mother had remained silent.

What else can I do? she wondered as night descended on the fifth day of captivity. *Maman is worse than ever.*

THE FOLLOWING AFTERNOON, unbound, filthy, and faint from hunger, they were once again in Major Werner's office. *Whatever our fate is,* Mariele thought, *we'll be together.*

When the major rose from his chair and began walking toward them, her mother gripped Mariele's hand hard and took a step backward. With her mother trembling next to her, Mariele lifted her chin and glared at the man.

His expression was menacing. "Well, Madame," he said, "my commandant has decided that Prussia does not make war on women, even ones who may have been duplicitous. You and your daughter are free to go."

Free to go. Mariele could not believe it. Maman sagged against her and might have fallen had Mariele not put an arm around her waist.

The major shouted for his adjutant, who arrived at a brisk trot, clicked his heels together, and saluted.

"Set up an escort for Madame and Mademoiselle de Crécy at daybreak," the major said. "Make sure they are taken to the Billancourt road and supplied with water and food for their walk back to Paris. You will understand, Madame, that it would not be safe for my soldiers to take you any farther."

9

SEPTEMBER 1870 – CAMILLE

THE BRASS KNOCKER was shaped like a woman's hand with long tapered fingers. Camille lifted it and let it fall. Immediately above the knocker was a small grill—the kind that allowed an inhabitant to peer out and check the identity of a visitor before opening the door. The combination of grill and knocker leant a rather sinister air to the small house where the Vigilance Committee meeting was taking place. When no one answered, she lifted and dropped the knocker again.

"Everyone comes in without knocking," said a young woman whose cheeks looked as if they'd recently been sunburned. "You must be new."

Camille's heart was thumping, partly from nerves and partly from the long climb to the top of Montmartre. "I am new," she agreed and smiled. "My name is Henriette Giraud. I heard Mademoiselle Michel speak and was inspired to come to one of her meetings."

The woman opened the door wider and stepped aside. "Come in, then. I'm Maxine Pierrefonds. The others are in the front room."

The dimly lit front room bubbled with conversation. Camille had expected the gathering to be larger and more anonymous, like the one she'd attended with André. Instead, this gathering felt like neighbors coming together to share news and gossip. She stood alone for a few minutes until Maxine beckoned from a spot next to the fire screen, where the woman stood with three others.

"Louise will be here soon," Maxine said. She introduced her friends, all young women dressed in plain garb with little adornment, then asked Camille where she lived. "We all live in Montmartre, but I've never seen you before."

Camille had prepared for this question. "I work for a family in the troisième and live with them."

"Must be a grand home if it's in the third arrondissement," said one of the women. "My sister is a chambermaid in the seventh. She tells me of fancy clothes and extravagant entertainment and jewels fit for a queen. Do they treat you well?"

The arrival of Louise Michel forestalled the need to answer. After shaking a few hands, Louise Michel stood on wooden box and began by thanking the women for their tireless efforts on behalf of Montmartre. "But there is much more to do," she said. "If we are to be successful, all vigilance committees must work together for the good of the workers of the city. The Comité Central urges us to do so in order to defend Paris and France."

Nods and murmurs of agreement followed.

Louise Michel raised her hand. The group fell silent. "Napoleon declared war against Prussia," she continued. "Never was there a declaration more frivolous. And who paid the price?" She paused and looked around, catching the eye of one woman and then another. "We paid the price. The working men and women of Paris and France paid the price in death and destruction. And now we will pay again as our brave soldiers and members of the National Guard defend the city, as we endure the poverty of lost livelihood, the lack of food and fuel. Soon, we will pay through the starvation of our children and the old and the sick." She paused once more, nodding slowly at face after face.

"Another government has arisen. Has it made peace with the enemy?"

"No!" a few women shouted.

"And why? Because of the vested interests of those in power who want to remain in power. Shame, I say. Shame on these men who proclaim themselves the leaders of France. They clamor for the return of Alsace and Lorraine. But what will be the outcome?" Louise Michel paused again, while the audience waited breathless for her pronouncement. "The outcome will be defeat and ruin, unless . . . unless, dear citizens of Montmartre, we rise up to claim justice. Justice for all citizens, not merely the wealthy. Justice for you and everyone here tonight."

"LOUISE MICHEL IS A POWERFUL SPEAKER," Camille said to André after he had helped her into the carriage, and they began moving swiftly toward the center of Paris. "She had the crowd mesmerized. I believe some would have followed her anywhere."

"Did she recognize you?"

"I don't think she noticed me. The room was lit only by a few candles, and I kept to the shadows."

"Good. What else—"

A dog dashed out from an alley and barked sharply at the wheels of the carriage. At the same time, André swerved to avoid a rotund man who stumbled onto the street almost directly in front of them. A high-pitched yelp followed.

"Damn! I think the carriage hit the dog." He pulled the horse to a halt and scrambled down.

"Is the dog all right, André? Do you need my help?"

"Can you reach behind the seat?" André replied a few moments later. "You'll find a blanket there, and if you cover your skirt with it, I can place the dog on your lap. His leg is bleeding. I think it might be broken."

The dog quivered as it lay on Camille's lap. She wrapped the blanket around the small animal and laid her hand on its head. "Where should we take him?"

"If that drunk hadn't stumbled onto the road, none of this would have happened," André replied. He sighed. "I know a man who's a doctor. I'll go there after I take you home."

"But wouldn't it be best to go there now?" Camille replied as the dog continued to whimper and blood trickled onto the blanket.

The carriage was already in motion. André glanced quickly at her. "If we do that, you won't be home until after midnight. What will your father say?"

Camille pursed her lips. "He's unlikely to notice, but if he does, I'll tell him about the dog. My mother thinks dogs and cats are odious creatures likely to bring diseases into the house, but Papa has a soft spot for them. I think this little creature deserves to be cared for."

"And how will you explain your clothes?"

She had forgotten about her clothes, the plain black skirt and roughly knitted top, and the scuffed boots with thick laces. "I don't know. I'll use the servants' entrance and hope that Father is asleep."

ANDRÉ'S ACQUAINTANCE wasn't at all pleased to be asked to look after a scrawny dog with a broken leg. "If I were you, I would just wring the dog's neck," he said. However, he was happy to accept André's money and his promise to return the following day to retrieve the dog. "But he'll probably never walk properly again," the man said.

When they resumed their journey, Camille returned to the question André had started to ask before the accident. "I believe Louise Michel and other leaders in the Comité Central are planning an uprising."

André listened intently as she related the woman's words. "Rise up to claim justice," he repeated the phrase. "Was there a date mentioned?"

"No. Although she encouraged everyone to attend the next meeting. I think she was setting the stage so that her followers understand the need for action. I have to confess, she almost persuaded me."

Was it Louise Michel's speech or her passion that was most persuasive? Standing among those who'd gathered, all of them clad in drab clothes and rough footwear, most with chapped hands and faces worn with fatigue, Camille sympathized with their plight. She tried to imagine how they lived day to day with the struggle to put food on the table and keep their children safe. *But there has to be another way to bring change than starting a revolution,* she thought.

"Are you willing to attend the next meeting?"

"I am. It's a week from tonight."

"You don't have to do this," he said. "It could be dangerous work, and I certainly wouldn't think less of you if you declined."

Camille squared her shoulders. "I'm doing it for Paris, for my family and friends, and for France. It's important, and I want to do something important. I'm privileged, Monsieur. Privileged to be part of an educated, wealthy class. With privilege comes responsibility." Her lips formed a rueful smile. "That's what my sister would have said if she were still alive."

André pulled the small carriage to the side of the street and stopped. "Please accept my sympathies. I didn't know that you'd lost a sister. How—"

"She died of consumption two years ago. We were very close. Some days I hear her voice telling me what to do. When you first asked me to help, Juliette told me quite clearly that it was an important duty to undertake." Camille turned to face him. "It's Juliette's approval I seek, Monsieur, not yours."

10

SEPTEMBER 29, 1870 – MARIELE

"THE MAJOR ORDER here to halt, Madame," said the corporal escorting them back toward Paris. His French was so basic and heavily accented that Mariele asked him to repeat the statement twice before understanding that their guides would be leaving them.

She looked around. In the immediate surroundings was a stone cottage with a dilapidated roof and a rusty scythe leaning against one wall. Weeds choked what might once have been a flower garden, and beneath a gnarled oak tree, a wagon with one missing wheel was propped on a large boulder. The cottage was situated on a slight rise, but, gazing into the distance, Mariele saw only forest to the right of where they stood and farmland stretching off to the left in undulating waves. Not a village in sight.

"Here, Corporal?" her mother asked.

Despite the almost lifeless tone in her mother's voice, Mariele heard the apprehension.

"*Jawohl*. We go," said the soldier.

"Just a minute," Mariele said. "How far is it to Paris?"

The men's puzzled looks made it clear the corporal and his

young companion did not understand. Mariele stretched her hands wide to show distance and used two fingers to illustrate someone walking from one hand toward the other. The corporal still looked puzzled; however, the younger soldier said something, and the two men talked back and forth.

"Ten, eleven *Meilen*," the corporal said.

"Ten or eleven miles?" Mariele repeated.

The corporal nodded, and the younger soldier offered her a leather rucksack. *"Wasser und das Essen."*

She took the pouch of food and water, then stood with her mother as the men turned their horses and trotted away. In a few minutes, they were mere specks in the distance, and Mariele and her mother were totally alone. She looked around once more. The cottage was clearly deserted, and if the Prussian soldiers had come to this point, it was likely that any families living in the vicinity had fled their homes out of fear. How far would she and her mother have to travel before finding help?

"Can you walk, Maman?" she asked.

Her mother's shoes were black kid-leather pumps fastened with three buckled straps, each toe decorated with a green velvet bow. After five days of confinement, the shoes were filthy. They were also distinctly unsuited to the distance they must now cover. Mariele glanced at her own sturdy pair of black boots and wondered why Maman had made such a choice.

"I'll be all right," her mother replied. "We're free, and that's all that matters. I don't care if I have to walk barefoot back to Paris." She shaded her eyes and gazed across the rolling countryside. "Your father will be surprised when he sees us." For the first time in days, her mother smiled.

"If we're on the Billancourt road, Paris must be over there," Mariele said, pointing in an easterly direction.

"But how do we know which road to follow?"

"I'm more concerned with how to avoid soldiers and thieves," Mariele replied. "Papa showed me a map of the forts surrounding Paris. I don't remember them all, but I do remember Fort de Vanves, which is not too far from Clamart and Fort d'Issy. They both should be in that direction." Mariele pointed toward a distant church spire.

"If that's the case, Fort Valérien should be over there." Her mother gestured in a more northerly direction. "Perhaps we can take refuge at one of the forts and ask the commander to send a message to your father." She seemed happy with that notion.

"I think we should avoid the forts, Maman. Our soldiers may be out on patrol. They'll have their weapons with them. If they encounter us, we might be in danger."

"In danger from our own soldiers?"

Mariele nodded. Time was passing. They needed to reach Paris before dark. With Prussian and French soldiers in the vicinity, the roads were unlikely to be safe. Instead, they would have to walk across the fields and through the forests and pray they didn't encounter anyone.

"Let's go through the fields behind this cottage," she said. "Mont-Valérien is visible in that direction. If we keep that as our beacon for the first few miles, we'll avoid the forts."

MARIELE WAS uncertain how long they'd been walking, although the morning sun was now higher in the sky and the temperature much warmer. Her legs ached, and the bottoms of her feet were bruised from the uneven terrain. She and her mother had passed through many fields where crops were ready for harvesting—corn, wheat, beets, and other root vegetables—and stepped across small streams, occasionally with the aid of a stone or two they'd placed in the water to keep their feet dry. A forest loomed in front of them, and she was debating whether to pass through it or try to skirt around the edges when her mother spoke.

"Can we sit for a while?" her mother asked. "I have a dreadful blister on my foot."

Mariele set down the rucksack. "Of course, Maman. And we'll have a sip of water too. Why don't you take your shoe off? Perhaps we should bandage your foot."

Her mother perched on a large stone near the forest's edge and breathed a sigh of relief. "I don't think I could have gone much longer," she said. "How far do you think we've come?"

Mariele shrugged. "I don't have a watch, but I think we've been walking for almost two hours. We may have covered three or four miles, and if those soldiers were right, we have seven or eight miles to go." Mariele didn't mention that since they weren't traveling in a straight line toward Paris, the journey would take longer. So far, her mother had been curiously compliant, not at all her normally decisive self. As long as Mariele could keep them moving, they should reach Paris before nightfall.

"It's a large blister," her mother said after removing her stocking and examining the base of her foot.

Although they'd been permitted to change their clothes before leaving Versailles, they had none of their luggage with them, nor could they have carried it on this cross-country journey, so their only possessions were the clothes on their backs and the small sack of provisions. Mariele lifted her skirt, grabbed the bottom ruffle of her petticoat, and tore a strip from the fine cotton garment. "Here, Maman. Let's wind this around your foot. The padding should make it more comfortable."

After securing the strip of cotton, her mother replaced the shoe. "It's tight," she said. "But it should be all right. If I were clever like you, I would have chosen boots for today." She shaded her eyes. "Let's sit a little longer. The view is beautiful."

It occurred to Mariele that it would be better to keep walking, but her mother was right, the view was indeed beautiful and the colors particularly striking: soft blue skies; dusky yellow wheat fields; sturdy evergreens marking the distant hills; and leaves with the first hints of gold and red. As she watched a long line of birds fly overhead, she thought she heard the babble of a nearby stream.

An explosion shattered the calm.

"What was that?" Her mother froze.

"Cannon, I think, but they're probably far away from us." Mariele hoped she was right, although the sound was louder than the cannon they could hear from their house in Paris. "We should start walking again, Maman. How is your foot?"

Her mother rose from the ground and took a few tentative steps. "It's fine," she said. "Much better now that it's wrapped. What direction should we take? I think the cannon are coming from over there." She pointed in a southerly direction. "Perhaps Fort d'Issy is firing on the Prussians."

"Let's go through the woods," Mariele said. "If there are soldiers about, they are unlikely to be in the woods." She picked up the rucksack and led the way.

TRAVERSING the woods proved to be more of a challenge than Mariele had anticipated, for the underbrush was dense and the lower branches of the trees and evergreens protruded like sharpened sticks to impede their progress. With no path to follow and no horizon to guide them, she soon doubted the decision to walk through the woods and worried that they would become hopelessly lost. To make matters worse, they were now climbing uphill.

Mariele stopped. "What do you think that is, Maman?" She pointed to her left, where a canvas tarp attached to four tree trunks could be seen about fifty yards away.

"It seems that someone has built a small shelter. Hello!" her mother shouted. *"Bonjour!"*

"Maman!" Mariele grabbed her mother's arm. "Be quiet. We

have no idea who might be living here in the woods. They might not welcome strangers."

Her mother looked stricken. "I'm sorry," she whispered. "I was just so glad to think that someone might be able to help us. Should we turn back or go in a different direction?"

The tarp flapped in the breeze. Mariele caught a whiff of smoke from a fire recently extinguished. Her eyes darted left and right, searching for movement. The forest was still. She put a finger to her lips, tugged at her mother's arm, and pointed to the right. "*Là-bas*," she said softly and headed downhill, away from the shelter.

They had only taken a few steps when a man leapt out from the bushes and blocked their way. "Who are you?" he shouted, his voice harsh and ragged. "Why are you here?"

"Monsieur?" Mariele's mother pleaded. "Please, Monsieur. We were captured by Prussian soldiers and are now making our way back to Paris. Can you help us, Monsieur?"

The man was bedraggled, his hair long and unkempt, his clothing torn in places, his face smudged with dirt and soot. He stepped closer. Body odor assaulted Mariele's nose. She wondered how long he'd been living in the forest, and at the same time wondered if he intended to do them harm. "This is my mother, Monsieur. We were left on the road not long after dawn, and we've been walking ever since. If you can point the way to Sèvres, we would be grateful."

She had no intention of going through the town of Sèvres. Under the circumstances, it was likely full of looters and thieves, since most of the townspeople had escaped to the safety of Paris. However, if they knew where it lay, they could make a plan.

The man gestured down the hill.

"Thank you, Monsieur. We're very grateful," her mother said. She stepped toward Mariele.

"Not so fast," the man said. He held out his hand. "I'll have that ring you're wearing, Madame."

Maman gasped. "Please, Monsieur. The ring belonged to my mother. She gave it to me just before she died. It is all I have of hers."

He snorted. "As if I care. Never knew my mother. She died giving birth to me. And now the bloody Prussians have taken everything else." He grabbed her hand. "Give it to me, or I'll take it off myself, and you won't like that."

An instant later, the man held a knife against her mother's cheek.

"Maman!" Mariele cried, her voice strangled with fear. "Give it to him, Maman. Your life is worth more to all of us than Grandmother's ring. Papa would say that too. I'm sure Monsieur will let us go as soon as you hand it over, won't you, Monsieur?" With a supreme effort, she made her voice calm and quiet, all the while holding her mother's gaze. "Just take it off, Maman. You can do that, can't you? Everything will be fine. I'm sure we'll be fine."

Her mother's eyes filled with tears. With great care, she wiggled the ring back and forth, edging it over her knuckle until she held it in her fingers. The man thrust out his hand, and she placed the ring onto his palm. "I hope it helps you, Monsieur."

Her mother's vulnerability was raw and vivid. Where had her once proud and forceful mother gone? Who was this meek, vanquished soul? Mariele took her arm. "This way, Maman. Watch your step. The earth is rather slippery."

IT TOOK MORE than thirty minutes to descend the hill and emerge from the woods into a field of corn with stalks high enough to reach their shoulders. They walked between two rows of corn until reaching another field, this one planted with onions. From there, Mariele could see a wooden hut and, a little farther off, a cluster of buildings framed by rolling hills.

"I wonder what town that is?" her mother said, one hand raised to shade her eyes. "It's not large enough to be Sèvres. Do you think that man was telling the truth?"

Mariele shook her head. "I don't know. But if he was, then we should continue in that general direction. Should we have something to eat first?"

They hadn't looked at the food the soldiers had given them, and now Mariele reached into the rucksack and pulled out a cloth so worn their cook would have thrown it into the rag bin. Wrapped inside the cloth were two thick slices of bread, a hunk of ripe cheese, and a few radishes.

"A feast," her mother said.

"WE NEED TO CONTINUE WALKING, MAMAN," Mariele said after they'd eaten half the food and rested for a while. "How is your foot?"

Her mother looked away. "Fine. It's fine. And you're right, we must get home to Paris."

"I think we went the wrong way through the woods, which means we still have quite a long way to go." After Mariele got to her feet, she reached out a hand to help her mother stand. "We'll cross this field, then keep close to the forest edge until we reach Sèvres. With luck, there may be a path we can follow."

The path they found bordered the forest but petered out as soon as they passed a small village, where an eerie silence prevailed, and every home had been abandoned. The only sign of life was an old man plodding alongside a horse-drawn wagon. Mariele led the way, clambering over thick roots and trickling streams and large boulders that had been left beside the forest when the fields were originally cleared.

She hadn't realized that her mother had fallen behind until

she heard her cry out, "Mariele! I need your help."

"Maman! Are you all right?" Mariele hurried back. "What has happened?"

"I think I've twisted my ankle."

Mariele knelt down to examine her mother's foot. "Let's take your shoe off."

After removing the shoe, Mariele discovered that her mother's left foot was swollen and bloody. The right foot was almost as bad. "Why didn't you tell me, Maman? We should have done something a long time ago."

"I suppose I should have sent for my maid," her mother said sharply. "In case you haven't noticed, we have no luggage with us, and certainly not an extra pair of shoes."

"You could have worn mine."

"And then what would you have done?"

"Let's not quarrel, Maman. I'll give you my boots. They may be a little big for you, but if you lace them properly, they will support your ankle. I can go barefoot for a while."

"You will do no such thing."

Mariele laughed at the absurdity of her mother's command.

"Why are you laughing?" her mother said. "I don't see anything that's the least bit amusing."

"I'm sorry, Maman. You're right. Our situation isn't the least bit amusing. We have to return to Paris before nightfall. You can't walk in those shoes. You've twisted your ankle." Mariele removed her boots. "Please put these on. And I'll give you my stockings as well. Can't you see that this is the most sensible thing to do?"

Her mother harrumphed. "Well, if you insist."

Five minutes later, they were once more walking at the forest's edge, making slow but steady progress. Mariele had one arm around her mother's waist and the rucksack slung over her shoulders. "We make a fine pair, don't we?" She wiped a bead of sweat from her brow.

"It would be easier to walk along the road," her mother replied.

"Yes, but not as safe."

After a few more steps, her mother spoke again. "Do you think we'll find Sèvres abandoned as well?"

"That's very likely, Maman. All those people who came into Paris after the emperor surrendered would have come from small towns like Sèvres. Papa said they were seeking refuge from Prussian attacks."

As they continued walking, stones, tree roots, and small shrubs dug into the soles of Mariele's feet. Now they were bruised and the skin scraped raw. When she began to limp, her mother forced her to stop.

"What's wrong, Mariele?"

"It's nothing to worry about."

"Let me be the judge of that. Sit on that stump over there so I can have a look."

Mariele was grateful to sit down. She watched her mother tear a strip from her own petticoat and dip it into a small stream. The world around them was still and quiet, except for two birds calling back and forth and the buzz of a bee hovering at the mouth of a fading blue cornflower. She closed her eyes and imagined a picnic spread out on a blanket beneath one of the wide-limbed oaks she'd seen along this stretch of the forest, Bertrand leaning back against the tree's trunk as they both enjoyed—

"We need to bandage your feet." Her mother's voice interrupted Mariele's reverie. "Now that I've wiped the dirt off, I can see that they are scratched and bruised. The left one is bleeding. You should put your boots back on. I'll wear my shoes."

"But you're the one with a twisted ankle. Your shoes are not fit for walking. We'll bandage my feet, just like you suggested, Maman. I'm sure I'll be fine."

Her mother sniffed. "Stubborn," she said. "Just as stubborn as your father."

Using strips of cloth from both petticoats, they bound Mariele's feet with several layers, then tied the ends around her ankles. Mariele stood and walked a few paces. "Much more comfortable," she said. "Although I look ridiculous. Thank you, Maman. Shall we continue?"

THEY SPENT an hour skirting the edges of Sèvres, keeping hidden whenever possible by walking within the forest's growth rather than at its edge. Occasionally, they had no choice but to cross a field or slink through an alley behind a row of houses. They made as little noise as possible.

The light had begun to fade when Mariele realized that not only would they have to cross the Seine at Sèvres, but they would also have to gain admittance to the city through one of its massive fortified gates. "We have no documents, Maman. How will we enter the city?"

They had been walking with arms linked, but now her mother withdrew her arm and turned to face Mariele. "We are Parisians. We will merely tell them where we live and your father's name. I'm sure it won't be a problem. Why would they doubt two women like us?"

Now that they were closer to Paris, her mother's spirits had revived and Mariele did not want to point out that in their present state, they looked more like servants than members of the wealthy class.

"I'm sure you're right. Now, look over there. I think that's the bridge we need to cross."

Like the sky, the Seine was tinged with pink. Spanning the river with a series of low arches, the bridge connecting Sèvres to the outskirts of Paris was a welcome sight. On the far side, a collection of low buildings flanked by trees glowed in the sunset. The bridge was deserted. Normally frequented by men and boys fishing for their supper, the banks on both sides of the river were empty.

Was it safe to cross? Mariele refused to consider otherwise. They had to take a chance. They were exhausted and hungry. Her mother's limp was more pronounced than it had been. Her own feet were so badly damaged, she could not imagine putting on a shoe for weeks. There was simply no other choice.

"It won't take us long to get across," her mother said.

Mariele wanted to run. Every muscle tensed, her entire body alert for signs of danger. "Let's hurry, Maman. It will soon be dark."

With each step that brought them closer to the other side, Mariele felt they were being watched. At the halfway point, a rifle sounded. Straight away, she pulled her mother down into a crouch. "Shh, Maman. Remain still." Mariele counted to one hundred. Everything around them was silent.

"Walk in a crouch if you can, Maman. We'll be less visible."

Once across the bridge, they continued straight, risking the openness of the road leading to Porte de Sèvres. Just like the other towns they had passed, Billancourt was deserted. Pigeons strolled along the roadside while rats scurried about, looking for refuse.

A dog barked and her mother jumped. "That startled me," she said.

Mariele squeezed her arm. "Not long now."

Night had fallen by the time the gate loomed in front of them: massive, impenetrable, marked by turrets and gun slits and, at regular intervals, the black, ominous protrusion of cannon. Mariele felt rather than saw the eyes that watched them approach. On either side of the gate, the walls of the city stretched stone by stone, stacked and interlocked to a height of fifty feet and protected by a wide, deep moat. *Surely*, Mariele thought, *no one can conquer the walls of Paris*.

Approaching the gate, she felt as small and insignificant as a mouse. The possibility that they might be turned away added to the chill that swooped in with the setting sun.

"Halt!" a gruff voice shouted. "No one can be admitted to the city after dusk."

Where did the voice come from? Mariele wondered.

"Monsieur," her mother called out. "We are two defenseless women, citizens of Paris. We were captured by Prussian soldiers six days ago and finally released this morning. Please, monsieur. We must get home to our family."

Silence.

Mariele and her mother waited, anxiety and fear building like the thick, swirling clouds of a threatening storm. She was so tired, so incredibly weary from their ordeal that she could barely stand.

"My name is Evangeline de Crécy," her mother said. "Wife of Philippe de Crécy, who is a well-known advisor to the government. I ask that you convey us to him immediately. He will verify our identities and reward you handsomely."

Her mother's voice was strong and commanding. Was this the same woman who had appeared so defeated and uncertain all day? The same woman who had wept inconsolably every night in captivity?

A harsh, scraping sound emanated from an iron door at the left side of the gate, then a creak as the door swung open. A soldier beckoned them forward. "Quickly!" he shouted.

The door clanged shut behind them. The soldier shoved two thick bolts into place. "This way. Follow me."

Mariele's mother maintained her bravado through an hour of interrogation with three officers of increasing seniority. Eventually they were permitted to depart unaccompanied through the deserted streets of Paris.

Her mother deflated immediately. She sagged against Mariele. "Can you take us home, *ma chérie?*"

"Of course, Maman."

11

OCTOBER 1870 – MARIELE

EXHAUSTED AND BEDRAGGLED, Mariele lifted the thick knocker accented with carved ribbons of brass and let it fall. She smiled limply at her mother and knocked again. Maman's cheeks were sunburned, and her hair—normally tightly coifed—now lay like thick ropes down her back. Their clothes were filthy, their hands scratched from the woods they'd traversed, their legs so fatigued they could barely stand. Mariele wore no boots; her feet, bound in strips of cotton torn from her mother's petticoat, were cut and blistered, the cloth damp with blood.

She was about to lift the knocker again when the door opened, and Eugène, his mouth wide with shock, looked at them, shaking his head but otherwise frozen into immobility.

"What . . . how . . . Madame . . ." he finally stammered.

"Please open the door so we can come in, Eugène," Mariele said. "Maman needs help. Is Monsieur at home?"

"Yes."

"Fetch him immediately. Maman, come sit on this chair while Eugène finds Papa."

Mariele sagged with relief. Since early morning, she'd been in charge. It had seemed odd to tell Maman what to do;

however, as they walked home, that was exactly what was required. Her mother had simply lost her ability to function, and there had been times when Mariele had taken her hand like a child and led her along step by step.

Although the house had been quiet when they first arrived, Mariele soon heard muffled voices followed by swift footsteps rushing along the hall, then clattering down the stairs.

"Evangeline!" her father exclaimed. "*Merde alors.* Help me, Theo. Right away. We must get your mother and sister upstairs."

While her father and Eugène assisted Maman, Mariele leaned on her brother's arm and followed them up the stairs to the petit salon, where two empty wineglasses sat on a small table between overstuffed chairs, and the embers of an earlier fire emitted a warm glow. Smaller than the main salon, the petit salon featured a walnut secretary topped with glass-fronted bookshelves, and a life-sized painting of golden chariots drawn by two black horses. Red was the room's dominant color.

"Eugène, find Suzette," her father commanded. "Ask her to draw a bath for Madame and one for Mademoiselle immediately. Theo, see what you can do to rekindle the fire." He knelt beside Evangeline and began to rub her hands. "You're freezing. I expected you to be in Rouen by now. What in God's name happened?"

When it became clear that her mother was unable to respond, Mariele recounted the events that had occurred since they'd first left Paris.

"They thought you were spies? How is it possible for two well-bred women to be taken for spies?" Papa asked.

"One of the officers questioned us each day," she said. She glanced at her mother to determine how much to reveal, but her mother seemed to be staring at something only she could see. "We . . . we kept each other strong."

"Shall I send for the doctor, Papa?" Theo asked.

"Yes. And ask Cook for some food. I'm sure she has leftovers from dinner."

Papa looked at each of them in turn, his face full of anguish. "This is all my fault."

"No, Philippe. You did what you thought best for our safety." Maman spoke for the first time. A little color had returned to her cheeks. "Mariele has been very strong," her mother added. "Strong enough for both of us. I don't know what I would have done without her. The Prussians are ruthless. They fully intend to conquer Paris."

The look of despair on her mother's face brought Mariele's thoughts back to the little room they had shared and the sound of her mother's weeping—ragged sobs mixed with pitiful whimpering. Mariele had been shocked to see her mother, normally in command of any situation she faced, reduced to such a wretched state. She reached out and squeezed her mother's hand. "We survived together, Maman. Didn't we?"

Theo returned, carrying a tray laden with two steaming bowls of thick soup and a small basket of bread. "I've sent for the doctor."

"This morning," Mariele said after taking a few mouthfuls, "they left us on the Billancourt road just a short distance from Versailles."

"You walked all the way home from Versailles?"

"And Mariele gave me her boots to wear," Maman said. Warmth and food and the familiarity of home seemed to have improved her mother's spirits, and she looked at Mariele with affection. "I don't know what I would have done without her."

"What did you encounter along the way?" her father asked.

"Very few people," Mariele replied, "and many deserted farms. Villages like Chaville and Sèvres were deserted too. Some of the houses have been looted. Most of the time, we walked along the forest's edge rather than the road. When we came close to Sèvres, we saw many French soldiers. A large group rode by on horseback, and I was glad then that we were not on the road." She nodded as much to herself as to the others, recalling the sound of hundreds of horses and the vibration that had echoed in her chest as they thundered by.

"Were you afraid?" Theo asked.

"We were," her mother replied. "But your sister was very brave."

"It was the sound of cannon that made me afraid," Mariele said. "You can't imagine it—so loud the heavens seem to be cracking open."

"Excuse me, Monsieur. The baths are ready," Suzette said. "Madame, Mademoiselle, I am so sorry to hear of your experience. A hot bath will make you feel much better, and I have laid out fresh clothes for each of you."

"Thank you, Suzette," her mother said. "I'll need your help before you retire for the night."

Mariele was pleased to hear a note of familiar imperiousness creeping back into her mother's voice. She turned toward her brother. "Theo, will you send a message to Bertrand? He'll be waiting for news, and I should let him know we are back in Paris."

"I'll take the message myself if Papa will permit me to ride Roulette."

Mariele followed her mother upstairs, and after shedding her clothes and unwrapping her swollen feet, she sank into the tub with a deep sigh. She must have dozed, for the water was tepid when she got out of the bath and wrapped herself in the large towel Suzette had placed on a stool beside the tub. Finally, dressed in a loose *sacque*, Mariele returned to the sitting room, where Bertrand was deep in conversation with Theo and her father.

Bertrand stood immediately. "Thank God you're safe." He wrapped his arms around her and whispered in her ear, "I can't bear the thought of what might have happened."

Mariele leaned against him, feeling his warm, solid body and the calm beating of his heart. She didn't care if it was improper to display such affection in front of her family, and for a long moment, she clung to him.

"Your father has told me how brave you were," he said with one arm still firmly around her waist. "I should never have let you leave. Pardon me, Monsieur de Crécy. I did not mean to imply you made the wrong decision."

"I've taken no offense, Bertrand. And it seems I did make the wrong decision. Would you like a brandy?"

"Thank you, sir. Most kind of you. I mustn't stay long, though. I joined the National Guard, and there are rumors of a Prussian assault, so I should be available for duty. Did you see the barricades on your way into the city?" He did not wait for her reply. "Great crowds are gathering daily in front of the *mairies,* waiting for news while soldiers are marching and people are singing 'La Marseillaise' at the slightest opportunity."

Mariele frowned. "If Parisians saw what Maman and I saw, they would realize how much danger our city faces. At Versailles, there were Prussian troops everywhere and an enormous field full of cannon and other artillery. The soldiers looked so serious and determined. We were suspected of being spies. Spies! As if Maman and I could ever be that clever."

"There is no doubt you are clever, *chérie,*" her father said. "Clever enough to withstand their questioning and walk back to Paris. As to rumors of an assault, there's great confusion in government circles. Some argue we should strike the Prussian army before they are well entrenched, while others say our army is of inferior size and we must wait for the provinces to send more troops and for our National Guard and Garde Mobile to strengthen." He was pacing back and forth in front of the fireplace now, his hands clasped behind his back. "To make matters worse, those who are socialists care more about establishing a republican form of government than they do about defeating the Prussians. They consider Trochu part of the old guard and dismiss his intentions as imperialist at heart." Her father threw up his hands. "But enough of that. I admire that you've joined the National Guard, Bertrand. Unfortunately, I'm too old to serve. You are welcome to visit again tomorrow. I'm sure my daughter will want to see you."

Despite the impropriety of being in her *sacque* without the usual corset and crinolines, her father made no protest when Mariele escorted Bertrand downstairs, where the hall clock's pendulum swung reassuringly back and forth.

"You could have been badly hurt," he said, holding her hands as they stood facing one another in the dim shadows.

"I was afraid," she said, "although I tried not to show it. The man who questioned us pretended to be kind at first, but he enjoyed frightening me. And the soldier who took me back to our holding cell seemed to take pleasure from hurting me." Mariele shivered.

Bertrand put his arms around her and pulled her close. He drew back a little and kissed her, gently at first and then with more insistence. His kiss aroused deep emotions.

"You should rest now," he said after releasing her. "I will see you tomorrow."

"Tomorrow," she echoed. "Yes, I would like that."

She watched him climb into the carriage and urge the horse forward. He turned and waved before disappearing through the gate. Mariele closed the door softly, then went upstairs to the sitting room, where her father was waiting.

"You did well, *ma bichette*," he said. "I'm so very proud. I shudder to think what Maman would have done without you. The doctor tells me that all she needs is rest. Now, as your Papa, I think the very best thing for you to do is get some sleep." He kissed her forehead. "Sleep well, my brave little one. We have many long days ahead of us."

12

OCTOBER 1870 – CAMILLE

CAMILLE CHECKED the clock hanging above the marble-topped console, its steady tick-tick-tick a reassuring sign amid the unfolding chaos of Paris. She was scheduled to be at the Odéon Theater by ten a.m. If she left now, she had time to walk through the Luxembourg Gardens, where dahlias were in full bloom and she could pass her favorite statues and the Medici Fountain, which always calmed her.

When they were younger, Camille and Juliette had often wandered through the gardens trailed by their governess, who enforced a strict regimen of daily walks and fresh air whatever the weather. As her illness worsened, Juliette would often dispatch Camille to take a walk for the two of them and toss a coin into the fountain. During the last six months of Juliette's life, Camille had tossed many coins accompanied by wishes for her sister to be spared. All to no avail.

"Monique!" Camille called out as she descended the stairs to the foyer.

"Yes, Mademoiselle?" The housemaid emerged from a swinging door that led to the kitchen.

"Do we have any fresh meat in the house?"

"We have chicken, and Monsieur Paradis has promised me some fish. I have no idea where he gets it, and I ask no questions, but he did say yesterday that he expected a few *daurade*." Monique wiped her hands on her apron, then pushed a loose red curl behind one ear.

Evidence of Parisian ingenuity continued to impress Camille. Despite severe shortages, the closure of the city's gates, and a tangle of regulations, both men and women found ways to circumvent restrictions. She wouldn't put it past Monsieur Paradis to pay young boys to fish in the streams outside the city gates. Children seemed to be invisible to the authorities.

"Make sure you get some fish, but we'll have the chicken tonight. Father mentioned bringing a guest home for dinner." She handed a few coins to Monique. "If that's not enough, tell Monsieur Paradis to put the rest on our account. And will you ask Madame Carnot to prepare her Armagnac chicken? She'll know what else to serve."

Camille's mother would have scrutinized every detail of the dinner preparations from the placement of candles to the choice of butter knives, but there was no time for such niceties now, and she had found that Madame Carnot enjoyed making her own selections. Keeping their cook and other members of the household content was critical to having the freedom for her other endeavors.

Victor ran down the stairs just as Monique disappeared. "Are you going out?" he asked.

Camille drew on one of her gloves. "I'm off to the Odéon. Are you busy this morning?"

He nodded. "I'm scheduled for evening Mass, but I have other things to do. Word has gotten around that we're looking after young children and our numbers are growing. Father Basil and I have our hands full. Shall I walk part way with you?"

"Yes, please. I need to talk to you." Camille drew an umbrella from a tall ceramic container by the front entrance. "It looks like it might rain."

"I'VE BEEN WANTING to talk to you too," Victor said a few minutes later, as they turned right onto rue de Sèvres. "But first, tell me what's on your mind."

Camille looked at her brother with affection. Victor never failed to put someone else's needs before his own. "I'll have a long day at the Odéon and Father was insistent this morning that I shop for more canned goods. At the rate I've been purchasing goods, we soon won't have any room left in the cellar." She smiled. "Would you have time to purchase a few items on your way to the church?"

"I think so. I can go to Monsieur Panisse's shop. I'll ask him to deliver. Do you have a list?"

Camille drew a piece of paper from her pocket. "Here's the list. We need canned goods like devilled ham and turkey, oysters, lobster, corn, and beans. I have to get some flour, rice, barley and tea as well, but those can wait for tomorrow. If Monsieur Panisse doesn't have all of these, ask him what other canned goods are available."

"I will."

"Father expects severe shortages. He reminds me almost daily, that money spent today will be money saved in the future. However, I'm sure he has a plan to ensure we have sufficient food to eat."

"Father and his schemes," Victor replied.

Camille turned her head. Victor's expression remained calm, but his tone had an edge to it. What did he know of their father's dealings? Did priests concern themselves with business matters? "Yes," she said. "Father and his schemes."

Victor continued as if she hadn't said anything. "With new restrictions on meat and bread and milk being rationed, prices are exorbitant. Everywhere I look beggars fill the streets. There are days when I think our father hasn't a charitable bone in his body."

A scowl contorted her brother's face, and Camille was surprised at the harshness of his words. "He only wants what's best for the family," she said.

Victor harumphed. "Maybe you're right."

They were quiet for a little while and then spoke of other topics: the vegetables growing in the hothouse garden; the prevalence of barricades and sandbags and tents; the balloons leaving Paris every day carrying mail or returning with news from the outside world.

"General Trochu and his commanders haven't had any success yet," Victor said. "And the Prussians are growing stronger."

"It's all so distressing," Camille replied. "I climbed to the top of the Arc de Triomphe yesterday and could see for miles with Father's binoculars. Great clouds of smoke burst from every direction as the Prussians fired on our forts. I don't understand why our government isn't negotiating for a peaceful resolution."

AT RUE DE GRENELLE, they stopped. "I'll leave you here, Camille," Victor said. "If he asks, tell Father I'll be home around seven." He placed a hand on her arm. "I'm so proud of what you're doing at the hospital. Such work requires great determination and strength, and it must be difficult seeing so many wounded men. I pray for you and the others every day."

Camille touched his cheek with her fingertips. "Thank you, Victor. But you forgot to tell me what you wanted to talk about."

Victor chuckled. "My mind is so muddled these days. I wanted to ask you whether you can think of someone who might be willing to help with the young children at the church.

Father Basil isn't really up to it. He's almost eighty and walks very slowly."

"I'd be glad to help. Give me a day or two. Many of my friends have left the city, but I'm sure I can find someone."

HER ELDEST BROTHER'S approval surprised Camille. He was more prone to criticize than to praise her, although she was willing to admit that some of her actions were less than laudable. As she approached Luxembourg Gardens, she considered which of her friends might help Victor. *Perhaps Mariele de Crécy would agree.* Bertrand had told them all about the failed escape from Paris, and she had new respect for her future sister-in-law. Withstanding severe questioning by Prussian officers and walking back to Paris from Versailles were impressive feats. She would send Mariele a letter tomorrow.

Once inside the gardens, Camille paused to toss a coin into the Medici Fountain and made a wish for the siege to end quickly. Though she knew she should hurry, she stopped to admire a few late-blooming roses and the deep reds and purples of Juliette's favorite dahlias. Twenty minutes later, she crossed the black-and-white tiled floor of the theater's lobby, hurried up the grand staircase, and entered the cloakroom, where her apron hung from a hook behind the door.

Given the nature of her work at the Odéon hospital, Camille had asked Monique where she might buy some plain, serviceable clothes and had acquired several items in practical colors. Today she wore a dark green dress that required no bustle and had fastened a black belt at her waist, from which she could hang keys should the need arise. A lace collar was the only nod to fashion.

Her duties were familiar now, and she was used to the sights and sounds, the way some soldiers clung to her hand, the empty beds of men who had died overnight, the fatigue, and her cold, chapped skin. As she approached the ward located on the main stage, she wondered how she might acquire a pair of boots sturdy enough for winter wear. The likelihood of purchasing them was slim, but perhaps Louise or Maman had left a pair that would fit.

Being at the hospital had given her a sense of purpose, and the soldiers—she had begun to think of some of them as *her* soldiers—made her feel needed. Instead of reading to them one by one, those who were able gathered around those who couldn't leave their beds, and she read stories to small groups along with occasional bits of gossip from Paris newspapers. She wrote letters too and spooned soup or thin stew into waiting mouths. Occasionally, she played cards, and Jean, a young man from Tours who was already half in love with her, was teaching her to play chess. The squeamishness she had felt on first encountering wounded soldiers had disappeared, and the hours flew by such that she was often exhausted when it was time for her to leave.

In the early afternoon, she took a break to have tea with the others in one of the larger dressing rooms. Camille liked these bold women whose experiences were so different from her own. They talked about life on stage, the men who kept them, and the ones they loved. At first, the conversations had stopped each time she joined them, and it wasn't until she expressly said she wanted to hear about their lives that they had relaxed in front of her. Marie Colombier had made a distinct impression, and Camille felt they were becoming friends.

Marie greeted Camille with enthusiasm. "Ah," she said, "our little socialite is with us again today." Marie laughed. "Now, don't take offense, *chérie*, I'm very happy to have you here, and I've told the great Sarah that you have talent and we must find more for you to do."

"Did you say that, Marie?" Camille felt a small flush of pride.

"*Bien sûr*," Marie confirmed with a nod.

"Well, I'm very grateful. I enjoy the work, but I would like to do more than read to our wounded or write their letters."

A petite woman with red hair entered the room, her hips swaying provocatively. She wore a ribbon around her neck that matched the vivid blue of her dress. As she came closer, Camille noticed the woman's black-rimmed eyes and rouged cheeks.

"*Bonjour,* Félicienne," Marie said. "Sarah mentioned you were planning to join us. Have you met Camille?" The woman shook her head. "Camille, this is Félicienne Dumont. Félicienne, Camille Noisette."

"I'm pleased to meet you," Camille said.

Félicienne smiled as she pulled out the pin securing her wide-brimmed hat and lifted the hat from her head. "Your surname is unusual, Mademoiselle. I've met a Monsieur Noisette. Perhaps you're related to him? I believe he has done well with certain large building projects."

"Most likely you've met my father, then, and not my brother," Camille replied.

"Your father. Ah!" Félicienne exchanged a look with Marie. "Yes, I was introduced to him at the Odéon. For some reason, the name stuck with me. Such an interesting man. And you have a brother as well?"

Camille wondered under what circumstances a woman like Félicienne would be introduced to her father. Although her red hair and voluptuous figure were striking, the woman's demeanor seemed coarse rather than refined like that of Sarah, Sophie, and Marie. *Surely Father isn't attracted to a woman like this.* She kept her smile fixed and her voice cool.

"Three brothers, actually," she replied. "The eldest is a priest. The second is in business with my father, and the youngest is only sixteen."

"Camille is a volunteer," Marie explained. "She reads to our men and sometimes writes letters for them."

"And I hope to do more," Camille said. "Marie, I must

compliment you on your glamorous dress, but surely you haven't worn that on the wards today."

Just then, Sarah Bernhardt entered the room. "Dressed like that, Marie must have been with her paramour last night. You should change, my friend. You won't want men to bleed on that lovely gown. Will you tell me who fashioned it for you, or will that be your little secret?"

Marie laughed. "I'll keep it a secret for now. Excuse me, ladies, duty awaits."

Sarah Bernhardt wore her nurse's uniform, a starched, voluminous affair that seemed none too practical but showed her dark hair and bright lips to advantage. "May I have a word with you, Camille?"

Camille followed her through the hall behind the main stage, where soldiers lay on narrow cots, then down a short flight of stairs to the front-row seats of the theater.

"Marie tells me you're interested in doing more than reading to our soldiers," she said when they were both seated. "Is that correct?"

"Yes, Madame. I was planning to ask you whether this would be possible." Camille hoped that her dedication and long hours had shown Madame Bernhardt that she was capable of more complicated tasks and dispelled the notion that she was a dilettante.

"This is excellent. I will have you trained to help with the nursing. I have it on good authority that we will soon have more casualties, so we must prepare. It's clear we need more nursing staff, and I don't wish the Odéon to have a reputation like that of the hospital at the Grand Hôtel. I learned just last week that they lose almost ninety percent of those who undergo operations." She went on to outline the training Camille would receive. "You will learn the basics, then learn more from the doctors and other nurses. It's hard work. Are you sure this is what you want?"

Hard work was exactly what she wanted. Although many of her friends seemed to savor idle chatter and endless rounds of visiting, she was tired of living for pleasure, without purpose or responsibility. With her mother away, she was getting a taste for household matters, but these were chores and not the least bit fulfilling. The hospital would be a fine place to contribute. She had plenty of time, as long as she reserved evenings for Louise Michel's meetings in Montmartre.

"Yes, Madame, and thank you. You won't be disappointed."

Sarah cocked her head. "I don't intend to be disappointed."

13

OCTOBER 1870 – MARIELE

MARIELE WOKE to the sound of drums and bugles playing a reveille. Soldiers were now lodged in every corner of Paris, including the grounds of Hôpital Beaujon, not far from their home. Beyond the morning reveille, she heard the distant pop of rifle fire, and the banging of hammers as the army enlarged their facilities. Making room for troops from the regular army, the Garde Mobile, and the National Guard meant that the city's public spaces had been repurposed into barracks, parade grounds, storage facilities, and practice facilities. Everywhere she went she saw men in uniform, and yet General Trochu seemed incapable of striking a decisive blow against the Prussians. At least that was what her father believed, often shaking his head as he repeated the sentiment.

Paris was no longer a place of beauty. Instead, work parties staffed by soldiers had erected barricades at most major crossroads, while along the wide avenues leading out of the city, the ground had been honeycombed, each hole filled with pointed stakes. The flag of the French Red Cross flew from many buildings, and on the Avenue de l'Impératrice, the American Ambulance had erected a series of canvas structures for treating the wounded, apparently served by a coal-burning stove placed in a nearby ditch to pipe warm, dry air into the tents. Mariele thought the approach ingenious.

She knew of many volunteer organizations serving the wounded, but the American Ambulance, formed in July by Doctor Thomas Evans, had the best reputation. There were even rumors of soldiers with notes pinned to their uniforms asking to be taken to this hospital.

Not long after she'd dressed, Suzette arrived with a letter. Mariele knew from the looping script that it was from Camille.

MY DEAR MARIELE ~~ *yesterday, while watching the conflict from the top of the Arc de Triomphe, I thought of you and the dangers you faced in Versailles and during the long walk home. I want you to know that I admire your bravery, and I am more convinced than ever that you will be a very fine wife for Bertrand. He is indeed fortunate.*

I have news about my duties at the Odéon. Sarah Bernhardt has asked me to train as a nurse. I am pleased to have earned her confidence. However, I will admit to you, and only you, that I am somewhat nervous at the prospect of such duties.

Speaking of volunteer work, Victor has mentioned the need for assistance with the young children he cares for. I immediately thought of you and your kindness. I haven't presumed to mention your name to him, but I know he would be very grateful for your help.

Please remember me to your mother and father. I hope you plan to attend the next salon evening, and I look forward to speaking with you there.

With warm regards,
Camille

MARIELE WALKED toward the window and looked out. *What do I know about looking after young children? I haven't the slightest idea how to entertain them or comfort them. Besides, Papa wouldn't want me to travel that far on foot.* She tapped the letter against her chin.

Later that morning, she went to her mother's suite. "Maman, you really should come out with me to see what's happening."

"I'm not up to that." Her mother plucked at the pleats of her dress. Her voice was brittle, and she sat near the window in the same chair she had used since returning from captivity.

"But if you don't try, you may never feel better. It's been three weeks since we returned. I wish you would tell me what's continuing to distress you."

Mariele had her own lingering trauma from their time in captivity. Every day, the sound of artillery and the sight of marching soldiers made her quiver. She told no one except Bertrand, who reassured her that these feelings would fade over time.

"There's nothing to talk about." Her mother rose from the blue-and-white striped chair and moved toward the window overlooking avenue Vélasquez.

They were in her mother's private sitting room, where the dominant color was blue, including the silk wall covering, the curtains, and most of the chairs. At her father's request, Mariele took tea with her mother every morning, bringing newspapers that remained seemingly unopened on the desk, each piled carelessly on top of the preceding day's news. She did her best to relay anecdotes of what was happening in the household or with friends who remained in Paris, but her mother did little more than raise an eyebrow or twist her lips into something approximating a smile. It was as if she were only half living.

Mariele laid a hand on her mother's shoulder. "Talking might help. That's what Papa said."

"You've been discussing me with your father?" Her mother's eyes narrowed.

"Don't be upset, Maman. We're all worried about you—Papa, Theo, and I—and it's natural for us to want to help." She paused to choose her words. "Robert would want . . . Robert would be worried about you too."

"Don't you dare tell Robert what happened. He has enough concerns." Sharp, staccato sounds. "You've asked me to come out every day this past week. I don't want to go out."

Her mother sounded like a petulant child. Mariele resisted the urge to snap. "Just a short walk, Maman. We don't have to go far."

Her mother crossed the room to where her needlework lay on a low hassock and slowly rewound a length of unraveled wool. "All right. If only so you'll stop pestering me. But not until after lunch."

MARIELE PLANNED THEIR ROUTE CAREFULLY: avenue Vélasquez to boulevard Malesherbes, then rue de Monceau, and finally a loop back to their home through Parc Monceau, where roses and hydrangeas were still in bloom. On rue de Monceau, they could visit a few shops, if Maman felt inclined to do so. She was pleased at the plan and smiled as she donned her bonnet and cape and waited for her mother. The day was sunny with a hint of cool air, and she hoped the outing would be restorative.

"Did you know that meat rations have been cut further?" Mariele said as they passed a small butcher shop on boulevard Malesherbes, the window listing outrageous prices for even the toughest cuts of meat. "I'm sure wealthy Parisians can still acquire adequate supplies, but I pity the poor and working-class citizens."

Her mother remained silent, and Mariele was searching for another topic when she finally responded. "The question will soon be how many of our citizens will starve."

"Starve? Do you really think it will come to that, Maman?" She hadn't imagined anyone starving because of the siege.

Surely the government would take sensible steps to allocate food for the poor.

"Your father said as much when he came to my rooms yesterday. He's certain the siege will last several more months, and the cold weather will soon be upon us. Fuel is already in short supply. The working class are agitating. I don't understand why the new government isn't seriously negotiating with Prussia. Your father says we are completely surrounded, and he is convinced the ultimate outcome will be surrender." Bright spots of color had appeared in her mother's cheeks.

Mariele was astonished to hear her mother speak at length. She had assumed the pile of newspapers meant that Maman wasn't reading the news, but clearly her mother knew much of what was going on. "What do you think we should do, Maman?"

"It doesn't matter what women like me think. It's men like your father who might have some influence."

Mariele slipped her arm through her mother's. "I've missed you, Maman. We've all missed your presence. I hope you'll consider coming down for dinner tonight. Last night Papa was talking about General Trochu. He said that the general should never have been given the responsibility for defending Paris. According to Papa, General Trochu is too old and too worried about his legacy."

"Your father mentioned those thoughts to me as well. What's uppermost in my mind is Robert's safety. I wish there was some way to get a letter from him."

HER MOTHER DID APPEAR at dinner that evening, entering the room elegantly dressed and coifed as if nothing was unusual about keeping to herself for so long. Mariele noted the astonished looks of both Papa and Theo, quickly converted to welcoming embraces. Throughout dinner, they kept the conversation on topics other than the siege. Theo told a story of a particularly formidable anatomy professor, which amused them all for a while, even Papa. Mariele had no idea whether his story was true or fabricated, but it was clear their parents appreciated his efforts.

A FEW DAYS LATER, a cold wind whipped the edges of Mariele's cloak, and she shivered beneath threatening clouds that promised yet more rain. She stepped carefully around a series of puddles lining the sidewalk. Camille's note had prompted her to act. The thought of hungry children whose families could not look after them appealed to Mariele's compassion. She hadn't informed her mother, nor had she asked Suzette to accompany her. Instead, she had dressed modestly and brought along an apron in case it was required.

A few raindrops splashed Mariele's face. She looked up. Ahead, the twin spires of the church beckoned, and she turned along rue Las Cases, making her way to the main entrance of l'Église Sainte-Clotilde. She paused to admire the statues of Clovis and his wife Clotilde flanking the entrance and a biblical scene of Christ on the cross that decorated the façade above. Once inside, her footsteps echoed as she made her way along the aisle toward the transept, passing several women on rush-covered kneelers, their hands clasped in prayer. Devotional candles flickered in the gloom while hints of incense lingered in the air.

"You've come," Victor said, appearing so silently Mariele was startled. "Thank you," he continued. "I knew my prayers would be answered, and Camille has assured me you're just the right sort of woman to help."

Just the right sort of woman. What did that statement imply? Did Camille think Mariele was only suited to looking after children while more difficult work, like nursing, required skills she did not possess?

"I'm pleased to see you, Victor. Why don't you explain what you need, and we'll decide if I'm indeed the right sort of woman?"

Victor chuckled, a rich, pleasant sound, which made Mariele realize she had never heard him laugh. "We'll go downstairs," he said. "I've left the children with Father Basil, but he has a difficult time keeping them under control. We have thirteen today, one as young as six months, and collectively they make a lot of noise, so we've transformed a large storage room into an area where they can play. My superiors disapprove, but I've told them we must help the poor in whatever way God sees fit. Watch your step. The stairs are narrow."

Mariele had never heard Victor so effusive. "Papa says the poor are suffering terribly with the colder weather and lack of food. Our housemaid has a cousin who died, leaving a child behind with no one to care for him. She thinks what you're doing is wonderful."

"And where is the child's father?"

"He's a prisoner of war, just like Robert."

Victor paused at the landing. "Forgive me, I should have asked about Robert. Have you had any news?"

"Just one letter. He says he's well and treated fairly enough in the prison camps, although their food is meager. But I doubt he would disclose anything that would worry Maman."

Victor placed a hand on her shoulder. "I will keep him in my prayers."

After descending the remaining stairs, Mariele heard shouting mingled with bursts of laughter. At the end of the corridor, Victor opened the door to a room bustling with children and an older priest who was sitting on a carved wooden chair while holding a little boy with big round eyes. A calico cat rubbed against the priest's leg, flicking its tail back and forth.

"Father Basil, you seem to have things under control," Victor said.

The priest raised his eyebrows but said nothing.

Victor's lips twitched with suppressed amusement. "Let me introduce you to Mariele de Crécy, who is engaged to my brother Bertrand."

After exchanging pleasantries, Victor explained that he thought Mariele might help by looking after the girls or the youngest children. "The older boys can be rough and boisterous, and the young ones miss their mothers."

"What do you do with them?"

"Our purpose is to provide a safe place for them during the day and feed them a noontime meal. For some, it's the only food they have all day. We're not to give religious instruction, although my superior, Father Anselme, would like to. However, the bishop said most republicans won't tolerate it. Sometimes we kick a ball around in the gardens." Victor chuckled again. "I used to be quite good at that as a youngster. Better than Bertrand, but don't tell him I said so."

He's a different person away from home, she thought, wondering at the reason for such a change in behavior. Perhaps he felt his father's disapproval, or perhaps Bertrand had over-shadowed him for so long that Victor no longer tried to stand out.

"So, what do you think?"

"I'm sure we can work out an arrangement," Mariele said. "I can bring some old toys with me the next time, and perhaps a few books."

"You're prepared to help, then?"

She nodded.

Victor made the sign of the cross. "Thanks be to God."

. . .

SHE WAS weary by the end of the day but satisfied with the obvious pleasure the younger children took in her presence. Some climbed on her lap while others held her hand or skirt as she moved about the room. The baby cried from time to time, and she found she could soothe him by putting the knuckle of her little finger into his mouth or giving him the tip of a cloth soaked in milk to suck on. Appalled at the ragged clothing and unkempt appearance of her young charges, she resolved to scour the house for anything that could be put to use. Suzette would know how best to help.

How is it that some members of society have so much and others so little? she wondered after the children had left for the day and she was tidying the room. She had taken her family's wealth for granted, rarely questioning the circumstances that determined generations of well-to-do ancestors. Her mother's family in particular had possessed fabulous wealth less than one hundred years before, although much had been lost during the revolution. *I wonder if that's why she married Papa,* she mused while placing a few tattered books into a basket near the hearth.

At six that evening, Bertrand arrived to escort her home. "I'll return tomorrow," she said to Victor.

When the subject of helping at the church had first come up, Bertrand had been concerned about the dangers she might encounter. Since Mariele had already experienced the paralyzing fear of being held captive, she had readily agreed not to walk home alone in the dark. Given the presence of beggars and rough-looking men loitering along the route, the decision had been the right one.

"I've agreed to help," she said.

Bertrand squeezed her hand. "I knew you would."

"You know me that well already?"

"I think I do. You care for people and enjoy being useful. You're like Camille that way."

Mariele reacted to Bertrand's statement without thinking. "I'm nothing like your sister."

"Really?" he said. "Are you implying there's something wrong with my sister?"

"No," she said quickly. "Not at all. I admire Camille very much, and I believe we're going to be great friends."

"But . . ."

"But she's beautiful and confident . . . and lively. She attracts attention wherever she goes and rarely hesitates to express an opinion. I'm nothing like that at all."

"I think you're beautiful."

She smiled at him. "Thank you, my love."

My love. The words had slipped out so easily and unexpectedly. Perhaps she would come to love him after all.

14

OCTOBER 1870 – CAMILLE

"MARIE COLOMBIER HAS SENT a message saying she's ill, which means we'll be shorthanded all day," Sarah Bernhardt said as Camille hurried into her uniform. "I may need you to stay longer than usual."

"I'm sure I can manage, Madame. I'll send a note to my maid so she can inform my brothers and father. Is Madame Guerard on duty?"

Bernhardt nodded. "Doctor Deschamps has two urgent surgeries. I'll help with one, but I need you to assist with the other."

Camille nodded. She'd already assisted with a procedure to set a serious fracture in a soldier's leg. The soldier had screamed when the doctor straightened his leg, which made her feel queasy, but she had forced herself to watch carefully and respond whenever the doctor asked for assistance.

"What type of procedure will it be?"

"An amputation. Do you think you can manage? I've told Doctor Deschamps this will be your first, and he said it would be quick."

A shiver radiated through her chest, and Camille clutched

her fists to keep from reacting. Amputation. Would it be an arm or a leg? She knew the doctors chose amputation for severe leg or arm wounds as the best way to keep patients alive, and even then, death occurred in almost half the cases. Speed was of the essence. "I'll do my best," she said.

During her training, Camille had been briefed on amputation techniques, a routine operation and, for too many soldiers, the only solution to the wounds experienced in battle. The concern was survival. Some soldiers bled to death; others died of shock or complications. Some who survived wished they hadn't. She had expected to help with one at some point and had heard many gruesome stories. The pit of her stomach churned.

"You'll find the patient in the alcove." Bernhardt squeezed her arm, then left as hastily as she had arrived.

Camille made her way to the refreshment room, an area designated for officers, and into an adjacent alcove, which at one time had been used for storage. She checked the pulse of the man dozing on a bed raised high enough for surgery and found it steady, if a little weak. While waiting for the doctor to arrive, she breathed slowly, in through her nose and out through her mouth, a technique that always calmed her nerves. The soldier began to moan.

"IN ADDITION TO PAIN, we have to avoid hemorrhage and septic shock," Doctor Deschamps said as he prepared for the surgery, setting out instruments on a small table beside the bed. "I will tie this belt around the arm just above where I'll make a cut. As you can tell, I've given the soldier a dose of laudanum to dull the pain; nevertheless, speed will be critical. Following the amputation, I will debride the stump and clean it with these cloths, which must be soaked in carbolic acid. Since this is your first procedure, your primary task will be to present me with tools as soon as I ask for them. I will also need you to check the patient's pulse. Is everything understood?"

"Can you name the tools again for me, Doctor Deschamps?" Now that the doctor was ready, she wanted to delay.

Deschamps pointed to each item, naming them as he did so. Camille repeated each term.

"Ready?" he asked.

The doctor applied a tourniquet above the wound and called for the scalpel. Camille took one more deep breath and handed him the instrument. During the next few minutes, she had no time to think; she merely did exactly what Doctor Deschamps commanded with a precision she had not imagined possible.

"Place this in the basket over there." Deschamps gestured with his right elbow to the far corner of the room.

Camille looked at the severed limb, its fingers twitching but already turning blue, blood dripping onto the floor. Her stomach heaved. She tried not to gag.

"Quickly," he said. "I need your help with the suturing."

She grabbed a scrap of linen, wrapped the lifeless lump in it, and placed it into the basket. As the doctor sutured the skin around the stump, she began to shake.

"Are you all right, Mademoiselle? Mademoiselle?"

"Yes," she said, feeling faint. "Just a momentary bout of nerves."

"Happens to everyone. Take that chair and sit near the captain's head. I'll send for someone to clean the floor as soon as I finish these stitches. When he wakes, can you soothe his brow and offer him a drink of brandy? The laudanum should dull the pain for a little while."

An hour later, Sarah Bernhardt stopped in for a moment. "You did well, according to the good doctor. I told him about your family, and he was impressed that someone like you has volunteered for this sort of work."

"Thank you, Madame. The doctor worked so quickly, I

barely had time to think. I felt wobbly at the end, but I'm sure I'll do better next time."

"So, there is to be a next time, is there?"

Camille nodded. Before the war, assisting with an amputation was unthinkable for someone of her class. But if women like her refused to step forward, how many men would needlessly die? Juliette would be proud of her.

"Excellent," Bernhardt said. "Stay with the captain a little longer, after which I'll need you in the green room."

"YOU DID WHAT?" Bertrand said as he drove Camille home. "Camille, it's outrageous that you're assisting with operations like that. Maman would be horrified, and I have no idea what Father or Victor would say."

"They won't say anything because you're not going to tell them," she said. "Promise me, Bertrand. What I'm doing is important work. Doctor Deschamps saved a man's life today, and I helped him. If I'm destined to spend the rest of my days as a wife and mother, the least I can do is be useful while our people are suffering so much. The captain was grateful to see me when he woke up. His exact words were, 'I might have died without your care.' So, you see, I'm making a difference."

"You could make a difference in less abhorrent circumstances, like Mariele is doing at the church."

Camille squeezed her brother's arm. "I wouldn't be at all good at that sort of work. I'm sure I would frighten the children."

Bertrand glanced at her. "Well, I suppose if it were me, I would want to wake up to a beautiful young woman too."

"So, you'll keep it to yourself?"

Camille had discovered long before, when they were still children, that her brother didn't like to be rushed or pestered into making decisions, so she waited while Bertrand made up his mind.

"All right," he said. "If it means so much to you."

"Thank you, Bertrand. You really are the best brother a woman could have. Now hurry if you can. I don't want to be late for Madame Lambert's salon."

DRESSED in a creamy shade of pink, Camille entered the salon, where music mingled with the thrum of conversation, and a pleasing mix of colorful gowns gave the room a graceful and glamorous feel. After the day's events, she wanted nothing more than the reassuring world of familiar faces and expectations. She wanted debate and discussion rather than the cries of wounded soldiers and the sweaty, fevered brows of men who might not last the night; the smell of perfume and fresh roses rather than the stench of gangrene or the sharp, metallic odor of blood.

For a moment, she didn't move but merely took in the scene. A world of civility and courtesy, of intellect and social graces, of power and influence, of cunning and subtle maneuvering. Her father had played this world well. Bertrand was destined to inherit the Noisette position in society. Perhaps to improve on it. *Unless Paris is destroyed by—*

"You're looking very serious, Mademoiselle Noisette," André said.

"I am serious, Monsieur Laborde." She tilted her head. "Haven't you realized that?"

André offered his arm. "Walk with me. I have something to tell you." His gaze was direct, and there was an undertone of urgency in his voice. "If we slip out onto the balcony, everyone will assume I'm flirting with you."

Camille admired the skillful manner with which André

guided them across the room, weaving around clusters of men and women, stopping occasionally to acknowledge a greeting, respond to a remark, or commit to a conversation later in the evening. She hadn't realized how well known he was in this particular circle of society, an admirable accomplishment for someone who hadn't been born in Paris.

When they reached the far corner, André released his hold on her arm, and she stepped out onto the narrow balcony. Camille pulled her shawl around her shoulders. "A cool night."

"I won't keep you long," he replied. "I've been made aware that there will be urgent meetings at the clubs tomorrow night. Are you able to attend?"

Camille thought for a moment. She was scheduled for the late shift, which began at noon. Perhaps she could make some excuse for leaving a little early. "I'll have to come straight from the hospital," she said. "There won't be time to go home and change."

André nodded. "I'll meet you outside the Odéon at seven. With luck, you can still be at the meeting before—"

"Ah, there you are, Camille," Mariele said.

Camille whirled around. "How lovely to see you, Mariele. Victor is so happy with your assistance. He has told me that the children adore you."

"How kind," Mariele replied. "Bertrand said you were here, and I've been looking for you." She dipped her head to acknowledge André. "Monsieur Laborde, we meet again."

"Mademoiselle de Crécy, you look very charming this evening. Bertrand is indeed a fortunate man. Tell me where I can find him."

Mariele pointed to a group who had moved beyond the main salon into an adjacent room where men gathered with brandy and cigars.

"You can tell me more the next time we meet," Camille said as André bowed briefly to each of them in turn.

. . .

MARIELE STEPPED ONTO THE BALCONY. "The stars are beautiful tonight." She tapped Camille's wrist with her fan. "Is Monsieur Laborde trying to charm you? I've noticed you with him on several occasions."

"Not at all. But he does amuse me," Camille replied.

"I have a delicate matter to discuss," Mariele said.

"A delicate matter? Now that sounds intriguing. How can I help you?"

Mariele blushed. "Bertrand has told me that we will live with your family for a while after our wedding, and . . . and I wonder . . . well, I wish to ask about your mother. She seems such a strong personality . . ." Her words dwindled away.

Camille was amused at the question. "Ah! Then you'll want to know how to handle my mother. She can be quite forceful and not at all easy to please. To tell you the truth, my mother's personality is one of the reasons I did not go to Lyon. We are like oil and water."

Mariele looked relieved to have broached the topic. "Perhaps we can take tea together and chat further. I'll send you an invitation." She raised her eyebrows.

"I would be delighted to help."

"Please don't tell Bertrand that I've spoken to you."

Camille smiled. "My lips are sealed."

15

OCTOBER 1870 – MARIELE

WITHIN A FEW DAYS, Mariele had become accustomed to the harried pace of looking after young children. She'd discovered that even with one child perched on her hip, she could soothe the cries of another or untangle a length of skipping rope or spoon food into a waiting mouth. That such accomplishments pleased her was a surprise.

She'd imagined motherhood in an abstract way, assuming that she would behave much like her own mother—by relegating childcare to a series of nannies, tutors, and instructors while maintaining a busy social schedule and keeping order in her home. Instead, she'd found that she rather enjoyed the weight of a baby in her arms, singing songs whenever the spirit moved her, touching the delicate skin of a two-year-old face, or seeing the wide, bright eyes of a little boy grow even wider when she brought a basket of toy soldiers one day.

After agreeing to help, Mariele had purchased four plain blouses and two sensible skirts with large pockets, and each day brought many handkerchiefs with her to wipe the spills and runny noses. She had six of the youngest children to look after: Lucille, a solemn baby who rarely cried; Antoine, a sturdy two-year-old who was tall for his age and had a mop of black curls; siblings Fabien and Sophie, who had the same plump cheeks and cleft chins; Charlotte, a lively six-year-old with perpetually tangled hair; and Philippe, who had an angelic smile but was always in trouble.

"I'm sorry to be late, Father Victor," Mariele said the morning after Madame Lambert's salon. They had agreed that she would call him Father Victor, just as the children did. "I had to spend extra time with my mother this morning."

With the baby whimpering in her cot, nothing more than a large wooden crate lined with a blanket, two of the older boys creating a ruckus in the corner, and a sobbing Sophie in his arms, Victor looked harried. "I was praying that you would arrive soon," he said. "You're so much better than I am with the young ones. Sophie has been asking for you ever since she arrived. I think she may have a fever."

Mariele produced a small bag of ripe plums and a few slices of cheese, which quickly established order among the little ones. Afterward, she entertained them with a story before sending the older ones off to play with the toys she'd brought from home: balls and spinning tops, wooden blocks, two dolls and a rather worn stuffed clown, ring toss, several picture books, and a badminton set that was proving to be a success, with all ages.

In the middle of the afternoon, she sought out Victor. "You were right," she said. "Sophie definitely has a fever. And she's quite fretful."

"Her mother should arrive soon," Victor replied.

"And what will happen tomorrow? If we aren't careful, the fever will spread to the other children."

At five, long after the rest of the children had been collected, there was still no sign of Sophie and Fabien's mother. "This is highly unusual," Victor said. "She's never been late before." He rubbed his chin and sighed. "What shall we do?"

"I'll take them home with me," Mariele said. "Suzette will

help, I'm sure of it. She comes from a large family and always asks about the children. The other day she told me that her mother expected her to look after the youngest of her siblings, even when she was only ten."

Relief flooded Victor's face. "Will Bertrand take you home?"

Mariele shook her head. "I sent him away an hour ago. I couldn't leave these two." Fabien had been clutching her hand and looking back and forth at Mariele and Victor as they'd been talking. She squeezed his little hand. "You'll come home with me tonight, *mon chéri*. You and Sophie. And you can meet my friend Suzette. You would like that, wouldn't you?"

"But where is Maman?" Fabien asked. "Why isn't she here to fetch us?" He tugged on Victor's cassock. "Where is Maman, Father Victor?"

Victor squatted so his eyes were level with Fabien's. "I don't know, Fabien. But I'm sure she'll be here tomorrow. Mademoiselle de Crécy will look after you and Sophie tonight. And, if you like, you can take the Pierrot—the stuffed clown—with you."

While Mariele fastened Fabien's sweater and secured her own cloak, Victor wrapped Sophie in a blanket and lifted the little girl into his arms. "I'll come with you," he said.

"I can manage, Victor. Don't you have Mass to attend to?"

"Father Basil will celebrate the Mass in my place. Bertrand would be upset if I let you travel by yourself."

"And we mustn't upset Bertrand," Mariele quipped.

MARIELE ALMOST LAUGHED at the look on Eugène's face when the butler opened the front door. "Mademoiselle Mariele?" he sputtered.

"These two children need a safe place to stay tonight, Eugène. If you could take Sophie from Father Victor, we can get them settled somewhere. Fabien needs dinner, and Sophie needs a little broth and then straight to bed. She has a fever."

Still looking astonished, Eugène held out his arms for the little girl.

"I'll bring the children back tomorrow morning," Mariele said to Victor. "Hopefully you will have news from their mother by then."

"I'm very grateful, Mariele. You're such a kind woman. Bertrand is lucky indeed." With a quick bob of his head, Victor climbed back into the carriage.

"Is that you, Mariele?" her father's voice called down from the second floor.

Mariele cringed. She had hoped to get the children established before facing her parents. "Yes, Papa. I'm sorry to be late. I'll be up as soon as I speak with Suzette."

"Shall we go to the kitchen?" Eugène whispered. "It's warm there, and I'm sure Madame Robinette will have some food for this little fellow. Now, don't let your clown drag on the floor, Fabien."

"Thank you, Eugène. I will explain all this to the family during dinner."

Eugène chuckled. "They will be a little surprised, Mademoiselle."

AFTER SETTLING the children with Suzette and one of Madame Robinette's scullery maids, who was little more than a child herself, Mariele ran up the back stairs to her bedroom and quickly changed for dinner. When they dined en famille, her mother permitted a less formal look, so she chose a fitted dress in dark green with embroidered lace cuffs and collar and fastened a simple strand of pearls around her neck.

Roughly forty feet long and twenty feet wide, the dining room was a luxurious space with three Flemish tapestries along

one wall and an elaborate gilded chandelier hanging from the
middle of the ceiling. A mahogany table that could readily seat
sixteen, and could be extended to host twice as many, anchored
the room. Wide windows trimmed with cascading drapes
graced the south and west walls of the room, while the east wall
contained an arched floor-to-ceiling mirror.

"What kept you so long today?" her mother asked as the
family sat down at one end of the table. "It's one thing for you to
help at the church, but quite another for Bertrand's brother to
take advantage of your kind heart like that."

"One of the mothers was late," Mariele replied. "I stayed with
her two children while Victor was dealing with other matters."
All true, she thought. *I'll wait to see what else Maman says.*

"Charity is all well and good," her mother said, "but those
receiving it should not abuse the gift." She lifted a spoonful of
soup to her mouth.

Mariele was happy that her mother no longer kept to her
rooms. She was even pleased to hear a little arrogance in her
mother's voice. However, having now spent more than two
weeks with the children in Victor's care, she was acutely aware
of the gap between rich and poor and how much the siege had
widened it. She wished her mother was more sympathetic and
understanding.

"Not everyone is born with the advantages we have," Theo
said as if reading her thoughts. "The amount of food on the
table tonight could feed at least twice as many people."

"Theo," her father said, "don't be rude to your mother."

"Theo's right, Papa." Mariele set her spoon in the saucer
beneath the soup bowl and clasped her hands together. "The
silver candlesticks on our table could feed a family for months,
if not a year. The money spent on my dress alone could buy new
clothes for all the children in Victor's care."

"Many Parisians are suffering more than usual," Theo added.

"Our family has much. Other families have so little. Some are starving. It's no wonder the poor are agitating."

"What would you have us do?" her mother replied. "Give away all our wealth?"

"Of course not, Maman," Theo replied. "But I, for one, am proud of Mariele's efforts."

"Thank you, Theo," Mariele said. "And now I should probably tell you that I brought two little children home with me this evening. Their mother never did arrive to pick them up. Suzette is giving them some food and will make up a bed for them to sleep in tonight. I will take them to the church in the morning. Hopefully, their mother will be there."

While speaking, Mariele had watched her mother and father for their reactions. Astonishment. Concern. Dismay. Shock.

Eventually her father replied. "While your actions are most kind, you might have warned us, Mariele."

"I'm sorry, Papa, but there wasn't time. I did what I thought best for Sophie and Fabien. They're very sweet. Didn't God tell us to welcome little children in His name?" Despite the churn of nerves, Mariele remained calm, her voice as close to everyday conversation as she could manage. Her father seemed to accept her actions, but her mother's lips were pursed, and she had yet to respond.

"What's done is done," her mother said. "I trust you will consult with your father and me in future."

16

OCTOBER 1870 – CAMILLE

AFTER SIX HOURS of wiping fevered brows, replacing soiled dressings, helping wounded men to sit or turn or lay back, spooning medicine into waiting mouths, and changing beds so that yet another wounded soldier could be accommodated, all Camille wanted to do was sleep. But André would be waiting, so instead she found an unused room that was little more than a closet and removed her nursing clothes.

More than forty days of siege, she thought as she dressed in the drab clothes she'd found at a secondhand store: a black skirt, a striped blouse, and a padded coat in a shade of brown that reminded her of cooked mushrooms. One sleeve of the coat had been mended at some point by its previous owner. After bringing them home, she had asked Monique to wash each item thoroughly to remove the musty smells and body odor that clung to them.

She hung her other clothes on a wooden peg on the back of the door and slipped out of the room. She would retrieve them tomorrow. As she made her way toward the main entrance, Camille wondered whether Bertrand was still on guard duty and whether Victor and her father were dining together tonight. Would they worry about her absence? No one in the house except Monique knew of these excursions, and she hadn't told Monique their real purpose. Should her father or brothers ask, the maid was instructed to say that Camille was indisposed. No man would ever question a woman who was 'indisposed.'

André's carriage was not in the plaza in front of the Théâtre de l'Odéon. The only vehicle waiting there was a dilapidated fiacre hitched to an old horse and a driver dressed in peasant garb. Camille paid the driver no attention and instead looked left and right, hoping André would soon arrive.

The driver waved at her. "Henriette!" he called.

Camille peered through the evening gloom. "André? Is that you?"

The man beckoned.

"You look as charming as I do," Camille said when she was close enough to appreciate André's garb. He looked tired, the fatigue evident in his red eyes and pallid skin. Whiskers had sprouted on his normally clean-shaven cheeks.

"Where on earth did you find those clothes?"

André laughed. "Tonight, I am Felix Cazabonne, a farmer from Meudon who fled to Paris when the Prussians approached."

"Well, Monsieur Cazabonne, you certainly look the part. Are you planning to attend the women's Vigilance Committee meeting with me?" she asked. "I've only once seen any men there, so you will stand out."

"No. I'm attending Le Club Rouge, which is also in Montmartre. Hopefully, this poor horse will be able to pull us up the hill."

The horse plodded along. The day's gloom had worsened, the clouds like a shroud over the city. Rain began to drip from the edge of the cab's canopy. Camille shivered. *How strange*, she thought, *to be out without a chaperone. Mother would be scandalized and worried for my safety.* And how ironic that at the same time as barricades spread throughout Paris to protect the city from harm, protections for young women had disappeared, the norms of social behavior abandoned under siege conditions.

WHEN CAMILLE ENTERED the house on rue Berthe, it was immediately clear that tonight's committee meeting would be different. For one thing, the crowd was much larger, and for another, several men were in attendance. Unlike previous evenings when there had been plenty of space to stand, this time she was forced to squeeze into a crowd of women stationed behind a well-worn settee. Excitement filled the air.

Although two lamps were lit, there was no fire in the grate, and had the room not been so crowded, Camille would have been chilled. She wondered if Maxine Pierrefonds, the woman who lived in the house and made it available each week for the committee, could afford wood to burn. Perhaps she rationed her supply to ensure hot meals for her five children. The contrast with Camille's circumstances reinforced the growing awareness of how fortunate she and her family were. Just last week, an enormous delivery of coal had arrived at the Noisette home. In addition, they had ample firewood stacked behind the house. Another example of the divide between rich and poor.

This was the fourth meeting she'd attended. Each time, Louise Michel had exhorted her followers to resist the government and rise up for change. With the passage of time, the mood of the group had changed. Instead of gossip and light-hearted conversation, the women grumbled and shook their fists as Louise cited the many hardships facing the working class: dwindling food supplies, with exorbitant prices for what little remained; rent increases imposed by wealthy landlords and extorted by their vicious collectors; coal making its way to the privileged arrondissements while wood was in such short supply that members of the gendarmerie guarded the trees in public parks; the spread of disease among children and the elderly; and the ever-present spectre of death. What would happen in December, when the cold weather arrived?

Suddenly the room bristled with whispers. From her place in the shadows, Camille peeked around the broad shoulders of the woman next to her and watched as Louise Michel entered the room with a tall man with white whiskers and prominent ears.

"Women of Montmartre!" Louise began. "Our people are organizing. Last week's demonstration at the Hôtel de Ville showed our strength. We will continue to demand elections to eliminate this false government that is no more than imperialists in disguise. France must take decisive action against the Prussians. Trochu does nothing. He is incapable of leading our brave soldiers and National Guardsmen into action. And who suffers while Paris is surrounded?"

"We do!" the women roared.

Louise raised her hands to quiet the group. "Thank you, friends. We are honored tonight to have Monsieur Gustave Lefrancais with us. He will tell us about the brave men who carried out that demonstration and our plans for the future."

The man bowed slightly to acknowledge the introduction. "*Merci*, Mademoiselle Michel. I see you have an enthusiastic group of supporters." He nodded to each corner of the room. "Indeed, the women of Paris have much to be proud of. Their support is vital if we are to reach our objectives. Last week, over seven thousand guardsmen responded to the call to overthrow the government. Some of them were your husbands, brothers, and sons. Proud men. Proud to call themselves Parisians. Proud to stand up for the rights of everyday men and women."

Gustave Lefrancais went on to explain that the government had stationed their own forces at the Hôtel de Ville, men he called traitors to the cause, and that these guards had prevented the demonstrators from presenting their petition for immediate elections. While Lefrancais was speaking, Camille wondered at the two opposing viewpoints of what was best for Paris and for France. It was as if each side operated from different realities, selecting different news to believe, repeating different rumors, and twisting each event in opposite ways.

"We will have it," Lefrancais said. "We will have our Commune, our grand democratic and social Commune. The light will descend from the heights of Belleville and Montmartre to dissipate the dark shadows of the Hôtel de Ville. We will sweep away the bourgeois like the janitor sweeps the apartment on Saturdays. And you"—he paused to sweep his arm around in a gesture that included every woman in the room— "you will lead the citizens of this great city, this great country.

"There are those who denounce us," he continued. "However, rest assured that we will ultimately prevail. Bread and firewood are scarce. Food prices impoverish our citizens. Soon there will be riots in the streets, when we should be using all our energy to defend our beautiful city. And where are our leaders?" Contempt spewed from his mouth. "Are they in Paris?"

"No!"

"Correct, Mesdames. The Assemblée Nationale is in Bordeaux, while Gambetta is in Tours. How can the Minister of War protect Paris when he is more than two hundred kilometers away? The answer, my friends, is that he can't. And so, we must protect our city and our citizens. I ask for your patience and support. Others have already taken steps. We will build on their efforts. Soon there will be concrete plans to take the government into our own hands and form a commune.

"Our armies are in disarray. Any day now, we expect Orléans to fall. New clubs are forming. We will all act together. Meanwhile, be strong. Support one another. Victory remains possible if we act together."

Lefrancais's speech stirred the crowd to long applause and

faces filled with passion. Camille joined in. To do otherwise would attract unwanted attention. As Louise Michel escorted her guest and the other men out of the room, the women around Camille and elsewhere clustered together in small groups, everyone talking at once.

"Wasn't he marvelous?" Maxine said, her eyes sparkling.

"*Certainement*," Camille replied. "Such an impressive man."

"Will you join us when the time comes, Mademoiselle Giraud?"

"Join us?" *Whatever does she mean?* Camille wondered.

"The uprising. Parisian women must come out in force if we are to free the city. It is our duty. My grandfather—bless his sacred memory—gave his life in 1830. If it's necessary, I will give mine for this revolution."

Revolution. The full intent of Louise Michel, Gustave Lefrancais, and all the women gathered tonight suddenly hit Camille. These people would settle for nothing less than the destruction of families like hers.

Camille forced a smile onto her lips. "Of course, I will join. As you say, Madame, it is our duty."

When Louise Michel returned, she circulated among the members of the Vigilance Committee, stopping to chat for a few minutes with each group. Camille was about to slip away to avoid being recognized when Maxine placed a hand on her shoulder.

"We're forming a small group to collect money for arms and ammunition. When the uprising comes, we'll need our own weapons. Why don't you join us, Henriette? It's important work."

Camille glanced at Louise Michel, who was speaking to a group less than six feet away. If she agreed to help Maxine, perhaps she could then make her excuses and get away before Louise moved any closer. If she declined, Maxine might detain her further. Both choices held risk.

The seconds ticked away. Maxine tilted her head and frowned. Louise Michel turned in their direction.

Too late, Camille thought. *I can't leave now.*

"Ah, our marvelous host, Madame Pierrefonds!" Louise said with gusto. "It's an honor to be in your home again tonight. Monsieur Lefrancais asked me to give you this token of his appreciation for your hospitality." She pulled a small pouch from her pocket and handed it to Maxine. "And who are these fine women?"

"And this is Henriette Giraud," Maxine said after introducing the others.

Camille nodded. "We've met before, Madame Michel. At Restaurant Polignac. Your speech inspired me to join this group."

Louise's eyes narrowed. "I remember that evening. You were with your fiancé, if I recall. Are you enjoying the Vigilance Committee, Mademoiselle? I imagine you are learning about our cause."

Camille considered how to respond. Too much enthusiasm might arouse suspicion, if not with Louise Michel, then with Maxine. "I don't think I would use the word 'enjoy,' Madame. But the cause is just, and I am certainly learning."

Louise held her gaze for a moment. "I'm sure you are."

ANDRÉ WAS WAITING AS USUAL, his carriage parked in front of a shuttered confectionery opposite the central fountain of Place Pigalle. Patrons at a nearby café, primarily men in uniform, drank wine or absinthe or some other beverage while deep in conversation with their companions.

"More talk of revolution, André. They plan to overthrow the government, establish a Commune, and take control," Camille whispered so as not to be overheard.

"We feared as much," André replied. "Tell me everything you recall. Even the smallest detail may be useful."

André probed relentlessly as Camille recounted the evening, asking for names, for descriptions of the men in attendance, and about the mood of the women involved.

"They're angry," she said. "They are imbued with a deep sense of injustice. And who can blame them? These families have so little while people like us have so much. And they're not prepared to wait for the government to make changes. I'm very worried, André. Paris will soon be at the breaking point. Despite my sympathies for the poor, we can't withstand an uprising as well as a siege."

The horse plodded along, and they rode in silence. With the streetlamps unlit, the only illumination came from the soft glow of café windows and the occasional lantern hanging above a door. On the sidewalk next to them, Camille watched a man wearing a battered homburg and carrying what looked like a riding whip lean over a café table to extract a cigar butt from the ashtray. He put it in his pocket and moved on to the next table.

"I spoke to Louise Michel this evening," she said.

"Did she recognize you?"

"I decided it was prudent to remind her we'd met at Restaurant Polignac."

"And?" His voice seemed impatient.

"She didn't seem at all suspicious."

"Good." He shook the reins, and the horse increased its pace. "Tell me the name of the woman whose house served as the meeting place."

"She's poor, André. I don't wish to cause trouble for her." An image of Maxine's angular face and threadbare shawl came to mind. "She has five children. The youngest still suckles at her breast."

André did not ask again, and they rode along in silence for a

few minutes, the clattering of the wheels against the cobblestones punctuated by the clip-clop of his horse's hooves. Along
the way, they passed street corners barricaded with stones and
rough planks, and Camille wondered at their seemingly random
placement. Tonight's Vigilance Committee meeting had lasted
longer than the others, and for the most part, the streets were
quiet.

"*Qui vive?*"

A sudden shout confronted them, and the horse pranced
sideways as André pulled sharply on the reins. Four members of
the National Guard emerged from the darkness.

"Bonsoir, messieurs," André said.

"Where are you going, and why are you out so late?" one of
the men asked while the others stood on either side of him with
their rifles ready.

"I am escorting this young woman home. She was tending to
the needs of my sick mother."

Camille admired André's quick improvisation. She kept her
eyes down and her hands clasped loosely in her lap, her heart
thumping so hard she thought the soldiers would hear it.

"Which regiment are you with?" André asked. "I joined a
battalion in the 5th arrondissement and just returned from my
training." He kept speaking in a calm, easy fashion as the men
relaxed and set down their rifles one by one.

"You should get home quickly, Monsieur," said the man in
charge. "It's not safe to be out so late."

"Of course, Captain. The house is less than ten minutes
away."

"I admire your quick thinking," Camille said after they had
traveled a few blocks farther. "Will it be safe for you to return
home?"

André nodded. "Next time I will wear my uniform."

"When will you convey the information about the uprising?"

"First thing tomorrow. My contact will be expecting me. It's vital that tonight's information is conveyed immediately. You've done well, Camille. Very well indeed."

André's praise pleased her. *Vital* was the word he had used, which meant she was part of something important. As with the previous times he had taken her home, she wondered about the identity of André's mysterious contact. She didn't ask and knew that he would think less of her if she had.

"What happened at the club you attended?"

"Some of these radicals think freedom can be achieved through torrents of tears and blood." André's tone was scornful. "They don't have the courage to give their own blood, but they are quick to call for others to spill theirs. I believe the leaders of Le Club Rouge are dangerous. They don't care if another civil war unfolds." He shook his head.

André was barely concentrating on where they were going. He'd let the reins go slack, and the horse ambled slowly of its own accord along boulevard de Sebastopol, heading south toward the Seine. The night was darker than usual, and with curtains firmly shut and no streetlamps lit, the eerie quiet was unsettling.

"At the same time," he continued, "they want to continue fighting the Prussians. They seem firmly convinced that Paris can conquer Bismarck. It's clear to me they have no military acumen at all. And they countenance no challenge to their ideas. One man was beaten and thrown down the stairs for daring to question the leadership of Gustave Flourens.

"They do not support any authority. They don't want to be governed, but they strive to govern others. They consider anyone who works in a public position to be a tyrant, and yet they imagine that their revolutionary government would somehow be considered legitimate. Did they learn nothing from the revolutions of 1830 or 1848?"

Despite the blackness, Camille could see his grim look. "Is there a specific plan?"

He nodded. "They're so angry that Trochu takes no action and furious that Thiers has gone to Versailles to negotiate with Bismarck, which they call treason. However, their plans are vague and hastily drawn. Flourens calls for demonstrators to occupy the Hôtel de Ville and for the National Guard of Belleville to imprison members of the government. He plans to immediately set up a Committee of Public Safety and has assigned men to seize the Prefecture of Police. Somehow this will miraculously lead to the establishment of a Commune."

"Did those gathered show their support?"

"Speaker after speaker came up to offer support," he replied. "Often they said the same thing as the person before them. Only a few were eloquent. However, most have no idea of history or geography and only the simplest notions of how to organize. They plan to gather at the Hôtel de Ville on October 31st."

"So, between us you have the information you need."

"Yes. All I need to do is meet with my contact."

A great flame appeared in the distance. "What's that?" Camille asked. "It looks like a vast fire. But what could have caused such a fire to rise so quickly?"

André stopped the carriage at the side of the road. "Look how the flames dart upward into the air. They're getting higher and higher. See over there!" He pointed to his left. "Sparks are spinning out from the flames like fireworks."

Camille tipped her head back for a better view. "There is so much light, it's almost like dawn."

They watched the display of lights fill the sky. Blood-colored flames burst all around.

"It's as if the heavens themselves are at war."

She heard the wonder in his voice. "Let's hope it's a good omen."

17

OCTOBER 1870 – MARIELE

SOPHIE'S FEVER DISAPPEARED OVERNIGHT. Mariele watched with interest as the little girl ate a good breakfast of preserved peaches with slices of ham and a fresh baguette, her bright eyes roaming the kitchen as Madame Robinette plucked a chicken and the scullery maid added wood to the stove.

"Mademoiselle," Sophie said, "will we have chicken for dinner?"

"No, silly," Fabien replied. "Maman will take us home tonight."

Sophie stuffed another slice of peach into her mouth. "But I like it here."

"I'm sure your maman has missed you," Mariele said. "She will want to see you tonight. Now finish up, *ma petite*. It's almost time to go."

Mariele took the children to Sainte-Clotilde in a hired fiacre and was just hanging up their coats when Victor entered the room with a plump woman wearing a black bonnet. "Can you join Madame Durand and me, Mariele? It's important." Victor looked both worn out and harried.

"Of course, Father Victor," she said.

Out in the corridor, just beyond the room where the children gathered, Victor asked Madame Durand to repeat her story.

"It's a sad tale, Mademoiselle. The children's mother was crushed against a stone wall by an omnibus. The driver didn't stop. They never do, when it's one of our sort. The poor, I mean. *Les misérables.*"

"Oh, mon Dieu," Mariele said. She made the sign of the cross. "Is she going to be all right?"

Madame Durand looked first at Victor and then at Mariele. "No, Mademoiselle. She's gone. May she rest in heaven. I knew she brought the children here, so I came to tell Father Victor. I have to go now. There's my work to be done. I need the money."

"Are there any relatives?" Victor asked.

The woman shrugged. "The children's father is off fighting somewhere. He's a soldier. Could be dead by now, though. Don't know of any other family." Madame Durand put her gloves on and wound a scarf around her neck. "Maybe the church can look after the little ones. It has plenty of money." With a nod at Victor and a quick bob in Mariele's direction, Madame Durand hurried away.

"Dead," Mariele said. "Their mother is dead. Just like that." *How fleeting life can be. Alive one day. Dead the next.* The children's mother probably hadn't even reached the age of thirty. She turned to face Victor. "What do we do now? Can the church look after them as Madame Durand suggested?"

Victor shook his head. "No. The only action the church takes in this sort of circumstance is to send the children to an orphanage."

"What should we tell them? Sophie and Fabien."

"Let me think," Victor replied. "For the moment, let's not mention it."

"They were happy at my house," Mariele said. "Although my mother wasn't at all pleased that I'd brought them with me. You should have seen the look on her face when I mentioned it at dinner." A sudden wail emerged from the children's area. "I have to go. Let's talk about it later."

As Mariele tended to the other children, she thought about Sophie and Fabien. The little girl had a beautiful smile and lively eyes. With her dark, curly hair, she was destined to be a beauty. Fabien was more solemn, as if the cares of the world were on his shoulders. Although brother and sister squabbled from time to time, he was protective of Sophie. Who would look after them? Did Victor even know where the family lived? Perhaps he could make inquiries with the army and get word to the children's father. Mariele pulled a piece of paper from her handbag and began a note to her parents.

AFTER LUNCH MARIELE left the children in the care of on older child and went looking for Victor. She found him on his knees in the nave of the church, where a few candles glowed and incense filled the air. She waited until he rose to his feet, noting the slump of his shoulders and the worry lines that creased his brow.

"I was praying for the children's mother," Victor said, "although why God saw fit to take her . . ." His voice dwindled away.

"The sisters at my school always said that God moves in mysterious ways. We just have to accept it and make a plan to help Fabien and Sophie."

Footsteps echoed against the marble floors as a middle-aged man, clutching a leather portfolio, made his way toward them. Thick sideburns sprouted from the man's cheeks. "Good day, Father Victor. I came to practice the music for Sunday and to work on a new composition," he said. "Will that disturb you?"

"Not at all, Monsieur Franck. Your beautiful music would be welcome. Why don't we sit and listen for a few minutes,

Mariele? Music soothes the soul, and mine needs a little of that. Almost as good as prayer."

They sat side by side on chairs with stiff backs and woven rush seats and waited for the organist to begin. In the echoing space of the church, Mariele heard the rustling of papers, the click and clack of organ stops being pulled or released, and the slide of shoes against the pedals as Monsieur Franck settled in. The ornate, stained-glass windows cast beams of color that glinted against the dust motes and illuminated the massive organ pipes anchoring the nave.

The music began softly, the pace as gentle as a slow-moving river, stirring her emotions with its simple, yet haunting refrain. The volume gradually rose as if the river were now tumbling toward a waterfall, the melody growing in complexity, diving and weaving around the same fundamental refrain. The organ pipes filled the church with majestic sound. Mariele waited for the crescendo and was surprised, when instead the piece returned to its earlier simplicity.

"That was beautiful," she said after the organ stopped.

Victor nodded. "Monsieur Franck became our *maître du chapelle* when the church was first consecrated. Now he's our *titulaire*. But he's a composer at heart. He once told me that the organ at Sainte-Clotilde is obedient to his thoughts." He smiled. "We are fortunate to have him."

"Indeed, you are." Mariele paused. A few notes rang out as if the organist was thinking about something else while his hands idly tapped the keys. "Victor, we need to decide what to do about Fabien and Sophie."

He sighed. "Yes. The matter has been weighing on my mind. I shall write to the army and ask them to let the children's father know the situation. In the meantime, I can contact—"

"In the meantime," she interrupted, "they will stay with me. I've already sent a note to my parents. I'm sure my father will appreciate the situation and give his blessing."

"That's too much of an imposition," Victor said. "Why don't I take them home with me instead?"

"Because they know me. I've been looking after them for a few weeks, and last night everything worked out so well. I'm sure we can manage while you contact their father."

Victor was standing now, pacing back and forth. "But I have no idea how long it may take to reach their father. He could have fought at one of the recent battles, which means he might be wounded or worse. You don't need to do this, Mariele."

She squared her shoulders and laid a hand on his arm. "I want to do this. Unless Papa forbids it."

BERTRAND ARRIVED JUST after four to take Mariele home. "Sophie and Fabien are coming with us." She placed an index finger against her lips to forestall his questions. "Their maman is sick and unable to come today, so they will stay with me for a few days. Papa has agreed."

With Fabien squeezed in between them and Sophie on her lap, Mariele chattered away to her fiancé as if nothing were out of the ordinary. They soon crossed the Pont de la Concorde, then entered the Place de la Concorde. "Look at all the tents," Mariele said to the children.

Two parallel rows of tents stretched out along the Champs-Élysées next to a long line of supply wagons. Soldiers mingled about, talking and laughing, some sprawled on top of loose heaps of straw, others standing or sitting on wooden crates or leaning against the lampposts at the edge of the road. A whiskered man played a tune on a simple wooden recorder, and two citizens passing by doffed their hats to acknowledge the men serving their country.

"Papa is a soldier," Fabien said. "He has a rifle. Look, Mademoiselle. That soldier is carrying a flag." He stood up and pointed.

"Take care, little one," Bertrand said. "Sit down. The carriage is moving." He smiled at Mariele, then raised his eyebrows.

"Victor will tell you everything," she replied.

As SOON AS the carriage swept through the gates, its wheels rattling against the paved courtyard, Eugène opened the front door and stepped beneath the porte cochère to greet them.

"Is this little Sophie and young Fabien?" he said. "Madame Robinette is anxious to see you. Come around to the back of the house with me." He held out his hands, and the children each grabbed one.

"Are you coming, Mademoiselle?" Fabien asked.

"Mademoiselle has other things to do," Eugène said. "Her maman and papa are waiting for her in the petit salon."

"Shall I come in with you?" Bertrand asked as Eugène led the children off.

"I wish you could, but I suspect my parents are upset with me, and your presence will not help, I'm afraid." She lowered her voice. "The children's mother died in a tragic accident. Victor is attempting to contact the father. Since they were here last night, I felt it would be less distressing if they stayed with us until we hear from their father. No doubt there are other relatives who can help." She touched his cheek. "I should go."

"I'll meet you at the church tomorrow afternoon. You can tell me how your parents reacted. Will your father be angry?"

She shook her head. "It's my mother I'm worried about. She wasn't the least bit understanding yesterday."

Bertrand bent his head for a swift kiss. "À demain."

A MIRROR HUNG JUST inside the front door, and Mariele paused for a moment to remove her hat and fix her hair, pinning loose curls and tucking a few strands behind one ear. The hallway clock chimed. She took off her gloves and pinched her cheeks for a bit of color, then crossed the foyer and climbed the stairs to the second floor. She would have preferred to change her clothes, but Eugène's tone suggested that the sooner she confronted her parents, the better.

In the time that had passed since Bertrand had drawn the carriage into the courtyard, she had weighed her options. Defiance was out of the question. However, an appeal to her father's compassion and fair-mindedness might work. Both parents were well aware that these were extraordinary times. She might even remind her mother that as a soldier, the children's father would be fighting against the likes of Major Werner and to secure Robert's release.

THE PETIT SALON was reserved for small family gatherings. Tonight, its double doors were slightly ajar, and the soft glow of her mother's new lamps beckoned. Her father had argued in vain to experiment with electric lights, however gas lighting prevailed. Mariele knocked and entered. Her mother and father were at opposite ends of the plush settee that anchored the room. Neither was dressed for dinner.

"Eugène said you wished to speak with me."

"We do," her father said. "Why don't you sit over there." He gestured at a single chair with a stiff back and wooden arms.

Mariele sat down, keeping to the edge of the seat, and arranged her skirt. The last time she had been alone in this room with her parents was the day they'd told her of Bertrand's proposal.

Bertrand's first proposal had been conveyed by Mariele's father. Shocked and not the least bit interested in engaging herself to a man she barely knew, she had defied her parents and rejected the offer. A few weeks later, Bertrand had surprised her at a café where she was having tea and had

convinced her to walk with him through the Jardin des
Tuileries, her maid trailing behind. In the ensuing months,
other outings had followed—the opera, a concert, an exhibition
of paintings, a boat ride along the Seine. During this time,
Bertrand had gradually engaged her mind and her emotions.
When he had proposed a second time, she had said yes.

"Did you receive my note about the children's mother?"
Mariele asked.

"I did," her father replied. A decanter filled with an amber
liquid was on the coffee table. He poured a small measure into a
glass and took a sip. "Your maman and I have discussed the
situation."

He swirled his glass, and as the liquid went round and
round, Mariele wondered if he was going to say anything else.
Her father was a thoughtful man who was guided by justice,
love of family, and service to his country. He had trained in the
law, but now acted as a senior government advisor. When she
was little, his height and gruff voice had frequently unnerved
her. It wasn't until she was older that she could appreciate his
wisdom and be secure in the knowledge that he loved her as
much as he loved his two sons.

"Yes, Papa. And what did you and Maman conclude?"

"While they stayed with us last night, we are concerned
about having two small children in the house for days or even
weeks." He held up one hand to forestall her response. "They are
not part of the family, nor the offspring of close friends who
might temporarily need a place to stay. Like all children, they
will make noise and disrupt the household. However, we both
realize that these are extraordinary circumstances, and I have
convinced your mother that we should do our Christian duty
and take them in for a short period of time."

Her mother cleared her throat. "They are to remain on the
ground floor. Madame Robinette has already cleared some
space, and Suzette tells me they were quite comfortable sleeping

in the small pantry. She's found some old clothes in the nursery, which they may use. The children will not be permitted in the family's main living areas. They will eat in the kitchen and are not to play in the garden. You will ensure that they are quiet and well-behaved." She raised her eyebrows. "Are these rules clear?"

Although inwardly bristling, Mariele remained calm. "Yes, Maman. And thank you both for being so . . . so charitable. I will, of course, take them with me whenever I go to Sainte-Clotilde."

The hard line of her father's face softened. "You should probably go and make sure Sophie and Fabien are comfortable."

Mariele rose. "Yes, Papa. I'm sure they would welcome a friendly face."

18

OCTOBER 28, 1870 – CAMILLE

IN THE DAYS after attending the Vigilance Committee meeting, Camille's anxiety continued to grow. André had assured her that he would communicate their findings to the right people, yet every day she was certain his mission had failed. As she went about the city, she noticed more National Guardsmen than usual on the streets, each armed with a weapon, and larger crowds gathering in front of public buildings, accusing the government of everything from misleading its citizens to outright treason. Many radicals denounced Thiers and his colleagues and called for their downfall, while others wrote articles designed to inflame Parisians to disobedience and revolt.

On Saturday, she spent a long, arduous day at the hospital. Despite growing used to the sight of blood, the howling cries of men undergoing surgery, and the putrid smells of septicemia and gangrene, she remained devastated by the degree of suffering. Walking home, she came across members of the National Guard tossing large bundles of newspapers onto bonfires while onlookers cheered and shouted.

"What's happening?" she asked an older man with one leg who was leaning on a crude wooden crutch.

"*Combat* said that General Bazaine is secretly negotiating with the King of Prussia to surrender Metz."

"But what are the guards burning?"

"They think the story is false. So, they've seized all copies of *Combat* from the news kiosks in order to burn them."

"Bazaine will never surrender!" a woman shouted. The crowd repeated her cry. "Those who believe these lies are traitors!"

"*À bas les traîtres*," came the reply. "Down with traitors!"

"What do you think, Monsieur?" Camille asked.

The man cleared his throat and spit on the ground. "If I were young and still had my leg, I would show those bastards what Parisians are made of. We drove them out of Bourget, didn't we? We can drive them out of Paris."

"I'm certain you would, Monsieur." Dusk was gathering, and with the crowd growing larger, Camille decided not to linger.

ON SUNDAY, Bourget was retaken by the Prussians, and on Monday, the newspapers reported the fall of Metz and the resulting capture of 170,000 additional French soldiers. Camille was reading a detailed report of the fighting when André entered the library. Michel, their butler, trailed well behind.

"The Reds have attempted a coup d'état," he said without bothering to greet Camille or her father properly. "I saw it with my own eyes. Their leaders, Flourens and Blanqui, were the instigators. They seized all members of the government and confined them under guard at City Hall."

"Impossible," Camille's father said. He'd just lit a cigar with a taper from the fire and now exhaled a drift of smoke. "The National Guard would not permit such a thing."

André clenched his fists. "On the contrary, sir, many members of the Guard reversed their weapons and sided with the radicals. Thousands were present at the Hôtel de Ville, most of them from the *faubourgs*. They formed a raucous crowd, shouting, 'Vive la Commune' and 'Down with Trochu,' and cheering those who appeared to make speeches. Then there was a call to arms, and many men rushed at the doors, forcing their way into the building. I heard four or five shots followed by drums and bugles.

"Within minutes, a mob had gathered, clamoring for the Commune. They shouted phrases like 'à Versailles' and 'à bas Trochu' and 'no armistice.' Even with the rain pelting down, the crowd kept growing. At one point, there was a pistol shot, and the people waiting outside went wild with fury."

André continued with further details of the episode, explaining that he had been able to get inside the building and watch the proceedings unfold. At several points in the account, Camille's father questioned him closely.

Although she'd known this event was coming, Camille's heart raced. "Were you in any danger, André?" she asked. "I watched a mob gather on Saturday after the *Combat* article was published, and yesterday's news of Metz also brought out many protesters."

"No, I wasn't in danger, but the crowd can turn at any moment. The streets are now decidedly unsettled, so I came to warn you. The leaders are calling for a Committee of Public Safety, and we all know where that could lead."

"Thank you for bringing this news, André," her father said. He stubbed his cigar in a silver ashtray. "I must leave at once. Our manufacturing facilities may be vulnerable. If the rabble were to take over the huge stocks of ammunition we have on hand, the results would be disastrous. Can you remain here with Camille? I don't know when Bertrand or Victor will return, and if the radicals prevail, the situation could turn ugly."

"Certainly, Monsieur."

Camille reached for his arm. "Please don't go, Papa. You may be in danger too."

He shook his head. "I have no choice, *ma chérie*. I must see to the business."

She wasn't surprised at his answer. "Then send word that you've arrived safely."

"It's just as we feared," she said to André after her father hurried out the door. "Everything they said at the republican meetings was true. What do you think will happen? Paris can't possibly survive a coup as well as a siege." She sat down once more on the library chaise.

"I agree with you," he said. "But counter measures are being put in place. Our Minister of Finance managed to slip away and reach the treasury. He is in communication with municipal and military authorities as well as battalions of the National Guard that favor the government."

THAT NIGHT the sound of bugles pierced the air, followed by the beating of drums, repeating every few minutes. The rappel had begun. Bertrand changed into his uniform as soon as he heard the call to arms, and Camille knew that André would be doing the same.

"Where will you go?" she asked.

"The call to arms means we must gather at our assembly points," Bertrand replied. "You and Victor should remain indoors. Hopefully, Father will have the sense to do the same."

Waiting was not Camille's preferred state. By midnight, she had abandoned her book and needlework and had begun to pace, occasionally pausing to stare out the window, hoping for some sort of clue. Bertrand did not return until after three in the morning.

"Trochu has taken control, and the provisional government is now restored," he said after downing the glass of cognac she poured for him in one gulp.

"What happened?" Victor asked.

"Our troops poured in from every direction toward the Hôtel de Ville, filling Place Vendôme and the nearby streets. We surrounded city hall and began chanting, '*Vive Trochu!*' and 'Down with the Commune!' Flourens and his men must have realized they were outnumbered, and by midnight many of them had slipped away. General Trochu released the members of government and sent out search parties for those in charge of the insurrection."

"We are fortunate, then," Victor said.

Fortunate, Camille thought. *There's nothing fortunate about what we're going through.* "Let's hope the situation doesn't get worse before it improves," she said.

THE COUP'S speedy demise restored a fragile calm to Paris. Citizens took up their daily struggles once more, searching for enough food to survive, anticipating further hardships, split into divided camps either grateful for reprieve or mourning lost possibilities. Every day the sounds of artillery grew louder as the Prussian army moved closer to the city's walls.

A week later, Camille spent the morning at home checking provisions and balancing the household accounts. In the afternoon, accompanied by the dull rumble of distant guns, she shopped for food, dismayed at the bare shelves and long queues of despondent women and children outside each establishment. In one queue, she noticed a woman wearing a soiled scarf holding a little girl whose eyes were shaded by hunger and whose fingers, wrapped around the woman's neck, were red and inflamed with chilblains. Camille was stirred by the hope-lessness apparent in the woman's eyes and slipped a few coins into her hand.

"Thank you, Mademoiselle," the woman whispered, stuffing the coins into her ragged pocket before anyone else could notice. "We won't starve tonight."

After purchasing some fabric for a heavy cloak, she stood by the Pont de l'Alma and gazed at the river. The Seine had always been a working river, full of color as skiffs, dinghies, and barges loaded with coal and other goods traveled east or west. No more. Now an eerie feeling prevailed, as if at any moment the river might erupt in the chaos of artillery launched from Prussian batteries. She watched a *bateau mouche* full of wounded soldiers move as swiftly as possible toward one of the designated quays for offloading.

These men would be taken to one of the many public or private hospitals in the area, perhaps even the Odéon, where tomorrow she might help them ease their pain and suffering. Camille shook her head. Fifty-one days of siege. When would it end?

To date, none of the military sorties ordered by General Trochu had been successful, and most Parisians were impatient, many clamoring for the government to seek a settlement, even if such negotiations meant loss and humiliation. The bour-geoisie were tired of playing at soldiering. Those from surrounding villages who had fled to the safety of Paris wanted to return home. The wealthy sought to reactivate their business dealings. Only men of fierce republican and left-leaning senti-ments were still spoiling for a fight.

André arrived at seven that evening to take Camille to another one of the republican clubs.

"Where exactly are we going?" she asked.

"To a club on rue d'Arras where the Ultras congregate.

They're the group leading the charge for turning government over to a commune. With the *coup d'état* attempt and the turmoil of the past week, I want to hear what's being said."

Camille grabbed his arm. "Do you think those who took our government hostage will attempt to take control again? I thought the recent vote proved that the people support the government of National Defense. Parisians voted overwhelmingly in favor of our leaders, including General Trochu."

"You're right, but I believe the radical factions will ignore what the people want. They mistrust the bourgeoisie, and it was the middle class and business owners who affirmed the plebiscite in such significant numbers. Men like Flourens and Blanqui may be in hiding, but not for long. I was there, Camille. I saw what happened. They dismissed Trochu and held the government prisoner, and the very men who should have defended our government did nothing."

Camille wondered at the passions that drove men to such treachery. "What if trouble breaks out tonight?"

"We'll leave if necessary. I won't expose you to any danger." He turned to look at her. "You're shivering. Why don't you move a little closer?"

"I'm fine," Camille said. She preferred not to move any closer to André. Having spent so much time in his company, her feelings for him were beginning to change, and she had yet to sort them out. At first, she thought it was admiration, but lately she found herself thinking of him at odd times of the day or night.

MEMBERS of the Club Rue d'Arras gathered in a large room with a gallery at one end and a long platform at the other. Sitting at a table just inside the entrance, a man and woman collected a few sous from each person for the purchase of more cannon. As with their other outings, André and Camille had worn workingclass clothes, and no one questioned their right to be there.

"Do you see that man on the platform with the graying beard and long nose?" André whispered. "That's Blanqui. I thought he was still in hiding after the coup attempt."

A man with stringy blond hair who stood next to Louis Auguste Blanqui was gesticulating wildly and shouting to be heard over the din. "Pimps and parasites," he said. "Just like Napoleon's government, we are governed by pimps and parasites and wanton panderers of special favors. These men know nothing of working-class matters, and neither do they care. They sustain an organized system of fraud and mendacity to line their own pockets. It's time to end our oppression!"

The speaker shook his fist, then bowed to the cheering crowd before sitting down. Another speaker claimed the platform, then another and another. They denounced Trochu, Favre, Napoleon III, the Catholic Church, the bourgeoisie, the Orléanists, former Empress Eugénie, and the wealthy, all the while extolling the working class and the values of fraternity, equality, and liberty.

Finally, Blanqui rose again. Everyone hushed. "My friends," he said, "we have much work to do. Paris has fallen on such hard times, no one knows how we will survive. But perhaps this siege is a blessing, for the longer it lasts, the more likely we are to convert others to our way of thinking. The past few days, while unsuccessful, demonstrate the strength of our cause. We are armed. We are resolute. We will prevail!"

The crowd roared its approval. Drums beat and bugles sounded. Everyone stood to sing "La Marseillaise."

Camille looked at André. "They're incensed with rage."

He leaned close. "And obsessed with the notion of taking power. I'm sympathetic to working-class problems, but this is madness. I fear they will make another attempt to control the government."

"And if they're successful?"

"It will be a repeat of 1848. They say they want a republic

that is truly egalitarian and representative; however, these men will be quite prepared to ignore the rights of anyone who disagrees. No one will be safe."

19

NOVEMBER 1870 – MARIELE & CAMILLE

AFTER TWO WEEKS, Sophie and Fabien were accustomed to the routine and rules and seemingly happy, although Fabien often asked about his mother. Victor had recommended that they tell the children that their mother was ill and could not look after them, until they had word from the father. Mariele had agreed.

Her routine had also changed. She now took her breakfast in the kitchen so she could wake the children up and help them get ready. She loved seeing their sleepy faces in the morning—the way Sophie reached her small arms above her head, yawning and stretching as she woke, pulling the covers tight around her chin; the way Fabien rolled out of bed with the stuffed clown still clutched in his arm.

Some mornings, she imagined a future with her own children to look after and wondered whether Bertrand would be the kind of father who indulged his children or one who was more reserved like her own had been. What would it be like to bear children? Would she be a good mother? With Sophie and Fabien and the other small children at the church, she had followed her instincts and had so far been successful. But a child of her own—surely that would be different.

"Mademoiselle, please help me," Fabien said, holding a pair of black leather boots with thoroughly scuffed toes. "Can't do the buttons."

Mariele knelt on the floor. "Sit still, Fabien. I can't do them up if you don't sit still." When she was done, she ruffled his tousled hair. "Bath tonight," she said. "I'll ask Nicole to have the hot water ready."

"I hate having a bath," Fabien replied. A few seconds later, his face brightened. "Can we play with Monsieur Theo's boat again?"

"We'll see," Mariele replied.

AFTER RETURNING from Sainte-Clotilde in the late afternoon, Mariele left the children with Nicole and went to see her mother. Located at the back of the house with windows over-looking the garden, her mother's suite consisted of three rooms: a bedroom, a dressing room, and a small sitting room. Each was decorated in a different shade of blue.

Mariele found her mother dressed in deep purple, standing by the sitting room window. The desk was open, and on it lay a sheet of paper, a pen, and an ink pot. A map of France lay on the coffee table and a stack of newspapers on the plush carpet.

"What are you doing, Maman?"

Her mother turned from the window. "Writing to Robert," she said. "In his last letter, he asked for details of what is happening. I've been reading the papers and following every-thing on that map so I can tell him." A wisp of a smile. "And you? What have you been doing today?"

"I went to Sainte-Clotilde as usual. Bertrand brought the children and me home. He's determined to see me home every day he can, which I appreciate, especially now that . . ." Mariele let the sentence trail off.

"Now that?"

Mariele wondered if her mother was so secluded that she was unaware of the desperation of working-class Parisians, the long lines for food, the demonstrations and rioters and looters on the streets. To say nothing of the artillery sounding from the forts encircling the city. "Now that . . . there are so many soldiers about."

Her mother frowned. "Are you sure it's safe for you to go to that church at all?" she asked. "I must speak to your father about the situation." She turned to look out the windows once more. "I've been watching a squirrel gathering nuts. A very busy squirrel. If his efforts are any indication, it's going to be a long winter."

Mariele saw her opportunity. "Speaking about winter, Maman, do you think we can spare a few blankets for the church? I found some old ones in the linen room. A few that are quite worn. Suzette said we haven't used them in ages. The church basement can be cold, and now that the weather has turned, the children need—"

"Yes, yes." Her mother waved one hand dismissively. "Of course. And you can ask Suzette to see if there are any warm children's clothes to donate. How are your little ones? Sophie and Fabien. I hardly even hear them."

Mariele stifled a chuckle. Her mother was the one who'd laid down the rules in the first place. In response, Mariele and the others—Madame Robinette, Suzette, Nicole, even Eugène—had been vigilant in caring for the children and keeping them out of sight. "Sophie's delightful, Maman. She chatters away to us all, and she's very curious. Fabien seems to be quieter. He misses his parents and asks about them every day. Victor and I haven't told him about his mother. We're waiting for a message from their father, although it's been so long . . ." She let the sentence trail away. Her worry was that the children's father had been killed in one of the recent military actions. What would become of the children then?

"Hmm," her mother responded. "Is there something else you wished to speak with me about? If not, I really should begin changing for dinner."

THEO WAS STILL STRAIGHTENING his tie as he hurried into the dining room. "My apologies, Maman. Doctor Picard's anatomy class ran late, and there was a disturbance blocking my route home."

"A disturbance?" Mariele's father set down his soup spoon. "What kind of disturbance, Theo? Nothing violent, I trust."

"No, Papa. More of a shouting match, really. Men with time on their hands and too much to drink. They spilled out of Club de la Résistance and blocked the street. Of course, others stopped to watch, and a crowd grew rather quickly. They were arguing about Trochu's military strategy."

What is it about Parisians that they are always certain they know better than those in authority? Mariele wondered, as Theo went on to describe the scene and what had taken place.

"And all of that led to a disagreement about whether Paris should continue to resist or negotiate peace," Theo concluded.

"Only the French government can negotiate peace," Mariele's mother said. "It astonishes me how Parisians always think their opinions are the only ones that matter. But let's not talk about the siege. I'm so weary of the topic." She beckoned to Eugène. "Please serve the fish, Eugène."

After dinner, Mariele and her family gathered for coffee in the library, where heavy damask curtains had been drawn and a fire crackled in the hearth. She wished that the children could have enjoyed the cozy atmosphere, imagining Fabien sitting on the fire bench and Sophie on her lap.

"Coffee, Philippe?" her mother said.

"Not tonight. I think I'll have brandy. Theo, do you wish to join me?"

They sat in their usual places: her parents in two wingback chairs, and Mariele and Theo on the settee. Robert's chair was as empty as it had been since he'd gone to war. A little silence ensued as the brandies were poured and the two men went through the ritual of swirling and sniffing and taking sips of the pungent liquid. A smile of satisfaction crossed her father's face.

"Madame Robinette told me this morning that prices have risen again," Mariele's mother said. "Ham is sixteen francs a kilogram, and a pound of fresh butter was forty-five francs. Forty-five francs! Outrageous! She bought two pigeons for twelve francs and two dozen eggs for almost nine francs. With two extra mouths to feed, we will soon have to economize."

"I'm sure we'll manage, my dear," Mariele's father replied. "The children do not eat very much."

Eugène entered the room, carrying an envelope. Mariele's father opened the letter, read it, and frowned. "Thank you, Eugène. Tell him I'll be there in a moment and bring some brandy to my study. Evangeline, please excuse me. I must speak with this gentleman on an urgent matter."

A hint of red touched her mother's cheeks. "Really, Philippe? It's late. Much too late for visitors."

Her father tossed the letter into the fire and watched for a moment as a flame caught, flared, and shriveled the paper into black ash. "Don't wait for me."

In the silence that followed, Mariele searched for a topic to divert her mother. Since her day had consisted of trivialities— stories, games, runny noses, lunchtime misbehavior, little bumps and bruises—there was little material to work with. However, Theo rescued the situation with a description of a surgery he had watched that morning and news of the engagement of one of his friends.

"What an odd time to get engaged," her mother said. "If Mariele wasn't already engaged to Bertrand, I doubt that your father and I would have entertained his proposal in the midst of

a siege. Who knows what might happen?" She set down her cup
with a rattle and turned to Mariele. "I'm sorry, dear. I'm sure
nothing is going to happen to your fiancé. The National Guard
are a defensive force. They won't be attacking the Prussians."

Mariele felt the color drain from her face. "I hope you're
right, Maman. Now, if you'll excuse me, I've had a long day and
should really go to bed." She laid a hand on her brother's shoulder. "Good night, Theo. And thank you for lending your sailboat to Fabien."

As Mariele walked along the hallway toward the stairs that
led to the third floor, she heard voices. Her father's voice was
clear, the other less distinct and yet familiar. She leaned over the
bannister sufficiently to see the two men and was surprised to
discover André Laborde was the man who had arrived unexpectedly. *What would bring Monsieur Laborde out this late?* She
wasn't aware of such a pressing connection between them.

The following evening, Madame Lambert's salon was
crowded by the time Mariele and Bertrand arrived, and the
mood of the room felt somber. With the cold weather and so
many women gone from the city, there were fewer colorful
gowns, fewer couples flirting in discreet corners, and much less
laughter. Mariele pulled her shawl closer.

"Are you chilled?" Bertrand asked.

"Just a little."

"Ah, Mademoiselle de Crécy," Madame Lambert said. "How
lovely you look in that shade. Monsieur, may I borrow your
fiancée for a few minutes? Why don't you join Monsieur
Garnier's group? I'm sure they could benefit from your experience with the National Guard."

Bertrand bowed slightly. "Six weeks of experience does not
make me very knowledgeable, Madame Lambert."

"Yes, but it's more knowledge than Monsieur Garnier has." Her eyes crinkled as she smiled. "Come with me, my dear," she said to Mariele. "I need your help."

Cecile Lambert was a beautiful woman, her slender figure enhanced by delicate eyebrows and shapely lips. However, it wasn't just her beauty that attracted attention. She also had a sharp mind, was extremely well read, and could discuss almost any topic with vigor and insight. In all the times she'd attended the salon, Mariele had never been alone with their hostess.

"How can I help, Madame?" Mariele asked after Madame Lambert had led her to a small table and chairs located next to the grand piano. On many other evenings, a pianist had entertained the group, but the piano's lid was down, and the bench was tucked in to suggest that there would be no entertainment that evening.

"Your father tells me that you are looking after destitute children. This is very admirable."

Mariele inclined her head. She'd never been comfortable with compliments and found herself tongue-tied when they came her way. Her two older brothers had always been the ones to stand out: Robert for his athletic capabilities and good humor; Theo for his intelligence and quick wit. As a daughter and the youngest, she had remained in the background.

"It's a small gesture to help Parisians who are less fortunate," she said. "Other women are doing more difficult work."

Cecile Lambert leaned forward. "In my opinion, the divisions that have afflicted Parisian society are in danger of tearing us apart. Our government is preoccupied with military matters. Others must find ways to heal these divisions if we are to survive this siege and repair our nation when it is over. Women can lead these efforts. Do you agree, Mademoiselle de Crécy?"

Women in the lead? Mariele turned the possibility over in her mind. Only one as influential as Cecile Lambert would hold such a conviction. "The thought had not occurred to me,

Madame. But now that you bring it to my attention, I believe we can have some impact."

"Excellent. At next week's salon, I would like you to describe the work you do and the suffering you see. I also plan to ask Camille Noisette to share her experiences, and afterward, I will appeal to my guests for their donations to the cause. Will you agree to help, Mademoiselle?"

The idea of speaking in public filled Mariele with dread until she thought of Robert, not only his bravery but the experience of being a prisoner. "I . . . yes . . . yes, I will. But I cannot promise to be a very good speaker, Madame."

"Just speak from your heart." Madame Lambert laid her hand on top of Mariele's. "You'll be fine."

CAMILLE HAD NOTICED Mariele with Cecile Lambert, their heads leaning close, and wondered what might have prompted such an intense conversation.

"You seem to be in a daze," she said with a little laugh when Mariele approached. "Are you all right?"

Mariele looked up and smiled. "I am. Just lost in thought, but I'm glad to see you. In fact, I was planning to speak with you about something that happened yesterday. Do you have a few moments?"

"How intriguing. Let's move away from the others so we can speak discreetly."

In a quiet spot between two potted ferns, Mariele described the meeting between her father and André Laborde. "You're well acquainted with Monsieur Laborde. Do you have any idea why he would visit my father so late in the evening? They kept their voices low, but the tone was urgent."

"That is indeed strange," Camille replied. She wondered if the visit had anything to do with the republican clubs. "I'm aware that they know one another, but I assumed it was a business connection, not a matter requiring a late-night visit. Shall we ask him? He's just over there."

"No, no, no. It's merely an idle question and none of my business, of course. Do you have a romantic interest in Monsieur Laborde? I suppose that's none of my business either, but I have often seen you with your heads together."

"Of course, you can ask such questions. You're going to be my sister-in-law. However, there's nothing romantic between us. I merely find him amusing, and we all need something amusing these days, don't we? Now tell me, did I ease your concerns about my mother?"

Mariele's cheeks grew pink. "Your advice was wonderful." She laughed. "And with you there as my confidant, I'm sure I will be fine. You haven't said anything to Bertrand, have you?"

"Not a word," Camille replied. "And you mustn't tell him of my schemes either. Now let's join the others. Bertrand probably needs to be rescued. Monsieur Garnier is holding forth again."

"OUR GOVERNMENT MUST SEEK AN HONORABLE PEACE," Monsieur Garnier said to the assembled group—some seated, some standing. "The countries of Europe depend on France. Their emperors and kings will come to our rescue and insist that the enemy depart. I'm in favor of Louis Blanc's suggestion that we ask for the arbitration of four powers—two monarchical and two republican. These powers will negotiate with Prussia and persuade the brute to depart. What say you, Monsieur Noisette? Or you, Monsieur Laborde?"

Camille wondered which of the two men would speak. She and Mariele had joined the animated discussion and now sat side by side on two tasseled chairs that were part of a loose circle of guests. André, who had offered his chair to Camille, stood with one elbow propped on the fireplace mantel. He looked decidedly annoyed.

"I fear that Prussia will pay no attention to the opinions of other European states," Bertrand said. "They are intent on punishing Paris and thus the rest of France."

"Well, then, all we need is for Trochu to prolong the resistance, so the provinces have time to muster their troops and come to our aid. Surely, we can then outwit Moltke," Garnier continued the argument.

Neither Bertrand nor André chose to answer the man, and the conversation shifted as one of the other guests lamented a recent decree stating that all horses, mules, and asses were to be considered property of the government.

Camille caught André's eye. She lifted her eyebrows and tilted her head to indicate that she wished to speak with him and was pleased to see him move away from the group. She tapped Mariele's shoulder. "Lovely to see you tonight, my friend. We'll talk again next week."

André was waiting for her in the corridor with his hands clasped behind his back. He looked pensive and perhaps a little worried. "You wished to speak with me?"

Camille ignored his brusque tone. "You've avoided me all evening. Is something wrong?"

"Not at all. There were a few people I had to speak to, and then, unfortunately, Monsieur Garnier insisted that I join that particular conversation. He certainly can be tedious."

"Hmm. And he thinks he knows better than our generals how to defend Paris."

A hint of amusement touched his mouth. "I'm sure you didn't pull me away to talk about Garnier."

"You're right. Mariele de Crécy told me of your visit to their home last night. I thought you might want to know that she's curious about why you would be speaking to her father. I'm curious too, although I have my suspicions."

He had drawn his head back as she'd spoken. "Damn," he said. "My apologies, Camille. One should never swear in front of a woman. Thank you for telling me, but please don't ask me any questions. It's something you needn't . . . you shouldn't know about. Trust me in this."

With anyone else, Camille would have continued to probe. However, André was different. She respected him and the mission they shared. In time, she would discover the truth.

20

NOVEMBER 1870 – MARIELE

INCREASING chill and low-hanging clouds marked the last week of November. Recent news included the discovery of handheld bombs in Montmartre, a call for priests to join the army, and a story about a group of officers from the fort at St. Denis having breakfast with Prussian officers located nearby. Mariele had grown accustomed to exaggerated stories like the one about breakfast between enemies, but her father had assured her that it had happened. She mentioned the incident to Suzette later that day.

"My husband believes the National Guard will save Paris," the maid said as she arranged Mariele's hair for an evening out. "Please sit still, Mademoiselle. I don't wish to poke you with these pins."

"The National Guard?" Mariele replied.

"Yes, the Guard is filled with strong, capable men. They will show General Trochu that he can rely on their strength."

"I see. I'm sure you're right, Suzette. My fiancé is also a member of the Guard, and I know we can rely on him." She thought Suzette's assertion—no doubt a repetition of her husband's opinion—to be highly unlikely based on what

Bertrand had said of the disorganization and ineptitude perme-
ating the National Guard.

"And he will see action soon. Two or three days from now,
he told me, and we will trounce the Prussians. Paris will be
saved."

"Really?" Mariele asked.

She was well aware that Parisians had turned angry and
defiant, certain of their city's impregnability and indignant that
outside forces—Britain, Austria, even Italy—had not come to
her rescue. Talk of exacting vengeance against the Prussians
swirled on every street corner, although the parades, bursts of
singing, and enthusiastic crowds that had gathered at the Hôtel
de Ville or the Strasbourg statue were no more. The streets had
become quiet—a restless quiet. Hope mingled with fear. General
Trochu's continuing vacillation caused men like her father and
Bertrand to doubt the military would ever take action against
Prussia. She was appalled to read of people dying of starvation
and expected there would soon be more.

"Yes, Mademoiselle. There, I'm finished. Are you pleased?"
Suzette held a mirror so Mariele could see the back and sides,
arranged in a cascade of curls.

"Thank you, Suzette. What would I do without your help?"

Mariele was nervous about the evening ahead and Madame
Lambert's request that she speak about her experience at
Sainte-Clotilde. She had practiced her remarks in front of the
mirror in her bedroom and had notes written on small slips of
paper in her purse. Mariele's biggest fear was that she would
become tongue-tied, as she had at the age of fifteen while delivering a recitation in class.

"YOU LOOK LOVELY TONIGHT, MARIELE," Camille said. She
handed her cloak to one of the footmen. "That shade of rose

complements your coloring beautifully. Don't you agree,
Bertrand?"

"I certainly do."

After greeting Madame Lambert, Camille went off to speak
with friends while Mariele and Bertrand circulated about the
room, hearing bits of conversation as people settled into groups
around the grand salon. In one corner, a young woman with
ginger hair played the piano while six men stood watching. In
another corner, two settees and four chairs were occupied by a
group of older men in animated discussion. One of them beckoned to Bertrand.

"Monsieur Noisette, will you join us so we can hear your
opinion of General Trochu's latest plans?"

Bertrand led Mariele over to the group.

"And what have *you* heard of Trochu's plans, Monsieur
Roche?" he asked as Mariele sat down and arranged her skirts.

Monsieur Roche pulled one end of his mustache a few times
before he spoke. "Well, we know the city's gates are closed to all
but military personnel, and there are more troops than usual
moving about. They seem to be gathering in great numbers in
the eastern parts of Paris. I've heard from a reliable source that
the army will head south to strike a blow at the enemy. But as a
member of the National Guard, you must know more than
I do."

"It's about time Trochu took some action," added a man with
dark hair and a distinguished air about him. "The longer he
delays, the more entrenched the Prussians will become, and
we've been under siege almost ten weeks now. Ducrot's the man
to lead us."

"I believe you're right, sir," Bertrand said. "Now please don't
repeat this, but in my opinion, General Trochu has been acting
more like a lawyer than a general, and we all know the only
fighting lawyers do is in the courts."

This statement caused much laughter, and to be polite,

Mariele allowed a smile to form while the words *going south to strike a blow at the enemy* reverberated in her mind. She had dismissed Suzette's earlier boasting about the National Guard, but now her maid's statements seemed to echo those of Monsieur Roche. She looked at her fiancé, but his face gave nothing away.

"Monsieur Wilcox of the American Consulate told me the Anglo-American Ambulance has been put on alert," said a man wearing a green waistcoat. "And that suggests they're expecting casualties."

"So," Monsieur Roche spoke again, "tell us what you know, Noisette."

"You're putting me into a very difficult position, sir. Unfortunately, I am unable to either confirm or deny reports of troop movements or disclose any military plans."

Although the men prodded Bertrand to say more, he refused to divulge any information.

"LADIES AND GENTLEMEN!" Madame Lambert stood by the fireplace and called for her guests' attention. She tapped a spoon against her glass for emphasis. "Thank you for coming tonight. It gives me great pleasure to see so many old friends in the midst of the terrible events going on in our city. I'm deeply grateful that you choose to spend your time here." She smiled and nodded. "This evening, I wish to ask for your help. As you know, many of our fellow Parisians are suffering greatly. They do not have sufficient food or supplies to keep their families fed, clothed, and warm. Deaths among the working class have increased. Others have lost fathers and husbands to the war and this terrible siege. It's a tragedy, my friends. A great tragedy.

"I've asked Mademoiselle de Crécy and Mademoiselle Noisette to tell you of their experiences. Mademoiselle Noisette is nursing at the Odéon Theater under the direction of Sarah

Bernhardt. Mademoiselle de Crécy goes to Sainte-Clotilde almost every day to look after young children in dire circumstances. Afterward, I will tell you how you can help. Mademoiselle Noisette, would you like to go first?"

Mariele watched Camille come forward and stand beside Madame Lambert. A footman appeared with a wide footstool, and Camille stepped up so that she was more than a head taller than their hostess.

"Thank you, Madame Lambert. Thank you on behalf of all the soldiers who have been wounded, and on behalf of Madame Bernhardt and my colleagues at the Odéon. In order to give you some idea of how our soldiers are faring, let me tell you what happened yesterday.

"The morning began as it usually does, with rounds. The night nurse took me around the officers' quarters, describing all significant changes and the condition of our new patients. She explained that three officers had passed away overnight, and that we had acquired four new ones—two amputations, one case of pneumonia, and one of pleurisy. We paused at the beds for each of these new patients so I could observe them. One of the amputations is not expected to live.

"After rounds, I spent time caring for my patients. Some had bandages that needed changing. Some were in pain. Some needed help with food and drink. Some merely wanted a kind word."

She went on to explain her other duties and, at one point, had the group open-mouthed while describing her first amputation. Applause broke out when Camille stepped down.

A few moments later, Madame Lambert raised her arms to quiet the room and gestured for Mariele to speak. Bertrand squeezed her hand and whispered, "Don't worry. You'll do a wonderful job."

Mariele clutched her notes and stepped up onto the stool. "Mademoiselle Noisette, I had no idea how brave you are. My own experience is vastly different from yours, however, it too paints a picture of what our fellow citizens are suffering. Let me start by telling you about the children at Sainte-Clotilde. When I began, there were thirteen ranging in age from six months to eleven years. Now we look after twenty-two. Who are these children, you ask?

"Well, Sophie and Fabien's mother was injured by a runaway wagon and died. Their father is in the army, and there are no relatives to look after them. Lily's mother is a prostitute. She moved into the city to protect herself and her three-year-old daughter, and this is the only way for her to earn a living. Anton's father used to work as a builder, but there is no work for him now. He has been forced to join the National Guard, which doesn't pay enough to feed his son." She continued this way, describing the challenges facing a few of the others.

"These children have little to eat. Their clothes are thread-bare and insufficiently warm now that the cold is upon us. Their homes are little more than shacks by the roadside. Their older brothers or sisters are sent out to beg, to gather scraps or small twigs for the fire, to run an errand or two on the streets. At times, the children Father Victor and I look after arrive with bruises or split lips, and on these occasions they sit silently all day, staring vacantly at something only they can see."

Engrossed in speaking about the children, Mariele had forgotten to look at her notes. She paused to check what she'd written.

"Few of them can read or write. Not one of them attends school. Their prospects are bleak at best. But one thing I've noticed, ladies and gentlemen—they all have hope. And I've grown to love them. Thank you, Madame Lambert, for giving me the opportunity to speak today."

Mariele blushed at the applause that ensued, and later, after Cecile Lambert asked for donations of money and supplies, several of the assembled guests came over to give their compliments.

"Your speech was wonderful," Bertrand said at the end of the evening as they settled into a carriage.

"Thank you, Bertrand. I have to admit that beneath my gown, my knees were shaking." She chuckled. "Your sister is an excellent speaker. I hope everyone will make a donation."

"I'm sure they will."

The night was cold and quiet, broken only by the sounds of distant cannon and the thud-thud-thud of patrols marching through the streets. Mariele tucked her hands into her muff. "I thought you were very discreet when Monsieur Roche kept pressing for information about the National Guard."

Bertrand snorted. "They didn't make it easy for me. Roche in particular."

"Well, I like the fact that you kept quiet. I'm sure you know much more than you let on. Even I've heard rumors. I'm worried, Bertrand. Worried that you'll be caught in the midst of battle by an explosion or rifle fire. So many dreadful things could happen."

He squeezed her hand. "Many things could happen, and that's one of the reasons my father suggested postponing the wedding."

"Will you tell me what you couldn't tell those men?"

He was silent, and she heard only the clip-clop of the horse's hooves and the dull boom of heavy guns firing in the distance.

"You know this must remain a secret between us."

She nodded.

"My battalion has been assigned to General Ducrot's command. Upward of one hundred thousand men will assemble in the Bois de Vincennes with the intent of crossing the Marne and ultimately engaging the enemy near the towns of Créteil and Mont-Mesly and destroying their batteries. My under-standing is that we'll commence action around midnight in three days' time."

"You'll be fighting, then." Her mouth had turned dry, and she could barely swallow.

"Yes, I'll be fighting. We won't know exact deployments until a few hours in advance."

"I see."

He squeezed her hand again but said nothing more.

"And Camille's friend André Laborde? Will he be part of it?"

"Yes, but he's assigned to a second force under General Vinoy. They're to create a diversion so we can cross the Marne without detection." Bertrand pulled the curricle to a halt in front of her home.

"What does our army know of the enemy? Will these efforts be successful?"

He wrapped the reins around one hand. "Their fortifications are said to be very well constructed. More solid than ours. According to our captain, the Prussians have established defensive emplacements beyond their main fortifications, and these are reinforced with stone, which will make them difficult to capture. Scouts have identified that these defenses are closed in on both sides so that they are as strong on the Paris side as they are on the opposite. They will be difficult to breach."

"And that's where you'll be fighting?"

He nodded.

She could lose him. The very thought brought an intense feeling of foreboding, that stole through every limb, every nerve, every muscle. She blinked once, twice.

"Please hold me," she said. "If this is all I'm to have of you, I want to remember the feel of your arms around me."

21

NOVEMBER 29, 1870 – MARIELE

FROM THE TOP of the Panthéon, Mariele and Camille watched the fighting to the south. The noise was deafening. The heavy booming of French guns was answered in equal measure from Prussian battlements. Shells flew through the air, their fuses lit, and burst over enemy lines. A harrowing din rose and fell with the intensity of the fighting. Although too far away to distinguish individual soldiers, they could track swarms of men moving this way and that. Mariele held a gloved hand to her mouth, her eyes wide with horror.

"Bertrand is out there somewhere," she said. "God keep him safe." Mariele gripped her friend's arm. "There will be many wounded. Will you go to the hospital?"

Camille nodded. "Madame Bernhardt asked me to come at seven for the night shift."

"Is it difficult? The nursing, I mean. The things you described at last week's salon sounded horrible."

"It was at first, but I'm used to it now, and at times there's a great feeling of satisfaction. I help the men more this way than when I was reading to them."

"I doubt I could be that brave."

Camille turned to look at her. "My dear friend, you can do anything you set your mind to. You will make Bertrand a splendid wife. One of these days, I will have to tell you some of the ways to manage him that I've learned over the years. He and I have always been very close. More so since Juliette . . ."

Despite the dreadful circumstances, Mariele was pleased that a friendship had bloomed between herself and Camille. Bertrand's sister had been a year ahead at school, one of the popular girls who always had a flock of other students clamoring for her attention. Camille had broken all the rules and flaunted her rebellious nature. Her sister, Juliette, had been just as beautiful but with a calmer disposition.

Whenever Bertrand mentioned Juliette, it was with a wistful tone or a sad smile, but Mariele had never asked about how his sister's death had affected Camille. She wondered if Juliette's death accounted for the air of bravado her friend carried and the false gaiety she'd detected from time to time.

Mariele pointed at the conflagration spread before them. "There are days when I wonder whether we'll ever get married and whether Paris will ever be the same after this."

With so much movement, it was impossible to tell who had the upper hand. Groups of soldiers formed up and charged; intense fighting ensued. Smoke from burning buildings and firing guns obscured the blue and red of the French uniforms. Absolute chaos.

"I'm so afraid," Mariele said finally. "Not for me, but for Bertrand and all the other soldiers defending Paris."

Camille's lips were drained of color. "I'm afraid too. Monsieur Laborde is somewhere out there."

When it became clear Camille had nothing further to add, Mariele squeezed her hand. "All we can do is pray. Pray for our men and our city."

"Yes. We can pray." Camille straightened her back. "Will you go to the church today? Victor tells me you are very good with the younger children."

"I'm glad he's pleased. Our numbers have increased, and he has found a second volunteer, so I'm not needed today. Sophie and Fabien are at home with Suzette, who is remarkably good with them."

"It was so kind of your family to take them in," Camille said. She shivered. "We should go down now. My feet are like ice. Our home isn't far away. Please join me. We'll warm up in front of the fire, and tomorrow we can read about what happened."

Along the way toward Camille's home, crowds of Parisians gathered at street corners, waiting anxiously for news, women and children of the poorer classes thinly clad and shivering in the cold. The streets were cluttered with ambulance wagons rolling slowly along, wheels groaning with the weight of so many men. A soldier called out in a husky voice, "A kiss, Mademoiselle, before I die."

With a flourish, Camille blew the man a kiss. "I wonder if some of these soldiers will be taken to the Odéon."

Strange, Mariele thought once they had settled in the library, *how the rules of etiquette have been abandoned with the siege.* Under normal circumstances, she would never have dropped into someone's home like this after an outing. The rules under which members of the *haute bourgeoisie* operated required written invitations properly accepted and a change of outfit from morning dress to an afternoon gown with matching gloves and a fan or shawl to reflect her family's wealth and her status as Bertrand's fiancée. Tea would have been offered in fancy silver pots with matching sugar and milk containers and, in all likelihood, a two- or three-tiered platter containing enticing delicacies. Instead, Camille brought their tea in a small brown pot.

"How much longer can we go on?" Camille asked as she added a log to what remained of the fire.

"I don't know." Despite the fire, the room held a damp chill.

Mariele pulled her shawl tighter for warmth. "We'll have riots if conditions continue to worsen. Papa told me yesterday that rations are to be further reduced. As it is, the poor are eating rats and dog meat." She shivered at the thought. "And there's almost no fuel available."

"Have you been to the Bois? André was there last week and said there are no trees left, just acres of stumps. He was shocked to see it looking so desolate."

"But what choice do the poor have?" Mariele responded with indignation. "They're desperate for fuel. *Figaro* reported over two thousand people died last week. Two thousand! And for the most part, working class. It's no wonder they're agitating for change. Sometimes I feel I'm doing too little. You should see the state of the children we look after, all hollow-eyed and emaciated. They'll freeze in the ragged clothing they wear. And Maman . . . well, let's just say that I'm disappointed with her. Ever since our ordeal with the Prussians, she's been different. I don't know whether it's fear or distress or sadness. Maybe it's nerves. She won't say. Friends have urged her to help with their volunteer efforts, but she hasn't done so. Not even once."

"Have you asked her why?"

"Yes, but she refuses to answer. What do you think could have affected her so, Camille?"

Camille hesitated before responding. "Perhaps one of the soldiers took advantage of her."

"Took advantage of her? What do you mean?" Mariele looked closely at her friend, who had turned away and was now adding a small amount of honey to her tea.

"Forget what I said," Camille replied. "I'm sure your mother has her reasons. I'm certainly glad mine isn't here. Mother wouldn't have coped very well either, and it's quite likely she too would have done very little."

Mariele smiled. "No one could have imagined this when we met last June. So much has happened since then. I feel like a different person. I've always been the quiet one. Always in the background. But the war has changed me."

"In what way?"

"I think it's made me more confident. Does that make sense? More willing to take charge. At first, the ordeal with the Prussians destroyed my confidence. The sound of cannon frightened me, and I kept seeing soldiers who reminded me of our captors, even though they were French. At night, even the slightest noise would make me quiver in my bed, and I had nightmares of getting lost and never finding my way back to Paris."

Camille reached out and squeezed Mariele's hand. "I had no idea that you were suffering like that. How terrible for you."

Mariele stared into the distance at something only she could see. "One night, Papa heard me crying. He came into my room, and we spoke for a long time. He told me about being an officer during the last revolution. I hadn't been aware that he had served in the army. He told me how he'd conquered his fears." She turned and looked directly into Camille's eyes. "He's the one who helped me."

"I hope you retain that confidence," Camille said. "If you do, I believe your marriage will be more successful."

"Do you really think so?"

Camille raised her eyebrows. "Bertrand needs a strong woman."

"Well, you're certainly a strong woman," Mariele said. "I've always admired that about you."

"Thank you, my friend. What needs to change is my boldness. Sometimes it wells up inside me and takes control. I've always been that way, although Juliette's death seems to have worsened that particular trait. Not particularly attractive for a woman."

"The right man will admire you for it."

Camille laughed. "If I can ever find the right man." She

paused for a sip of tea. "Do you think Paris will ever be the same?"

"Will *we* ever be the same?"

"I'm not sure I can return to the idle life I led before . . ." Camille's voice faded away.

"I agree," Mariele said. "Hopefully, we will both marry soon after the siege ends, and then have other responsibilities to keep us occupied. I've seen the way André Laborde looks at you. Has he made his interest known?"

Camille frowned. "Monsieur Laborde isn't interested in me. I'm sure you're mistaken."

Mariele was embarrassed to have spoken so candidly. And yet she was certain she'd seen meaningful glances between Camille and André. She had definitely seen the man watching Camille closely. "Look at the time," she said. "Maman will be worried, and you need to go to the hospital. Promise me you'll be careful, Camille. If General Ducrot's sortie fails, Prussian guns will soon be able to reach the Left Bank."

Camille's look was somber. "If that happens, the hospitals of Paris will have civilian casualties to deal with too."

22

DECEMBER 1870 – CAMILLE

FOR FIVE FULL DAYS, Parisians trembled with anxiety while kept in ignorance of what had occurred on the field of battle south and east of the city. When defeat was finally announced, along with the tally of casualties, the city roared like a wounded animal. Everywhere she went, Camille heard people exclaiming, "We will die rather than surrender!"

Late one afternoon, Bertrand returned unscathed, although his uniform was coated with dirt and blood. Other than delivering warm embraces to each member of the family—Camille, Victor, and his father—he declined to answers questions about his ordeal, except to say that it was brutal, and he would tell them more at dinner. "Camille, please send Michel with a note telling Mariele I'm safe," he called as he climbed the stairs. "Tell her I'll visit as soon as I can."

"THE FIGHTING WAS INTENSE," Bertrand said after a toast to his safe return. "I imagine you've heard that General Vinoy led a force from St. Denis and Genevilliers to distract the Prussians. However, my battalion was with General Ducrot, and we began in the Bois de Vincennes, while others were located in the nearby villages. Our initial objective was to throw bridges over the Marne, and once across the river, to attack the enemy's lines with the ultimate objective of joining up with the army of the Loire."

Not a mouthful of food was eaten as Bertrand continued his story. "Unfortunately, the Marne had flooded its banks, which created a disaster for the first attempt to cross. At least a thousand troops were lost." He shook his head, his eyes clouded in memory. "The next day was the main attack. My battalion was with a force assigned to cross the Marne using pontoon bridges and then drive Prussian advance units from Champigny. In places, the fighting was hard hand-to-hand combat, but we managed to force them out."

As Camille's father poured more wine, he squeezed Bertrand's shoulder.

Bertrand took a gulp of wine before continuing. "During the next phase, we advanced up a plateau toward Villiers. Fighting uphill cannot be sustained for very long, and the enemy was so well entrenched that our efforts stalled. I heard rumors that General Ducrot had called on III Corps to attack from the north, but they failed to do so in time. If they'd arrived sooner, the outcome might have been different. On December first, there was a truce so we could bury our dead."

Bertrand didn't say what that effort had cost him, but Camille could tell by the look in his eyes and the set of his mouth that it was an ordeal he would never forget.

"The following day was a stalemate. Minor skirmishes without significant progress from either side. Our men were exhausted, cold, hungry, demoralized. Some of my comrades lay writhing in agony, waiting for an ambulance to take them away. I could do nothing for them except offer a drink of water or the comfort of my hand. Most died before help arrived. On the fourth, Ducrot ordered the retreat."

To Camille, Bertrand looked like some of the soldiers she'd nursed—defeated and demoralized, his eyes empty of emotion, as if to feel was too much to bear.

"I'm grateful to have you back, son," Camille's father said. "We all are."

"I'm sure you acquitted yourself with bravery," Victor added. "God answered my prayers."

Bertrand tilted his head. "Based on what I saw, I don't think God had anything to do with it."

THAT NIGHT, cold and frost blanketed the city, but by ten the next morning, the light was bright and bracing. Camille had received no news of André, not that she had expected to, and she tried hard not to imagine the worst.

"I must go to the Odéon later this afternoon," she said to her father and brothers. "Every bed we have is full, and still they keep bringing more. Some of the wounded are lying on the floor."

"But you didn't return until almost midnight," her father replied. "Surely someone else can look after the men today." He turned at the sound of the door opening. "Yes? What is it, Michel?"

"A letter for Mademoiselle Camille, sir."

The letter hovered between the servant's outstretched hand and Camille's. She did not recognize the bold slanted letters of dark blue ink. *Perhaps it's something about André*, she thought, suspended in the space between ignorance and knowing. She pressed her lips together and took the letter from the Michel's hand. The fine linen paper was cool to the touch and featured a watermark shaped like a family crest. She slid one finger beneath the flap of the envelope and extracted a sheet of paper.

"Who is it from?" Bertrand asked.

Camille held up her hand and scanned the writing. "André

Laborde. He's been wounded. In the leg. He's bedridden with his leg elevated to prevent swelling. He wants to see me."

"Why would he want to see you?" her father asked. "Does he have intentions where you're concerned?"

"No, Papa. We're friends. Just friends."

"Well, it's good to know he's all right," Bertrand said. "I quite like the man. His banking skills have become such an asset to us. Since I'm going out for an errand, I'll take you there myself."

A SERVANT LED them to a small sitting room that faced east to catch the morning sun. As they were ushered in, Camille admired the floral wall covering and the pale gold of the settee and chairs and wondered who had selected them. A series of portraits lined two walls, and an ornate clock topped with bronze angels stood on the mantel. The window looked out across an interior courtyard to the ivy-covered building next door.

André's pale, pinched face broke into a smile as soon as he saw them. "I'm so glad you're here. Bring some chairs over so we can talk for a while. This leg is a nuisance. Edmond, can you arrange refreshments?"

"Yes, Monsieur. I'll bring tea as soon as it's ready. Don't forget Doctor Larousse will be here at noon."

"Yes, yes. I know Larousse is coming. And you can let Coco in."

Seconds later a small, brown dog scurried into the room and leapt up onto the chaise, his whole body wagging as he licked André's face. "Enough, Coco. Enough." André pushed the dog away.

"Is that . . .?" Camille said.

André nodded.

Bertrand looked back and forth at the two of them. "Is there a story about this little mutt?"

"No real story," André replied without looking at Camille. "I told your sister about Coco one evening at Madame Lambert's. His leg was damaged by my carriage when I swerved to avoid something. After the surgeon fixed his leg, I brought Coco here to heal." André chuckled as he scratched the dog's head. "He seems to have made it his home."

Surprised by the presence of the dog and the lie André had just told Bertrand, Camille drew her chair close. "You look exhausted," she remarked. "And thin."

"I am, but the doctor says I'll mend."

"Tell us what happened," Bertrand said from his perch near the foot of the chaise.

André waved a dismissive hand. "Camille doesn't want to hear about all that."

"Yes, I do," she replied. "And don't think you need to spare me. I've seen far worse at the hospital."

She had dressed with care in a gown the color of ripe plums and had arranged her hair in a simple chignon, leaving wispy curls to dangle near her ears. A hint of jasmine wafted from the perfume she had dabbed on her neck and wrists just before leaving.

"I'm sure you've read reports in the papers." André's voice was hoarse and less forceful than normal. "I was with General Vinoy's troops south of the city. We began near Villejuif, and our intention was to push forward in the direction of Choisy to attract the Prussians away from the attack led by General Ducrot. After significant bombardment in the early hours of the morning, we advanced but met with fierce resistance and were ultimately ordered to retreat." André paused and stroked Coco's head.

"We advanced again the following day and were forced to retreat once more. All the while our forts and batteries hit the Prussian lines. At one point, I was surrounded by casualties—both French and Prussian—but there was no time to help them.

I couldn't even check whether they were alive. It was chaotic, and not everyone acquitted himself with honor."

As André relayed these events, Camille watched his face. Though his voice was calm, he was clearly agitated, his eyes turning inward in recollection, his hand twitching.

André continued recounting the battle for another ten minutes. "On the third day, a piece of shrapnel tore a hole in my leg, and I was lucky enough to be dragged to safety by one of my companions."

For a few moments, no one spoke. Camille glanced at her brother. The grim line of his mouth was evidence that he too had seen such things.

"And what about you, Bertrand?" André said. "I can see you were not wounded."

"Thankfully. But perhaps we can share that story another time," Bertrand said. "You look tired. Camille, I think we should go."

"Could you leave us alone for a few minutes?" André asked.

Bertrand cocked his head and smiled. "Of course, my friend."

"You could have died," Camille said as soon as her brother left the room.

"Yes, but I didn't."

"And what of our secret work? How will you be able to attend the clubs now?"

"That's one of the reasons I wanted to see you. Can you be my eyes and ears?"

"Your eyes and ears?"

"Can you go to the Montmartre Vigilance Committee meeting this week, listen to what they're saying, and report back to me? Ask questions about the other clubs while you're there. I don't expect you to go to the clubs I usually attend. They're mainly for men, but you may be able to query Louise Michel and discover what's being planned."

"I've only spoken to her once before. Usually, she's inundated with women wanting to question her."

He nodded. "We're . . . I'm worried that this recent loss will have unexpected consequences. Any information you can glean will be helpful."

THE FOLLOWING EVENING, after a long day at the hospital, Camille walked to Montmartre, a journey of more than an hour. The last twenty minutes were uphill, and she was exhausted by the time she arrived at Maxine's home. As she'd done before, she had changed into drab working-class clothing before leaving, including a long woolen cape to combat the cold.

"You haven't been here in several weeks," Maxine said as Camille hung her cape on a wooden peg.

"My fiancé was wounded," Camille explained, trying to look seriously concerned for her non-existent fiancé. "I had to care for him. You know what men are like when they're sick."

Maxine put her hand on Camille's shoulder and laughed. "We love them anyway, don't we? But why are you bothering with marriage? Marriage is bondage, as far as I'm concerned. Women would be much better off if we abolished the institution."

Camille was astonished at Maxine's opinion. It had never occurred to her to be with a man outside the bonds of marriage. "I see that you have radical ideas."

"That's why we're all here, isn't it? You will be glad to know that we've raised sufficient funds to acquire some weapons. They may soon be useful."

They exchanged a few more words before Maxine went off to greet some new arrivals. Camille looked around. The group seemed on edge—less chatter than on previous occasions, fewer smiles, and more whispers, as if each woman was expecting another blow to fall. Hollow cheeks suggested hunger, while red-rimmed eyes suggested sadness and sleepless nights. In one corner, a woman was weeping.

About fifteen minutes later, Louise Michel swept into the room. "Comrades!" she called out. "Forgive me for being late. I was visiting with our wounded." She unwound a thick scarf from around her neck and tossed it aside. "I spit on General Trochu, who has caused so much suffering. I weep for those who have lost loved ones. I bleed for those whose husbands and sons and lovers are wounded." She paused to catch the eyes of those gathered. "And what is our fate now? We cannot afford to eat. We cannot care for our children. We cannot warm our homes. Is this life? Is this liberty? No, *mes amies*. It is not. And how should we correct this injustice? We must rise up again and again until the rich are vanquished and the people are in charge once more."

Some of the women present shook their fists. Others shouted, "Away with Trochu! Resist to the death! *Vive la République!*"

Louise Michel allowed the outcry and the boiling conversation that followed to continue for almost a minute before raising her arms. "This provisional government headed by Thiers cannot save Paris. It is useless. This government says our clubs should be closed. They say we are planning a revolution. They say we are lawless and ungovernable. But I say we should stand up and fight for our country. All of us. Each and every one of us, my friends, must be prepared to fight. We will expel the Prussians. We will save Paris."

Cheering began, and Camille raised her voice with the others until Louise Michel quieted the group once more.

"The current social order carries within itself the seeds of misery and death for all freedom," Michel continued. "Women have more to fight for than men. We fight for our rights as well as the future of Paris. The right to divorce, to work for reason-

able wages, to be educated, to be equal in the eyes of the law. We
want universal free education for our children that is not under
the control of the church. We demand to be part of the leadership of this great uprising that will lead to a new society."

A young woman who Camille judged to be no more than
sixteen responded. "We must shoot the priests. They prevent us
from doing what we want. Women are harmed by going to
confession. I urge all women to denounce the priests and banish
the nuns who do their bidding and deprive us of our just
wages."

Louise Michel walked over to the young woman and raised
her hand high in the air. "Listen to our youth. They are the
future. We can be happy without the sacraments of the church.
Another evil of the present society is the rich, who only drink
and amuse themselves without ever considering the working
class. We must get rid of them, along with the priests and nuns.
We will only be free when we have no more bosses, no more
wealthy people, and no more priests."

"What shall we do?" someone cried.

"We shall set up a woman's movement for the defense of
Paris." Louise Michel had to shout to be heard. "We will organize to recruit volunteers for nursing, for canteen work, for
construction and staffing of barricades. We will distribute food
and succor for those in need. Ultimately, we will help abolish
existing social and legal structures and eliminate all privileges
and forms of exploitation. We will help replace the rule of
capital by the rule of labor. Think of it, my friends. True liberty,
equality, fraternity, and sorority."

Louise Michel's voice echoed with passion. Commitment
and hope shone from every fiber of her being, as if the slightest
spark would set her on fire. As soon as she stopped speaking,
the assembled women surrounded her, touching her clothing,
her hands, her arms. They called out to Louise, demanding a
turn to add their support for such a noble cause, to repeat what-

ever phrase still pulsed within them. It seemed to Camille that these women would follow their leader into battle without the slightest hesitation. Even if such a battle led to death.

"I COULDN'T GET close to her, André. She was mobbed by the women in attendance. I waited at least thirty minutes before leaving to make my way home. I can tell you that I didn't feel the slightest bit safe walking through Montmartre after ten o'clock. The streets were full of drunks and other belligerent men."

It was late morning on the day after the Vigilance Committee meeting. Camille had dressed simply, thrown a heavy coat over her shoulders, and walked to André's apartment. When he had opened the door, Edmond had not hidden his disapproval of a woman visiting his employer without a chaperone.

"Tell me what she said," he demanded. He seemed out of sorts and spoke without his usual polished tone or the light banter he favored when in her company. Coco's tail thumped in greeting, but the little dog remained curled up on the carpet.

"Are you all right?" she asked after relating as much as she could recall of the meeting.

"If you must know, this useless leg is causing me a great deal of pain." He shifted his position and winced. "*Nom de Dieu!*"

When he didn't apologize for cursing, she knew it must be bad. "Can I get your medicine?"

"No. I have none left, and the doctor won't come again until tomorrow."

"I see." She chose not to debate the matter with him. "Louise Michel is advocating revolution. The women who were there last night are totally supportive. I'm sure from what was said that other radical clubs are planning an uprising of major proportions. They won't make the mistakes they made in October. She told the gathering that when the day comes, they will need women to serve at ambulance stations and field kitchens, to build barricades, to administer funds, to organize soup kitchens and other tasks. When the day comes, André."

"Was there any indication of timing?"

Camille thought carefully. "I have the impression that it won't take place until after the siege is over."

"Thank you, Camille. You've done well. Very well indeed."

She'd been sitting on a chair a few feet away from the chaise on which André lay, and now she stood, crossed the room, and opened the door. "Edmond!" she called. He appeared in less than thirty seconds. "Please fetch a basin filled with hot water, some carbolic soap, and a roll of linen bandaging."

"What on earth are you doing?" André demanded.

"I'm a trained nurse. Since the doctor isn't coming until tomorrow, I'm going to clean your wound and change your dressing. If you let it fester, gangrene might set in."

"But . . . but . . ."

"I insist," Camille said in the same tone she used with a difficult patient. "Edmond, I need those items right away, please."

Under the valet's watchful gaze and André's tight-lipped scowl, she cleaned the wound and rebound his leg. "No signs of gangrene," she said as she secured the dressing.

André's look was indecipherable.

23

DECEMBER 24, 1870 – MARIELE

As CHRISTMAS DREW CLOSER, the shops had so little to offer that Mariele had a difficult time finding gifts for the children. Eventually she settled on a spinning top for Sophie and a wooden sailboat for Fabien, as well as small items she planned to place inside their shoes. She wrapped each in plain paper and hid them in her wardrobe.

With the passage of time, she'd grown close to the children. Their questions and innocent comments made her see the world differently. Sophie had become so attached, she occasionally called her Maman instead of Mademoiselle, although Fabien was always quick to correct her. Fabien's demeanor was changing too. He spoke less and less of his mother and father, almost as if he no longer expected to see them again. It broke her heart when she saw the bewilderment that came over his face from time to time, and she wanted to scoop him up and hold him tight and make sure that nothing ever hurt him again.

Victor had written to the army on three separate occasions, but there was never any response. Just last week, he had asked Mariele if the children were too much of a burden.

"Of course not," she'd declared. "I love looking after them."

ON CHRISTMAS EVE, she sat with them in the kitchen while they ate their dinner, and then, with Sophie on one side and Fabien on the other, she played Christmas carols on the drawing room piano.

"Mademoiselle, what's that?" Sophie asked, pointing to the mantelpiece after Mariele finished playing.

Mariele picked the little girl up and brought her closer to the fire. "This is an ivy plant," she said. "Isn't it a beautiful green? If you touch this leaf, you will find that it is silky smooth. And this other plant is mistletoe. Did you know that people kiss beneath the mistletoe?"

Sophie shook her head. "Why?"

"It's an ancient custom," Mariele replied. "Kissing under the mistletoe on New Year's Day is supposed to bring good luck. Now let's put your shoes by the fireplace so Père Noel can find them." She put Sophie down.

"But I need my shoes," Fabien said.

Mariele smiled. "Père Noel won't take them. He will fill them with treats, which you will find tomorrow." She turned at the sound of the door opening. "Maman?" she said. "Do you need me for something?"

Her mother shook her head.

"Treats?" Fabien replied as if nothing had occurred. He drew the word out into two long syllables. "What will they be, Mademoiselle?"

"Sweets, perhaps," Mariele's mother said. She crouched down beside Fabien. "Do you like sweets?"

Fabien nodded slowly, his eyes so wide they seemed to fill his face. "*Oui*, Madame."

"Then I'm sure you shall have some. But little boys and girls must be in bed well before Père Noel arrives. Nicole will help you get undressed. Mademoiselle has other things to do."

Mariele was astonished to watch her mother ruffle Sophie's curls and thread her fingers through Fabien's hair. "He reminds me of Robert at that age," her mother said with a sad smile.

"WE HAVE much to be thankful for," Mariele's father said as he proposed a toast later that evening. "We have survived three months of siege. We have food on the table and a comfortable home. Robert remains safe as a prisoner of war. Theo continues his studies. Mariele is serving the poor. We are looking after two small children. Each of these is cause for celebration.

"Many others are much less fortunate, but I believe our government will soon negotiate peace terms, and after that, we can begin to return to normal." Papa raised his glass, and everyone followed his example.

Yes, we are fortunate, Mariele thought, looking around the table at her family and the guests invited for dinner: Madame and Monsieur Lyons from the British embassy; her grandmother, who had aged significantly in the last six months; Madame and Monsieur Lazare, longtime friends of her parents; and Julien Degrasse, one of Theo's friends from medical school whose family had left the city in early September.

"Yes, Papa," Mariele said, "we do have much to be thankful for; but most of Paris faces only brutal cold and the possibility of death. Our citizens are freezing from lack of fuel, starving from lack of food, and dying by the thousands."

Reports of working-class conditions shocked her, and she was well aware that the children who came to the church were luckier than most, since the basement was warmed with a fire and they had one decent meal each day. However, the streets along her route to the church were filled with near-starving children and the desperate parents responsible for their care.

"Mariele's right," Theo said. "And our soldiers are dying—if not from battle, then from pneumonia, smallpox, and cholera. The radicals continue to demand change. They denounce General Trochu as a traitor and a fool. They speak of revolution and are desperate enough to take action. I fear that even if peace is negotiated, the city will be under threat."

"Mariele and Theo," Maman said, "we have guests, and it is Christmas Eve. Perhaps we can all talk about something other than the siege while we dine."

Mariele's mother had arranged the dining room beautifully: crisp white linens, sparkling stemware, glowing candles, and a garland down the middle of the table. She had paid an exorbitant price for two small chickens and had arranged for their cook to begin the meal with oyster soup and end with *tarte tatin*. After her admonishment, conversation touched on many topics but steered clear of politics and military matters.

To acknowledge the festivities, her mother had opened the grand salon, where the group retired after dinner.

"Will you play for us, Mariele?" she asked as their guests took coffee and Eugène passed a tray of candied fruit and chocolates.

Mariele had anticipated her mother's request and rehearsed a selection of light music, careful to avoid all composers of Germanic heritage. She had neglected her music since the siege began, and tonight the pieces filled her with nostalgia. When she rose and turned to acknowledge the applause, she saw Bertrand standing beside her father.

"What a wonderful surprise," she said softly as he kissed her cheeks. "I thought I had to wait until tomorrow to see you."

"Your mother invited me," he whispered.

How strange for her mother to arrange such a surprise—

particularly strange given her reclusive behavior—and yet, thinking about it, she realized that her mother had been more animated this evening than she'd been in a long time and had taken the time to visit with Sophie and Fabien. *I wonder what has happened.*

"You played very well tonight, *ma chérie*," her mother said.

"Thank you, Maman, and thank you for inviting Bertrand to be with us."

"Why don't you and Bertrand spend a little time together in the morning room? I'll send Eugène in with some brandy."

"What's come over your mother?" Bertrand asked once they were settled. "Not that I'm objecting to having a few moments alone with my fiancée."

"I have no idea."

A FEW DAYS LATER, Mariele went to her mother's sitting room and found her embroidering a lily of the valley on a white handkerchief.

"Do you have time to talk?" she asked.

Her mother tilted her head. "Of course."

"It was very kind of you to invite Bertrand to visit on Christmas Eve and very considerate of you to think that we might wish for a few minutes alone with each other," Mariele said, a blush forming on her cheeks.

Her mother set aside her needlework. "I haven't forgotten everything about being young, you know."

After trailing a finger across her mother's desk, Mariele idly picked up a paperweight, the glass globe filled with what looked like miniature blossoms in shades of blue and red. She twisted it in the palm of her hand.

"You seemed in good spirits on Christmas Eve. I'm pleased

for you and for Papa. He's been so concerned about you. Are
your worries behind you?"

Her mother became still, as still as a startled fawn. "My
worries?"

"Yes, Maman. You and I both know you haven't been yourself since our attempt to leave Paris. I've asked you about it
many times. Now that you're feeling better, can you tell me
what happened? It's been very distressing seeing you like that. I
keep blaming myself—thinking I should have done something
more to help you."

Her mother rose from the chaise and walked over to the
window. "You couldn't help me," she said in a voice so quiet
Mariele could barely hear her. "It was my job to protect you in
whatever way I could."

"Why did I need protection?"

When her mother turned around, she had a sad smile on her
face. "Because you're young and beautiful."

"What do you mean, Maman?" Her mother had never called
her beautiful, and Mariele was astonished.

"Major Werner was not a nice man. He threatened to do
certain things to you unless . . ."

"Unless what?"

"Unless I . . . unless I cooperated."

Cooperated? What on earth did that mean? Mariele recalled
Camille saying something about soldiers taking advantage of
her mother. Had something terrible happened to Maman? "Why
didn't you tell me? We could have decided what to do together.
Exactly what kind of cooperation did he demand?"

"It's no longer important. I finally told your father, and he
understands what I had to do."

"But *I* need to understand as well. Please tell me, Maman.
Please."

Her mother turned away again. "I can't . . . I'm too ashamed."

Mariele gently placed her hands on her mother's shoulders. She was as tall as her mother now and, given the siege conditions they'd been living with, almost as slender. "Under the circumstances, there is nothing to be ashamed of. If you were threatened or felt I was threatened, I'm sure you did what any mother would have done, and I love you for it, Maman."

Mariele noted the softening of her mother's face and her wistful smile. *When was the last time I told Maman that I love her?*

"Thank you, *chérie*. It's a difficult topic to speak about. The major is a violent, despicable man. He threatened to violate you. To take away your . . . your virginity. I couldn't allow that." She shook her head, and Mariele could feel her mother's shoulders tighten. "At first, I pleaded with him, and when that had no effect, I bargained with my own body. He laughed at me. 'Why would I accept an old married woman when I could have your daughter?' he said.

"He thought I had knowledge of our government's plans because I told him of your father's connections. I had only mentioned your father because I thought the major would surely release us if he knew of Philippe's position. I was a fool."

Her mother seemed to be talking to herself, and Mariele did nothing to disturb her. The revelations were shocking. To think that without her mother's intervention—whatever it had been— she might have been disgraced, unable to marry Bertrand, and forever tainted. Unable to marry Bertrand—she considered the possibility, realizing how devastated she would be without him.

Her mother continued. "A fool. A simpleminded fool. I saw that Major Werner wanted to be a hero. If I told him what I knew, he could relay that to his superiors. I played for time, but not very successfully. He . . . he tortured me with small cuts in hidden places. I never showed you."

"Oh, Maman." Mariele turned her mother around and embraced her, swaying back and forth as if she were the parent and Maman her child. "How terrible that you had to endure that," she whispered. "But why didn't you tell me? I could have comforted you. I could have . . ." What could she have done? In reality, they had been trapped and at the mercy, such as it was, of Major Werner. Her mother had used the only weapons she had—her body and her knowledge. "Oh, Maman," she said again.

"Eventually, I told him everything I knew. Your father had papers in the house, and sometimes I would read them. Occasionally, he told me little details when we were alone together. The major was patient. Once I began to talk, he knew he could extract it all."

"You read Papa's private papers?" There had never been any suggestion in her mother's words or deeds that she could be duplicitous. Why would she have violated Papa's—her husband's—sanctuary?

Maman looked embarrassed. "Every marriage has difficulties, some more severe than others. You will discover that, and I hope yours are of minor consequence. Your father and I . . . we've had difficulties for quite a while, and I was hurt by the way he treated me." She moved away from Mariele's embrace. "I won't say anything further. It's a matter between the two of us. One day I was searching for something and instead found confidential documents concerning the defense of Paris. Out of curiosity, I read them. I shouldn't have, but if I hadn't read them, I wouldn't have had anything of value for Major Werner."

"And you've told Papa."

"Yes," Maman whispered. "I couldn't keep it from him any longer. The Prussian army has used the information I gave them, and every day that has passed since we've returned, I've seen the consequences."

The color had drained from her mother's face. An air of bewilderment settled upon her like a veil. She had faced an impossible choice: her daughter or her country. Mariele's heart ached for her. What would she have done if the choice had been up to her?

"Did he understand?"

A long, drawn-out sigh. "Yes. When I finally explained everything, he understood."

Her mother's lips formed the briefest of smiles.

JANUARY 1871 – CAMILLE

THE FETID ODOR assailed Camille's nose as soon as she entered the Odéon. Although she had become accustomed to the work of nursing, and experienced satisfaction from her efforts, her senses revolted from the smell of wounded men, their moans and cries, their glassy-eyed stares, their twitching bodies. She braced herself for another day and prayed that no one would die in her care.

When the hospital had first opened, only five wounded men had been delivered to the Odéon. In the days that had followed, Sarah Bernhardt had joked that she would have to advertise for more wounded or go out to the battlefields and find them herself. Now they took care of more than seventy-five men, all parts of the theater filled to capacity.

As she went to the wardrobe room to change into her nursing clothes, she wondered what the day would bring.

"Camille, I need you to help with laundry this morning," Sarah Bernhardt said.

The laundry was Camille's least favorite task. Bandages soiled with pus had to be burned, but others could be cleaned and reused, a process involving scrubbing with carbolic soap followed by washing in great vats of boiling water mixed with carbolic acid. The bandages then had to be hung and dried. Bernhardt had hired four women to do the heavy work under the supervision of one of her trusted colleagues. Clearly, today was Camille's turn.

After completing her laundry duties, it was almost one o'clock. Camille planned to change quickly and get something to eat from the kitchen, where Bernhardt's cook managed the immense coal stove located in the public foyer and turned out enough food for the wounded men and those who staffed the hospital. She was famished, and although the best food was reserved for the wounded, the cook always had soup available for the nursing staff.

Camille had lost weight from working long, strenuous hours, as had most of the volunteers. Sarah Bernhardt, who worked from early morning to late at night, had become so thin, she was almost skeletal. The actress's face now featured sharp angles and haunting eyes, but this seemed to enhance her beauty rather than take away from it. Sometimes, when a late convoy of wounded arrived, Sarah even worked through the night. Camille knew that both Marie Colombier and Madame Guerard were worried about their friend.

Camille spent the afternoon in the officers' section and returned later that day to the wardrobe room, where she found Sarah, Marie, and Félicienne.

"Why don't you join us?" Marie said. "Madame Guerard is on duty, so we're having a brief respite. Sarah has just heard that another convoy of wounded will soon arrive. Tonight will be busy."

Camille had become accustomed to changing her clothes in front of these women. She shed her soiled uniform and stripped down to her corset and pantalets, all the while listening to the women's chatter.

"Are you going out tonight?" Félicienne asked.

Camille planned to attend the Vigilance Committee meeting, but she wasn't about to disclose that detail. Instead, she smiled. "Perhaps Madame Lambert's salon if I'm still awake. My brother often escorts me."

"Will your father be there?" Félicienne smirked. "I saw him just the other night with Madame Chevilly. They seemed very . . . very friendly."

"Be quiet, Félicienne. Camille doesn't need to hear your gossip," Sarah reprimanded. "I'm sure it was nothing, *ma chérie*," she continued, turning to face Camille. "Your father does admirable work for the defense of our city."

Gossip, Camille thought. *But that doesn't mean it's false.* Since her mother was in Lyon and most of her friends away from the city, this was an ideal time for her father to escort Madame Chevilly around Paris.

But Papa should be faithful to his marriage vows. At the very least, he shouldn't flaunt his mistress in public.

As she climbed the hill to Montmartre, Camille was still thinking about Madame Chevilly. Perhaps she should confront her father with the gossip she'd heard. Or maybe she should discuss the matter with Bertrand. He was eminently sensible and spent a great deal of time with their father every day. *Does every husband have a mistress?* she wondered. *Are wives supposed to ignore them?*

Camille shivered and quickened her pace. The weather had been unrelentingly cold, and she wished she had her fur-lined gloves. However, they were too elegant for the kind of woman she was pretending to be. She tightened the shawl around her coat and shoved her hands into the pockets.

The street had begun to narrow, its cobblestones rough and uneven. A wagon pulled by a boy who couldn't have been more than thirteen emerged from a dirt path and turned down the hill toward her. Wooden wheels creaked and groaned. As the wagon drew close, she recognized the smell of death. A quick glance confirmed the bodies of two adults and a child.

Sadness welled up inside her. In the morning paper, she'd read that the death rate had risen to four thousand a week, more than four times the rate before the siege began. To make matters worse, the Prussian army had begun its bombardment of the city, targeting the Left Bank and striking the Panthéon, Les Invalides and Salpêtrière Hospital. Even the beautiful Saint-Sulpice had been shelled. Sarah Bernhardt had warned them all to take as much precaution as possible when coming to the Odéon.

When will this end? Camille was keenly aware that if the siege didn't end soon, it would be compounded by an uprising pitting citizen against citizen within the walls of Paris. An uprising that could lead to anarchy and another bloody revolution. The note she'd received from André yesterday had said it was imperative for her to discover the timing of such an event.

MAXINE STOOD at her front door with two other women. "We're meeting at Saint-Bernard de la Chapelle," she said to Camille. "A combined meeting with women from Belleville, Villette, and La Chapelle. Eugénie and Lucie are walking over there now if you wish to accompany them. I'm staying here to direct others."

Camille nodded at the two women. "Thank you," she said. "I'm grateful to walk with you. Is it far?"

"Fifteen minutes if you hurry," Maxine said with one hand on the doorframe. "And take care. The streets are restless tonight."

Eugénie and Lucie set a brisk pace with Camille following close behind. Maxine was right; the streets were indeed restless. Men called out to one another in loud, raucous voices. Some broke into song. Others stood silently, chassepots held across their chests, ready to fire if the need arose. A drunk stumbled into them. *"Excusez-moi, mesdames,"* he slurred, glassy-eyed and as gaunt as a starving whippet. A cat leapt down from atop a wooden gate.

As she strode along, her breath forming small clouds of frozen air, Camille heard the limp cries of hungry children and saw the occasional drift of smoke above the narrow houses that lined the streets. The crack of a rifle exploded nearby, and she wondered at a world where gunfire and cannon were everyday occurrences.

"Almost there," the woman called Lucie said.

Camille stumbled on a broken cobble and would have fallen if a member of the National Guard hadn't reached out to grab her arm. "Steady, Mademoiselle. Now, where are you all rushing off to? Why don't you ladies keep me company for a while."

"We're off to the Club de la Révolution," Lucie replied. "Come with us. We need soldiers to be part of the uprising."

"What do women have to do with an uprising?" the guard scoffed. "You should be home tending to your families and looking after your men."

Eugénie snorted. "Come on, Lucie," she said. "We don't need the likes of him at our meeting. He's one of those who only have one use for women." She made a rude gesture with her hand and laughed.

Two LANTERNS LIT the arched entrance to Saint-Bernard de la Chapelle on an otherwise dark street, where shadows concealed the poverty of nearby homes and the rats that scurried between piles of refuse. Only one side of the enormous double door at the central portal was open. Camille followed Eugénie and Lucie into the church. She deposited a few centimes into a basket by the door and looked around.

Women filled almost the entire nave, whispering, chattering, and laughing, their voices echoing through the cold, cavernous space like hundreds of birds trapped in a cave. Only the soft glow of candles reflected the sacred function of the church. Had she not been here on a mission, Camille might have been caught up in the as yet undefined possibility of so many women coming together with purpose.

She moved toward the front, determined to find a space where she could hear the speakers clearly, and found a chair on the righthand side. The chair teetered back and forth on uneven legs. Camille nodded to the woman next to her, then sat and waited.

The crowd grew restless. A few stood, calling out to friends and neighbors. "Don't have all night," one woman shouted. "What are we waiting for?" shouted another. "My children are alone," said a third. "Can't leave them forever."

Finally, Louise Michel and three other women appeared at the front of the nave, where a wooden riser had been placed. Each one mounted the steps. After conferring with one another, a woman with strong facial features and curly hair raised her hand.

"Women of Paris!" she shouted as the crowd grew quiet. "Women of Paris! My name is Paule Minck. I'm here tonight with Louise Michel, Victoire Béra, who some may know as André Leo, and Maria Deraismes, all leaders in the movement for women's rights. Tonight, we plan the way forward. Tonight, we demand our rights. Tonight, with your strength and support, we begin the journey to a new France. Will you join me, mesdames and mesdemoiselles?"

A roar of assent filled the church. Paule Minck raised her hands again.

"Four years ago, we founded La Société du Droit des Femmes. We called for schools for girls, civil equality for married women, and equal working opportunities. We still call for these rights." Minck's eyes blazed with passion. "But now, *mes amies*, now we face bombardment and starvation. The working people of Paris have almost no food or fuel. Our children are dressed in rags. They eat rats to survive. They are cold. They are sick. They are dying." She paused to scan the crowd.

"And what has our government done? Has it called out our National Guard to conquer our enemy and end the siege? No! Has it rationed food so that everyone has something to eat? No! And now, now that Paris is almost destroyed, the government is negotiating with Prussia. Mark my words, there will soon be an armistice. Will that bring justice for the working people? Will that bring fair wages? Will that bring relief from sickness? Will that bring our loved ones back?"

Cries filled the air. Tears spilled. Women shouted "no" again and again. They condemned the leaders of the government, men like Thiers and Trochu and others. They rose as one, shaking their fists, clamoring to tear apart a system and the people who had condemned them to a life of poverty and injustice. Camille had never seen anything like it.

Louise Michel spoke, followed by Maria Deraismes. Finally, Victoire Béra took her turn. She began by unfolding a piece of paper.

"Democracy will only triumph with women," she began. "In our own time, it is ideas more than the force of arms which wins the battle. Any human being has the instinct for preservation. It is not the beard which controls this instinct, but a superior passion. Parisian women today have that passion." Béra's quiet demeanor did not match the emotion of her voice. She looked down at her paper.

"Now women's help is necessary. It's up to the women to give the signal to the greatest mobilization which will sweep away all hesitation and resistance. Working-class women are anxious, enthusiastic, and ardent to give themselves entirely to the great cause of Paris. Our souls are committed to the struggle. Our eyes are filled with fire, not tears. We will participate actively in the struggle.

"My companions tonight, and many others, have already provided an example. They are the pride of their admiring brothers in struggle, whose ardor has been doubled because the women are present. When daughters, wives, and mothers fight alongside their sons, their husbands, their fathers, Paris will no longer have only the passion for liberty, it will be wild with it. We cannot have a revolution without women!"

The crowd roared its approval.

"Revolution is liberty and responsibility for any human being, male or female. Who is suffering more today from the crisis, from the high costs of goods, from the lack of work? We all know the answer. It is women who are suffering more. And it is women who are subjected to all sorts of abuse. Does the government care?"

"No!" came the shouts from the women.

"Women must join with the men to fight this revolution. Along with our usual duties to tend the wounded and feed our soldiers, we must take up arms, build the barricades, make the ammunition, and, along with our brethren, take control of the government. We don't have much time if we are to be successful. A month, perhaps two at the most. The men are already organizing. We must begin now. *Toutes pour tous!* All for all!"

Victoire Béra's speech was met with cries of support and a frenzy of movement and conversation. Camille used the opportunity to slip away.

"THEY'RE CALLING FOR REVOLUTION AGAIN," Camille said as she paced back and forth in André's small salon, while he sat with his foot propped on a hassock covered in silk brocade. "And they're asking women to participate in the fighting."

"Participate in the fighting?" he echoed. "They want women to take up arms?"

Camille nodded.

He rubbed a hand across his chin. "Did they mention when?"

"Six weeks, two months at the most. That would suggest early March. And the women are truly supportive. I've never seen such passion. They could have grabbed their muskets and marched into battle right away. What will you do, André?"

"I'll send a message to my contact. He'll make sure it gets to the right people."

Camille stopped pacing. "Is it safe to put this information in writing? I could meet with your contact if you wish. He might appreciate firsthand knowledge, and he might have questions."

She watched André's face for an indication of his reaction. His brows lifted. His mouth twitched. He pulled himself into a more upright position and narrowed one eye.

"You're right. It could be dangerous. But it could also be dangerous to have another person know his name. I trust you, Camille. But what if your role is discovered and you are threatened?"

Camille stooped to scratch Coco's head. "And what if you're threatened? Would you not refuse to disclose any information? I would do the same. While I understand the reforms these women seek, I am utterly opposed to the measures they and the men are planning. Peaceful means are required to secure change, not violence. Violence didn't work in the first revolution, nor in 1830 or 1848. It only led to bloodshed and destruction." Camille was surprised at the passion and conviction that filled her voice. The system was unjust, but civil war was never the answer. Previous revolutions had taught them that.

"Let me consult with my friend," he replied. "It's his decision, not mine."

25

JANUARY 1871 – MARIELE

THE PRUSSIAN BOMBARDMENT continued attacking the forts and ramparts surrounding Paris. Artillery shells now reached parts of the Left Bank, wounding or killing civilians every day. Wagons and handcarts filled with household goods rumbled along Left Bank streets as Parisians moved to safety on the Right Bank. A Prussian shell made a hole in the dome of the Panthéon, and in the Jardin des Plantes, all the glass of the conservatories had been shattered. According to rumors, Fort d'Issy would soon fall. Each time Mariele walked to Sainte-Clotilde, the route became more difficult, with rubble accumulating on the sidewalks and in front of buildings that had been hit.

"You can't be going out today," her mother said. "The bombardment was furious yesterday and all last night. It won't be safe."

"The children need me, Maman. I'll be careful. Eugène has volunteered to escort me. Camille is the one who's in the most danger. The Prussians seem to be targeting hospitals."

"Whatever possessed her to volunteer as a nurse?"

Mariele cut a slice of bread. They were still able to purchase bread from the local bakery the family had frequented for years, but the quality was poor, nothing like the light, crusty baguettes of the past. She had a bit of cheese to go with it and a cup of weak tea. "She feels her talents are more useful as a nurse. The last time we spoke about the hospital, she told me she's used to the terrible wounds."

She wasn't about to tell her mother of the kinds of wounds her friend now thought commonplace. Maman already had reservations about Camille and would be horrified to know of the conditions under which she worked. With an inadequate supply of painkillers and other medicines, operations were often conducted amid the piercing screams of wounded soldiers. Mariele had come to realize that Camille shared these stories with her as a way to cope.

"That dress looks big on you," her mother said. "I think you've lost weight, and now your real beauty is blossoming. Don't you think so, Philippe?"

Mariele's father looked up from the newspaper. "You look very becoming, *ma chérie*. But is Victor Noisette asking you to do too much?"

"We must all do our part, Papa. Hopefully, the siege will be over soon."

"If only sense would prevail, we could end the siege now," her father said. "Unfortunately, our politicians fear the reaction of the people. Every time there is talk of negotiation, radicals on the left denounce the government and threaten revolution." He shook his head and resumed his reading.

These days it was unusual for her father to join them at breakfast. His business interests normally required him to leave soon after daybreak, and today it was already nine o'clock. But nothing was normal anymore. Papa had explained his involvement in a special government committee managing the city's supplies of food and other essentials. There were days when his face was so fatigued by the time he came home that Mariele thought he might be ill.

"Maman, would you like to come with me today? Our numbers have grown, and an extra pair of hands would be very welcome."

"Certainly not. It's bad enough that you're associating with these young ruffians."

"They're not ruffians, Maman. They're poor. Not everyone has the money Papa has to cope with this siege. Some like Sophie and Fabien have even lost one of their parents since it all began, and two of the children who used to come to the church have themselves died."

Mariele thought of little Suzanne, who had succumbed to smallpox, and an older boy named Pascal, who had been kicked by a horse that reared out of control at the sound of an explosion.

"You must be very careful, just as your mother says," Papa cautioned. "Violence on the part of the radicals is increasingly likely."

"Yes, Papa. I'm leaving Sophie at home today. Suzette says she has a cold. Will you look in on her, Maman?"

"I will. She's a sweet little thing. I can see that you are very fond of her and Fabien." Her mother took another sip of coffee and dabbed a napkin on her lips. "Make sure you take a fiacre home," she said. "Your father and I will see you at dinner."

WITH MORE YOUNG children than usual to look after, the day had been busy. They now had two rooms for the children; the older ones continued to use the original space, while she looked after the younger ones in an adjacent but smaller area. These rooms were always cold despite the fire that gave off a little warmth, and she had taken to reading a story at the end of the day with the children gathered near the fireplace so they could warm up before going home.

Today's soup had been thin: a concoction of root vegetables and lentils and no meat at all. She had brought a little cheese with her and some crusts of bread Cook had saved so the children could dip them into the soup to soften the crusts before eating. Even little Rosalie, the youngest of the group, had eaten every last drop.

"Is it time to go, Mademoiselle?" asked Fabien.

"Yes, *mon petit*. I'll just slip off my apron and then we'll go."

Mariele took a moment to rearrange her hair before putting on her coat. Then she peeked into the other room to say goodbye to Victor. "Fabien and I are going now."

Victor frowned. "It will be dusk soon," he said. "If you can't get a cab, come back to the church and I'll see you home."

The street was quiet. Not a cab in sight.

As they waited, Fabien hummed a little tune, which brought a smile to Mariele's face. She glanced around. A man pushing a cart full of garbage stopped to button his coat in front of a shop with windows boarded up. A gust of wind nipped her cheeks.

"I'm cold, Mam'selle," Fabien said.

Mariele debated whether to return to the church. She'd walked home many times and there were always people about. No need to bother Victor. Maintaining an air of bravado, she gripped Fabien's hand and walked briskly along boulevard Saint-Germain, where a few lights still illuminated the street, passing the Ministry of Commerce and Public Works before crossing rue du Bac, where the Church of Saint-Thomas-d'Aquin stood next door to the Artillery Depot. Bertrand and his family attended this church, and Mariele smiled as she remembered a recent discussion about whether their wedding should take place at his family's church or hers. She knew what her mother's opinion would be.

Mariele continued to hurry along, paying little attention as a shop owner rewound the striped awning that overhung the street and a man with a silk-tasseled walking stick passed by.

Fabien tugged on her hand. "Mam'selle, please don't go so fast."

She crouched down to speak to him. "Your legs aren't as long as mine, are they? I'll slow down, and because you're being so good, let me see if I have a treat in my bag for you."

Fabien waited patiently while she searched for a small tin of jujubes. "Here they are," she said from her crouched position, looking up to show the tin to Fabien.

The whistling sound was faint at first, and Mariele ignored it as Fabien poked his finger among the candies. The sound grew louder, becoming almost a screech. Watching nearby pedestrians scatter, the thought of imminent danger crossed her mind. She dropped the tin of candies and grabbed Fabien's hand. *What should I do? Where should we run?* Panic suffused her, hot and urgent. It dulled her senses and left her immobile. "No. No. No!"

Louder and louder.

"Run, Fabien! Run with me!"

Mariele turned back the way they'd come, her hand gripping the little boy's as tightly as she could, and they ran.

The sound at impact was deafening, a roar so intense her ears seemed to explode. The blast lifted them into the air, and she felt herself tumbling uncontrollably as she struggled to hold onto Fabien. And then, nothing.

26

JANUARY 1871 – CAMILLE & MARIELE

"But where is she?" Camille asked as Bertrand shoved his arms into a thick woolen coat and his feet into a stout pair of leather boots. "She's such a dependable woman. Even if she walked, she's so familiar with the route, she wouldn't go astray, and just the other day, she told me that she always tries to take a cab home." Every muscle in her body tightened.

"I have no idea. Madame de Crécy's note says she never returned. Since Mariele's father has been detained at work and Theo is not at home, she's asked me for help. Is Victor here?"

"In his room, I think. He came in late and said something about narrowly escaping an explosion."

"*Merde.*" Bertrand thundered up the stairs, returning a few moments later with Victor trailing after him.

"When she left, she had Fabien with her," Victor said.

"You let my fiancée take a little boy into God-knows-what dangerous streets? Why didn't you insist that she wait for a cab?"

Victor hung his head. "I'm sorry, Bertrand. I was seeing to some of the other children. Mariele said she planned to get a cab. I told her to return to the church if she couldn't find one."

Bertrand snorted. "With the Prussian army bombing our boulevards, she never should have been there in the first place." He buttoned his coat. "Camille, send Michel to secure a cab so you can attend to Mariele's mother. With no one else at home, she may need someone to comfort her. But only if you can get a cab. I don't wish to worry about you as well."

Camille nodded. She had never seen Bertrand so distressed. Where on earth could Mariele be? They both knew the dangers of being out on the streets, particularly in the evening, and now that the Prussians had begun to bomb Paris daily, the danger was even more severe. "What do you think has happened?"

Bertrand dragged his fingers through his hair. "I don't want to think about it. It's eight o'clock, pitch black, and the sky is blazing with artillery. This is a nightmare."

"If you wait just a moment, I'll come with you," Victor said.

Bertrand grunted. "Be quick. There's no time to waste."

MARIELE REGAINED CONSCIOUSNESS SLOWLY. Her head throbbed. A heavy weight rested on her chest. She lifted her right arm, and a jolt of excruciating pain swept from one end to the other. Her left arm was trapped. All was dark. Scratching the nearby ground with her fingers, she felt nothing but dirt and stones. *Where am I?*

For several minutes, her sluggish brain refused to cooperate until, bit by bit, an image formed. Running. Fabien. Noise. Tumbling.

"Fabien," she croaked. "Fabien!"

Voices. A church bell tolling. The sharp clang of metal against stone. Mariele struggled once more to move her arms and legs, but except for her right arm, she could move no other part of her body. "Fabien," she shouted again. "I'm here, little one. Be still. Help will come." Her body trembled. Her heart thumped.

With the exertion of shouting, dust had entered her mouth and lungs, and she coughed uncontrollably. *Think, Mariele, think. What would Papa do if he were trapped like this?* She knew the answer. Papa would remain calm and assess the situation logically.

They'd been caught in an explosion. Debris had fallen on her and Fabien, and he seemed to be lying on top of her. *Perhaps I grabbed him at the last moment to protect him.* She could not move, but she was conscious, able to breathe and speak. It was likely they were trapped beneath a mound of rubble just like the ones she'd seen on other streets after the Prussians had begun bombing Paris. Since it was already dusk when she and Fabien had left the church, it would be dark by now. But many others had been on the street when the explosion occurred, and the authorities would know of the incident. Someone, or perhaps more than one person, was digging nearby. *They'll find me and Fabien.*

Reasoning helped calm her nerves, and she breathed slowly in and out, trying not to inhale more dust. She wiggled her left toes. *Yes, those are working.* But the toes on her right foot would not move, and the weight of Fabien on her chest grew heavier and heavier. How long would it take for those digging to reach her? What if they couldn't reach her?

The sounds of digging—the scrape of a shovel against the dirt, the clang of metal against rock, the grunts of exertion—had gone on for what seemed like more than an hour when she finally saw a flicker of light. "Help," she called out, her voice hoarse with exhaustion.

"Don't move, Madame. We'll have you out soon," someone said. "We have to remove each piece of stone and dirt with great caution."

After another stone was removed, more lights appeared, and

she saw that several women held lanterns on long poles to illuminate the area while a man wearing a kerchief wrapped around his head lifted the rock trapping her right shoulder.

"There's a small child here too," he said.

"Be careful," Mariele said. "He's only five."

She gasped when the final weight was lifted off her chest and watched the man with the kerchief hold the limp form in his arms. "Fabien?" she whispered.

"*Je suis désolé, Madame.* Your son has been killed by the explosion. We think his body sheltered you enough to keep you alive."

"Fabien," she said once more and began to cry.

AWARE OF A BANDAGE on her left cheek and another across her brow, Mariele lay on a cot in a dimly lit room, her right arm set in splints and her right leg bandaged from hip to knee. Two men had carried her on a wooden door to the nearest hospital. A nurse had asked for her name and address when she had arrived, and a doctor had dealt with her injuries, but no one had paid the slightest attention to her for hours. Pain pulsed through her body, and she gritted her teeth to avoid calling out.

The smells were disgusting: a mix of blood and vomit, body odors and decaying flesh, soot and disinfectant. Cold and hungry, Mariele shivered. She was in a hospital—that much was clear—but how would anyone know where to look for her? Her parents would be frantic with worry.

And where had they taken Fabien? She couldn't shake the image of the little boy's broken body, his head matted with dried blood, his fingers cold to the touch, one leg twisted at right angles, his eyes open and lifeless. Why? Why had a beautiful little child been destroyed while she had lived? What would become of Sophie, who followed her brother everywhere, copying his every move, listening open mouthed to the stories

Fabien told of their mother and father? Sophie adored her older brother.

Tears trickled down Mariele's cheeks and onto the thin pillow beneath her head. Sobs wracked her body. She wept for Fabien, for Sophie, for Paris, for herself. Pent up sadness and fear spilled out. *When will this end? When will the killing stop? How can I find the strength to go on?*

SHE DOZED in fits and starts and was sleeping when someone touched her hand.

"Mariele. Mariele, can you hear me?"

The voice was familiar. She opened her eyes and blinked away the crust of tears that had formed.

"Bertrand? Is it really you?" Never had his presence offered such profound relief. She wasn't alone. Bertrand was with her.

"Yes, it is, my love." He knelt beside her. "I've been searching for you for hours. You can't imagine the scenarios that have gone through my mind. I don't know what I would have done without you." His voice was agitated but controlled, his hand gripped hers, and if she wasn't mistaken, his eyes brimmed with unshed tears.

"Fabien . . . Fabien. Oh Bertrand, Fabien is dead."

"Little Fabien," he replied. "How?"

Through tears and sobs, Mariele told him what had happened and how the little boy's body had protected hers.

"I'll never forgive myself," she said. "If I'd waited for a cab, he would still be alive."

Bertrand kissed her hand. "It wasn't your fault. You weren't to know that a projectile would fall at that precise moment. Sometimes fate takes an unexpected twist."

"But how will I tell his father?"

"Don't think about that now," he replied. "Let's just get you home. Your mother is worried sick about you."

"What will I tell Sophie?" Mariele asked as tears began again.

AFTER MARIELE TOLD Sophie that Fabien would not be returning, the little girl refused to leave her side. With a thumb in her
mouth, she clutched Fabien's small stuffed clown and traipsed
from room to room, rarely more than an arm's length away.
During the day, she draped herself alongside the chaise where
Mariele lay or curled up like a small puppy on a cot beside
Mariele's bed. She watched with big brown eyes whenever the
doctor came or Bertrand visited, and sat patiently on the floor
while Suzette helped Mariele get dressed.

Sophie rarely spoke, except to the stuffed clown she called
Pierre. Occasionally, large tears would unexpectedly drop from
her eyes, and a bewildered look would appear on her face. The
child's distress broke Mariele's heart.

27

JANUARY 22, 1871 – CAMILLE

"MARIELE WILL BE CONFINED for at least another two weeks," Evangeline de Crécy said. "The doctor was very clear about that. And Camille, I need your assistance. Please tell my daughter it is unthinkable to return to your brother's church. She could have died in that explosion."

"But Maman, I didn't die," Mariele said. "My leg is healing, and the doctor said my broken arm will not prevent me from getting about."

"Your mother is right," Camille said. Sophie had curled up on her lap with a thumb in her mouth, and Camille now ran her fingers through the little girl's silky curls. "You must be cautious. Bertrand asked me specifically to tell you that, as your fiancé, he wishes you to remain at home until the siege is over. It seems that won't be long, now that Trochu has been removed as head of the army. My father reported just last night that there's talk of capitulation."

Camille had a day off. At Bertrand's request, she had made her way to the de Crécy home to see her friend. Although pale, Mariele appeared healthier than the last visit, and from the way she moved both leg and arm, it seemed she was indeed much improved. The leg had sustained a deep wound. According to the doctor, Mariele had been fortunate that Fabien's body had applied sufficient pressure to stanch the bleeding. The arm was fractured—a clean break—and was expected to heal quickly. Camille could make a positive report to her brother.

The women were in Madame de Crécy's sitting room, an elegant space decorated in blue and white. While Mariele's mother recounted a long story about damage to her cousin's home, Camille considered the dangers of living in Paris. Just yesterday André had stopped by to encourage her to give up nursing. A source had informed him that the radical clubs had gone beyond agitating for the establishment of a commune and now spoke of the need for violence to secure rights for the working class. "They're armed," he had reported, "and I don't trust them. I predict we have more to fear from them than we do from the Prussians. And you shouldn't go to the Vigilance Committee meetings anymore. Montmartre is at the boiling point."

While she hadn't agreed to André's suggestion, she had told him she would think about his advice.

"Thankfully, the bombardment has eased," Camille said in reply to Madame de Crécy's story. "Last week the Odéon suffered some damage, but the worst is that all the seats and props have been chopped up for firewood. It will take ages to refit the theater once the siege is over. Madame Bernhardt said she might have to raise the funds personally."

"I thought I would find you here," said Philippe de Crécy as he entered the room. "Camille, how delightful to see you. How is our patient? And our little Sophie?"

Camille observed that Mariele's father had a way of commanding a room as soon as he entered it. He exuded confidence through his erect bearing and the forceful sense of energy emanating from everything about him—eyes that were piercingly direct, shoulders that seemed capable of taking on great responsibility, movement that was purposeful and yet elegant. *A man born for power and influence.*

"She seems to be recovering very well, Monsieur," Camille said. "And I'm delighted to see it."

"You're home early, Papa," Mariele said. "I was just telling Camille how much better I'm feeling. Doctor Charbonneau says I'll be able to go out soon."

"You may be able to go out," he said. "However, I don't want you going back to that church."

"But you said yourself that the bombardment is easing."

Mariele shifted on the chaise as she spoke, and Camille noticed the grimace that accompanied this motion.

"That may be," he replied. "However, the situation is volatile. The Belleville battalions have marched through the streets, demanding the commune, and yesterday some of the Garde Mobile fired their weapons into a crowd, killing five civilians. Today gunshots at the Hôtel de Ville caused the crowd to stampede. Many hate the thought of capitulation, so I doubt we'll return to anything approximating normal for some time." He ran one finger along a marble-topped chest of drawers. "The streets aren't safe for young women like you and Camille. No one can tell what a half-starved and exasperated Parisian population will do."

"Perhaps we should hide our valuables," Evangeline de Crécy said. "We all know what happened the last time the mob took over Paris." She paused, her brow furrowed. "Do you think Robert will soon return?"

Philippe de Crécy pulled the curtain back and peered out the window. "The situation might be dangerous for Robert," he said, letting the curtain fall back into place. "Now that Blanqui, Flourens, and other revolutionary leaders have been released, I fear for the safety of officers like Robert when they return. They're being condemned as traitors to the working class. How defending your country can lead to such an accusation is beyond me, but these are not men of reason; they are men of singular intent and inflamed passions. If a new government forms, it will likely be under the leadership of Adolphe Thiers, who will negotiate the terms of peace. I know France will lose some territory, and the radicals will be up in arms about it." Agitation clouded his face. "Evangeline, I wish to speak with you in private. Will you join me in the library?"

After Mariele's mother and father left the room, Camille rose from her chair and placed Sophie, who had fallen asleep, on the end of the chaise. She covered the child with her shawl, then crossed to the window. Earlier, the windows had been rattling, but now only the low muttering of distant guns and the solemn beating of drums could be heard as trails of smoke rose in the distance. She pulled a chair close to where her friend lay with her injured leg propped on a pillow. Mariele's face was pale, her hands alternately pleating and smoothing her skirt.

"Your father is clearly concerned," Camille said.

"More than concerned, I think, based on the tone of his voice. Usually, he would not wish to alarm Maman or me by sharing such information." At that precise moment, an explosion rattled the windows once more. Mariele startled at the sound. "You must remain here tonight. The streets won't be safe. And don't argue with me, Camille. Bertrand would never forgive me if I let you go home under such conditions." Mariele's eyes widened as she placed the tips of her fingers on her lips. "Do you know where he is?"

"He said he was on duty today. He's been assigned to the fort at Saint-Denis, and yesterday I heard the Prussians are bombarding it from six separate batteries." Camille's attempt to relay this information without emotion failed. Tears slipped down her cheeks. "I'm afraid, Mariele. What if something happens to my brother?"

"Don't say that! I couldn't bear it if something happened to Bertrand." She reached for Camille's hand. "He has become so dear to me." A smile quivered on her lips. "I believe I've fallen in love with him."

"And he loves you. He's told me so on several occasions, and my brother isn't one to readily share such emotions. He's always been stalwart and self-possessed, but when he speaks of you, I can see his vulnerability. You are just the right woman for him."

"I'll pray for his safety." Mariele's voice had dropped to a whisper.

"And so will I."

28

JANUARY 23, 1871 - CAMILLE

MONSIEUR DE CRÉCY took Camille home. She remained silent, respecting his need to concentrate. The route to the seventh arrondissement was fraught with difficulties—main streets blocked by crowds and marching soldiers, mounds of debris inhibiting passage along narrower routes, explosions that caused the horse to snort and skitter. To make matters worse, thick fog shrouded the city.

"*Merde*," he said as the horse jostled nervously. "My apologies, Camille. My wife would be furious with me for using such language."

"I've heard worse at the hospital, Monsieur," she replied with a smile. "With what we've seen this morning, I'm truly grateful you're taking me home."

"And I'm grateful for the work you've done with André Laborde. The information you've passed along has been most helpful. Has he told you that he and I are working together to protect Paris from radical factions?"

She'd been right. Philippe de Crécy was indeed André's contact. How astonishing to know that this well-respected man was involved with clandestine activities. "No, Monsieur. He said nothing about you. You should know that I'm honored to help my city and would gladly do more should you need me to."

Mariele's father looked grim. "It's too dangerous now and likely to become more so. You are in enough danger at the hospital. If you were my daughter, I would insist that you stop your nursing."

She smiled, despite the serious nature of their conversation. "My father knows that it's difficult to stop me when my mind is made up."

Philippe glanced at her. He didn't smile, but there was a slight loosening in his mouth. "I know you and my daughter have become close. However, you must not tell her anything about your visits to the clubs or my part in these activities."

"You have my word, Monsieur."

IT WAS WELL after ten when she entered the house, and her footsteps echoed as she climbed the stairs from the foyer to the main floor. "Hello?" she called out. "Is anyone home?"

She heard a distant patter of footsteps and soon saw Monique rounding the corner. "You're back at last, Mademoiselle. You had your father and brothers very worried until Monsieur de Crécy's message arrived. I think your father was about to send Monsieur Victor to the Odéon in case you had gone there after your visit with Mademoiselle Mariele."

"I'm fine, Monique. Mariele's family took good care of me. Is no one here this morning?"

"No, Mademoiselle. Monsieur Victor is at the church, as usual. Monsieur Bertrand is still on duty, and your father has gone to see someone at the Ministry. He said to consult you about dinner once you arrived, although Madame Carnot has very little that's fresh to prepare. And he left a note for you."

PARIS IN RUINS 217

Monique took an envelope from her apron pocket and gave it to Camille.

"Thank you, Monique. Tell Madame Carnot to do her best with whatever is on hand. The streets are not safe, so she's not to leave the house for any shopping. Will you draw me a bath and then help me change?"

As soon as she reached her room, Camille opened her father's letter.

Camille, I am writing in haste. Your absence last night gave me great anxiety until Monsieur de Crécy's message arrived. Your brothers are well, as am I. Today I am at the Ministry of Supplies for negotiations, but I expect to be home for dinner. Talk of capitulation is everywhere, and I am certain the government will soon surrender. Last night Victor and I hid many of our valuables. Under no circumstances are you to leave the house.

Your loving father.

She bristled at the last sentence. Her father had no appreciation of her responsibilities at the hospital. Madame Bernhardt was expecting her, and patients needed her. Why was the work of women always of so little consequence? It was just as Louise Michel and Victoire Béra said. Women were expected to fulfil a certain role under the direction of men, not make decisions for themselves. While bathing, she continued to brood, ultimately convinced that her responsibility to the hospital outweighed her father's direction.

To appear inconspicuous on the streets, Camille used one of the dresses she'd worn to Montmartre—a drab brown wool—as well as a cape and hat. In such clothes, she looked like a typical working-class woman. She added thick gloves and a knitted scarf for extra warmth, then hurried from the house.

Despite last night's talk of capitulation, bombardment

continued that morning, interspersed with sporadic intervals of silence which, when combined with the fog, created an atmosphere of ominous uncertainty. She picked her way along smaller streets, avoiding the main boulevards that were certain to brew unruly crowds, and planted her feet with care to avoid slipping on icy debris. Fear had never been a concern before. She had enjoyed the risk, taking pride in being bold, working with purpose. But Philippe de Crécy's warnings and her father's note had unsettled her, sowing doubts that undermined her confidence. And then there was Mariele's catastrophe. Luck had been on Mariele's side. Luck and a sweet little boy called Fabien.

With tents and soldiers occupying the Luxembourg Gardens, Camille skirted north of the gardens to pass Saint-Sulpice before angling south again toward the Odéon. Nothing looked out of place until she rounded the corner to the front entrance and saw that one of the theater's massive columns was badly damaged. She rushed inside.

"Is everyone all right?" Camille asked Madame Guerard.

"Thank goodness you're here. Félicienne and Celeste have not arrived. Félicienne's disappearance does not surprise me. She's been neglecting her duties for weeks, but I'm worried about Celeste."

Celeste Aubry, another of Bernhardt's friends, was a recent addition to the nursing staff. Camille had only met her twice. "Was there any damage to the theater?"

"The noise was deafening, but no one was hurt. Some plaster fell in the entrance foyer, but otherwise it was not serious."

"Thank God we were spared. Where do you need me today, Madame?"

"Sarah needs help updating the records before Sergeant Durieux arrives. She has gone out with the wagons to collect wounded soldiers from the Châtillon Plateau. I told her not to put herself in such danger, but you know how she is. Do you know where she keeps her ledger?"

Camille nodded.

"Afterward," the woman continued, "you can relieve Marie in the green room."

With so many men housed at the Odéon, the task of updating the records of admittances, deaths, and discharges was time consuming. Regular soldiers were housed in the green room and the main foyer while officers were in the theater's former refreshment room. As Camille went from location to location, checking the records, a few men called for her attention, further delaying the task.

While she worked, she recalled her father's note. Why would he and Victor hide their valuables if the government planned to surrender? She considered two possibilities. Prussian soldiers rampaging through Paris was the obvious one, a possibility that sickened her for the damage it might bring to the city and the potential for wanton violence. A second possibility involved the radicals clamoring for change and a communal form of governance. If members of the National Guard and Garde Mobile had opened fire on ordinary citizens, what would they be prepared to do with a commune in place?

Camille didn't remember much of her history lessons, but she did recall studying the reign of terror that had descended on Paris not once, but twice in less than one hundred years. Looting had been rampant. Many innocent people had died. And now she'd experienced the passions of those agitating for change and seen the way crowds of inflamed people behaved.

"You're finally here," Marie said, mopping the brow of a young officer. "I've been on duty since midnight, and my feet are so sore I can barely walk."

"I'm sorry, Marie. Madame Guerard asked me to update the records, and you know how particular Sarah is about that."

Camille could tell from her grimace that Marie had lost all

patience and cared not a whit for the matter of paperwork. "We lost seven men on this ward since I came on duty yesterday," Marie said. "Those arriving are in worse condition than usual, and the doctors cannot keep up. Several whose wounds were eminently treatable died, gasping for breath, imploring me for help until all that remained were limp bodies and lifeless eyes. It makes me furious."

Camille heard the unmistakable sound of an exploding shell, and the two women jumped. "They're falling much closer to the theater," Marie said, "even though we have an ambulance flag on top of the building. You would think the Prussians are deliberately targeting us."

"The whole neighborhood seems to be under attack. You go home. I'll take over."

After Marie reviewed each patient's condition, Camille set to work freshening bandages, shifting the men into more comfortable positions, and feeding those who needed help with the day's soup and a tisane of water and brandy. All the while bombs continued to fall, a lethal rain of exploding fragments followed by the crackle, spit, and sputter of death, claiming bodies one by one without reason or rationale.

Midafternoon, the doctor came to check on each patient. Before leaving, he issued instructions for Captain Tremblay, an officer recovering from severe leg wounds, to attempt a few steps around the room. "Just to the doorway and back."

Camille finished her other tasks, then turned to the captain, placing one arm beneath his shoulder to help move him into a sitting position. "Now swing those legs around so I can help you stand."

It took all their combined strength to bring him to a standing position, but once there, the man was able to shuffle step after step toward the door, leaning heavily on her for support. "Why don't you sit for a moment while I tidy the sheets?" she said, pulling a chair close with one foot.

"I never imagined taking a few steps would be so tiring," the captain replied.

In the midst of helping her patient sit down, Camille froze. The hair on the back of her neck prickled. The sound was like nothing she had heard before—a piercing whine that grew louder and louder and louder. When it came, the crash was ferocious as the bomb tore through the ceiling and landed on the only empty bed in the ward, splitting it in two.

Camille screamed. A collective gasp echoed as each person in the room recoiled in dread, waiting for the explosion that would kill them all. Nothing happened.

Steam escaped. The bomb hissed and sputtered. Still nothing.

Her nerves were so tight, she thought they might snap. Death could be moments away. Was it safe to move? She could run and possibly escape the blast, but what of the soldiers who depended on her? She looked at the gaping hole in the ceiling and the bed where Captain Tremblay had been a few minutes earlier. No one moved. No one said anything. *You're a nurse,* she said to herself. *Your duty is to care for these men.* She turned her thoughts to whom to help first.

"Could be faulty," Captain Tremblay said. As the most senior officer in the room, the others looked to him for guidance.

"How long before we can tell?" Camille asked.

The captain shrugged. "I have no idea."

She would have to decide on her own. "For those who can walk, leave the room as quickly as possible," she said decisively. "If you can help someone else, please do so. I'll help Captain Tremblay first, and then find an attendant to assist those who can't walk."

The bomb never exploded. Eventually it was carted off by two members of the National Guard. When Sarah Bernhardt ultimately returned and heard the news, she made the decision to move their patients into the cellar. "Even if it's damp, our men will be safer," she declared. "We'll start tomorrow."

CAMILLE RETURNED the following morning to find the theater in chaos. Wounded men were waiting in the foyer on stretchers. Those who could walk were being escorted or shuffling on their own accord toward a doorway to the left of the grand staircase. Madame Guerard seemed to be in charge.

"We are all grateful for the courage you displayed yesterday," Madame Guerard said. "I have no idea how many men we would have lost if that bomb had exploded. I'm surprised your father has permitted you to return today."

"I said nothing to my family, Madame. They are already worried about the work I do here, however, I feel it is my duty to continue. Now tell me, what can I do?"

Madame Guerard smiled. "You are bold and fearless, Camille. I suspect this is what Sarah admires about you. Change quickly. Then you can help move the patients. Doctor Deschamps has promised to come by later this afternoon to check on our men. Guillaume has made the cellar as comfortable as possible, but I'm worried the damp conditions will not be good for our soldiers."

With so many beds, the move was a lengthy process. They positioned regular soldiers at one end of the vast cellar while officers occupied a section at the other end, the two groups separated by paneled screens formerly used in the theater's dressing rooms. In the late afternoon, Camille and Madame Guerard were checking every patient when Sarah Bernhardt arrived.

"We need more wood," she said to the two women. "We've already burned so many theater furnishings, it will take a fortune to reopen the Odéon. But our men will suffer terribly if we can't keep them warm."

"Would Mademoiselle Hocquigny be able to help?" Madame Guerard asked. "After all, she's the head of all the ambulances for the ministry. Surely, she will recognize there's no use looking after the men's wounds if we allow them to freeze to death."

"You're right, my friend. I will attempt to see her tomorrow. Camille, how are your patients?"

"Except for Captain Tremblay, whose wound opened up during the move, everyone else has successfully made the transition. I'm very worried about him. I've done my best, but he really needs Doctor Deschamps's attention."

Camille's last words were almost lost with the shattering sound of another explosion and the crumbling of plaster and dislodged stone. Fear lit the faces of those nearby.

"The infamy of war," Bernhardt said, her well-trained voice resonating across the cellar. "What has happened to humanity when our enemy deliberately targets buildings flying the ambulance flag? Will there ever be a time when wars are no longer possible? When the ruler who wages war is dethroned and imprisoned? This horror is like poison seeping onto our streets, affecting every man, woman, and child."

There was hopelessness in her voice, something Camille had never heard from the tireless actress, who looked after each wounded soldier like a mother looks after her child.

Camille feared there was worse to come. "My brother believes we'll face even greater danger if the revolutionaries take control."

~

"MADAME BERNHARDT HAS to close the hospital," Camille said to André as he walked her home a few evenings later. "The basement is too damp, and no matter how hard we try, the rats keep finding ways to come in. Doctor Deschamps has declared it unfit for our wounded."

"Where will the men go?"

"Sarah has arranged for some to be moved to another hospital and for others to lodge temporarily at a small hotel on the Right Bank."

He offered his hand to help her step around a large pile of debris that blocked part of the street. "Will you continue to help?"

"I'll be at the hotel for a few days, but most of those men will soon be able to go home."

"You sound disappointed."

She tucked her arm into his. "I am disappointed. We all are."

"But you did some wonderful work, and you truly made a difference."

"Thank you, André. I'm pleased with what I was able to do."

She hadn't told him of the bomb that never exploded, nor had she told her father or brothers. They would have prevented her from continuing at the hospital, and Sarah needed her, as did the soldiers. The truth was that she enjoyed being involved and the sense of accomplishment that came from testing her capabilities. What had begun as an impulsive decision had become more meaningful than she could ever have imagined.

"It's all but over," André said. "When the second sortie failed, I knew we'd run out of options. The National Guard was a disgrace, running away from the fight rather than standing up to our enemy. Most of them did little more than bluster and drink and brag. Not one effective battle against the Prussians in over four months." He shook his head in disgust.

"Father expects the siege to lift in a few days. He said negotiations are underway."

André nodded. "The cost will be enormous. France will give up Alsace and Lorraine and be forced to pay reparations. And we have lost our military prestige. The balance of power will be in Prussian hands. King Wilhelm will now unite the German people and create a much stronger country on our border."

"And what will the radicals do?"

"That remains to be seen. Unrest continues to build. In my opinion, unless the government enacts serious change, the radicals will try to take control again."

29

FEBRUARY 1871 – MARIELE

AN EERIE QUIET came over the city after the armistice took effect on January twenty-eighth. In the days that followed, Mariele read articles condemning those in charge, for despite a force of more than two hundred thousand soldiers, Paris had failed, and thousands had died of disease and starvation, and bombs and bullets. The papers railed at inept generals and cowardly soldiers and those who had profited from all that had been lost.

Gradually, the city came back to life. Theaters reopened, trains resumed service, mail arrived from the outside world, and food began filling the shops and markets of every arrondissement. Her father explained that one of the terms of the armistice was that France could elect a new government, which would finalize negotiations for peace.

February remained cold and damp. Bit by bit, Mariele's days resumed old patterns as friends returned and social activities began again. With her parents' blessing, she and Bertrand set a wedding date at the beginning of April, for he was certain his mother and siblings would return from Lyon by then, and she was equally certain her brother would be released once peace negotiations were completed.

"ROBERT!" she cried at the sight of her brother sitting with her parents in the morning room. Her mother looked radiant, and her father's smile stretched from ear to ear. "I'm so happy to see you."

He was thin, his face gaunt, his uniform tattered and filthy. He was the same and yet totally different. In his eyes, she saw maturity and something else, an emotion she'd seen in the eyes of soldiers on the streets of Paris—as though the monstrosity of war had wiped away every shred of youth and every shred of hope.

Mariele widened her smile to ensure he saw nothing of her understanding and rushed over to embrace him. During all the months he'd been away, she had prayed for his safe return, fearful that one day they would receive devastating news. And yet here he was. She clung to him and wept.

"I hope those are tears of joy," he said.

"Of course, silly. And relief. We have so much to catch up on. If you've already told Maman and Papa, you'll just have to start all over again. I don't want to miss a word of what you've been through. And we all have so much to tell you."

"I think I should take a bath first. I arrived less than an hour ago and have been with Maman and Papa ever since. I'm sure everyone will benefit if I wash and remove these clothes."

"You can tell us everything over dinner," her mother said. "Go on upstairs. I'll see if Madame Robinette has something special to serve. And since we'll be *en famille*, there is no need to dress formally for dinner."

. . .

"SEDAN WAS A DREADFUL BATTLE," Robert said, closing his eyes for a moment and shaking his head.

"You needn't tell us, *mon chéri,*" Maman said. "Not if it's too difficult for you."

Mariele watched her brother's sad, sweet smile form.

"Perhaps the telling will ease my thoughts," he said, pushing a few crumbs on the table into a tiny mound. "The Prussians had twice, if not three times as many soldiers as were under French command. The center of our position was the fortress of Sedan, and our flanks extended north and south from Givonne to Mézières. We thought we were safe with most of our men in the fortress at Sedan and the rest fanned out north and south to protect us. Safe," he said, his voice dropping, "until we saw the masses of Prussian infantry whose ranks came at us like the surrounding hills and forests weren't even there."

No one made a sound or even moved as Robert told them how Prussian forces kept them under fire while other enemy divisions moved north and west to encircle Sedan.

"When Marshal MacMahon was wounded, first one general and then another took over, and there was so much confusion. Our cavalry charges were unable to make any inroads, and our artillery was outgunned." He looked away and sighed. "In the early afternoon, General Ducrot and General LeBrun organized a massive charge. We might have broken through if it wasn't for the arrival of Prussian reinforcements. The sound was deafening. Our batteries roaring at every point of their lines. We tried to withstand the onslaught, but there wasn't enough ammunition to be effective.

"The enemy must have deployed almost one hundred guns against us, and they were accurate. As soon as we took up a new position, they found us again. Our men were shot down so quickly, it was carnage of the worst sort. At one point, fires were burning everywhere I looked, and hundreds of men lay in the mud, crying out for help."

When Robert stopped to take a sip of wine, Mariele noticed the shock on her mother's face and the grim looks of Theo and her father.

"Our emperor raised the white flag in the early afternoon, but General Wimpffen continued the fight for another few hours. I wasn't in the fortress of Sedan, but I heard tales of dead bodies everywhere, of men scrambling over one another to find a point of safety, and of the crush of soldiers and gun carriages struggling to force their way inside. Bugles and trumpets rang out on all sides. And then it was over. Later that night I saw men cutting up dead horses so they could roast the meat and have something to eat. I don't know the numbers of casualties, but I've heard rumors of more than ten thousand French soldiers lost."

"Thank God you weren't one of them," Maman said.

Mariele's only view of soldiers fighting had been from the Panthéon, and that had been awful enough. Robert's account made her realize how much worse it had been.

"How did they treat you after the surrender?" Papa asked.

Robert tipped his head back and forth. "Well enough. We had food of a sort and roofs over our heads. I did everything with my men, and we formed a strong bond. However, almost six months of captivity is a very long time to be without purpose. Those of us who are junior officers tried to keep the men as busy as possible." He shrugged. "As you might expect, some men tried to escape, and many were dragged back or shot upon capture. With the cold and snow, these past few months have been the worst."

Conversation turned to the conditions in Paris and the events of the siege. "We marched through the villages close to Paris. They've been devastated," Robert remarked as he swirled the last of his brandy.

Mariele's father nodded. "I've been to see many of them as part of a committee assessing damages. It's clear that what wasn't destroyed by Prussian bombs has been taken by looters. A travesty. It will take years to rebuild."

"And who will pay for that?" Theo asked. "France already has to pay five billion francs in reparations to Prussia. Five billion!" He shook his head. "What I also don't understand is why the National Guard has been allowed to retain their arms."

"A very good question," said Robert. "If the regular army had to disarm, why not the city's armed soldiers? Papa, do you know the reason for this decision?"

"Not the full story. What I've heard is that Favre begged Bismarck for this concession because he feared the National Guard would rise up in rebellion if their arms were confiscated. So, France has been allowed to retain one army regiment and the guards to retain their weapons."

"That seems dangerous to me," Robert said. "They can still rebel, and now they have the arms on hand to be dangerous."

Maman raised her hand. "I've had enough talk of war to last me a lifetime. Now I must go to bed." Before departing, she hugged Robert and ruffled his hair. "I'm so happy to have you home at last."

"But you haven't told me what happened here. To each of you and to our city."

"Tomorrow night," Papa said. "We can tell you all about our escapades then."

30

MARCH 1871 – CAMILLE

WHEN THE PRUSSIAN army entered Paris to occupy the city for two days—a deeply humiliating condition of the peace treaty—no stores or restaurants remained open, the fountains were dry, the shutters closed, the streets empty of omnibuses and carriages and wagons. Defiant Parisians gathered along the route to witness the enemy. They booed and hurled insults as the first soldiers passed. However, by the time the full contingent—thousands of well-armed men in precise formation—had marched past the Arc de Triomphe and along the Champs-Élysées accompanied by martial music, the crowds were silent. Not a sound except the tramping of boots and the occasional sharp command could be heard.

After the last Prussian soldiers marched by and Parisians slunk away to lick their wounded pride, Camille and André began to walk toward the Place de la Concorde.

"Paris is like a woman ravaged by a throng of soldiers," he said. "She's damaged in body and soul. And what will her people do? Food remains so expensive. Work is difficult, if not impossible, to find. And to make matters worse, rents suspended during the siege are now due. Many families will face utter destitution.

"If the emperor was here, he would be torn limb from limb for putting our country through such humiliation. He chose war only to glorify himself and secure the throne for his son. Not to serve the people of France."

André sounded bitter and disillusioned; two emotions Camille didn't associate with him. "I can't shake the feeling that worse is to come," she said. "It's criminal that the government has chosen this moment to cut the pay of National Guardsmen. Discontent is already threatening to erupt in working-class districts."

"Defeat, poverty, death." André shook his head. "Just the right conditions for rebellion. Did you know that a few days ago, former Guard members seized two hundred cannon and hauled them to various strongholds in the outskirts?"

"Two hundred cannon?" Camille said. "That's incredibly dangerous. Why would the army permit such a thing?"

André kicked a loose cobble. "The army is in disarray," he said. "The radicals fear Thiers and his cronies will allow the monarchists to rule. They pass this falsehood around to stir unrest. Meanwhile, they promise to rule in favor of the working class."

"But what would they know about governing a country like France? It's ridiculous to think that hat makers and street sweepers can make sensible decisions in such complex circumstances."

"Precisely." André shoved his hands into his coat pockets. "Yet everywhere I go, people cry out, 'Vive la Commune.' They see treason and conspiracy in every act of the government. They see negotiated peace as betrayal. And they believe that only the people can save the people."

All around them, the crowd was dissipating, silent, morose, and slumped in defeat. Camille walked alongside André. She didn't care where they went. She just needed the comfort of his company.

Since September, they'd spent many hours together. She admired his thoughtful consideration of politics, his intellect and curiosity, and his willingness to serve his country. Although he had seemed playful and carefree when she'd first met him, Camille had come to realize that he cared a great deal about humanity and struggled to reconcile his well-to-do upbringing with notions of justice and compassion.

"Do you still sympathize with the republicans?" she asked.

"At one time, I did. Now my sympathies have turned to fear. A spark could set their emotions aflame, and the consequences for Paris might be worse than what we've already endured. The people I've shared your findings with are seriously alarmed. However, the conditions imposed by the Prussians have made it impossible to take action against the radicals. Your father is well connected. What does he think?"

Camille sighed. "I have no idea. Now that the siege is over, he's too busy concocting new schemes to make money."

"Now, that sounds harsh. Has your mother returned?"

"Not yet. Father and Victor visited her and my siblings in Lyon. Afterward, Maman wrote to him, saying she did not want to disrupt Paul and Laure's schooling. He didn't insist, and I assumed I knew why, but the dangers you've described make me wonder if Father is also concerned for the future."

"He should know more than most."

"Indeed. But enough about my father. Now that you're no longer in the National Guard and Paris is returning to normal, I'm looking forward to a ride in the Bois with you. That is, if you still wish to spend time together." Camille intended her words to be lighthearted and to erase the anger that had clouded his face.

"If I still wish to spend time together."

She couldn't tell by the tone of his voice if he was mocking her. For a moment she thought she'd overstepped some invisible boundary between them.

André pulled her by the hand into one of the covered walkways leading north from rue de Rivoli. "You are indeed a foolish woman. Have you no idea of my feelings for you?"

His kiss took her breath away, a mingling of lips and tongues that stirred a flame deep within, his body close to hers in a way that held promise. When he drew back, he said, "I've wanted to kiss you for a very long time."

Had he kissed her months before, Camille would have said something bold or playful. But now, after so much strife, so many fearful days, so much death, she told him the truth. "That took my breath away. Will you kiss me again?"

She thought she was prepared for his second kiss, but this time his hands cupped her face, and he looked at her with such tenderness she felt like she might melt. His kiss was gentle at first, then passion overtook them both.

MORE THAN TWO WEEKS LATER, Camille slipped out of the house in one of the drab outfits she'd worn to the Vigilance Committee meetings. Awakened at six by the faint sound of drums and bugles, she was anxious to meet André and find out what was happening.

On Tuesday, leaders of the National Guard had issued a proclamation: *"Soldiers, children of the people! Let us unite to save the republic! Kings and emperors have done quite enough harm."* The proclamation went on to exhort regular soldiers to ignore their orders and support the founding of a new republic. André expected that a major confrontation between government troops and the National Guard would soon take place.

"I want to see what's happening for myself," he had said to

Camille after stating his intention to climb the hill to Montmartre.

When she had expressed a desire to go with him, he had resisted. "Those agitators are so stirred up, there could be violence. Particularly if the government sends soldiers to deal with the leaders."

"Aren't the mayors negotiating a return of the cannon?"

"They are, but . . ."

"But what? I'm the one who attended the Montmartre women's club to gather information. And after you'd been wounded, I walked there by myself in the dark. Besides, you're a former National Guardsman. I'll be safe with you."

"You're impossible, Camille. Why do you always want to court danger?"

She had shrugged. Embracing danger was the path she'd followed since Juliette's death. Had she become addicted to danger the way others were addicted to opium or absinthe? Danger made her feel alive. The siege had certainly provided many opportunities. Perhaps this new threat would provide more.

She had smiled at André. "We'll look after each other."

"Well, make sure you wear something suitable."

DRESSED IN ROUGH WORK CLOTHES, he was waiting for her just outside the Noisette home. As they crossed the Pont Royal, he relayed the latest information. "The government has decreed that the National Guard should surrender their weapons. Everything is in chaos. Hopefully, the government will take charge and rescue the rest of Paris. We cannot live our lives with the threat posed by the Communards."

"Do the drums and bugles signal the beginning of trouble?"

"I don't know why the general alarm sounded, but I doubt

it's a good sign. We'll go to the Butte Montmartre. Many of the cannon are there, so it seems a good place to observe what's happening. We'll leave if there's any trouble."

Near Place Pigalle, they stopped to read a government placard signed by Adolphe Thiers and other leading officials protesting the attempt by so-called "Red" leaders to set up an alternate government. The notice declared that offenders would be brought to justice and the cannon restored to the state's arsenal. Others had also gathered to read the document until one man, wearing the uniform of the National Guard, tore it from the post, shouting, "*Vive la Commune!*" and then thrust the proclamation at the faces of those assembled. Finally, he brandished his rifle and forced the small crowd to scatter.

André took her hand and pulled her down the street.

Camille was shocked at the man's violence. "How many other members of the Guard are against the government?" she asked when they were far enough away.

"I don't know," he said tersely. "Battalions from working-class neighborhoods like Montmartre, Villette, and Belleville are more likely to side with the rebels. That's a lot of men. And they all have weapons."

With André leading the way, they walked briskly and in silence. A fine rain that bordered on mist had begun to fall, and Camille rearranged her shawl to cover her head. Nearing Place Blanche, they encountered many men and women and more than a few children heading up the hill. Rumors flew. According to one, the cannon that had been held back from the Prussians were in the open fields of Montmartre. These had been captured by government troops while those situated on a lower plateau remained under National Guard control. The crowd grew denser the higher they climbed.

André stopped to ask a shopkeeper what had occurred.

"The government tried to take our cannon, but we're fighting them," she said. "Those cowards came during the night.

Now we've made the troops understand their duty to the people, and many have refused to use their guns. They'll be joining us soon. *Vive la Commune!*" The woman gave a satisfied smile.

National Guard captains sporting red belts on their uniforms as well as high boots and rifles led their troops forward.

"*À la Butte!* To the top!" many of the soldiers shouted.

Crowds jostled and pushed. The road narrowed. Camille and André reached Place Saint-Pierre, an open area where the cannon rested surrounded by government troops. Attempts to stop the wave of people determined to stand up for their rights proved futile. Within minutes people were climbing on the gun carriages, over the caissons, under the wheels, and surrounding the horses hitched to the cannons.

"It's bedlam here," André said. "We should leave."

"Unharness the horses!" a woman shouted.

"We want the cannon! Cut the traces!" cried another.

Perched on a boulder with André standing on the ground to her right, Camille saw a series of women passing a knife from hand to hand until it reached someone close enough to cut the harnesses attaching the horses to the big guns. Shouts continued. The crowd surged forward. A horse reared in fright, unseating its rider, a government soldier, who was kicked again and again by those who swarmed around him.

Camille looked to her right, expecting to say something to André, but he was no longer there.

"André!" she shouted. "André, where are you?"

On her left, two regular army soldiers clambered down from a perch where they'd been waiting, ready, if necessary, to shoot members of the National Guard. Instead, they now embraced the very men they were ordered to take prisoner. A woman joined them, shedding tears of joy. "We are all brothers and sisters," she said.

Noise and confusion bubbled up behind Camille. As the crowd surged forward, she was almost swept away. "Camille!" She heard André calling and struggled to keep her footing.

"André!" she shouted, looking frantically in all directions. Screams and laughter mingled together. A young boy threw a rock at one of the artillery officers. Cabbages flew through the air, pelting government soldiers. National Guardsmen cheered.

The crowd surged again. Camille lost her balance and tumbled from the boulder. Someone grabbed her wrist to help her stand, and she turned to thank him.

"I've got you, Mademoiselle. You don't want to fall in this crowd," said a rough-looking, gray-haired man.

"*Merci,* Monsieur." Fearful, she attempted to turn back.

"You won't be able to force your way through there now. Too dangerous. And soon they'll be out for blood. I've seen it happen before. Be careful."

The man pushed his way forward, and she was on her own once again, struggling to stay close to the place where she'd last seen André, but the jostling continued, pushing her along step by step.

From the open plateau where the cannon were, the crowd followed a well-worn path before turning north onto rue du Mont. Camille breathed heavily as she and the crowd climbed farther up the hill, rough cobbles giving way to dirt paths. Where the path turned sharply right, a windmill turned slowly. Now even thicker with people, the crowd slowed, inching toward a crossroads where a guard stood on a makeshift platform, beating a drum.

"Bastards!" the woman beside her said. "The government will pay for what they've done. They can't take our cannon."

"They're traitors," another woman said. "My son died for nothing." She raised an arm, her fist clenched, and once again shouted, "Traitors!"

Although the rain had stopped, the clouds remained thick

and dark. Ahead was a church, and Camille, wondering if she might take refuge there, attempted to force her way through the tangle of bodies, only to have the crowd resist her efforts. A bugle sounded. Cheers filled the air.

"*À la rue des Rosiers,*" a man up ahead shouted, and the crowd picked up the cry. "To des Rosiers street!"

Camille stumbled and placed a hand on the shoulder of the woman in front of her to regain her balance.

"*Laissez-moi!*" the woman growled. "Keep your hands to yourself." She had turned as she spoke, showing a weathered face, cracked lips, and lank gray hair escaping the scarf wrapped around her head and shoulders.

"I beg your pardon, Madame. I lost my balance. Do you know where rue des Rosiers is?"

"Not far from here," the woman grunted.

"And why are we going there?" Camille walked alongside the woman.

"No idea, but we'll soon find out. I hope our men capture some of Vinoy's soldiers. We have plans for the likes of Vinoy and those loyal to him."

Rue des Rosiers was little more than a laneway flanked by narrow two- and three-story houses, several surrounded by walled gardens. Shouts could be heard. With hundreds crowded into the laneway, Camille could barely move, her face so close to the man in front of her she could see the ring of dirt around the inside of his collar and a small scar on his left earlobe. The air was ripe with sweat and garlic and unwashed flesh.

A sudden need to bear witness made Camille wriggle forward, pushing and maneuvering to pass through the mass of people. Chanting began, the words gradually picked up by the crowd. "Death to the traitors! Death to the traitors!" Over and over and over. Like a beast aroused by the scent of prey, the crowd roared its rage.

Finally, a space opened up, and Camille was able to slip

around the side of the house at 6 rue des Rosiers. What she saw made her recoil in horror. Two men stood six feet apart against a stone wall that separated two houses. One was an officer, the other a bearded man dressed in a black suit, holding a hat in his right hand. In the middle of the yard were a dozen men from the National Guard, their weapons shouldered, ready to fire. Men and women, even children, stood in defiant clumps to witness the proceedings.

A drum rolled, its rat-a-tat encouraging citizens to shout even louder. A rough-looking man who seemed to be in charge held his hand up. *Rat-a-tat. Rat-a-tat.* The man dropped his hand, and shots rang out in quick succession. The officer slumped against the wall and crumpled to the ground. A roar went up. Then a moment of silence before the chanting began again. "Death to the traitors! Death to the traitors!"

They've just executed a man in cold blood. Camille recoiled with fear and disgust. Despite months of nursing, nothing had prepared her for such ruthless savagery. Shock swept through her, followed by a shiver that would not stop. Hemmed in on all sides, she could not escape.

The drum rolled again. The man in charge raised his hand. The second prisoner braced his shoulders and looked at his captors with defiance. *Rat-a-tat. Rat-a-tat.* Shots burst again. The prisoner toppled onto the officer. Two men slaughtered like animals.

"Death to the traitors! Death to the traitors! Death to the traitors!" The chants were louder than before. Even children added their shrill voices.

She watched in horror as those who had executed the men stepped toward the bodies and fired into them repeatedly. The bodies jumped and twitched as bullets riddled them. Then a man who was clearly drunk walked over to the bodies, unbuttoned his trousers, and urinated on them. He was followed by others, while the crowd jeered and yelled obscenities and people began to dance around as if the occasion were some sort of festivity.

Camille clamped a hand over her mouth. Nausea swirled in the pit of her stomach. The men and women she'd observed had behaved like animals, their humanity discarded like a ragged cloak. She felt a crushing sense of doom.

She had to get away. Back to safety. She cursed her brazen foolishness. What if someone recognized her from the Vigilance Committee meetings? If they discovered her real identity, would she be considered a traitor merely because of her family's wealth? Her father, because of his business dealings? And Victor? Were priests also considered traitors? What would happen if this mob mentality took over? Where would the danger end?

31

MARCH 18, 1871 – MARIELE

"IT'S TRUE. Two men were killed. General Clément-Thomas and General Lecomte," Camille said.

Mariele was in the library of the Noisette home with Bertrand, Camille, and André. Camille's eyes were scattered, her voice ragged. André's clothing was torn. One eye was swollen and bruised, and a jagged cut, the blood crusted over, was on his forehead.

"I couldn't escape the crowd," Camille replied. "People pushed and shoved. They were all trying to get to a small street called rue des Rosiers. It felt like a bad dream, a nightmare. I can't get the image of those men out of my mind." She covered her face with both hands.

"Are you feeling unwell?" Mariele asked, truly concerned for her friend. "Perhaps you should lie down."

"No!" Camille shook her head. "I don't want to be alone."

André moved closer to Camille and held her hand.

"How can people do such a thing?" Mariele asked. "I've seen what the Prussians are capable of, but these are our fellow citizens." She tried to imagine being in the midst of such an inflamed mob as two men were murdered. For there was no other word for what had happened. Soldiers hiding behind some code of command had murdered two generals. Something cold and ominous sliced through her.

Bertrand stroked his mustache. "And where exactly were you, André? Father would be furious to know you left my sister in such danger."

"You must believe I had no intention of leaving her, Bertrand. But someone in the crowd knew me. He and his friends dragged me off into an alley, where they confronted me about my feelings for the working class and the National Guard. One of them even demanded that I join the cause right there and then, take up a rifle, and help them overthrow the government. They gave me this as a souvenir." He pointed at his black eye and the jagged cut just above it. "And then I couldn't find her. You have no idea how frantically I tried."

Bertrand looked at André and then at Camille. Mariele noted that the worry lines on her fiancé's face were more pronounced than ever, as if he'd suffered one too many shocks.

"Well, my dear sister," he said, "if you expect me to keep this from Father, you must promise not to be so foolish the next time our friend here wants to investigate the lower classes."

"You have my word," Camille replied.

"There won't be a next time," André said, "I will never expose Camille to those radicals again."

THE FOLLOWING MORNING, Mariele attended church. While the priest intoned the prayers of the Mass, she prayed for Paris and its citizens, and for an end to the threats of unrest. Midafternoon, accompanied by Suzette, she took a cab to the Noisette home to check on Camille.

Overnight, improvised barricades had appeared at critical intersections in the central part of Paris—the Hôtel de Ville, the

rue de Rivoli, avenue Victoria, and the Quai de Gesvres. These
barricades forced the driver to alter his route across the Seine.
The streets had a restless energy about them. People gathered
here and there, their faces angry or despairing, the conversations loud or whispered. Military men rode purposefully along
in groups of two, three, or more.

Camille was delighted to see Mariele and pressed her to stay
on for tea. Confident that Bertrand would drive her back to
avenue Vélasquez, Mariele sent Suzette home in the same cab.

"My sister is impossible," Bertrand said later, while negotiating
a turn onto a narrow street that paralleled the now barricaded
rue de Rivoli. "Your mother will be shocked if she hears about
Camille's experience."

"Well, I don't intend to tell her, and with Robert finally
home, Maman's not objecting to anything these days. Has
Camille always been so . . ." Mariele searched for a suitable word
that wouldn't offend her fiancé. *Bold* or *rash* might be too
strong. Perhaps *daring* or *fearless* or *spirited*.

"Outrageous?" Bertrand said. "And yes, she's always caused
trouble. But after Juliette died, she became more brazen.
Mother has given up trying to rein her in. And Father . . . well,
for the most part, he laughs at her escapades. But I don't think
he would laugh about this one. Do keep it to yourself, *ma chérie*.
I don't wish to give your parents any reason to disapprove of
my family."

An unexpected consequence of her engagement to Bertrand
had been a growing friendship with Camille. During the siege,
they had been together on many occasions and shared their
concerns, which brought comfort to both women—Camille had
said as much more than once. However, this most recent
episode was beyond horrifying.

Mariele shivered and turned up the collar of her coat. "I

think my parents have grown quite fond of you. Papa certainly respects your business acumen, and just the other day, Maman said she finds you charming."

In truth, she was pleased that her mother approved of Bertrand. "He's impressed me," her mother had remarked one day after the siege ended. "He's steadfast and capable. Admirable qualities. And it's clear that he loves you." At this, her mother had brushed a lock of hair away from Mariele's face and smiled.

"Well, that's a relief," Bertrand said. "I'm sure you're all delighted to have Robert with you once more. I hope he's there when we arrive; I'd appreciate a word with him. He'll know what's going on. Rumors are that Thiers has things under control, so it will soon fizzle out. But I think we should take our honeymoon outside France. We both need to get away."

"I've always wanted to visit London," Mariele said. "What about Camille and André? Do you think he will ask her to marry him?"

"I'm not aware of any specific plans, and he certainly hasn't asked permission. Father would have told me. I suspect they're waiting for Mother to return." He chuckled. "Maman will be so relieved to have Camille married."

ROBERT TURNED up shortly after they arrived at the de Crécy home, and Mariele's father insisted that Bertrand stay for dinner. "Robert will appreciate hearing of your exploits in the National Guard. Apparently, those under Prussian captivity had a rather boring time of it."

While Bertrand and Robert spoke, Mariele changed for dinner into a gown the color of blue hydrangeas with a multi-tiered skirt and a V-neck both front and back. She'd lost weight during the siege, and the gown's narrower waistline, taken in by a seamstress, flattered her slimmer figure.

Bertrand seemed a little flustered when he complimented
her. "You look beautiful this evening, Mariele. And you as well,
Madame de Crécy," he added as he escorted Mariele's mother to
her chair.

They had just finished the first course when Eugène arrived
with a message. "I'm terribly sorry, Monsieur, but the man who
brought this insisted you would want to read it straightaway. I
hope I've done the right thing."

"What is it, Philippe?" Concern flashed across her mother's
face.

"A moment, Evangeline. I need to read it first." He extracted
a pair of silver-framed glasses from his breast pocket.

When Mariele's father finally lifted his head, his face was
ashen. "The letter is from a senior official I know. The National
Guard has sparked a revolution and called for Thiers and Favre
to step down. The Tuileries and Hôtel de Ville have been occupied. Thiers and most of his government have fled Paris for
Versailles. *Incroyable!"*

Her mother gasped.

"Mon Dieu!" Robert said. "This is a catastrophe."

"What . . . what does it mean?" Mariele asked. "Surely our
government wouldn't just leave the city." She looked from her
father to Bertrand and then Robert. "Surely not. Papa?
Bertrand?"

Theo exhaled slowly. "Can you tell us more, Papa?"

Her father picked up the letter and began to read. *"Late this
afternoon, National Guard insurgents erected barricades throughout
Montmartre. They then gathered several battalions and marched into
central Paris. With many defections, and fearing that even more
soldiers would abandon the army and join the National Guard,
government troops withdrew to the Left Bank. Leaders of the Guard
collected several battalions and occupied Place Vendôme, Hôtel de
Ville, the Tuileries, and the Prefecture of Police. The Ministry of*

Finances is currently under threat. General Vinoy has concentrated his troops at the École Militaire and the Champs de Mars."

Robert pushed back his chair and stood. "I must go, Papa. My services will be needed."

"No, Robert. You can't leave us again. Please, Robert. Please." Mariele's mother reached toward her son, her face torn with anguish.

Robert crouched beside her and held her hand. "This is my duty, Maman. I must join General Vinoy and defend our country. Please try to understand."

"He's an officer, Maman," Theo said. "Officers are duty bound to lead. Can I help you in any way, Robert?"

"Would you secure me a fiacre, Theo? I assume the streets are still somewhat safe."

Robert embraced his mother and father before turning to Mariele, who stood to put her arms around him. "Come back to us," she whispered.

Mariele watched Robert leave the dining room, his steps purposeful, his shoulders braced, his head high. What was he thinking? Did he feel duty bound to serve his country or eager to subdue this new enemy, an enemy pitting Frenchmen against one another? Alarm engulfed her like a rapidly spreading fire.

AFTER ROBERT'S DEPARTURE, Mariele's mother staggered from the room in tears.

"I'll go and comfort your mother if I can," Papa said, his voice weary with concern. "Please excuse us, Bertrand. I hope to see you again soon. There's no need for you to leave."

"Of course, Monsieur. I'll stay with Mariele and Theo for a little while. Convey my thanks to Madame de Crécy. Let us hope the government crushes this insurrection as quickly as they did last November."

"Papa looks almost as upset as Maman," Mariele said when she could no longer hear his footsteps.

Theo nodded. "This turmoil is affecting all of us. The university is in disarray, coping with students and professors who left during the siege and are now returning and others who have decided to find a different life elsewhere. I never know whether there will be a class at all. But that's nothing compared with our government leaving Paris." He walked to the window and pulled aside the curtains to peer out. "I have a bad feeling about this. A very bad feeling."

"I agree with you, Theo," Bertrand said. "People have little, if any, money to spare. Jobs are scarce. This coup attempt is only going to make things worse."

Mariele set down her knife and fork. "My appetite is gone. Do you think it's merely an attempt, Bertrand? If the government has fled the city, they must think it more than an attempt. Why didn't Monsieur Thiers ask the army to take control as General Ducrot did in November?"

"I don't know," Bertrand replied. "But what Camille and André experienced yesterday suggests that the situation may worsen before it improves. One spark and everything could go up in flames."

Theo gulped the rest of his wine. "Maybe this is the spark."

IT WAS ALMOST midnight when Mariele accompanied Bertrand to the front door. With the limited information at hand, they had discussed and debated the uprising's potential for more than three hours until Theo had finally declared it was time for him to go to bed.

"I won't say anything if Bertrand wishes to stay longer," he said with a feeble smile.

Bertrand shook Theo's hand. "Thank you, Theo, but I have

worked hard to be in your mother's good graces and certainly don't wish to risk damaging her opinion of me now."

Mariele escorted Bertrand to the front hall. He put his arms around her. "I will send word tomorrow of my whereabouts. No doubt Papa will have formulated a plan."

"If it really is a coup, how will we survive this? And our beloved city, how will Paris survive?"

"I don't know, my love. I don't know."

When she could no longer see Bertrand's carriage, Mariele closed the front door and slid the bolt into place. Her mind was numb. Camille's account of bloodshed followed by news of the government fleeing the city and Robert's departure filled her with despair. Was there to be no end to the suffering of Paris and its citizens? How many more would die to satisfy the demands of radicals? Which of those dearest to her would be lost?

32

APRIL 2, 1871 – MARIELE

ON PALM SUNDAY, after church and a light meal, Mariele managed to convince her mother to get some air. Dressed in subdued colors, they walked among the crowds on the Champs-Élysées. Everywhere Mariele looked, red flags signaled the reign of the Commune. She pointed at a barricade blocking the entrance to rue de Marny.

"It's just like before, Maman. As if we're under siege again."

Her mother nodded. "These supposed leaders intend to destroy the National Assembly because they believe the February elections were not representative," she replied. "Look around. They're marshaling troops to fight against the French army. Civil war will follow. And what will happen to Robert? I can't bear the thought of him being in danger once more."

Mariele linked arms with her mother. There was nothing to say. Robert would do his duty regardless of the dangers he faced. What kind of courage was required to take up arms and risk one's life? Was her brother naturally courageous, or had he learned to be so? When they were young, Robert was always the one who led the way, with Theo and herself taking the role of willing followers. Robert smiled and the world seemed to smile in return. She squeezed her mother's arm.

"Your papa said this morning that a collection of bootmakers, perfumers, and clerks know nothing about governing," her mother said. "He called them ruffians and criminals, and I agree. A commune is nothing but a mirage. All they want is power. And they are all from Paris. What about the rest of France?"

"Maman, do you know where Papa goes every day? Does he have connections with this new government?"

"He tells me nothing." Bitterness laced her voice. "But I have only myself to blame for that."

"I wonder if he had anything to do with the negotiations between members of the Commune and the National Assembly."

Her mother shrugged in response.

Mariele sought another topic. "How many of our friends have left Paris?"

"Most of them," her mother replied. "When your papa urged me to go, I told him that once was enough for me. I'm staying in Paris with you and Theo and your father. Hopefully, the army will soon prevail, and Robert will return."

"Theo has told me that he has to find new routes each day to attend classes. He's often harassed by guardsmen who think he's shirking his duty. Bertrand has been forced to rejoin the National Guard. Those in charge of the Commune say that any man who doesn't join the guard will be imprisoned or shot."

The sound of boots thumping across the cobblestones made them step back against the windows of a shop featuring hats and umbrellas. Mariele and her mother watched a battalion of National Guardsmen march by, shouting, "À Versailles! À Versailles!"

"What do you think will happen, Maman?"

"I have no idea, but I think it best that we return home. Your papa won't want us to be in any danger."

Mariele and her mother turned along rue Balzac in the direction of Parc Monceau, and when they turned again on rue Faubourg, she saw a number of horse-drawn ambulances coming toward them.

"Those are wounded men," Mariele said. "Members of the National Guard. Do you think they were shot by soldiers in the army?"

Her mother nodded and gripped Mariele's arm so tightly she imagined a bruise would form. "Pray for your brother."

TWO DAYS LATER, Mariele gathered together a basket of food and prepared to visit Sainte-Clotilde. Her father had forbidden her from working at the church, but she knew from Bertrand that Victor continued to care for destitute children. Only the promise of taking Suzette along had secured her mother's agreement to the outing.

The scent of meat pies filled the kitchen.

"May I come, Riele?" Sophie asked when Mariele told her where she was going. After Fabien's death, Sophie had started to call her 'maman'. When Mariele had encouraged Sophie to use her proper name, the little girl had difficulty with the pronunciation and had adopted the term Riele.

"It's too far for you to walk, sweetheart," Mariele replied. "Why don't you help Madame Robinette make jam tarts? She told me this morning that she needs a good helper like you."

Madame Robinette held out her hand. "Let's get a bib to tie around your neck so you don't get jam on your clothes," she said. "Mademoiselle Mariele won't be gone long."

Sophie took the cook's hand. "À bientôt, Riele. We'll make a tart for you."

. . .

"MAMAN WOULD PREFER that I stay at home all day every day," she grumbled as she and Suzette climbed into a small carriage.

"Mothers always worry about their children, Mademoiselle, no matter how old they are. With so much turmoil, I'm glad I don't have any."

"And your husband? What does he think?"

"He thinks life will return to normal once the Commune is firmly established."

Mariele did not reply. Suzette did not intend for her words to be offensive. They were from different classes, each class believing their own version of events, and there was little point trying to convince their maid that the Commune had neither legitimacy nor the skills to govern.

"Do you support the Commune?"

"Well, yes, Mademoiselle. They speak for the working class and will right all the wrongs we've experienced. Already they've resolved the matter of overdue rents. Papa earned almost nothing during the siege. If he hadn't had his Guardsman's pay and the little I was able to contribute, they could have starved. When Thiers took control and reinstated rent payments, my parents faced being put out onto the streets. They had no way to pay six months of rent."

"You could have asked Maman for help."

"Possibly, but . . ."

A quick glance at the maid's face told Mariele all she needed to know. "But you don't think she would have."

Suzette looked embarrassed, and for a while they traveled in silence, listening to the sounds of the streets, the clatter of wheels on cobblestone, and the crack of the cab driver's whip. Bright sun had marked the day along with hints of warmth, but now a chill was gathering.

"Would you prefer to wait for me here?" Mariele said to Suzette as she placed one foot on the carriage step and, with the driver's assistance, climbed down to the sidewalk. "I shouldn't be too long."

"I'll just go along to a shop I saw a few streets away. Your mother asked me to buy some ribbon to repair one of her bonnets."

Mariele entered Sainte-Clotilde through a red door to the left of the main entrance. Despite the soaring height of its ceilings, the church was dark and chill, only two parishioners kneeling in prayer. A few candles had been lit, but not as many as she recalled from the days of the siege, and only muted light streamed through the glorious stained-glass windows. A sense of sadness and despair hung in the air.

Victor did not know she was coming, and she made her way briskly along the aisle and down the stairs.

"Mariele!" Victor smiled as he greeted her. "How wonderful to see you. The children have missed your kindness."

A few children gathered around her, one tugging her skirt while another lifted round blue eyes and simply stared up at her. Fire crackled brightly in the fireplace, and some of the older ones were seated at a long table waiting for Victor, dressed in his usual black cassock, to finish the book he'd been reading to them. Mariele sat on a low chair near the fire and pulled two little boys onto her lap. Although Sophie continued to be her constant companion, she had missed the pleasure of these children, their simple ways and eager faces.

"I brought meat pies for everyone to take home," she said.

AFTER THE CHILDREN LEFT, Mariele sat beside Victor. "Not as many children as we used to have," she said, "although that's not surprising, given that the siege ended two months ago."

"Yes, and with the latest decrees against the church, I suspect the numbers will dwindle further. It's a difficult time for our people to believe in God, and yet we soldier on."

"Did the Commune really eliminate stipends for all Parisian priests?"

Victor nodded. "And now they've declared that all Church property will be considered national property. Even worse, I read this morning that *Le Père Duchesne* has advocated the robbery of all churches."

"That can't be right," Mariele said, putting a hand to her mouth in astonishment. "Why would a newspaper advocate such an extreme position?"

"If you ask me, it's because the Commune needs money. My father said the treasury was empty when they captured it, and I'm certain the leaders of the uprising are furious. Today they announced that all Frenchmen are prohibited from leaving Paris." He looked at his watch. "You should go home now. It will soon be dark, and the streets may turn rough. I'll escort you outside. Did you come by carriage?"

"Yes, the driver and Suzette are waiting for me."

Victor nodded. "I'm glad you had the sense to come by carriage."

They walked toward the front, where a stooped priest was in the chancel lighting candles set in tall silver candlesticks. "Father Georges is preparing for Mass, but only a few of the faithful still come."

Mariele missed being at the church and the hubbub of little children in her charge. In the time she'd spent with them, she had even helped some learn to read and to know their numbers, but for the most part, she'd given them comfort and a place where they could laugh and play. If only for a short while, the work had offered a sense of purpose, and Mariele looked forward to a time when she would have her own children to care for.

Suddenly, she realized Victor was waiting for her to speak. "I'm sorry, Victor. I was lost in thought. What did you say?"

"I was saying that there seems to be a disturbance outside. You stay here while I see what's going on."

An instant later, the front door burst open. Five members of the National Guard entered the church, brandishing rifles. Mariele gasped.

"You!" one of the men said to Victor. "Stop right there." He aimed his rifle at Victor's chest.

At the sight of a rifle trained on Victor, Mariele became very still. A woman who'd been praying in one of the small chapels made the sign of the cross and scurried out a side door. Father Georges had stopped his preparations for Mass and seemed frozen in place.

"Drag that other priest down here. Don't waste any time. And you," he poked the rifle into Victor's chest, "you are going to tell us where to find the valuables."

Without thinking, Mariele closed the gap between herself and Victor. "Leave him alone," she said. "He's a priest doing God's work. What sort of men are you to burst in here?"

"God's work?" the man scoffed. "Well, we're doing the people's work. These bastard priests are nothing more than thieves stealing from the poor for thousands of years." He spit on the ground. "You'd better get out of here if you don't want any trouble."

"He's right, Mariele. I'll be fine. Get into the carriage and go home."

"Like he said, he'll be fine. But before you go, I'll have that little trinket around your neck." The captain reached forward and ripped the gold chain from her neck.

Mariele's eyes and mouth opened wide. "Give that back," she demanded.

"The Commune needs it, Mademoiselle, and we'll take whatever we want." He jerked his head at Victor. "If you don't want to see her hurt, you'd better tell us where to find what we've come for."

By now, the other guardsmen were at the front of the church, one standing behind Father Georges, holding the priest's arms tight, while another tossed candlesticks and a silver chalice into a burlap bag. Finished with that task, they threw the priest onto the floor and cracked his head with the butt of a rifle.

"*Merde,*" Victor said. "Stay here, Mariele."

Mariele had seen violence during the siege but always from a distance. Watching such deliberate cruelty perpetrated on a man old enough to be her grandfather was sickening. "You're animals," she said, shaking from head to toe. "Animals."

Victor took a step toward the chancel. The captain jammed his rifle into Victor's chest. "Don't even think of moving."

"I'll give you what you're looking for," Victor said. "But first, let this young woman go."

"Doesn't work that way. Once we have what we came for, then we let her go. Grab her," he said to a thick-chested man who looked no older than her brother Theo.

Mariele was grabbed from behind, her arms wrenched so tightly, she feared her buttons might pop. The feel of the man's breath on her neck made her skin crawl, and in an instant, she was back at Versailles being threatened by Major Werner and a young soldier called Johann. With great effort she kept still, sensing that to struggle might put their lives at risk.

She watched Victor lead the other men up the central aisle and through a door on the right side of the chancel. Behind that door was a storage room containing felt-covered shelves filled with gold and silver chalices, censers, plates, and candlesticks, some of which were jeweled. When she'd seen these treasures, the effect had been dazzling.

After the men returned, carrying three large sacks that clanked and clanged as they walked down the aisle, the leader said, "Let's go." He prodded Victor with his rifle.

"Let him be," Mariele shouted. "He's given you what you

wanted. He looked after your children during the siege, feeding them and keeping them warm. You should be grateful to him. Take your loot and go."

"That may be, but for now he's coming with us. The Commune has plans for priests."

Victor turned to face her. "I'm sure I'll be all right," he said. "Tell my father where I've gone."

Helpless in the face of four armed men, Mariele clenched her fists and watched while the men led Victor out of the church. When the door slammed shut, the thud echoed off the stone and marble surfaces of the church.

33

APRIL 4, 1871 – MARIELE

BLOOD RUSHED through Mariele's body making her feel both dizzy and nauseous. Stunned at the sequence of events, she could not decide what to do. Should she check that Father Georges was alive or try to follow the men who'd taken Victor away? She looked toward the chancel, then toward the entrance. Turning away from the door, she ran up the aisle and was relieved to see the priest beginning to move.

"Are you all right, Father Georges? Let me help you sit up. They've taken Victor away, and I don't know what to do. Is someone else here at the church?" Mariele knew she was babbling but couldn't stop.

"They took Victor, you say?"

"Yes, yes. Where's Father Anselme?"

"Father Anselme?"

The man seemed to have lost his wits. "Just sit quietly, Father Georges. I'll look for one of the other priests."

Almost thirty minutes passed before Mariele was able to leave Sainte-Clotilde, and as she scrambled into the waiting carriage, she shouted, "Go! Go! Be quick, Laurent. Take me to Monsieur Noisette's home."

Holding a gloved hand to her mouth, Suzette said, "What is it, Mademoiselle? Why did the National Guard take Father Victor away with them?"

"Those men were despicable. They denounced the Church, then they stole many sacred items of silver and gold and acted like common thugs. I have no idea where they've taken Victor."

Laurent turned the carriage around, and within minutes had them rattling along at a fast pace, dodging other vehicles, a cracking whip urging the horses to greater speed. They slowed at the intersection with rue de Sèvres and turned right, then careened through a series of narrower streets to the Noisette home.

All she could think of was Victor. Where had they taken him? And why? What plans did the Commune have for priests? If only she'd left immediately rather than helping Father Georges, Monsieur Noisette could already be on his way to find his son. *No one is safe in this city anymore*, she thought. *No one.*

"Here we are, Mademoiselle."

Mariele climbed down from the carriage and ran to the door, shouting and knocking at the same time.

"Is Monsieur Noisette home?" she cried out when the butler appeared. Without being invited, she entered the house. "Father Victor has been taken by the National Guard. I must see his father immediately."

"*Mon Dieu*," he replied. "Monsieur is in the library. If you would follow me . . ."

Mariele swept past him and ran up the stairs. "Monsieur Noisette! Monsieur Noisette!" she shouted.

"Good heavens, what is all this commotion? Mariele, my dear, what are you doing here?"

"Oh, Monsieur Noisette. You cannot believe what has happened." Mariele related the story. "I couldn't stop them. They took Victor . . . Oh, Monsieur, it was dreadful." Mariele had spoken so quickly, she was breathless.

"*Incroyable!* This is outrageous. Are you certain, Mariele? Are you sure it wasn't some sort of misunderstanding? You're distraught. Let's go to the petit salon, where it's comfortable. Bertrand should be home soon. I'll pour you a brandy and fetch Camille. Once you are settled, you will tell me the story again."

While waiting for the others to arrive, Mariele paced up and down, reliving the details. Fear and anxiety overwhelmed her again. Like floundering through a maze in the dark, the nightmare of the past hour refused to release her.

Footsteps clattered down the stairs, and a moment later Camille burst into the room, her eyes wide, her manner agitated.

"Mariele!" Camille said. "Father tells me you have terrible news about Victor. You're shivering. Take a sip of brandy and sit with me near the fire where it's warm." She looked over her shoulder. "Father, I don't like the look of Mariele's face; I think she might be in shock."

Camille lifted the glass to Mariele's lips and tipped a generous portion into her mouth. The warmth of the brandy slithered down her throat and spread quickly through her body. She closed her eyes and sighed.

The butler entered the room. "Excuse me, Mademoiselle Camille. Monsieur Bertrand has sent word he will return as soon as possible."

"Thank you, Michel," Camille said. "Will you please tell Madame Carnot that dinner will be delayed?"

"Certainly, Mademoiselle. Will that be all?"

Camille nodded, then took Mariele's hands in hers and rubbed them vigorously. "You're freezing. Father, fetch my shawl from that chair by the window."

With the shawl draped around her shoulders, Mariele said, "I think I'm all right now. But someone must go quickly to find Victor."

They were losing valuable time, and the men who had taken

Victor seemed more ruthless than reasoned. Just as they had cracked the head of Father Georges, they might take precipitate action against a priest who, in their minds, had already perpetrated crimes against the people. Mariele's hands trembled.

"Before I do that, tell me the story again from the beginning," Monsieur Noisette said. "I want to go through the details once more. They'll be important when I ask the authorities for information." He had tossed a brandy down his throat earlier, and now, while waiting for Mariele to gather her thoughts, he splashed more into his glass.

Mariele took several deep breaths, then closed her eyes to visualize the events that had occurred less than two hours earlier. With slow deliberation, she relayed what had happened, answering every question Charles Noisette asked. How many men? What did the leader look like? Exactly what did he say about priests and the Church? What valuables did the men take? Were they all National Guard? Which man hit Father Georges with his rifle? Which one threatened her? On and on until Charles Noisette was satisfied and Mariele exhausted.

"Here you are," Bertrand exclaimed, swiftly crossing the room to kneel in front of Mariele. "My love, are you hurt? Father's note disclosed very little. I hurried away as soon as I could."

Bertrand's father quickly relayed the story. "You and I must go immediately to the authorities. But before we go, change into your uniform, as that might influence those to whom we'll be speaking."

"I can certainly put on my uniform, Father, but I won't pretend to be one of those Communards who are destroying our society. They're brigands of the worst kind," Bertrand said, his voice harsher than Mariele had ever heard.

"You'd be wise to keep those opinions to yourself. Discovering your brother's whereabouts takes precedence, and if you can't guarantee the appropriate conduct for such a delicate mission, there's little point in going with me."

Mariele watched her fiancé struggle to control his emotions. He was normally deferential and reasoned with his father, and she was surprised at his confrontational tone.

"All right, Father. I'll change as quickly as possible. Mariele, is that your carriage waiting outside?"

"Yes, and Suzette is in the kitchen. Go, go! You're wasting precious time. Laurent and Suzette will take me home."

"Send a note to Camille as soon as you're safely home," Bertrand said.

"I will, and you'll let me know when you discover Victor's whereabouts?"

"We'll let you know whatever we discover," Charles Noisette replied.

AFTER THE MEN LEFT, Camille added a few logs to the fire and pulled two chairs close to the crackling flames. "Come and sit here, my friend. The warmth will be good for you. I'll ask Monique to get us something hot to drink."

A few minutes later, Mariele held a cup of broth in her hands. Each sip spread heat through her body. "I'm no longer shivering."

"You've had a shock," Camille replied. "Shock often causes the body to shiver. It's a natural reaction." The fire popped, and a small piece of charcoal leapt onto the floor. Camille rose quickly and swept it back into the fireplace. Afterward, she slid a wire mesh screen in front of the flames. "How did Victor react to being taken away?"

Mariele thought for a moment or two, recreating the scene in her mind. "He was calm," she said. "But there was a fierce look on his face. Victor is always so kind and gentle. I've never seen him angry, but he was definitely angry at the way those men treated Father Georges and the church's property. And the way they treated me."

"Were you afraid?"

"Not at first. I was more indignant than afraid. But when they threatened me, I couldn't help thinking of what happened at Versailles. The major who questioned us and the soldier who led me back to our cell were horrible people. Johann—he was the soldier—took pleasure from hurting me, and those men today also took pleasure from intimidating me. If the leader hadn't interfered, one of those men might have . . ." The thought was horrifying. The very thing her mother had protected her from might have happened at the hands of her fellow citizens. Mariele's hands shook.

"Victor is strong," Camille said. "His faith gives him strength, but he also has a natural fearlessness. Even when we were children, he was the brave one. Victor, Bertrand, Juliette, and I were always together, and Victor was our leader. Father was so disappointed when he chose to become a priest."

This was an insight into the family that Mariele had never heard. "I had imagined Bertrand in that role. He has such confidence."

"He does. After Victor went to the seminary, Father brought Bertrand into the business. Even after a long day at school, he was expected to spend several hours with him going over the accounts, hearing about the day's events and any concerns there might be. Some days, Juliette and I would stand outside the study and listen. I learned many fascinating details that way."

A clock began to strike the hour.

"I must go," Mariele said. "Thank you for sharing these stories, Camille." She gathered her jacket and gloves. "You will let me know what your father discovers about Victor, won't you? I will be praying for his safe return."

Camille nodded. "I'll be praying for his return as well."

34

APRIL 1871 – CAMILLE & MARIELE

DESPITE HER FATHER'S best efforts, which Camille imagined might have included bribery, he and Bertrand were unable to secure Victor's release. Housed in the Conciergerie prison, which was famous for the incarceration of Marie Antoinette, denied the use of fork or knife, and restricted in all movement beyond a small inner courtyard, Victor remained under arrest, along with several other clerics. When the family learned that the Archbishop of Paris, Monseigneur Georges Darboy, was also being held, Camille consoled herself with the thought that being in the archbishop's presence might protect her brother.

With little to do and most of her friends absent, each day passed slowly. To find one segment of Paris at war with another was shocking. To realize that the National Guard, a militia designed for the protection of Paris, had turned against the government and now supported the Commune was difficult to believe. Although Camille tried to understand how the working class felt, recalling the women she'd met at the Vigilance Committee meetings and quizzing Monique or Eugène on the matter, she held the view that French citizens should never take up arms against one another to resolve their differences.

Conditions continued to deteriorate. Camille and her family no longer used the large rooms of the house. These had been closed off after they had covered the furniture with heavy cloth and stored valuables in a locked room on the third floor. Instead, they used the petit salon and took their meals in the library, where her father had made space for a round table and four chairs. She found the arrangement cozy and was surprised that she did not miss the grandeur of their former lives. With less space to keep warm, the rooms they did maintain had fires crackling each evening.

News spun wildly across Paris. One day she heard of an assault planned by the National Guard to capture Saint-Cloud, one of the city's forts currently held by the army; the following day there was a report of a massive demonstration in front of the Hôtel de Ville. Rumors of further food shortages would be followed by declarations of ample food available at Les Halles. Camille and her brother and father relished each bit of information they heard concerning the buildup of government forces around Versailles. The latest rumor claimed that the Commune would soon be defeated—as early as the following week—because military reinforcements from the southern regions of France had finally arrived.

Just like Bertrand, André had been forced to join the National Guard. Camille rarely saw him and worried about him constantly.

By April seventh, government troops began to bombard the walls of Paris. The shelling brought back memories of the siege, although this time it was French troops who fired on the citizens of Paris. Soon the bombardment reached as far as the Arc de Triomphe and the Champs-Élysées. Once again dust and ruins cloaked the city. Forays beyond the walls resulted in enormous casualties for the National Guard, and the hospitals filled with wounded soldiers. Camille was torn. Her nursing skills could alleviate some of the suffering, but she abhorred the Commune and all it stood for.

One afternoon, Mariele came to visit. After inviting her into the library, Camille asked if she would like any refreshments.

"No, thank you, Camille. I'm terribly sorry to come unannounced, and I won't inconvenience you for long. But I need your help."

Camille tilted her head. "I'll help any way I can. What's made you so agitated?"

Mariele smoothed the skirts of her rather plain day dress. "The Commune has ordered all medical students to assist at the hospitals, and Theo has been assigned to Hôpital Beaujon. I volunteered to go with him, but he says what they need most is women with nursing experience." She took a deep breath. "Would you be willing to come with me? Teach me what you know. Just until I've learned how to be useful."

"Of course," Camille said without hesitation, "although I only had a few months of experience. When do you need me?"

"I'm going there tomorrow."

Mariele's decision to nurse at the hospital was a surprise. While her friend had grown increasingly confident, Camille never expected her to tackle the grim conditions of nursing. After agreeing when and where to meet, Mariele asked about Bertrand.

"I haven't seen him since the day Victor was taken. He has sent a few brief letters but says little about his duties with the Guard, and I'm sick with worry. Papa says the streets are filled with violence and that thousands have left the city."

"Bertrand is fine. I saw him at breakfast this morning. My father's reports are the same as your father's. With no work or income, many Parisians are in desperate circumstances. Soon it will be worse than the siege. I'm surprised your father has agreed to your plan."

"He hasn't, but I must do something. Theo is an excellent

medical student, but he lacks Robert's confidence. I believe my presence at the hospital will help him. I suppose that sounds like boasting, but I seem to have acquired new capabilities this past year."

"You aren't boasting at all," Camille said. "But my brother won't be pleased to hear of your plans."

Mariele shrugged. "What will be, will be. Forgive me, Camille, I haven't asked about André. I know you have feelings for one another. Have you seen him recently?"

"Four or five days ago now. His battalion remains within the city walls, but he expects they will soon be assigned to one of the forts."

"How can they possibly fight against our government?"

"They don't have a choice. Men like Bertrand and André, who were in the Guard during the siege, either fight or go to prison. Or worse," Camille said. "I heard of some who've been shot for refusing to join the National Guard."

"Everything is in such dreadful turmoil," Mariele replied. "Maman is desperate to hear from Robert."

"I'm sure she is. And what about Sophie? I thought you were expecting her father to come for her."

"We were, but now it seems he's been called for duty once more. I must go. When Maman thinks I've been gone too long, she becomes frantic with worry."

Camille embraced Mariele. "Do you have a carriage to take you home?"

"Yes. My mother insisted." She pulled on her gloves. "Thank you, my dear friend. I don't know what I would do without you."

～

AT THE HOSPITAL, Mariele surprised Camille. She had expected her friend to be squeamish, but instead Mariele was observant and curious, asking questions not only of Camille, but also of Theo and the doctors who were present. After only a week of training, in Camille's estimation, Mariele was competent enough to handle some patients on her own. Docile and demure. Those were the words Camille would have used to describe Mariele eight months ago. But not anymore. Instead, she thought of her friend as confident, assured, and valiant. She looked at Mariele fondly and chuckled.

"I'm surprised you've found something amusing in all this," Mariele said. She had a basin of water and was wiping blood from a man's face.

"I'm thinking of how strong and resilient you've become. After you're married, Bertrand will discover that his wife is not the slightest bit submissive."

EACH DAY MARIELE took time to follow developments in the conflict. As April unfolded, fighting continued in the outskirts west of Paris, gradually encroaching into the city proper. She walked to the hospital amid the smell of gunpowder and clouds of smoke and sounds of war—the shouts of those in command, the drums calling men to their posts, the cries of wounded men.

Each day, those manning the barricades and patrolling the streets seemed more desperate. On the elevated area of the Trocadéro, Communards, well supported by the National Guard, installed heavy guns to fire on government troops and made several attempts to recapture the strategic town of Neuilly and the bridge there that crossed the Seine.

Hostages now numbered in the hundreds, and speculation was that they would be traded for safe passage should the time come. Lawlessness prevailed. Starvation loomed.

Mariele, Camille, and Theo attempted to ignore the happenings beyond the confines of Hôpital Beaujon. Instead they served the wounded. It was brutal, exhausting work with only rare occasions to celebrate success.

MARIELE MOPPED up another pool of blood. "I don't think he's going to survive, Theo. He's lost far too much blood."

Mariele and her brother were in an open room with twenty narrow metal-framed beds filled with wounded soldiers. Occasionally, a man screamed with pain, but for the most part, patients moaned and muttered in distress. Three doctors and seven medical students did their best to save those with a chance of survival; Mariele was one of six who assisted. After ten days, her skills had improved, and she could now anticipate Theo's needs and have instruments or sutures ready before he asked for them. Treatment was crude. In one corner of the room was a barrel full of limbs waiting to be carted away, for amputation was the easiest way—often the only way—to save a man's life.

Laid out on a narrow table to Theo's right was a box containing a large saw, several knives, including one with a long, curved blade, forceps, small scissors, a cloth strap and tourniquet screw, a metal scoop, a few needles, and ligature thread. Theo's sleeves were rolled up. Sweat dripped from his brow.

Theo looked at her, a look of exhaustion combined with anguish. The day had not gone well, beginning with a man whose left leg was almost completely severed at the knee, followed by a series of urgent amputations, and now a soldier with a hole through his abdomen. They had lost six men already. The man in the bed in front of them would be the seventh.

"I can't lose another one," Theo said, shaking his head. "Why did I ever think I'd make a good doctor?"

Mariele gave him an encouraging look. "I'm amazed at what

you're doing under these conditions, and you're only a second-year student. Can you suture the wound here?" she asked, pointing to a spot where blood continued to seep into the abdomen.

From the very beginning, she had decided to look at the human body as an intricate series of connected parts, both a puzzle and a miracle. Although she had been shocked the first time she had looked at an open wound, she had developed a keen interest in understanding how it all worked.

Theo leaned over for a closer look. "That might work. I've tried everything else."

While Theo prepared a suture, Mariele stanched the blood one more time, then held the wound open using two forceps so Theo could sew a few small stitches. When he was finished, he took the man's wrist and felt for a pulse.

"It's weak, but it seems steady," he said.

"And the bleeding has stopped," she observed.

Theo wiped his forehead and pulled his shoulders back. "I'll close the rest of the incision. If you can clean up after that, there's a patient in the corner who needs my help."

35

APRIL 15, 1871 – MARIELE

ANARCHY, Mariele thought. *That's what has happened to my beloved Paris.* Everywhere she went she saw evidence of civil society's descent into inhumanity. Mansions of the wealthy ransacked. Church poor boxes raided. Crowds cheering as men prepared to demolish a statue of Napoleon III. False accusations leading to the arrests of innocent people. These and other horrors made her weep.

The fighting continued day and night, with shells falling in many quarters of Paris as government troops gradually gained ground. Soon the Commune would fall, but what atrocities would happen in the meantime?

Another day had dawned, and from her bedroom window, she looked out on Parc Monceau. In years past, the view of the park would be one of blossoming trees and lush green, of governesses watching their young charges play and women exchanging gossip while strolling through the gardens. Instead of these peaceful happenings, she watched members of the National Guard form into groups and ready themselves for battle.

When will it end? she wondered. *How many more people will die before it does?*

She couldn't voice such thoughts at home since her mother feared for Robert's life every hour of every day. Her mother lived for news of her firstborn. But when he did find time to write, his letters were so delayed, they described events already long past, which did nothing to allay her fears. Her father was more stoic; however, he too resisted talk of the conflict, claiming that his few hours at home were the only respite he had. As for Theo, he was hanging on by a thread; with so many wounded to treat and punishing hours at the hospital, he had shrunk into skin and bones. Mariele wished she could talk to Bertrand, but she hadn't seen him in weeks, and if not for Camille, she would have no news of her fiancé at all.

A week ago, Suzette, whose husband was a fierce supporter of the Commune and a member of the National Guard, had left the employ of a family the insurgents referred to as traitors, so Mariele now helped with household chores in addition to her duties at the hospital. She also had Sophie to care for.

Whenever Mariele was home, Sophie remained at her side. At that very moment, the little girl was perched on the loveseat, holding a children's book in her hands, pretending to read to the stuffed clown that had been Fabien's favorite toy. Once lively and full of chatter, Sophie had become quiet and shy. The change broke Mariele's heart.

No child should have to endure such loss, she thought.

At the sound of something shattering, Mariele jerked away from the window and rushed to the stairs.

"Mariele! Did you hear that?" her mother called out.

"Yes, Maman. I'm going to investigate. Sophie, you stay here. Don't move."

Mariele hurried down the stairs and found glass strewn across the dining room floor and Eugène holding a large stone.

Outside, a group of men were shouting, "Bastards! Royalists! Traitors! Soon the likes of you will have nothing." One of the men heaved another stone, which crashed through the salon window.

"Step away from the window, Mademoiselle. It isn't safe."

"Thank you, Eugène. But they seem to be leaving. I know Papa has gone to work, but if Theo is here, he might be able to fetch my father." Mariele was amazed that she wasn't more frightened. A year ago, she would have been scared witless, but perhaps she had already experienced so many shocking events that one more made little impact.

"No, Mademoiselle, he went to the hospital early this morning."

"What is it, Mariele?" Her mother spoke from a vantage point halfway down the stairs.

"A few troublemakers have thrown stones through the window, Maman. Eugène is here to help me clean up."

"Send for your father. With the bombardment getting closer by the hour and now this, I believe we should leave the house without delay. We are no longer safe. My sister's home is in a better area of the city. She'll take us in." Her mother turned around and went back up the stairs.

"I'll fetch Monsieur de Crécy," Eugène said.

"Yes, go now, Eugène," Mariele said. "I'll get rid of the glass. Perhaps you can board up these broken windows when you return."

AUNT ISABELLE REPLIED IMMEDIATELY. *Come at once,* the letter said. Mariele wrote a brief note to Camille telling her of their relocation and asking her to advise Bertrand as well. She closed the letter by telling Camille to send a message to 17 rue des Archives if she needed to reach her.

The following morning, Mariele's family packed a few bags

and took the carriage to her aunt's grand home in the third arrondissement. Although Mariele's family was considered well-to-do, the Challumel family was considerably wealthier.

"Won't Aunt Isabelle's home also be at risk?" Mariele asked, Sophie sitting on her lap.

"Possibly," her father said, "but it's surrounded by thick walls, and for now it's beyond the reach of the bombardment. I'm sure your uncle has the gate locked at all times."

Although Sophie's presence caused raised eyebrows, the family was easily accommodated in the many guest rooms on the second floor while Eugène, Madame Robinette, and Nicole were given rooms in the servants' quarters. Theo left for the hospital not long after their arrival, and, claiming pressing business, her father declined lunch.

"You'll be back for dinner?" Mariele's mother asked.

He nodded. "I'll send a message if I'm detained." Just before leaving, he instructed Eugène to return to their home twice a day and check for intruders.

Her aunt and uncle were ostentatious, and nothing was more so than their home, a four-story *hôtel particulier* on rue des Archives. From the lavish entry hall with gold-trimmed doors and yellow damask walls to the ceilings decorated with ornate frescoes and the grand interior conservatory, the Challumel home shouted its wealth.

Lunch was served in the small dining room, where one wall was filled with shelves displaying china figurines and another lined with oil paintings, which were flanked by a pair of gold pedestals topped with ornate sculptures. The meal was an elaborate, stilted affair as her aunt and mother discussed fashion and family, literature and shared history, and studiously avoided any mention of the ongoing struggle to govern Paris. Previously, Mariele had viewed her aunt through the eyes of a child, forming an impression of kindness and devotion to her cousins and uncle. Now she saw conceit, arrogance, lack of compassion, and little attempt to refrain from criticism.

"I have no idea why you've let some ruffian's daughter come to live with you," Aunt Isabelle stated.

Mariele opened her mouth to respond, but her mother cut in. "She's a delightful little girl, Isabelle. Our home is much livelier for her presence. Mariele did a wonderful job looking after those children. It's unfortunate that more women did not see fit to help."

Isabelle sniffed. "One might be able to admire such kindness to the poor, but surely you agree that no young woman of our class should be looking after soldiers, Evangeline. I'm surprised you have allowed such a thing. Mariele's fiancé will be having second thoughts about marrying someone of such bold character."

"She's not being bold, Isabelle, she's helping, and I admire her for it. Most women of our *class,* as you call it, have shirked their responsibilities by either fleeing the city or retreating to the boudoir. I'm ashamed of myself for doing so little. As for Bertrand Noisette, he has told me directly that he firmly supports Mariele."

Her mother's words were astonishing. In the months since Mariele had begun volunteering, not once had Maman voiced her approval. Perhaps being the younger of two sisters, and the one who was always made to feel inferior, was the impetus for her mother's statements.

"Thank you for your support, Maman. Aunt Isabelle, lunch has been delicious; however, I'm sure you will appreciate that I must abandon you ladies for my duties at the hospital." *There,* she thought. *I've made my point that I won't be bullied, least of all by an aunt who does nothing to support our city in its time of need.*

· · ·

MARIELE'S FATHER did not return that evening, nor did he send a note, and although her mother made light of the situation, Mariele knew she was worried. When he failed to return the following evening and Eugène reported another incident of vandalism at their home, Mariele's uncle arranged to meet with the prefect of police.

"He merely shrugged his shoulders when I asked him to investigate," Uncle Auguste said upon his return. "He said, 'We are at war, Monsieur, and I have no resources for trivial matters such as the disappearance of someone from the *haute bourgeoisie*.' I could have smacked the man for his insolence."

"Well, I'm pleased you didn't," Aunt Isabelle said. "I'm sure you're worried, Evangeline. Who else should we contact?"

Her mother squared her shoulders and lifted her chin. "I'll draw together a list of men who might know of Philippe's whereabouts."

"I'll contact whomever you advise," Uncle Auguste said, "and visit your home tomorrow morning to assess the damages."

"Thank you, Auguste. Isabelle, I'm sure you will understand if I excuse myself from the table. Philippe's disappearance is an urgent matter."

Mariele tried to contain her fear. Where would he have gone? In the past, he had always sent word if he was detained, and never had he been absent more than a short while without letting them know. Had he been taken hostage like Victor? Or worse? She'd read of some men being shot on the spot for suspected anti-Commune activities. Paris was in such turmoil that anything could happen.

Her mother rose from the table with quiet dignity, her face drained of color and her lips drawn into a thin line, not in a disapproving manner, but in a manner that suggested tears were not far away. Mariele tried to imagine the fear her mother felt. To have one son fighting against the Commune, another treating the wounded in a hospital that could be bombarded at any moment, and her husband—the one person on whom she relied for comfort—suddenly disappear must have felt like tumbling into a bottomless abyss.

Mariele set aside her napkin and pushed back her chair. "Excuse me, Aunt Isabelle. I'll come with you, Maman. We can send letters out more quickly if we work together."

36

MAY 3, 1871 – CAMILLE

ANDRÉ ARRIVED one morning while Camille was writing a letter to her mother, a task she performed weekly. Despite her dislike for letter writing, she undertook the duty with sympathy for her mother, and had just finished reporting, for the fourth week in a row, that there was no news of Victor.

"Shall I show Monsieur Laborde into the petit salon?" Monique asked.

"Of course. Tell him I'll be down shortly," Camille said, rising from her desk. "And please return to help me dress."

Within ten minutes, she was properly clothed in a morning dress of floral chintz, her light brown hair tied loosely with a black ribbon. She wore no adornments except her favorite gold necklace and locket, which had belonged to her great grand-mother, and did not stop to apply rouge or a spritz of perfume. As she hurried down the steps and along the gallery, a crashing boom rattled the windows, and the glass prisms of the chande-lier at the salon's entrance clanged against the brass frame.

Camille joined André at the window. "That sounded close," she said. "Can you tell where it hit?"

"I don't have a clear view from here, but there's smoke rising

near Les Invalides," he said. "The government is slowly gaining
ground. Several forts have fallen. The Commune should soon be
finished."

She put her arms around him and rested her head against his
shoulder. "Thank God you're here. I've been so worried. Each
day brings news of fresh disasters, and I'm so terribly afraid I'll
read your name in the list of casualties."

André held her tight. "I've missed you. You have no idea how
good it feels to have you in my arms."

Camille drew back. "Why are you in uniform?" She'd rarely
seen André in his National Guard uniform. Indeed, they had an
unspoken agreement that he would not appear in such garb. A
sinking feeling overwhelmed her. "You're going on duty again,
aren't you?"

He nodded. "My battalion has been ordered to protect the
gates at Saint-Cloud. At all costs."

"At all costs? You mustn't go. You have to find a way to leave
Paris. If something happens to you . . ." Her words dwindled
away. What would she do if André was seriously hurt or worse?
Their feelings for one another had intensified. Because of the
insurrection, they hadn't made any commitments, and she had
urged him not to speak to her father until the Commune had
been destroyed. The situation was impossible. All able-bodied
men were required to join the National Guard. Failure to do so
would result in arrest, possibly even death. If those in charge of
the Commune knew of André's clandestine activities, he would
be executed. The risk was enormous.

He pulled her closer. "You know I have to go. If I refuse
orders, I'll be shot as a traitor."

The warmth of André's arms brought a moment of comfort,
followed almost immediately by a sinking feeling of doom. "I
don't think I can bear it any longer."

He tilted her chin. "Yes, you can. I know you're strong
enough. And when I return, we shall marry right away."

"Right away?"

"Yes, right away." His kiss left her breathless.

That kiss, along with thoughts of having André as her husband, kept her going as the days unfolded and Paris succumbed to further fear, misery, fury, and revenge. She was shocked when the Communards appointed a Committee of Public Safety with immense powers to seize property, arrest individuals, and direct the course of the insurrection. And further shocked to learn that the committee had mines placed at one hundred and forty points within the sewers, to be detonated if deemed necessary to blow the city apart. Shelling continued as government forces gained ground. Lawlessness grew. Chaos reigned.

Camille went out only in broad daylight, wearing working-class clothes and a scarf over her hair. She no longer worked with Mariele at Hôpital Beaujon—the journey to get there was too fraught with danger—but instead helped at a nearby hospital. Her hands were so badly chapped from long hours of nursing that not even those gave away her wealthy background.

One afternoon on the way home, she passed several bodies lying beside the road. Although she was no stranger to death, Camille shuddered at the lifelessness of the men's eyes. When a shot rang out from somewhere behind her, she spun around in fear. In an alley perpendicular to the street, a member of the National Guard aimed his rifle and fired. A man toppled to the ground less than ten yards away.

Camille scurried to a nearby barricade. She kept her head low and wondered how to escape. Shots alternated back and forth. Without warning, a member of the National Guard leapt over the barricade and crouched beside her. "Move over," a rough voice said.

Camille froze. The butt of a rifle hit her shoulder.

"Move over. Didn't you hear me?"

The voice belonged to Maxine Pierrefonds from the Montmartre Vigilance Committee. Camille shifted a few feet over. *What if she recognizes me?* More shots rang out.

Maxine wore a red scarf around her neck, the symbol of the Communards. She readied her weapon, rested the rifle's barrel against the top of a sandbag, squeezed the trigger, and fired. "Damn," she muttered. She readied her weapon again. Fired a second shot. "Got him."

Camille heard a man howl and a weapon clatter against the cobblestones. Although her instincts were to rush over and help him, she gripped her hands until her knuckles turned white and forced herself to remain still.

Maxine sat back on her haunches and checked her rifle, then looked at Camille. As recognition dawned, there was no smile, no softening of her features. "What are you doing here, Henriette? I thought you lived in the third arrondissement. This is the seventh. Most people don't stray very far from home these days."

"I'm . . . I'm helping at one of the hospitals," Camille replied. Her throat was so tight she could hardly speak.

"Why aren't you working for the Commune?" Maxine demanded as she reloaded her weapon. "Everyone on the Vigilance Committee is doing their part. Louise Michel and others are with the National Guard like me. Many are on the barricades or driving the ambulances. Some make cartridges or fill sandbags." Suspicion lurked in her eyes. "I didn't take you for a coward."

"Nursing is hard work," Camille responded with a flash of indignation. "I'm helping save the lives of our soldiers."

Maxine wiped a hand across her face, leaving a smudge on her cheek. "I suppose."

The alley was deathly quiet. From her perch behind the barricade, Camille could see very little except shuttered windows and closed doors. The moans of the wounded soldier were now merely faint whimpers. The sun had disappeared behind the ornate towers of a church, leaving shadows, and in their wake, a creeping chill.

"You'll have to wait here until it's safe," Maxine said. "We've trapped a pocket of Thiers's soldiers in a courtyard across the way. Bastards! They should be fighting with us, not against us."

Camille wondered how soldiers from the regular army could have made their way into Paris. As far as she knew, the army remained focused on taking the forts surrounding the city. Once those had capitulated, the infantry would attempt to break through the city gates. She thought of André and said a quick prayer.

Maxine removed her scarf, reached up, and waved it. She popped her head above the barricade for an instant and sat back down. "Only three of us left," she muttered. She eyed Camille once more.

"Why aren't you wearing red?" she asked.

The question caught Camille off guard. "I . . . I forgot it at home."

"Well, it's lucky for you that I have another one." Maxine pulled a tattered red scarf from her breast pocket. "I'll tie it for you," she said, moving closer.

The prickling began in Camille's belly, and quickly spread to her chest and limbs. *Dear God, no! My necklace.* Her heart pounded. Camille jerked away just as Maxine reached for her hair.

"What's wrong?" Maxine hissed.

"I'll tie the scarf myself," Camille replied.

Maxine was tall and large boned. She grabbed Camille's arm and twisted it. "Why?" she demanded. "Aren't we comrades, or are you hiding something?" With her other hand, she lifted Camille's hair. "And what's this?" Maxine pulled the necklace and locket out from beneath Camille's dress.

"I stole it," Camille said. "It belonged to my mistress. She has so much jewelry, I knew she wouldn't miss it. Now let my arm go."

"Well, then, you won't mind donating it to the cause." Maxine gripped the necklace and pulled so hard it broke.

"Give that back," Camille exclaimed without thinking.

Shots echoed across the alley. Maxine twisted her head. There were no answering shots, and it was impossible to know who had fired their weapons. She turned back toward Camille. "Something's not right. You're in the wrong arrondissement. You're not wearing red. And you have a gold necklace. What else do you have?"

She pushed Camille against the barricade, cracking Camille's head against a thick piece of wood. With one arm across Camille's neck, Maxine searched the pockets of her dress and pulled out a small pouch full of coins. "Did you steal this as well?"

A riot of thoughts clashed inside Camille's head. What course of action would allow her to escape? What lies could she add to those already told? Or would those lies only endanger her further? Victor had already been incarcerated. Would that be her fate as well? Or worse? The Communards were more desperate now, less likely to show any mercy.

Maxine had dumped the coins onto the ground—a collection of centimes and francs worth more than most families could scrape together in two or three months. Camille had only brought them with her to buy medicine for the hospital from a supplier Sarah Bernhardt had used. Unfortunately, her nursing duties had taken longer than usual, and she'd been unable to make the purchase.

"A housemaid doesn't have this kind of money," Maxine stated with disgust. "You're one of them, aren't you? One of the rich we want to destroy." She reached for her weapon and thrust it against Camille's chest. "Why did you come to our meetings?"

Camille's thoughts spun wildly. What fabrication would

convince Maxine of her innocence. Still pinned against the barricade, she stared into the woman's eyes, searching for a scrap of sympathy. "I believe in your cause."

"That's a lie." Maxine snorted. "If you believed in our cause, you wouldn't have disguised yourself, pretending to be someone of our class. I welcomed you into my home. You even held one of my children." She jabbed the rifle into Camille's chest once more. "Were you spying on us?"

"No! I'm not a spy. Maxine, you must believe me. Take the money if you want. Take the necklace too. I'm not a spy."

Maxine stood, her musket now aimed at Camille's chest. She pulled the lock to full cock, placed the butt of the weapon against her right shoulder, and squinted.

Camille's thoughts slowed. Mere seconds separated her from life and death. An image of André came into focus. They had kissed and held one another. She wished they had been intimate.

Farewell, my love. What joy we might have had. Camille closed her eyes and formed André's name on her lips.

A rifle sounded. Blood and flesh splattered against her face and clothing. Camille's eyes flashed open just as Maxine crumpled to the ground, her musket discharging against the barricade, spraying sand and splinters in all directions. A gaping hole had appeared in the right side of Maxine's head. Blood still pulsing from the fatal wound. Her brown eyes were open and lifeless, the necklace and coins scattered on the ground.

Camille gasped. Shock held her motionless for a heartbeat or two. Whoever had killed Maxine might now be planning to storm the barricade. They might want her dead as well. More rifle shots rang out. Each one made her cringe.

How can I escape?

The alley wasn't safe. Behind her was a narrow lane, barely wide enough for two men to walk abreast. If she kept low to the ground, she might be able to move away from the skirmish and find safety. Camille lay face down. Using her elbows, she pulled herself forward inch by inch, thankful that the lane was dimmed with shadows.

The earth smelled of garbage and urine and animal droppings. A rat scuttled across the lane and disappeared into a cracked pipe made of clay. She breathed through her nose, fearful that she might ingest something foul and diseased. She lost track of time. Her muscles screamed fatigue. Her clothing was filthy. Finally, she saw a doorway just ahead that offered a bit of shelter. Camille pulled herself into a crouch and, huddling within its frame, looked back toward the barricade.

Although the light had faded and dusk was near, she could see Maxine's body spread out upon the cobbles, her head pillowed against a sandbag. From this angle the wound on her head wasn't visible, but a crow was busy pecking away at the woman's face. Camille averted her gaze. Her stomach heaved.

After a moment or two, she wiped her mouth and looked back. The alley now seemed deserted. Shadows had deepened in the laneway. She had to get home or face more danger once the streets were completely dark. She rose to her feet and, keeping her back against the wall, edged her way along until she reached an open street. From there she followed a circuitous route, crossing each intersection at a run after waiting until just the right moment following a round of shots, when she knew those firing would be reloading their weapons.

Closer to home, she passed a small guillotine on which three rats hung by their tails. Beneath them was a sign: *Fate of Thiers, MacMahon, and Ducrot.* Camille sobbed and began to run.

37

MAY 13, 1871 – CAMILLE & MARIELE

"I FORBID you to go to the hospital anymore," her father said the following morning. He selected a piece of cheese and a slice of bread from the meager breakfast buffet and took his seat at the circular table. "The situation on the streets is untenable. Yesterday, the Champs-Élysées was completely deserted as everyone fears the shelling. And rightly so. Government troops surround Paris. I heard yesterday that these anarchists ordered the destruction of Adolphe Theirs's home and have begun to tear it apart stone by stone. They're nothing but thugs. If I could get you out of the city, I would do so, but there seems to be no possibility."

"You're right, Father. It's too dangerous, even for me."

He looked surprised, and Camille recounted the previous day's events, omitting all mention of Maxine. "If someone had questioned me, I might have been arrested merely for the way I speak. But what about you? Surely, it's not safe for you either. Or for Bertrand and André. I'm so glad Maman and the others aren't here."

He nodded. "I plan to stay in my study this morning. With so much unrest, business has ground to a halt." He put on his glasses and picked up the newspaper.

"Have you heard anything about Victor's release?" Camille asked before her father could get immersed in his reading. She asked this question every morning. The answer was always the same.

"No, but I have finally secured permission to visit him tomorrow. I had to bribe a few people, but at least I can now see him."

The bribery didn't surprise Camille. Lacking funds, the Commune seemed to thrive on bribes, and in all likelihood, her father was no stranger to that method of influence. She knew not to ask if she could accompany him. The authorities would resist having a woman involved and might refuse admission altogether. "Where is Bertrand?" she asked. "He hasn't been home for several days."

Her father shifted on his chair and looked away for a moment. "He'd be in danger if I told you."

"In danger? He's already in danger by being in the National Guard."

He fixed his gaze on her. "You mustn't breathe a word of this to anyone."

Camille's eyes widened. She nodded in agreement.

"Your brother is no longer fighting for the insurrection. He has escaped to join our government troops."

She sucked in her breath. Without warning, she felt as if a vicious current had her in its grip, pulling her down beneath the water. She couldn't breathe. Their lives were disintegrating, everything about the way they had lived—family, friends, society—upended in a frenzy of war and rebellion. The Paris she loved was in ruins. She'd already lost Juliette. André or Bertrand could die at any minute. Victor was in prison. Nothing was secure anymore.

"Are you all right, *ma chérie?*" her father asked. "You've gone very pale."

"Just a little faint," she replied.

He poured more tea into her cup. "Put some sugar in it," he said. "Sugar will help." He passed the sugar bowl and cleared his throat. "The catacombs have secret passageways. A man who was familiar with them led Bertrand through. I paid him handsomely for his help."

Camille pushed her plate away. Food was the last thing she wanted. "I'm surprised you let him go. Last September you didn't want him to join the guard, and now you're helping him join the army."

He spread out his hands and shrugged. "Bertrand made it clear to me that he would find a way with or without my support. Your brother is a determined man. Let's just say he was very persuasive."

Camille offered a small smile. "I wonder who he takes after? Does Mariele know?"

"Good heavens, no. Now not a word about Bertrand, Camille. Not a single word." He waited for her to acknowledge him. "And speaking of Mariele, a man I know told me Philippe de Crécy is missing."

"Oh no! How can that be? Is the Commune condemning lawyers now? I haven't seen Mariele since they moved in with Madame and Monsieur Challumel. She and her mother must be very worried. I will send a message straightaway." Camille pressed a napkin to her lips. "Can the Communards hold out much longer?"

The roar of cannon almost drowned out her words. It was followed by the whistling of shells and the rattle of muskets. "Our troops are getting closer," Camille said. "Surely it won't be long now."

Before responding, her father poured himself a second cup

of tea. "It's difficult to secure accurate information, but I heard yesterday that Fort de Vanves has fallen, and last week Fort d'Issy was abandoned. Government forces are also in possession of the forts at Neuilly, Meudon, and Sèvres, and there are rumors that they are under the walls of Paris, exchanging shots with insurgents near the Muette gate. The end will come soon."

"And Saint-Cloud, Father? Do you know what's happening there? André told me his battalion would be at Saint-Cloud."

"I believe it's still holding on. But it won't last much longer."

"The end can't come soon enough for me. Then our family will be together again, and André and I can get married." But what if he didn't survive? From her nursing, she knew firsthand of the losses suffered by the ill-trained and badly led battalions of the National Guard. André was not a coward. But poor leadership had already resulted in hundreds, if not thousands, of unnecessary deaths.

"If he returns," she said.

Her father patted her hand. "Let us pray for that."

CHARLES NOISETTE never returned from his visit to see Victor at the Conciergerie.

Alone in the house, except for Monique and Michel, she paced the small salon up and down for hours before finally acknowledging that he was not coming back. She sent Michel to her father's primary office, but he returned saying that no one had seen Monsieur Noisette. In the morning, she wrote notes to various friends and acquaintances and received the same answer. There was no one else to ask, no one to consult, and with fighting in every corner of Paris, the streets were too dangerous to visit his other haunts.

"What shall I do?" She tapped her pen against the inkwell, spattering drops of ink across the blotter.

Bertrand had disappeared; Victor was in prison; the rest of her family was in Lyon. André was beyond the walls of Paris, fighting for a cause he didn't believe in. Her world had fallen apart.

"Can I get you anything, Mademoiselle?" Monique asked. "You've barely eaten all day."

Eat? Who can eat at a time like this?

"Don't fuss, Monique. Even the thought of food makes me ill. I have to do something. I can't stand waiting like this. I'll go mad. Come with me. I need to change."

The fighting would only get worse. Government troops were reported to be retaking the city section by section, block by block. The seventh arrondissement would soon be a battle zone—today, tomorrow, a few days at the most. The Communards had already shown what happened to those who got in their way. The Noisette home and all that was in it could be destroyed as desperate men fought for their lives.

An hour later, she was ready to leave in one of the shabby work dresses she wore to the hospital, carrying a small bag in which Monique had placed a proper gown, a pair of silk-and-leather shoes, and a few precious items. Just before leaving, she wrapped a black shawl around her shoulders.

"Take whatever food you need and shelter at your own homes until this is over," she said to Monique and Michel. "If you hear of either my father or Bertrand's return, try to send them word that I'm with Mariele de Crécy at the Challumel home," she said. "Lock the doors and secure the gate when you leave."

"Be careful, Mademoiselle," Michel said. "Are you certain I can't escort you?"

"Thank you, Michel. But I believe it's safer for all of us this way. Take this." She gave each of them a small bunch of coins. "It isn't much, but I—"

Monique grabbed her hand. "Thank you, Mademoiselle. I will pray for you."

"Pray for Paris, Monique. Pray for Paris."

When the gate clanged shut, Camille looked around for signs of life. To her left, the street was deserted. Only a scrawny cat stirred the scene. In the distance to her right, members of the National Guard stood behind a six-foot barricade composed of bricks and stones and upended wagons. Red flags marked each end of the barrier. Most of the men held rifles, and one crouched on a platform, ready to shoot a rapid-fire *mitrailleuse*.

She turned left. Walking slowly along the street, she kept as close as possible to the buildings lining the route. At the next intersection, seeing more soldiers both left and right, she continued straight across the road, her destination the Challumel residence, situated almost directly north on the other side of the Seine. Camille couldn't think of anywhere else to go.

Choosing a safe place to cross the river would be critical.

"A safe place," she muttered. She had no idea which bridges were in the hands of the army and which ones were held by the revolutionaries.

Camille ducked at a sudden burst of machine gun fire and a sharp blast of rifles. Shouts of rage and cries of anguish followed. From every direction, she heard the deadly sounds of destruction. She hid in the narrow space between two buildings until the firing stopped, then proceeded a few more paces to another street corner. Camille continued in this way, alternating her route left, right, and straight, for another ten minutes until she reached a point where Pont Saint-Michel came into view.

With the bridge heavily barricaded at both ends, she turned right. Perhaps Pont au Double or Pont de l'Archevêché, both narrow bridges joining the Left Bank to Île de la Cité near Notre Dame Cathedral, might be less fortified. She scouted each bridge before choosing Pont de l'Archevêché, where there was no evidence of armed men, although the crossing was more exposed.

Despite the smoke of continuing bombardment that drifted across the sky, the heat was oppressive. Dressed in a black shawl and heavy clothes, sweat trickled down her back and between her breasts. Should she cross during a lull in the conflict or when the nearby fighting was in full fury and the soldiers less likely to see her? There was no right answer; both were dangerous.

"You can't stay here," she muttered.

The distance wasn't far. Huddled beneath an arched walkway, Camille estimated she could run across the bridge in two or three minutes. Would running attract more attention than walking? Indecision paralyzed her.

A few feet away, a pigeon fluttered its wings and pecked at the ground. A shot rang out. The bird lifted its head and cocked it one way, then the other before continuing the search for food. Camille gathered her courage. With a burst of energy, she scurried to the other side of the street and huddled against an abutment that marked the entrance to the bridge.

From her new position, she could no longer see the far end of the bridge, and a hint of panic frayed the edges of her self-control. What now? She was no longer beneath the arch, a position of relative security. Instead, she was an easy target for snipers situated in the surrounding buildings. Should she go back?

If she crossed the Pont de l'Archevêché, she would be on Île de la Cité and would have to negotiate a second bridge to get to the Right Bank. For the moment, the machine guns and rifles were silent. Camille took a deep breath, stooped low, and ran as fast as she could.

～

WHEN SHE FINALLY REACHED THE Right Bank, Camille stopped to get her bearings. She couldn't afford to rest long. Picking her way along once familiar streets, she was dismayed at the devastation: sacked hotels and damaged homes, pock-marked buildings, and rubble everywhere. The fourth arrondissement had deteriorated rapidly in the week since she had last been there. A great roar sounded to her right, and she wondered if crowds had gathered at Place de la Bastille, always a rallying point for the working class. Turning left instead, she followed a small alley leading toward Place des Vosges.

"Stop!" a soldier shouted, his rifle pointing directly at her chest.

Camille had failed to see a man standing behind a pile of sandbags at the end of the alley.

"Who are you?" he barked.

"Just a housemaid, Monsieur," she said, doing her best to speak the way Monique did. "Please let me through, sir. My employer has sent me home."

A shot rang out, and the man spun around to return fire.

"Get down," he said, pulling her behind the sandbags, where he crouched low to reload his rifle. Another shot echoed, this one zinging off the building to her left. And another. Camille huddled into the corner. The soldier stood, fired another shot, and immediately ducked down again.

Why did I ever think I could safely walk across the city? she thought as the soldier fired two more shots. The man had accepted her identity without question, and although he did not speak to her, he glanced her way from time to time with what she took to be encouragement. As the minutes unfolded and the sniping continued, fear replaced shock, seeping through her body as if her blood had become ice and her limbs heavy weights. She could barely think, let alone act.

Time slowed. The soldier rose once again, rifle cocked. A sharp crack sounded, and the soldier's head blew apart, bits of flesh and blood spurting in all directions as his body crumpled to the ground. Camille was too stunned to scream.

"Got the bastard," she heard someone shout.

"Be careful," another voice called out. "There might be another one behind those sandbags."

Dressed in government blue and red, the soldiers who soon appeared hauled Camille to her feet. Her limbs were so numb she could barely stand.

"What the hell are you doing here?" one of them said, gripping her right arm.

Camille opened her mouth to speak, but no words came. He shook her and asked the question again.

"I'm just . . . just a housemaid, sir. I took shelter here. I only want to get safely home."

"Just a housemaid," he echoed. "What do you think, Pascal?"

"I think we have more important things to do than question this little bitch. If he was a friend of hers"—at this point, the soldier gestured at the headless body—"then she's already got what she deserves."

Camille held her breath as a brief argument occurred, one of the soldiers making obscene gestures while the man who seemed to be in charge struggled to maintain control of his men.

"You're free to go, but you'd better get out of here quickly. There will soon be more soldiers coming through here."

Camille scurried away from the men and across the road. To avoid further detection, she passed close to the walls where there were slivers of shade and darted across each open stretch she encountered. At every turn, debris filled the streets—not just the stones of damaged buildings, but broken bits of furniture, children's toys, discarded flags, shattered glass, and other scraps and fragments of lives lived.

Finally, hungry and more frightened that she wanted to admit, Camille reached the Challumel home only to find the gates barred and the courtyard deserted. *What am I going to do now? What if they've left Paris?* While this was unlikely, it was possible Monsieur Challumel had sufficient funds and connections to escape, even as government soldiers recaptured parts of the city. She walked all along the wrought-iron fence that bordered boulevard Haussmann and the street running perpendicular to it, searching for an opening. The fence was totally secure.

Returning to the main gate, Camille looked up at a second-story window and saw a woman's figure gazing out. She drew the shawl away from her face and waved an arm back and forth to attract attention. The figure paused, then turned away. *Don't go,* she thought. *Stay and look at me.* Camille waved again, even though no one was there, then waved again more urgently when she saw the figures of two women standing at the window.

Time passed. Hope dwindled. The sounds of fighting drew nearer, and the air sharpened with the pungent smell of gunpowder. Camille was about to turn away when one of the grand entrance doors opened and a man dressed in black emerged from the residence. A few moments later, he approached the gates.

"Madame asks for your name and your business here," he said.

Camille gripped the iron bars of the gate to remain erect. "My name is Camille Noisette. I'm seeking my future sister-in-law, Mariele de Crécy, and her mother, Evangeline de Crécy. They are staying with Monsieur and Madame Challumel."

"How do we know you're telling the truth? You don't look like a woman Mademoiselle de Crécy would associate with."

"But I am, Monsieur."

Just then, Mariele appeared at the doorway. "Please unlock the gate and let the woman in, Valois. She's my friend."

"How on earth did you get here?" Mariele asked as soon as the gate was barred once more and the front doors locked.

"I'll tell you the story later, but right now I've come to ask for help. My father is missing, and despite many inquiries, I can't discover his whereabouts. I thought your uncle might be able to offer some assistance. I had no one else to turn to. And I'm ... I'm ..." Camille burst into tears.

38

MAY 20, 1871 – MARIELE

FOR DAYS, they remained inside, the great gates of the Challumel home barred, every door locked, the ground-floor windows covered with wooden shutters to keep intruders out. Sounds penetrated their self-imposed prison: shells exploding, rifle fire cracking, debris falling, men shouting orders, others crying out in pain. Occasionally, they heard the piercing scream of an injured horse. Each silence was soon broken as fighting renewed again and again.

Waiting was unbearable. Her mother was so distraught, Mariele feared she might go mad, and nothing she or Aunt Isabelle did made any difference. Sophie wouldn't leave her side. She trailed after Mariele with her thumb in her mouth and the little clown clutched in her hand. Theo had sent word he'd been forced at gunpoint to remain at the hospital, but there had been no message from Papa or Robert or from those dear to her friend Camille. They could only endure each day and hope.

Trapped inside, Mariele and the others received infrequent bits of information concerning the insurgency. In the third week of May, a note arrived with news that government troops had seized Saint-Cloud and established their headquarters within the city proper at the Trocadéro. The army was in possession of Point du Jour, Grenelle, Porte de Sèvres, the Ceinture railway line, and the Arc de Triomphe, each site offering a strategic position in the battle for Paris. It was clear that the end was near, and with this news, hope flickered.

"The Communards are fighting ferociously and without mercy, attempting to hold on," Mariele's uncle said a few days later. Despite his wife's protests, he'd left the house early that morning dressed in a servant's clothing on what he had referred to as a scouting mission. "I'm told they're defending the barricades to the last man as our military advance street by street. You would not believe the number of dead bodies lying in heaps along the streets."

After imparting this news, her uncle left the room, muttering about the need for a brandy.

All they could do was wait. With a book in hand, Mariele glanced out the window. What she saw made her recoil.

"Maman! Aunt Isabelle! Camille! Come upstairs to the window," she shouted from the corridor. "Paris is on fire."

The three women came to Mariele's room and together looked out at the conflagration destroying Paris. Smoke and flames rose to the south and west. From time to time, a wild burst of flames shot high in the air as an explosion echoed through the city.

"*Mon Dieu*," Aunt Isabelle said, holding one hand to her mouth. "This is unbelievable."

"God in heaven," Mariele's mother exclaimed. Horror marked her face. "They've set fire to the Tuileries Palace. That beautiful, beautiful building."

"And look over there." Camille pointed west. "The Louvre and the Palais Royal are also burning."

"There are fires everywhere," Mariele said. "I think that's the Ministry of Finances. And over there, the Orsay barracks."

From where they stood, the Seine looked like molten lava, like a fire-breathing snake winding through the city. Ash clouds billowed like giant mushrooms. Cinders flew. Her mother moaned, a wrenching sound more animal than human.

"Maman!" Mariele put her arms around her mother. "Hush, Maman. Hush."

Sobs wracked her mother's frame, gulping sobs from deep within. Mariele continued to hold her and whispered soothing phrases.

"We'll be all right, Maman. It's almost over. I'm sure it's almost over. Hush, Maman. There now, hush."

Finally, her mother spoke. "What if Robert or Theo or your papa is caught in those fires? What if I never see them again? My sons. My husband." Her voice was racked with pain.

"I know, Maman. I'm terribly worried about them too. And about Bertrand." She spoke as if her aunt and Camille were not there. "Do you remember telling me that I might come to love Bertrand? Well, Maman, I do love him. And I know the fear you feel. We must be strong, Maman. You and I must be strong. Let me take you to your room. Perhaps Aunt Isabelle has something to help you rest. Camille, will you look after Sophie?"

My beautiful Paris, she thought after seeing her mother to her bedroom and returning to stand by the window. What possible reason could there be for destroying the grandeur of centuries? What sort of twisted minds made such a decision? *I hate them. I hate what they've done to us, the fear, the anxiety, the loss.*

"This is monstrous," she said, more to herself than to the two women standing beside her, transfixed by the destruction unfolding before their eyes. "How will we ever rebuild our city and our families?"

For days, Mariele and the others watched the inferno engulf Paris with crimson fury. The city was like a demon tearing itself to pieces; a demon sparked by atheism, anarchy, and insane pride. She wondered what would be left of Paris and how it could possibly rise again. Would she find her home demolished, if not by insurgents, then by fire? When would Papa, Robert, and Theo return? And Bertrand? Was he dead or alive?

39

MAY 29, 1871 – CAMILLE

BY MAY TWENTY-NINTH, when an eerie calm had descended, Bertrand arrived in the blue and red of the French army. Camille, who had returned to the family home two days earlier, rushed down the stairs and flung herself into his arms.

"Thank God, you're here. I've been frantic with worry, and I have terrible news. Father is missing, Bertrand. No one knows where he went. I sent messages to everyone I could think of, but he's disappeared. And the streets were too dangerous for me to go out looking for him."

"Slow down, Camille. Father has disappeared?" Bertrand's thick eyebrows pulled together into a frown.

She nodded. The panic she'd experienced more than a week before returned, and her head began to pound. "He had permission to see Victor at the prison and never came back. He might have been shot or caught in an explosion or . . . and the city was in such a dreadful state, with bombs going off and French soldiers capturing street after street, and Communards everywhere. And then the fires. I couldn't think what else to do in order to find him, and I was alone, Bertrand. I was so afraid and alone."

Camille felt secure in her brother's arms, a feeling she hadn't experienced for weeks. Now that he was home and the Commune destroyed, perhaps life would return to some semblance of normal. She imagined André, Victor, and her father coming through the front door and her mother returning with Paul and Louise and Laure. They would be a family once more.

"Father would not just disappear," Bertrand said. "He would have let you know his whereabouts if it was in his power to do so." He released her and crossed the room to the window, where he pulled back the curtains.

"That's what I thought, but then I remembered what he told me about how you escaped, and I wondered if he might have done the same. I was so worried; I even stayed with Mariele and her mother during the last days of the Commune. You can't imagine how terrible it's been."

Bertrand turned away from the window. "I think I can imagine, but I had no idea you were alone. Is there any news of Victor?"

She shook her head. "A few days ago, we heard that they shot the archbishop along with eight other priests. The names have not been released. I'm so afraid Victor is one of them. Dozens of other hostages were killed before it was over. Now that the government is in charge once more, I'm praying for news."

"And Mariele?"

"She was at her aunt and uncle's home when I was with her. They were very kind to me. She's so worried about you and Robert. And her father."

"Her father?"

"Yes. Just like Papa, Monsieur de Crécy disappeared one night." Camille had been twisting her handkerchief, and it now looked as if it would never be suitable to use again.

"I understand the National Guard took many hostages," he said. "Perhaps our fathers are among them. I will telegraph

Maman. With Father missing, I'm sure she will want to return to Paris."

"I'm sure she will. And you, Bertrand? What happened to you?"

"I escaped Paris before the final onslaught and reported to General Vinoy at Neuilly with a letter describing the sabotage efforts I and other members of the National Guard had conducted. Vinoy immediately assigned me to an infantry battalion, and I participated in several battles as we retook the city." His voice was rough and weary.

"After taking the streets around Parc Monceau," he continued, "General Clinchant sent us to capture the barricades at Place Moncey, then to silence the artillery on the Butte Montmartre. That's where we encountered the most resistance. We had orders to remain in control of Montmartre, but I wish we'd been given further targets to take."

Camille was surprised at the fierce look on her brother's face as he relayed the story. He looked nothing like the personable businessman he used to be. Instead, he looked like a man capable of murderous revenge.

"You must have been in great danger," she said.

Bertrand nodded. "Yes, but you put that from your mind in the midst of battle. You can't think of anything but the orders you have and the men who mean to kill you. You must destroy them." He looked away. A few moments later he spoke again. "What has happened to André?"

Camille placed a hand over her mouth and closed her eyes for a moment. "I don't know," she said in a whisper. "The last time we spoke, he was going out to defend Saint-Cloud."

"I see," Bertrand said, but he offered nothing more.

"He could be dead or wounded. He could be a prisoner. I have no way of knowing."

The uncertainty and deadly chaos of the last ten days had drained almost every bit of energy, leaving her lethargic and depressed. And now a wave of anguish flooded both heart and soul. André, Father, Victor—were any of them alive? She couldn't bear the thought of losing even one of them. The only relief she'd had in the past few weeks had come from Mariele. Her friend had had more than enough to worry about, but somehow they'd been able to comfort one another during the horrible final days of the Commune.

The following day there were rumors that some hostages were being released. Hoping to find Victor, Camille and Bertrand walked to Île de la Cité. As they approached the Conciergerie, a brooding medieval fortress with peaked turrets and impregnable walls, Camille thought of the hundreds of French citizens who had perished within its confines over the years and prayed that her brother had been spared.

At the gate, Bertrand presented their papers to the guard, a thick, bearded man who examined the documents closely before waving them through the massive archway. "Go left," he said. "Take the first covered corridor, where you'll find doors to the great hall."

Camille didn't recognize Victor at first, not until she saw his hands clasped together, his fingers interlinked as if ready to pray at a moment's notice. Emaciated and hollow-eyed, with a ragged beard and mud-encrusted clothing, her brother stood in the poorly lit great hall with more than one hundred other hostages.

"There he is, Bertrand, next to the table in that corner," she said, pointing.

Together they embraced Victor, clinging tight, whispering words of comfort, rocking back and forth, choked with emotion.

"We'll take you home now," Bertrand said finally.

40

MAY 29, 1871 – MARIELE

MARIELE WAS in the upstairs sitting room with her mother and Aunt Isabelle when the butler appeared.

"*Oui,* Henri?" her aunt said, a frown appearing on her overly powdered forehead.

"There is a man claiming to be Monsieur de Crécy at the front door, Madame. I didn't want to let him in without your permission."

Mariele's mother flew out of her chair. Within seconds, she heard footsteps running down the curving staircase. She was about to follow when her aunt raised her hand.

"Give your maman and papa a few minutes alone," she said with a small smile. "They haven't seen each other in weeks."

Mariele remembered when Bertrand had returned, her heart fluttering and her nerves so jumpy she could hardly speak. She'd wanted everyone to disappear so she and Bertrand could kiss at length and whisper of love and the misery of being apart. "Of course, Aunt Isabelle. You're absolutely right. I'll just check on Sophie. Nicole was giving her a bath."

Her aunt snorted. "That child could find dirt even at Monsieur Worth's salon, and we know how fastidious he is. But she's a pretty little thing. When do you think her papa will return?"

Mariele wasn't sure she wanted Sophie's father to return, although the thought implied that he'd died in the fighting and brought a rush of shame. After six months, her attachment to Sophie was almost maternal. The little girl still followed her everywhere, dragging the stuffed clown along with her.

When her parents finally appeared, her father had his arm around her mother. Both were smiling.

"I was in Versailles," he said after accepting a glass of wine, "delivering information about the Commune's plans to General Ducrot. Then, because of the dangerous situation in and around Paris, I was forced to remain there until government troops were sufficiently in control. Yesterday, it was finally deemed safe enough for me to return."

He told them he had carried out such missions for weeks, disguised as a poor man fishing on the banks of the Seine. "I pretended to be a simpleton. No one pays attention to a man who is old and stupid, although I was roughed up a few times. Now that it's over, I can tell you that several brave men and women collected information for me to pass on. You would be surprised who came forward to help." Her father tipped his head and looked away.

Mariele was astonished to learn of his bravery. "But if you'd been caught, Papa, you could have been executed." She shuddered at the thought.

"Your father has served our country well," Mariele's mother said. "I'm very proud of him."

"And where is Theo?" her father asked.

"During the last few weeks, he was confined to the hospital," Mariele replied. "The Communards wouldn't let him leave. I worked alongside him until Maman thought the streets were no longer safe."

"They would barely let him sleep," her mother added. "The

last note we had was at least a week ago. You wouldn't believe how terrible it has been, Philippe. Buildings on fire and street battles everywhere." A bewildered look came over her face. "As if the world had gone mad."

THE FOLLOWING MORNING, Theo returned. He was gaunt, his clothing soiled and ragged, his eyes haunted by sights only he could see.

"What were the final days like?" Mariele asked after he'd bathed and changed.

Theo glanced down and shook his head. "Too horrible to describe. But one thing is clear—I won't be returning to medical school. I can't face it. I need to do something different with my life."

The only family member unaccounted for was Robert, although Mariele's father had brought news of the disposition of his battalion during the last week of the conflict.

Paris remained full of fury, but this time it was government forces bent on revenge, indiscriminately butchering those thought to be guilty of insurrection. A mere whisper of involvement could lead to death, and thus ten weeks of murder, assassinations, pillage, and terror culminated in more blood.

AT THE BEGINNING OF JUNE, Mariele's family returned home. Although the day was warm and sunny, the sky remained clouded with smoke from the fires that had engulfed the city. Debris littered avenue Vélasquez—stones and great planks of wood, discarded weapons, spent cartridges, kepis, torn garments, canteens, torches—forcing them to abandon the carriage and pick a path on foot through the ruins. Her father unlocked the gates and the great doors beyond the porte-cochère, and they went inside.

"I'll check for damage," he said. "Theo, can you take our valises upstairs? Eugène will soon be here, but no doubt there will be other tasks for him. Mariele, help your mother settle in, then speak to Madame Robinette about dinner. She promised to help us get organized."

An hour later, Nicole arrived with a message. "There's a man here to see Monsieur," she said to Mariele with a brief bob of her head. "But I don't know where to find him."

"Thank you, Nicole," Mariele said. "Maman, I'll go downstairs to find Papa and return in a few minutes."

Her father was in the gallery looking out the window onto Parc Monceau. "Our beautiful park may never be the same," he said as Mariele approached.

She stood by his side. "It looks ruined. Hardly a tree left. Papa, someone wishes to speak with you."

Mariele followed him to the front hall. Nicole hadn't mentioned that the man was in uniform. "Monsieur de Crécy?" he said.

"*Oui.*" Her father did not advance to greet the officer.

Mariele's heart thudded. She reached for her father's hand and held it tight. *No*, she thought. *This cannot be.*

"I am Brigadier Deluce, your son's commanding officer. I . . . I very much regret to tell you Robert died two days ago defending France."

Her father staggered back as if the officer had struck him. "Robert?" he said. "My son Robert? Are you absolutely certain, sir?"

For a moment, Mariele's heart stopped. Then it thudded once more, awake to the news of death. Her brother. *No, no, no. Not Robert. Not on the very last day of battle. Not now that Paris has been saved to rise again in beauty and serenity.* She felt the color drain from her face and the chill creep across her chest. Her body rebelled against this new and devastating truth.

Deluce nodded. "Is there somewhere we can sit, Monsieur? Somewhere comfortable where I can describe what happened? Robert distinguished himself and will be remembered as a man of great valor."

Her father's face was white, his shoulders slumped, his eyes staring at something only he could see. He remained silent for a moment or two, as if marshaling whatever shreds of strength remained.

"Mariele, please keep the brigadier company while I fetch your mother." He turned toward the stairs, then looked back at her. "Will you be all right for a few minutes, *ma bichette?*"

Tears gathered in her eyes, but she blinked them away. "Yes, Papa. Will you fetch Theo as well? I believe he's upstairs in his room."

He nodded. "We'll find you in the petit salon. That will be best for your mother."

Papa climbed the stairs like her grandfather did, one slow step at a time, his hand clutching the railing. He paused at the landing to extract a handkerchief and wipe his eyes, then looked up at the remaining stairs. She saw the hesitation and knew he was filled with sorrow, and yet somehow, he would have to be strong, for the news would break her mother's heart.

Moments later, a wail rent the air. The sound of unbearable pain. On and on it went until finally subsiding into whimpers. Minutes ticked by, excruciating second after second. But when her mother ultimately appeared with Papa's arm around her waist and Theo's hand holding hers, she was in command of her emotions.

"Thank you for coming, Brigadier Deluce," she said.

"Madame, my sincere and deepest condolences. Your son was my very best captain. It was an honor to have him in my brigade."

Once they were seated, Brigadier Deluce looked at Mariele's father, whose face was as gray as stone. He gave the barest nod.

"The last few days were difficult," the brigadier said. "Our brigade was one of those that took the bridgehead on the Pont d'Austerlitz, your son in a pivotal role, crushing the barricades and pursuing those fighting as far as the Mazas Prison. From there, we abandoned our artillery and continued on foot. The following day—this would have been Saturday—we were ordered to Père Lachaise Cemetery, which was fiercely defended. Robert and his men endured murderous fire as they cleared the cemetery foot by foot. He never faltered, and his men followed him without question."

The brigadier stopped to mop his face, which was mottled with emotion. "On Sunday, we continued with one last assault, this time on the heights of Belleville, a scene of terrible carnage and the last stand of Commune forces. Those men acted with such fury as I have rarely seen, and I can only conclude this was a response to the knowledge of their own impotence. Once again Robert distinguished himself.

"Afterward, he and others under my command conducted a house-by-house search for those who had gone into hiding, and it was during this time that Robert was shot by a sniper. Despite the efforts of our medical personnel, he did not survive. Your son was a man of great courage who was prepared to give everything for France and our beloved Paris."

Mariele and her family had listened to Brigadier Deluce's accounting in silence. Occasionally, the faces of her mother and father twisted in pain, but for the most part, they were stoic in their grief. She knew they were grateful for every bit of information he disclosed so they could imagine their son's bravery, his daring, and all the fine qualities he had displayed under such frightful conditions. Theo held his mother's hand throughout.

Snuffed out on the last day of conflict. Mariele was numb.

Her brother cut down at the age of twenty-four. Impossible to accept.

When the brigadier finished, her mother asked a single question. "When can we have Robert's body?"

"At any time, Madame. I will arrange for it immediately, and if you would be so kind as to inform me of the funeral arrangements, it would be my honor to attend."

Theo showed the officer out and returned with a bundle wrapped in cloth. When Robert's cap, sword, and dress uniform were revealed, Mariele began to sob.

41

JUNE 1871 – CAMILLE

IN EARLY JUNE, Paris was still smoldering. On the streets, people whimpered and wept, mourning the loss of thousands of citizens and reeling at the brutal executions that had marred the last few days of conflict. As Camille sought food from newly opened shops, she grieved for her city. The charred remains of once grand monuments and the wreckage of bombarded buildings lined the route. Here and there, she passed decaying corpses partially covered with whatever rags could be found. The soul of Paris had disappeared.

Bertrand was waiting anxiously for her return. At Camille's request, he'd visited a number of sites where members of the National Guard were incarcerated until finally finding the one where André was being held.

"But why has he been arrested?" she asked. Though the day was warm, this news brought a deep chill to her body.

"He's accused of supporting the rebels. The government seeks retribution, and there will be court-martials for those who go on to trial. I've heard reports of more than thirty thousand arrests. Some of them are even women. It may take a long time before he's released."

Camille was furious. "He didn't *support* the rebels. He was forced to participate. Just like you were. If he hadn't, he would have been shot."

Bertrand raised his hands in a calming motion. "At least we know he's alive."

"I'm sorry, Bertrand. I'm not angry with you. Thank you for finding him. I know it hasn't been easy."

"What hasn't been easy?" Victor asked, entering the library.

"Looking for André. Bertrand has been searching for days and has finally found him. But he's been arrested, and that can't be a good sign. Were you able to discover anything else?" Camille asked, turning back to face Bertrand. "What can I do to get him released?"

"Nothing, I'm afraid. They won't let you into the prison since you're not his wife or a member of his family. However, I know some people who might be able to help. I'll do whatever I can."

Camille braced her shoulders. "While you do that, I have someone I need to visit. And don't worry, I'll take Michel with me and send word if I'm going to be late."

"I'd be happy to come with you," Victor said. "I feel restless and a walk would do me good."

"Are you sure you're strong enough?" Camille asked.

RUBBLE LITTERED the streets on their route to the de Crécy home—large stones, discarded uniforms, spent cartridges, torn flags, the carcass of a dead dog, its bones picked clean, charred bits of wood from barricades that had been set on fire, an over-turned wagon that was missing two of its wheels. A few feet from the gated entrance on rue Vélasquez, someone had abandoned two gilt-framed paintings, but not before slashing them with a knife.

In response to Camille's knock, the butler cracked the door

open a few inches. "Mademoiselle Noisette and Monsieur Noisette," he said. "Please come in. I'll fetch Mademoiselle Mariele for you."

"Thank you, Eugène. But I'm here to see Monsieur de Crécy if he's available."

Except for a twitch of his lips and a brief bow, Eugène gave no indication one way or the other of his employer's presence. "Why don't you wait in the library while I see if Monsieur is here."

"I'll stay here," Victor said. "Take your time."

Camille had been grateful that Victor hadn't asked any questions as they'd walked to the de Crécy home. Her brother had a knack for sensing when such probing wouldn't be welcome. Instead, he'd spoken about plans for the future including a desire to establish a home for destitute children.

ONCE IN THE LIBRARY, she removed her gloves finger by finger and tucked them into her purse. In addition to the usual grouping of settees and chairs, the library contained a games table with a chess board ready for use. Next to a chest of drawers enhanced with gilded filigree were several large landscapes encased in heavy frames. She walked over to examine one of the paintings.

"Do you approve of that one?" Philippe de Crécy asked. "Daubigny painted it last year for my wife. I particularly like the reflections on the water."

Intent on the pastoral scene, Camille had been startled when he spoke. "It's soothing," she said, turning to face him. "And we all need a little soothing right now. Before I tell you the reason for my visit, let me express my deepest condolences, Monsieur. Mariele often told me stories about Robert. How is Madame coping?"

Philippe clasped his hands behind his back, his shoulders

sagging. "Not well. She hasn't been out of her suite since we had the news. But tell me the reason for your visit."

Camille respected his need for brevity. A man who had just lost his eldest son had no patience for small talk. "It's André Laborde. He's in prison, and I fear for his life. You and I both know that he served France well. Is there anything you can do, Monsieur? Bertrand says he has connections. However, I suspect your connections would be more effective."

"Did you tell your brother about our . . . our alliance?"

Camille shook her head. "Of course not, Monsieur. I know how to keep a secret."

"Leave the situation with me, Camille. I will speak to the right people. And thank you for the part you played. Every scrap of information was useful to us. I'm sorry that your courage will go unrecognized for now."

"Thank you, Monsieur."

"Would you like to speak with Mariele?"

"I think not. Victor is waiting for me in the foyer. Please tell her I will call on her soon."

"THE PAPER SAYS the military are releasing hostages at Mazas Prison this morning," Bertrand said a few days later. "Those deemed falsely arrested. Victor and I are planning to be there. Father might be one of them."

"I'd like to come with you," Camille said.

Victor placed his hand on top of hers. "I don't think that's wise. The crowds may be unruly, and I'm certain the conditions are dreadful. Mazas is worse than the Conciergerie, and it is known for holding more of the criminal elements."

By the time her brothers returned in the late afternoon, Camille was so worried, she had almost been sick to her stomach.

"He wasn't there," Bertrand said, handing his hat and walking stick to Michel. "We spoke with a few officials, but they have no record of him being at Mazas. And we also went to La Roquette Prison."

"So, where is he?" Camille asked. "Do they have any idea what has happened?"

Victor and Bertrand exchanged a look.

"Tell me," she demanded. "What do you know?"

"We don't *know* anything," Victor said, his voice calm and soothing, his hands loosely clasped. "But there are rumors of executions carried out in the last days before the Commune fell. We don't have any information; however, Bertrand and I feel we should investigate."

"Do you mean you're going to look at dead bodies?" she asked.

Victor nodded.

"Well, this time I won't wait at home, so don't try to convince me otherwise."

"It's not a good idea, Camille," Victor said. "The bodies will have begun decomposing. You don't want to see that."

"I've been a nurse, you know. I've seen many unpleasant things."

If Victor and Bertrand could look at dead bodies, she could as well. And if her father was one of them, she would honor him by keeping her composure. *If.* Why would someone have taken him as a hostage? What could he have possibly done?

"Why do you think he might have been taken hostage?" she asked.

"I don't know," Bertrand replied. "But he was known to be an astute businessman. And . . ."

"And what? Being astute isn't a reason to be condemned. What aren't you telling me? I know Father's scruples have not always been the best, but what do you know that I don't? Tell me, Bertrand."

Bertrand looked at Victor, who returned his gaze with a small shrug. "He was stockpiling goods during the siege—food and other items—and he sold them almost exclusively to upper-class Parisians."

"I've heard of others who did that, and they weren't taken hostage."

There was something else Bertrand hadn't disclosed. She could tell by the way his voice hesitated.

"And?" she prompted.

Bertrand took a deep breath. "And he was involved in a stock fraud that took place last August. Father and others spread a false rumor of French success against the Prussians. People went crazy. The Bourse went up wildly. Do you remember? Crowds thronged the streets singing 'La Marseillaise,' and when news of the fraud spread, thousands rushed to the stock exchange to get their money back. But it was too late. Father made a lot of money, which he used to buy the food and other goods I spoke of."

Camille felt as if she'd been punched in the stomach. She opened her mouth but couldn't speak. Her knees were so weak, she had to sit down. Faith in her father had been destroyed. Worse still, she now knew it was likely she would never see him again. Someone must have denounced him. Someone who knew what he had done. She closed her eyes and lifted a hand to her mouth. "Oh God."

No one spoke. No one moved. Silence enveloped the room. A long, excruciating silence. *Nothing will ever be the same*, she thought.

"He wouldn't listen to me," Bertrand whispered. "I tried, Camille. But he just wouldn't listen."

Victor held her hand. A shred of comfort. "Bertrand and I need to go. We have to discover if Father is there. Let us pray that he isn't."

"I'm coming with you," she said.

Victor continued to hold her hand as they traveled across Paris, passing the remnants of barricades, homes destroyed by bombardment, and alleys filled with refuse and the remains of lives once lived. Shops had reopened, and omnibuses traveled the boulevards as life slowly returned to the streets. The acrid smell of smoke hovered over the city, and the hiss of smoldering fires could still be heard. Cannon remained in place at Place de la Bastille and other intersections, although now soldiers in blue and red stood guard over them. As their carriage traveled farther east, they encountered the sullen faces of working-class Parisians and children dressed in rags.

How pitiful it all is. Hubris caused this destruction. Hubris and unbridled power. Napoleon III, Bismarck, Trochu, Thiers, Blanqui —those were a few of the men whose pride and lust for power had destroyed Paris and thousands upon thousands of lives. Camille vowed to remember their treachery and the damage both sides of the conflict had done to so many men, women, and children.

Camille shaded her eyes, as they approached the gates of Père Lachaise Cemetery. Bertrand descended from the carriage to speak to an official who, along with three soldiers, guarded the entrance.

"WE'RE to follow the path on the left," Bertrand said as he climbed back into the carriage.

Camille gripped Victor's hand and said a silent prayer for strength as the carriage moved into the cemetery's vast grounds. Gnarled trees sprouting the bright green of new growth stood guard over tombs—some bearing crosses, some with steeply sloped peaks, a few surrounded by wrought-iron fencing, still others marked by angels—crowded at all angles alongside the path and up the gentle rise to the right. As the path curved, hugging the outer perimeter of Père Lachaise Cemetery, she watched the parade of somber gray tombstones.

"I think this is the place," Bertrand said at last.

Camille took his hand and descended from the carriage. She saw a group of men and women huddled on the left near an open pit. Bertrand linked his arm with hers, and with Victor on her other side, they approached the gathering. The area was slick with mud, forcing her to step carefully past mounds of dirt and decaying. A woman standing near the pit began to wail.

To steady herself, Camille took another deep breath.

"Wait here," Bertrand said. "Victor, stay with Camille."

She watched her brother make his way toward a man wearing a black top hat. After a few moments of conversation, the man escorted Bertrand to an area where five bodies lay on a large wooden slab. His face when he returned told her everything she needed to know.

"It's Papa," he said.

Someone had attempted to clean his face, although remnants of dirt remained in the crevices of his eyes and the corners of his mouth. He wore the same gray suit she had last seen on him two weeks before, and his hands had been placed together on his chest, but his feet were bare, and she wondered whether someone had forced him to remove his shoes or they'd been taken from him after he died. She clamped her lips tight to stifle the cry that filled her mouth.

Her father was gone, and a part of her died with him. The man who had infused her with strength, chuckled at her escapades, and taught her to embrace life was gone. She could no longer hear his voice or seek his advice, no longer argue with him or listen to his business conversations. He wouldn't be there for her marriage to André or the birth of her first child. Like a windswept desert, her soul was desolate, its landmarks lost.

BERTRAND TELEGRAPHED LYON, and their mother returned two days later, along with Paul, Laure, and Louise, each of them stricken with grief. With her father's death, as well as that of Mariele's brother, both families were plunged into mourning, and although she attended the funeral for Robert de Crécy and Mariele attended the funeral for Camille's father, the two women had little time to share their sorrow. The days passed slowly. The nights were excruciating.

Camille mourned her father in silence, taking long walks through Paris while barely noticing the city's slow resurgence from the destructive depths of insurrection. She avoided places where friends congregated and instead found small streets in parts of the city she had never before visited. She sought solace in churches with dim interiors and shards of color glinting through stained-glass windows. She was also angry. Angry that her father's greed and underhanded dealings had resulted in his death. Angry that someone had betrayed him to members of the Commune. *If only you'd been content with less wealth and prestige, Papa. If only you'd stopped to consider the consequences.*

Camille's mother took grief in stride, donning black like a badge of honor. Never once did she express regret concerning the absence that had kept her from Paris for almost nine months, and Camille wondered what that signaled. Stoicism? Muted emotions? Love that had faded? Bertrand made the decision to conceal their father's misdeeds from the rest of the family, a decision both Camille and Victor supported, for what could be gained from such a disclosure?

She longed for André. Just to have his arms around her and hear his soothing voice would make her feel less alone. Against Bertrand's advice, she went to the prison where her fiancé was being held, but without proof of their engagement, she was unable to see him. The sergeant-at-arms told her it might be weeks before his trial.

42

JUNE 1871 – CAMILLE

"I MISS FATHER," she said to Bertrand, who was in the study looking through stacks of papers.

"I do too. Even when I disapproved of his decisions, I admired his business sense and the gusto with which he tackled every day. I wish I'd stood up to him more, though. I might have been able to change his mind, and he might still be alive."

"You shouldn't think like that, Bertrand. He was always so determined to have his way. A lesson for all of us, I suppose. Now tell me, what are you doing here?"

"Maman has suggested I take over his office. Since I'll be running operations, I need to know the details, so I'm going through his files. I'm familiar with most things, but still, I've found some surprises."

"Did you find the confidential government documents he acquired last summer?"

Bertrand stopped what he was doing to look at her. He frowned. "How do you know about those?"

"I was in here one day looking for you, and I found them on his desk. I planned to ask you about them, but when I tried to raise the topic, you dismissed me."

"I did? I don't remember that. What did you want to know?"

"I suppose I wanted to know if Father had bribed someone to get access to those documents."

"He might have, but in truth I have no idea. He didn't tell me everything."

"I thought Mariele's father might have been involved. One of the initials was PDC. And since it was not long after you proposed . . ." She let her words drift away.

Bertrand nodded slowly. "There was . . . I don't . . . I suppose that's possible," he said finally. "But Monsieur de Crécy is a very honorable man."

"More honorable than . . ." She let the implication hang in the air, waiting for her brother to comment. Bertrand said nothing.

"I wish . . ." Camille started, then stopped.

"Yes, what do you wish?"

"Sometimes, I wish I were a man. Then I could be involved in the larger world. But there's no point wishing for something impossible."

"You would be good at it. You're smarter than many of the men I do business with." Bertrand slipped a few papers into a folder just as the butler rapped on the door. "Yes, Michel," he said.

"A letter for you, Monsieur."

Bertrand slit the envelope, extracted a sheet of paper, and scanned the words. "Philippe de Crécy has testified on André's behalf, and André will soon be released."

Camille threw her arms around her brother and kissed his cheek. "That's the best news I've had in a very long time."

SHE STOOD at the street corner and looked east at the massive structure of gray stone. La Roquette Prison. Camille had refused her brother's offer to bring André home and had instead awakened before dawn, dressed in modest clothing, and taken a carriage to the eleventh arrondissement, disembarking a few blocks away.

Even at this early hour, the streets teemed with life as shops opened, beggars stirred from their nighttime posts, chickens squawked, and wagons rumbled by, carrying produce to the more fashionable districts of Paris. Camille lifted her skirt and stepped around a steaming pile of horse dung.

Wearing a kerchief on her head, she carried nothing to indicate her status in life. Relations between rich and poor remained fraught. Skirmishes continued, some resulting in death. Bertrand had expressed it well a few days before: "Just because someone raised a flag, doesn't mean the war is over." She thought about that now and shoved her right hand deep into her pocket to confirm that the money was still there. The authorities may have agreed to release her fiancé, but a bribe might yet be required.

Up close, the prison seemed impenetrable. An outer wall at least ten feet high surrounded the five-story building. Round turrets marked each of six corners, and a central dome soared high above the rest. Set back from the streets and with no surrounding trees, the prison exuded fear and hopelessness.

Camille joined a group of women waiting near the main gates, many with young children. Most bore the ravages of siege and conflict. Nearby a woman suckled her baby, occasionally brushing a fly from her child's pinched face. The rising sun brought heat and humidity. Sweat trickled down her back. Time passed, one long minute after another.

Finally, an outer gate constructed of iron bars rolled to the side and a guard emerged. "Visitors over there," he shouted.

Most of the waiting women and children moved left to cluster around a narrow wooden door. Camille watched them stop to talk to the guard before passing through the door one by one. Although she wanted to ask about those being released, she knew not to draw attention to herself. The gate rolled back into place.

The sun rose higher. The heat intensified. Crows flew overhead, cawing in discontent. A knot of hunger tightened.

She heard a sound that reminded her of the swish of ball gowns brushing the floor. The sound grew louder, now like a faint drumroll. Louder still. Then a shout. "Halt!" The gate rolled aside. A narrow door opened. A guard emerged, followed by a man dressed in rags, shielding his eyes against the summer sun. The guard unlocked the shackles on the man's wrists and ankles and shoved him forward.

Every nerve in her body tensed. Camille waited as prisoner after prisoner emerged. She had thought the experience of Victor's release and witnessing her father's pitiful remains would have prepared her. But today was different. Waiting for the man she loved was an excruciating process.

Suddenly, he was there, his tall frame little more than skin and bones, his eyes rimmed with dark shadows. He saw her and tried to smile. She rushed forward to embrace him.

"You're here," he said.

"Of course, I am, my love."

43

JUNE 1871 – MARIELE

A FEW WEEKS after Robert's funeral, Victor Noisette and a bearded man with a crutch appeared at the door.

"Victor, how lovely to see you," Mariele said, wondering why Victor had brought this man to the house, and why he looked slightly familiar.

The two men had been in the vestibule, and now Mariele escorted them into a small waiting room on the ground floor.

Victor cleared his throat. "I have good news, Mariele. Let me introduce you to Gustave Decamp, Sophie's father. He has just returned from serving our country."

Mariele's polite smile slid from her face. She couldn't breathe. Her lungs felt as though they'd collapsed. "Sophie's father?"

"Are you all right?" Victor took her hand. "Perhaps you should sit down."

Mariele sat on one of four upright chairs positioned on either side of the fireplace. Despite the concern on Victor's face, she said nothing. Indeed, she could barely think.

The appearance of Monsieur Decamp implied the loss of Sophie. Every part of her rejected that notion: her arms and lap

that had cradled the little girl's body, her voice that had sung
lullabies or spoken words of encouragement, her legs that had
run or skipped or jumped when they had played games
together, her body that had curled beside Sophie's sleeping
form, her mind that had constantly thought of ways to amuse,
to teach, to console. What would she do without her?

Mariele raised her head. "Monsieur Decamp, I'm sure you
are anxious to see your daughter."

The man nodded. "Father Victor told me how kind you've
been, Mademoiselle. Losing my Jeanne and my little Fabien . . ."
His voice petered out, and a certain vacancy filled his eyes. A
few seconds passed. "Losing them is a dreadful thing. But I have
my little Sophie. Did you know she looks like my wife?"

Her throat tight with unshed tears, Mariele took a deep
breath. "Let me fetch Sophie for you, Monsieur. I think she's in
the kitchen."

WITH A PINAFORE COVERING her dress and a pink ribbon in her
hair, Sophie sat at the kitchen table, her height boosted by two
thick books, so she could play with a set of wooden blocks.
"Riele!" she exclaimed. "Have you come to play with me?"

Mariele fixed a bright smile on her face. "No, sweetheart, but
I do have a surprise for you."

"A treat?" Sophie's eyes widened.

"Yes, a wonderful treat. Your Papa is here."

"My Papa?" Sophie wrinkled her forehead. "Why is Papa
here?"

"Your Papa has been a soldier. He's a very brave man. And
now that he's finished being a soldier, he wants to look after
you. He has missed you very much."

"But you look after me, Riele. And Madame Robinette and
Nicole. And sometimes, Monsieur Theo." Sophie's lip quivered.
She turned away from Mariele.

"I promised your father we would look after you until he could come back. He's back now, *ma petite*. Your papa needs you."

"Because Fabien is gone?"

Sophie's words cut through Mariele's heart. "Because he loves you." Mariele swiveled the chair away from the table and picked Sophie up. "Let's go see your papa."

On encountering her father, Sophie hid behind Mariele's skirt, clutching Fabien's clown. Victor knelt beside her. "Why don't you show the clown to your papa? I'm sure he would like to see him."

Gustave Decamp leaned forward in his chair. "Sophie, *ma petite*, please come to Papa. I want to meet your friend. Does he have a name?"

Mariele nudged Sophie forward.

"His name is Pierre, Papa." Sophie edged a little closer, her hand extended. "And he's lost one eye. See?"

Gustave examined the toy. "Perhaps we can get him a new eye. Would you like that, little one?"

Sophie nodded. "Yes, Papa."

Mariele stepped back and watched as Sophie and her father spoke. She admired the patience Monsieur Decamp displayed, speaking in quiet, reassuring tones as he let his daughter lead the conversation. After several minutes, he reached down to pick her up, and she came onto his lap willingly and nestled against his chest.

"Papa?" Sophie said.

"*Oui, ma chérie?*"

"Are we going home now?"

"Yes, we are." Gustave's voice was rough with emotion.

"Can Riele come with us?"

Gustave Decamp glanced at Mariele.

How can I let go of this beautiful child? Mariele wondered. *How can I never see her again?* For eight months, she had looked after

Sophie. Soothed her, cuddled her, played with her, taught her songs and manners, read to her, helped her get dressed. After Fabien died, Sophie had clung to her and slept in her bed. Mariele had hugged her and dried her tears and had tried to explain the tragedies of Sophie's young life. As if she had become Sophie's mother.

But Sophie belonged to Gustave Decamp.

"I can't come with you, sweetheart. But you can visit with me if your papa agrees. You will always be welcome in my home." Mariele crouched in front of Sophie. "And you will always be in my heart."

"Well, isn't Mademoiselle de Crécy kind to you, Sophie. Can you say thank you?"

A tear trickled down Sophie's cheek. "Thank you, Riele."

Mariele squeezed the girl's small hands. "It's very exciting to have your father back after all these months. I know he has missed you so very much. Now, while you talk to your papa, I'll gather your things together."

She didn't wait for anyone to acknowledge her words but walked briskly out of the room and along the corridor toward the kitchen. After a quick explanation, she asked Nicole to collect Sophie's clothes. "I'll find a satchel and fetch some of Sophie's things from my room. It shouldn't take me long. Madame Robinette, can you please assemble a basket of food to send along with Sophie's father?"

Only a few items were kept in Mariele's bedroom: a selection of ribbons, a small hairbrush, a nightgown for the times when Sophie had refused to leave her side, a few storybooks, and a sweater she'd knit while they'd been living with Aunt Isabelle. She placed them carefully in the satchel and returned to the kitchen.

"Monsieur Decamp, it has been a pleasure looking after Sophie," Mariele said after introducing Madame Robinette and Nicole. "She is a delightful little girl." She turned toward Victor.

"Eugène has secured a cab to take them home. The fare has already been looked after."

"*Au revoir, ma petite,*" Nicole said. She gave Sophie a kiss on each cheek.

"Be good for your father," Madame Robinette said. "You're a big girl now. Your papa will need your help."

Mariele picked Sophie up. One last hug. One last caress cheek to cheek. "I hope you are always happy, my little one."

She stood at the door with Nicole and Madame Robinette and waved until the carriage disappeared out of sight.

"THE STREETS ARE CROWDED AGAIN," Camille said when she visited a few weeks later, "and all the shops are open for business, even some that were damaged. I suppose life goes on despite the grief we've experienced."

"How is your mother?" Mariele asked.

"She's been amazingly stoic. To think that she hadn't seen Father since last September, and now . . ." Her voice faded away.

Mariele touched her friend's hand. "I'm sure you're giving her great strength."

Camille nodded. "We're all trying to help. Victor prays with her every morning, and I know Maman finds that comforting. Paul has grown so much, I almost didn't recognize him when they returned. And Laure is going to be a real beauty. I hadn't realized how much I'd missed them." She paused to reflect. "I remember . . ."

"You remember?" Mariele prompted after a moment or two of silence.

"Losing my father reminds me of losing Juliette. I think back on that time and how the family drew together to support one another. We are doing the same thing now. Life will never be the same, but at least I know that life adjusts and creates new threads to hold us together."

"Family is so important," Mariele said. "I see how gentle my mother and father are with one another now. It gives me comfort to know that something good has come from Robert's death." She pressed a handkerchief to each eye. "I will surely cry if I go on much longer. Please tell me about André. Has he been released?"

"Yes, thank God. He was held in the most dreadful, lice-infested place and charged with participation in the insurrection. He didn't really participate, but he was forced to join the National Guard, just like so many men, otherwise the Communards would have killed him. What came to light were the actions André took on behalf of the government. He and others infiltrated the republican clubs and reported their plans for rebellion. Your father spoke on his behalf." A few heartbeats of silence followed. "And what about Theo? He doesn't seem to be himself."

Mariele shook her head and sighed. "He has quit medical school. I believe the horrors he dealt with were too much for him, and Robert's death has also been very hard. He's slowly improving. I told Papa just yesterday that I think Theo should travel for a while; perhaps seeing other parts of the world will help him recover. We have relatives in Nice and Rome. Papa agrees and plans to write to them." She sighed again. "We're all fragile. Maman never smiles. Papa retreats to his office for hours. Theo is either in his bedroom or out of the house. I thought the camaraderie we developed working together at Hôpital Beaujon would allow me to be close to him, but that doesn't seem to be the case." She offered a little smile. "I'm so glad you're here today. Have you and André set a date?"

"Yes, but it's not as soon as we'd like. Maman prefers us to wait until October or November. She says she can't face the thought of organizing a wedding until then, especially given the plans you and Bertrand have made. I decided not to argue with her. Not now after everything that has happened. But I'm worried about you. You haven't been the same since Sophie left."

Mariele felt her face grow warm as tears filled her eyes again. In the first few days after Sophie's departure, she had withdrawn from her family, barely noticing the comings and goings of her father, mother, and Theo, rarely participating in the subdued dinner conversations that had become the norm following Robert's death. Accompanied by Nicole, who trailed a few paces behind, she'd taken to wandering the streets of Paris with no purpose at all other than to fill her days. Even Bertrand had been unable to soothe her.

She looked at Camille, the woman who had unexpectedly become such a dear friend. "When Fabien died, I was overcome with grief and responsibility. It was my fault he died. That's what I told myself. If only I'd left him at home that day. If only I'd waited for a cab to take us home. If only we'd left earlier. If only. If only.

"Sophie was inconsolable. I became her safe harbor. You remember what she was like in the first weeks after the explosion, don't you?"

Camille nodded.

"She became my shadow. Wherever I was in the house, she would find me. She needed me, Camille. I've never been needed like that before. In the months since then, we had become so close. And now, it's as if I've lost my own child." A tear slipped down her cheek.

Camille reached out and squeezed Mariele's hand. "Perhaps you'll have a child with Bertrand soon. I've watched you with Sophie. You'll be a wonderful mother."

Mariele attempted a smile. "I hope so," she said. "I hope something will take away this feeling of emptiness."

～

THE WEDDING WAS a quiet affair held in early August. Because both families were in mourning, Mariele had chosen a simple gown of striped dove gray rather than the cream silk fashioned more than a year earlier by Emile Pingat. Nonetheless, with its tight sleeves and the velvet-bound frills edging the skirt and train, she felt the gown flattered her figure.

An hour before the ceremony, she joined her family in the petit salon.

"You look beautiful, *chérie*," her father said. "Bertrand is a lucky man."

"Thank you, Papa."

Theo and her father were dressed in black with gray waist-coats and plain white shirts. Her mother's new black silk acknowledged the occasion with a narrow strip of ecru lace at both neck and sleeves.

Mariele embraced each in turn.

"I have something for you," her mother said, holding a small velvet box. "My mother gave these to me on my wedding day, and I want you to have them."

The box contained a string of pearls. "How beautiful, Maman. I will treasure them. May I wear them today?"

"Of course. They will complement your dress. Robert would have been proud to see you looking so lovely."

Her lips quivering ever so slightly, Mariele smiled at her mother. It was the first time Maman had referred to Robert without tears.

BERTRAND HELD out a white-gloved hand to assist Mariele as she stepped from the carriage. "You're beautiful," he said. "And I'm the most fortunate man alive." He linked his arm with hers as they proceeded into the council chamber of the *mairie* where the civil ceremony would take place.

Chattering guests mingled in the large room. Tapestries graced the walls. Heavy curtains swooped across the windows, and a plush red carpet added an air of great ceremony. Near the front, three men waited at the magistrate's bench. On the left, a man sat with a pen, inkwell, and leather-bound book on the desk in front of him, while on the right, another man held a sheaf of papers. Wearing his blue, red, and white sash of office, the mayor stood in the middle.

Her father shook the mayor's hand before taking a seat on the left. Mariele waited at the door with Bertrand at her side.

"We are gathered for the marriage of Bertrand Thomas Noisette and Mariele Simone de Crécy," one of the clerks intoned. "Would the bride and groom please come forward?"

The ceremony was brief, and Bertrand held her gaze as he slipped a gold band on her finger and repeated his commitments. As they turned to face the assembled guests, he whispered, "I can hardly believe this day has finally come."

Mariele smiled at him. "We have years ahead of us."

AT ÉGLISE SAINT-PAUL SAINT-LOUIS, light streamed through the cupola's windows. Gaslit chandeliers flanked the aisle, while candles graced the altar. The priest, wearing splendidly ornate vestments and surrounded by clouds of incense, celebrated Mariele and Bertrand's nuptial Mass, assisted by a smiling Victor. During the small but elegant reception held at Mariele's home, they mingled with guests, the only note of sadness occurring during her father's toast, when he said how proud Robert would have been knowing of his sister's service to her country during the insurrection and how pleased Bertrand's father would have been to see the two families together.

"Today was lovely," Camille said as she and André prepared to leave. "And you look very elegant, Mariele."

"That's a word I associate with my mother," Mariele said.

"She's taught you well, then. Are you looking forward to your *voyage de noces?*"

"I am. I've never been to London, and your brother has made many plans. But we're only away ten days, as I don't wish to leave Maman alone for very long. She's still grieving terribly, and Theo will soon be leaving on his travels. She knows the change will be good for him, but . . ." Mariele stopped to wipe away tears. "And your mother too continues to grieve. She will need Bertrand close at hand."

"Don't be sad, my friend. This is your wedding day. I'll visit your mother while you're away. I enjoy her company." Camille squeezed Mariele's shoulder. "I see Bertrand heading this way, so I'll leave you to your new husband."

"Are you ready, my love?" Bertrand asked as he joined her. "The carriage is waiting."

"I have to change first," Mariele replied.

The previous night, her mother had taken her aside. "You know it's your duty to be intimate with your husband," she'd said. "He will want to consummate the marriage right away and will expect you to follow his wishes."

"Of course, Maman."

"You may find it a little unpleasant the first time. Bertrand will show you what to do. Are there any questions?"

She'd had many questions. However, even the thought of asking her mother had made her blush. Bertrand loved her. She was certain of that. Their first time together would be fine, and if not, time would ease any discomfort.

"Don't be long," Bertrand said. "We haven't had a moment alone all day."

Alone, she thought. *With my husband*. A man she had come to love and admire.

"You wish to be alone with me?" she asked, a little smile playing on her lips.

44

OCTOBER 1871 – CAMILLE

"WHY ON EARTH would Maman disapprove? André and I are to be married in four weeks' time, and you and Mariele will be our chaperones." Camille turned away in frustration and glanced out the library window.

Two months had passed since her brother's wedding, and the family had gradually settled into a new routine, one that acknowledged her father's absence and Mariele's presence. Bertrand now sat at the head of the table and, even more importantly, had taken over their family business. His days were hectic, and after dinner he often spent time in his father's private study or in the suite of rooms allocated to the newly married couple. Camille missed his company profoundly.

"Yes, but you know how conservative our mother is," Bertrand replied.

"Well, Maman is making me crazy with endless discussions and debates about the most trivial of matters. If anything causes me to end this engagement, it will be our mother's behavior. Yesterday she spent hours worrying over the exact shade of black for her dress. I told her black is black, but she paid no attention."

"You said yourself there are only four weeks left." Bertrand spread jam on his brioche.

Camille sighed. Her brother was always so logical. "I know. I just need to get away for a few days. Being with you and Mariele would be marvelous. And Mariele needs to get away too. Haven't you noticed the way she forces a smile whenever Maman begins one of her instructional moments?" Camille shook her head.

She had imagined the loss of a husband might alter some of her mother's character traits, perhaps allowing nostalgia to creep in along with the realization that family was to be cherished. But no. If anything, the opposite had occurred.

Bertrand smiled, although she could tell it wasn't a genuine smile. "Yes," he said, "there have been a lot of instructional moments."

"Please, Bertrand. If Maman thinks it's your idea to go away for a few days, she's much more likely to support it."

"All right," he said. "As you say, Mariele will enjoy getting away. I'll speak with Maman."

Bertrand's persuasive skills were a marvel to behold. He adeptly flattered their mother, appealing to her pride of family with a story about wanting to forge a closer bond between the two couples, and to the embarrassment she felt over leaving her daughter during nine months of siege and civil war.

"A few days away will be of great benefit, Maman," he said.

"Well," Maman replied. "If you believe this is acceptable, I will trust your judgment, but just a few days. And you must return before Thursday for Camille's final fittings."

"Of course, Maman."

∽

THEY TOOK A TRAIN TO AMIENS, where a carriage was waiting for the drive to Beaufort, a small town in northern France.

Camille wondered why Bertrand had chosen this location but, grateful for his intervention, had not questioned him even once. Being with André was all that mattered.

The experiences she had shared with André had brought them closer, and she was more convinced than ever of her love for this intelligent, courageous man, a man who brought a smile to her face with ease, whose nearness made her body yearn for more, whose embrace—and they had found some occasions to be alone despite her mother's careful oversight—filled her with promise. His laughter made her happy. His silence was warm and comforting. The thought that they would soon be husband and wife, sharing a home and sleeping side by side, gave her joy.

Birds scattered as they passed, and brown cows lifted their sleepy heads. Pungent scents of autumn leaves and freshly mown hay permeated the air. On a slight rise to the right was a farmhouse framed by a cluster of trees and a tangle of bushes on one side, and two sturdy outbuildings on the other. On the left, farmland and forest made a patchwork pattern of green and brown and yellow. A church spire glistened in the distance, and a high ridge marked the horizon.

"Beautiful scenery," André said as they rounded a bend, the open carriage squeaking and bouncing on the narrow dirt road.

"Definitely not Paris," Camille said.

"Well, you were the one who wanted to get away," Bertrand remarked with a wry smile.

"André's right. It's beautiful," Mariele said. "Gaston, can you tell us how much farther it is to Beaufort?"

"About ten minutes, Madame."

"And where exactly are we staying?" Camille asked, imagining rustic accommodations with uncomfortable beds and small rooms.

"It's a small hotel owned by the Ducette family," Bertrand replied. "Father's banker is the brother of the owner. When he heard we planned to be in Beaufort, he insisted on making the arrangements. He's been very kind to me since father's death. Although the town is small, there are rich coal mines in the vicinity."

"Well, then, we must be sure to visit them," Camille said.

"I plan to do exactly that," her brother said. "They might make a good investment."

"And hence the reason for our destination."

"Don't mock, Camille. You don't know the losses Father suffered during the siege. It hasn't been easy taking over the business, and now that I'm in charge, I'm looking for opportunities to restore our fortunes."

"Oh," she said, embarrassed to have spoken without thinking. "I'm sorry, Bertrand. I had no idea."

The carriage turned another corner, revealing a long, low building with narrow windows and black smoke billowing from each of the four chimneys. On a rise not far from the road, a windmill spun lazily in the breeze.

"We're coming into town now," Gaston said.

Soon they turned onto rue Principale, where cobbled streets lined with squat, red-roofed houses ran perpendicular to the main street. Camille watched a boy pushing a handcart piled with cabbages and an old woman dressed in black sweeping her front step. As they drew closer, the houses became larger, with wide front doors and lace-curtained windows.

"This is Place Saint-Georges," Gaston announced. "A market takes place here every Saturday."

Place Saint-Georges was a circular space dominated by a fountain with a central plume of water ringed by six smaller plumes. The fountain was enclosed by a low stone wall, where two girls perched, each with a basket at her feet. A church and its tall belfry anchored the intersection, and five streets fanned out in all directions, one marked by the statue of a rearing horse.

Gaston navigated the carriage around the fountain, avoiding

a number of horse-drawn wagons and handheld carts as well as pedestrians crossing this way and that, then drove north along rue de la Paix, gradually ascending a steep rise. At the crest of the hill, he stopped in front of a spacious four-story limestone building.

"Monsieur Ducette's hotel," Gaston said. "They will be expecting you. Please proceed into the house. I'll bring the baggage to your rooms."

A short, rotund man with bushy eyebrows and a bald head appeared at the front door. "I bid you all welcome," he said. "Madame Ducette and I are pleased to have you stay with us. My brother has mentioned your family many times. Come in, come in." He waved one arm to encourage them through the door. "I'll escort you to your rooms straightaway as I'm sure you've had a long journey. We'll serve dinner tonight at eight, so you have plenty of time to relax."

"BEING AWAY from Paris seems to agree with Camille," Mariele said as she put away their clothes. "She hasn't been herself since your father's death. I've been worried about her."

"You're right," Bertrand said. "And if anything had happened to André, I don't know how she would have coped. I've always thought of her as such a strong woman. In the past, nothing deterred my sister, and she really did do the most outrageous things. Father . . ."

Bertrand stopped speaking, and Mariele glanced at him as she placed her toiletries on the dressing table along with the perfume bottle he had purchased for her more than a year before. She went to him and cradled his cheeks in her hands, feeling the soft bristles of his beard. "Are you all right?"

He nodded. "My father would shake his head at her antics and try to hide the smile they prompted."

"She'll be married next month. It makes me happy to see how much she and André love each other. He'll help her return to her old self. That's my hope, anyway. Would you like to take a walk before we change for dinner?"

Bertrand put his arms around her and said, "I have another idea."

~

"MY ROOM IS DELIGHTFUL," Camille said after they were seated for dinner. "Chintz curtains, Chinese accents, and a set of shelves containing old perfume bottles in every shape and color. I just stood at the window for a while, looking out over farmland, and in the distance, I could see a village and the spire of its church. How different from Paris. This hotel is a wonderful choice, Bertrand."

Located at the rear of the hotel, the dining room was a spacious area with windows overlooking the garden, where roses still bloomed with a profusion of colors and a vine clung to an arched trellis at the edge of the property. The room contained four tables covered in white linen, although theirs was the only one occupied. A fire glowing brightly in the hearth and floral paper in green, pink, and white gracing the walls above the wainscoting created an aura of comfort and calm.

Monsieur Ducette appeared, bearing a carafe of red wine. "You've settled in, I trust. I hope you've found the rooms comfortable."

"Very comfortable," Bertrand said. "How did you come to run a hotel here?"

"Ah," he said. "That's a long story." He glanced at them as if seeking permission to continue, and Bertrand raised his eyebrows in encouragement. "The home has been in our family for almost two hundred years. Originally, my ancestors owned much of the land you can see beyond the windows. The land was a grant from King Louis XIV for service during the Dutch war, and it provided the family with a comfortable living for many, many years. My great-great-great grandfather built this house, and his descendants, including me, were all born here. Unfortunately, my grandfather got into financial difficulties—I never knew the details, but I suspect it was gambling—and my father was forced to sell off most of the land. My brother and I inherited when he died. The house came to me, and the remaining land went to Stéphane. He sold the land, and I converted the house to a hotel. *Et voilà*, here we are."

"It's a lovely hotel," Camille said. "Do you have any children, Monsieur?"

"Yes, a son, who is studying for the law, and our daughter, Blanche. She is helping me tonight. You will meet her. Gaston, who met you at the train station, is my wife's nephew. So, you see, it's a family affair. Now it's time for me to tell you about our menu for this evening."

"DELICIOUS FOOD, MONSIEUR," André said after finishing the first course. "If you offered this kind of food in Paris, your restaurant would become famous."

"*Merci*, Monsieur. Madame Ducette does most of the cooking, and now my daughter helps her. Ah, there you are, Blanche. These are our guests."

What a striking looking woman, Camille thought as Blanche Ducette approached their table. Taller than most women, she had a willowy figure and hair so blonde it was almost white. When she walked, she seemed to glide across the floor in a fluid movement that called to mind swans drifting across a pond. "A pleasure to meet you," Camille said.

When they finished dinner, it was well past ten. "Time for bed," Mariele said. "What shall we do tomorrow?"

"Why don't you two have the morning together while André

and I visit the mine I mentioned? Will that suit you, André?"
Bertrand asked.

"Of course."

"Monsieur Ducette mentioned a place where we can have a picnic and go boating afterward," Bertrand said.

Camille touched André's hand. "That sounds idyllic."

45

OCTOBER 1871 – CAMILLE

CAMILLE SLIPPED ON HER NIGHTGOWN, one of five purchased for her trousseau, and crossed to the window to gaze at the night stars and a moon that lay bright on the horizon, only slightly obscured by streaks of cloud. She felt calm and peaceful, as if the rolling land and quiet sounds of the country warmed her soul.

She would be a good wife and mother. She would gather in her restless spirit and bold outlook and replace them with warmth and happiness. The thought made her smile.

She lingered at the window, feeling no chill from the air that settled on the earth, creating dew to nourish the land. A layer of mist had formed on the ridge to the north, and she imagined it falling gently down the hills to blanket fields and villages in northern France. André would be her future; André and the children they would have together.

One last bold act, she thought.

Tiptoeing down the corridor, she passed three closed doors before stopping in front of one labeled *Lille*. Someone had given each bedroom the name of a city in the environs. Camille's door bore the name *Cambrai*, which made her think of the cambric that came from that city, a fine linen she had chosen recently for a traveling outfit to take on their honeymoon. She touched the doorknob and twisted it to the right.

"André?" Camille whispered as she entered the room.

At first, there was no answer, and then a sleepy murmur, "Camille?"

She closed the door, taking care to make no noise. "Would any other woman be in your bedroom?"

"What are you doing here?" André's voice was husky and deeper than usual.

"I thought . . . I thought . . ." What exactly did she think? Was this the way she wanted to consummate her love for him? Was he as eager for her as she was for him? Would he think less of her? "Is it all right?" she asked. "We'll be husband and wife very soon."

André pulled the covers back and rose from the bed. He was naked, his slim torso broadening to wide shoulders, his chest sprinkled with curly hair. She allowed her eyes to travel the full length of him.

"Are you sure? There's nothing that would give me more pleasure, but I can wait a few more weeks."

"I know. And so could I, but there's something about this place that makes me want to be with you now. It's so peaceful. There are no memories here and nothing to remind us of what we've been through. It feels right." She stood a few steps from him, wanting to touch him, to see his eyes fill with desire. André wouldn't be the one to make the first move.

She took a step closer. Another step. Another. And then she reached for him, and he wrapped his arms around her.

"I want you more than I've wanted anything else in my life," he said.

He kissed her, a kiss that lingered and deepened until she was completely breathless. A kiss that touched the innermost part of her. Urgency surged, a need to feel every inch of him against her skin. As if reading her mind, he took her nightgown off and pressed against her.

"I . . ."

"Shh," he said as he picked her up and placed her on the bed.

Lying beside her, he caressed every inch of her body. Heat flooded her face as his fingers explored further. A feeling of unexpected intensity gathered, and she felt as if at any moment she might explode. When she thought he'd given her all the pleasure possible, André spread her legs and gently entered her, pressing into her until she felt the full length of him deep inside. As he rocked back and forth, intensity built once again, this time the feeling even more urgent. Suddenly, she shuddered, a thousand spasms exploding within her. André thrust again, and then he too shuddered in climax.

Whatever she had expected, it wasn't the intense feeling of contentment that permeated her as they lay together, André's chest nestled against her back, his arms holding her close. She imagined hundreds of nights like this as their lives unfolded. She would give him everything she could, certain that he would do the same.

He was her home, her foundation, her future.

46

OCTOBER 1871 – MARIELE

BERTRAND AND ANDRÉ left the hotel before nine, and Mariele arrived in the dining room for breakfast not long after to find Camille sitting with a cup of *café au lait*, humming a little tune. *She looks distracted*, Mariele thought. *But in a pleasant way, none of the brooding looks I've caught on her face recently.*

"Were you up early?" Mariele asked as she looked over the food arrayed on the sideboard: a choice of *tartines*, fresh baguette, sliced ham, thick sausage, and a selection of fruit. "Was your bed uncomfortable? Bertrand and I slept wonderfully well. It must be the country air."

"Hmm," Camille said. "I didn't get as much sleep as I normally do. But I agree with you about the country air. It's rather magical. And to think that I've always considered Paris the only place I could possibly live."

Mariele laughed. "I can't imagine you anywhere but Paris. From the moment we met, you seemed to have that indefinable attitude and elegance of a true Parisian. Do you realize you intimidated me?"

"I did? You must forgive me, Mariele. I had no intention of intimidating you. What I wanted was to be your friend. Even, perhaps, a dear friend. I haven't had such a friend since Juliette died."

"You are a dear friend," Mariele replied. "A very dear friend."

Blanche entered the room. "Would Madame like *café au lait?*" she asked.

"Yes, please," Mariele replied. "I would enjoy that very much. And what a delicious-looking breakfast. If I were to eat like this every day, I would gain far too much weight."

"But you're on holiday, Madame. You should indulge a little on holiday."

"I agree with Blanche," Camille said as she helped herself to ham and cheese and a large piece of baguette. "After everything that has happened, a few days of indulgence will be good for us."

BEAUFORT WAS BUSTLING by the time they walked into town, Mariele in a dark green skirt and sage-colored jacket nipped in at the waist, Camille in a black skirt and a jacket of pale fawn. Touring the shops lining the main square, they walked past a florist where metal tins filled with a profusion of colors flanked the doorway, a bakery whose shelves held tempting desserts and a depleted stock of the day's fresh bread, and a dressmaker's shop offering fine fabrics and ribbons and lace. In addition, they noticed a shoemaker, a butcher, a *poissonnerie,* a pharmacy, and a café.

"Café Pitou," Camille said as they crossed the street. "Why don't we go in?"

Situated on a corner, the café had windows on two sides from which they could watch the comings and goings of the little town. Once seated, Mariele removed her gloves and undid the buttons of her jacket. "It's warmer than I imagined."

A stout woman wearing a bibbed white apron bustled toward them. "Good morning, ladies. What can I get for you?"

"*Bonjour*, Madame. Two cups of *café au lait*, please," Mariele replied.

"Lovely little place," Camille said after the woman returned to her spot behind a spacious counter to prepare their coffees.

Patrons filled a few other tables: a man and woman leaning close to one another; two old men playing chess; a young woman with a little girl dressed in pink; and a priest wearing glasses that sat at the end of his nose. Lace curtains hung on the lower half of each window.

"Are you happy?" Mariele asked after taking a sip of her coffee. "We've talked a lot about the wedding, but Bertrand and I want you to be happy."

"I will be, although as you know, Maman is being difficult. I'm sure it's because she's still overwhelmed by Father's death. Louise has been unexpectedly kind, perhaps because she likes André very much." Camille smiled. "Of course, he can charm anyone."

"Has he found a place for you to live?"

"Yes. Just the other day, he found an apartment in the fourth arrondissement, a few blocks from rue de Rivoli. It's going to be perfect, but we're taking a suite at Hôtel du Louvre for the first month while we furnish our home."

"Do you remember promising you would help me cope with your mother? And instead you're abandoning me." Mariele pretended to pout.

"I don't think you'll have any trouble with Maman, although if you had asked me twelve months ago, I would have had a different answer. You've changed. In fact, you've changed a great deal, and I admire you even more."

Mariele placed her hand on top of Camille's and gave it a little squeeze. "Thank you for saying that. The past year hasn't been easy."

Camille pursed her lips and shook her head slowly back and forth. "No," she said. "Nothing this past year has been easy."

"But I'm glad to see that you're happier now. Bertrand and I were so worried about you."

"'Bertrand and I.' How lovely that sounds. Soon I'll be able to say 'André and I.'" Camille sipped her coffee and glanced out the window for a moment. "Just yesterday I told myself that it's time to put away my bold and reckless behavior. Time to grow up. I want to be a good wife, and I thought I would never say those words. A good wife."

"You will be a good wife. You two are so well suited. And please don't eliminate all your bold behavior. That's one of the things I most admire about you. Do you know, there were many times this past year when I said, 'What would Camille do?' before deciding on a course of action?"

"*Vraiment?*"

"Yes, really."

"We've learned from one another, then, and I hope we'll continue to do so."

Mariele detected a certain wistfulness in Camille's voice and smiled at her friend. A change of topic might bring a smile back to her face.

"Have you noticed how hard Bertrand is working?" she asked. "He's so determined to learn everything about your father's business. He wants to finish certain projects and close the munitions operations as quickly as possible so he can return to what he considers the primary focus of property development. With so much destruction throughout Paris, there will be ample opportunities."

"My brother's very clever. But I hope . . ." Camille trailed off.

"What do you hope? Don't leave me in suspense."

"I hope he has more scruples. I loved my father very much, and it pains me to say these things, but if you can guide Bertrand in any way, make sure you guide him on a path of integrity."

Mariele wondered what Camille was referring to. Bertrand

had never given even the faintest hint to suggest his father's business dealings were anything other than sound and effective. She hadn't expected this topic to become as serious as the last.

"I will," she said slowly. "I certainly will."

"And make sure you know about the business, Mariele. A wife shouldn't concern herself only with household matters. My mother made that mistake, and I imagine yours has too. Although very different personalities, they're both too confined by social convention."

"You're beginning to sound like one of those women campaigning for women's rights, Camille."

"I hope not," Camille said. "I don't approve of their tactics. But I've always had more interest in what men do than what women are expected to do to fill their time."

Mariele smiled. "Such a weighty conversation for what is supposed to be a holiday." She glanced at the clock mounted beside a picture of Napoleon III. "Look at the time, Camille. The men will have returned by now, and we promised to be ready for our picnic."

They strolled arm in arm back through the square and began the climb up the hill to the hotel. Light glinted off lampposts and a brass doorknocker shaped like a lion's head, and they passed several clumps of golden leaves alongside the road. Halfway to the top, Mariele nodded at a woman pushing a wicker carriage, her sleeping baby covered with a white crocheted blanket. *Perhaps that will be me next year,* she thought. *We certainly make love often enough. And I've become a very willing participant. I wonder how it will be for Camille and André.* Mariele blushed at having such thoughts.

As they crested the hill, André and Bertrand came into view, and Mariele waved her hand to catch their attention.

"The four of us will be great friends, won't we?" Camille said.

They'd been through more together in a year than most

friends shared in a lifetime. Mariele recalled the first time they'd met—the inadequacy she'd felt encountering Camille's beauty and bold personality. She thought of how each of them had contributed in their own way during the tumult and terror that had consumed their city. She thought of the people they'd lost and the destruction of Paris.

Without Camille, I might never have gained the confidence to be who I want to be.

"Yes," she said. "We'll be the greatest of friends."

THE END

AFTERWORD

First and foremost, thank you for reading *Paris in Ruins*. It gives me great pleasure to know that readers have enjoyed my novels, and it is an honor to have captured your time and attention for a little while.

Paris in Ruins was prompted by readers' questions about an earlier novel titled *Lies Told in Silence*. That story begins in 1914, when a young woman called Helene Noisette leaves Paris along with her mother, grandmother, and younger brother to escape the threat of war by moving to the fictional town of Beaulieu in northern France. Helene's grandmother, Mariele, is a widow in her mid-sixties, a woman whose past holds tragedy and secrets.

To my delight, readers were taken with Mariele and the role she played in Helene's coming of age. They wanted to know more about her. *What could Mariele's story be?* I pondered this question for a while and eventually asked: *What if I went back to a time when Mariele was a young woman and the historical events that might have shaped her life?* I did the calculation and landed in 1870. A quick search led me to the Franco-Prussian war, the siege of Paris and the Paris Commune. Wonderful! War, destruction, death, starvation, and a ruthless insurrection – all that drama. Surely, I could cook up something.

A second character threads her way through *Lies Told in Silence* – Camille Noisette, Mariele's sister-in-law. Although Camille died before 1914, she features in that story through the memories of Mariele and through her house, which is located just outside the village of Beaulieu.

Two capable women. A friendship. A siege and an insurrection. Throw in a dash of unscrupulous behavior, some clandestine activities, an element of romance, the desire to protect those you love and to serve your country, and voilà, as the French say.

Authenticity is crucial to historical fiction. Weaving the right blend of facts and fiction will transform a reader in time and place while staying true to the historical record. As with all my novels, research—deep, wide-ranging research—occupied a major portion of the writing process. I have not knowingly departed from the historical record.

While I can speak a little French, reading the language is much more difficult. Fortunately, I discovered many English sources including some remarkable firsthand accounts of those living in Paris during this time. *Elihu Washburne: The Diary and Letters of America's Minister to France During the Siege and Commune of Paris* by Michael Hill was one such source. I also read *Diary of the Besieged Resident in Paris* by Henry Labouchère, *The Divine Sarah* by Arthur Gold and Robert Fizdale along with excerpts from *My Double Life* by Sarah Bernhardt, *Paris Reborn* by Stephane Kirkland, *My Days of Adventure; the Fall of France 1870-1871* by Ernest Alfred Vizetelly, *Journal of the Siege of Paris* by Denis Bingham, and *The Insurrection in Paris*: Related by an

Englishman Davy. *The Franco-Prussian War and Its Hidden Causes* by Émile Ollivier. Surprises emerged at every turn.

To give life and accuracy to some of those who led the Paris Commune, I dipped into a range of sources: *History of the Commune of 1871* by Prosper-Olivier Lissagaray (translated by Eleanor Marx, daughter of Karl Marx); *Unruly Women of Paris* by Gay Gullickson; *Paris in 1870-71*: a lecture delivered at Simla on 1st July, 1875 by Lieutenant R. C. Hart (Sir Reginald Clare Hart); *Les Clubs Rouges Pendant le Siège de Paris* by Gustave Molinari; *Les Clubs Politiques en 1870-1871* from the website Paris Révolutionnaire; *Journal du Siège (1870-1871) par un bourgeois de Paris* by Jacques Henri Paradis; *Women in the Paris Commune* from the website Workers' Liberty and many others. Wikipedia pointed the way in several cases and a friend helped with translation.

Beyond the siege and the Paris Commune, I collected articles on a range of topics related to 19th century France and Paris: art, literature, and journalism; fashion; French government; industry and economics; language and slang; law and civil code; life and society with a particular interest in salons of the time; medicine, including an article about conducting an amputation; technology; women in the 19th century; Paris maps and landmarks.

Of great assistance was a trip my husband and I took to Paris in 2016. Each day we walked for miles, taking pictures at what seemed like every street corner. We visited museums and several beautifully restored grand homes. We went to Versailles. We climbed the hill to Montmartre and walked its narrow streets. We went to the top of the Pantheon and the Arc de Triomphe. We visited a fan museum. I even found a book titled *Fashion Design: 1850-1895* while browsing in a used bookstore on the Left Bank. Another prize from that trip is a map of Paris 1871 which was on sale at one of the museums and now hangs in a lovely frame beside my desk. I used the map regularly to understand the city's layout as well as the existence of particular streets during the time of *Paris in Ruins*.

Three weeks of immersion in the world of Paris was not only a spectacular trip but also a wonderful way to absorb the feel of the city, to watch the people interact, to listen to the language, to see the trees and flowers in bloom, and to let my imagination roam.

Many people are involved with bringing a book to fruition. *Paris in Ruins* is no exception, and I am grateful for their generous support and the time and talents they offered. Jenny Toney Quinlan of Historical Editorial provided editing support and designed the striking cover. Emma Cazabonne who runs a blog called Words and Peace and does translation work helped research some French sources related to the Paris Commune. Beta readers Ian Tod (yes, he's my husband), Pamela de Leon, Rob Stephenson, and Maggie Scott gave invaluable advice on how to improve the story. In particular, Maggie went above and beyond to offer superb editorial guidance that prompted significant revisions. My sincere thanks also go to authors Margaret George, Patricia O'Reilly, Jeffrey K. Walker, David O. Stewart, Patricia Sands, and Margaret Chrisawn for reading and endorsing *Paris In Ruins*.

On the marketing front, friend and fellow author Patricia Parsons helped shape the book's two sentence 'hook' as well as the back cover copy. To my delight, she and her husband Art surprised me one day with a book trailer they'd put together. Thank you, Patty and Art! And Keri Barnum of New Shelves Books provided publishing and promotional expertise along with a steady hand as we prepared for release day and executed the launch.

Other writers have given their time and encouragement via

email, Facebook, Zoom calls, and that old-fashioned medium of the telephone. This welcoming and knowledgeable community of historical fiction authors is a real blessing. Many volunteered to help spread the word when *Paris In Ruins* launched—it's a real privilege to have their support.

I am grateful too for the love and support of friends and family. No doubt their eyes glazed over at times when I launched into yet another tidbit of research I'd discovered or complained about one of the many challenges associated with writing fiction. My husband Ian can't be thanked enough. Not only does he offer encouragement and unwavering support, he's also an insightful reader and the person responsible for the production activities involved with getting a Word document into readable e-book or paperback form. He always has a sympathetic ear and can be counted on for honest, but tactful feedback at every decision point. Throughout our marriage, we've always been a team. I couldn't do this kind of work without him.

And finally, I love hearing from those who've read my novels. All comments are welcome. You can reach me at mktod@bell.net. I can also be found on Facebook, Twitter, Goodreads, my author website, or on my blog, A Writer of History.

M.K. (Mary) Tod – March 2021

PS – if you enjoyed **Paris In Ruins**, please check out my other novels: *Unravelled, Time and Regret,* and *Lies Told in Silence.*

ABOUT THE AUTHOR

Paris in Ruins is M.K. Tod's fourth novel. Mary began writing in 2006 while living as an expat in Hong Kong. What started as an exploration of her grandparents' lives and a way to keep busy ultimately turned into a full-time occupation writing historical fiction. Her other novels include *Unravelled* which was awarded Indie Editor's Choice by the Historical Novel Society, *Lies Told in Silence*, a World War One novel featuring a French family, and *Time and Regret*, a dual timeline story about a woman searching her grandfather's World War One past. Beyond writing historical novels, Mary blogs about reading and writing historical fiction at her award-winning blog A Writer of History and is known for her highly respected reader surveys. She lives with her husband in Toronto, Canada, and is the mother of two adult children and two delightful grandsons.

CPSIA information can be obtained
at www.ICGtesting.com
Printed in the USA
LVHW091914011121
702138LV00004B/675